Balaam Gimble's Gumption

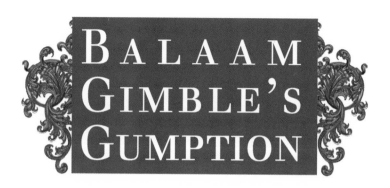

BALAAM GIMBLE'S GUMPTION

MIKE NICHOLS

JOHN M. HARDY PUBLISHING
ALPINE & HOUSTON

2004

First Printing: November 2004

1 3 5 7 9 10 8 6 4 2

ISBN 0-9717667-5-4

Printed and Bound in the United States of America

Cover Design - David Timmons
Austin, Texas

John M. Hardy Publishing Company
Houston, Texas

www.johnmhardy.com

To the memory of Jerry Flemmons,
who in his too-short life had two hearts, each of gold.

Acknowledgements

A novel has one parent but many midwives. My thanks to my agents, Mike and Susan Farris; to all the friends who dared to critique a hypersensitive friend's manuscript; and to the best neighbors a man ever had: the wildlife of Limestone County, Texas.

Balaam Gimble's
Gumption

❧ Prologue ❧

On that day in April, just before Balaam Gimble put his shovel into the ground, the small Texas town of Willoughby was blithely minding its own—albeit languishing—business:

- Rudy Janacek was overhauling Cecil Bell's tractor engine and wondering if Cecil had ever changed the oil in that poor engine in his life.

- Juanita and Richard Greer were anticipating their seventh wedding anniversary.

- J. D. Vernon, avid outdoorsman, was reading a catalogue of hunting accessories and weighing the merits of the new deer-attracting scents.

- Nanetta Wilson, polish and cloth at the ready, was gliding across the considerable floor space of her home, just *daring* a speck of dust to show its face.

Elsewhere on that day in April:

- Two hours away in Houston, David Wilson, dutiful son unto Nanetta, was sitting in a glass-skinned office tower, thinking about lipstick.

- Two states away in Denver, masseur Ernie Ruiz was kneading a client's deltoids.

- Also in Denver, wealthy developer Howard J. Liggett was feeling fit as he played golf with a group of potential investors.

But then, on that day in April, Balaam Gimble had to go and put his shovel into the ground. And within six months:

- The town of Willoughby would have five hundred unneeded Mason jars, four unneeded bed-and-breakfast rooms, and a collective broken heart.
- Nanetta Wilson would have a broken hip.
- David Wilson would sabotage a job that paid him $60,000 a year.
- Rudy Janacek would be addicted to Internet pornography.
- Juanita and Richard Greer would be separated.
- Ernie Ruiz would be mauled by Bambi and have to escape on a riding lawn mower; that would *not* be the low point of his day.
- Howard J. Liggett would be, to quote his chief physician, "not at all a well man."
- J. D. Vernon, not to be outdone, would be dead.

Later, looking back on it all, Balaam Gimble would say that if he had known on that day in April that he had the power to do so much good in the world, he'd have used an even bigger shovel.

❧1❧

"Did you know that this town once had a dress shop? Imagine not having to drive all the way to Waco to find out you're no longer a size seven!"
———Donna Jean Janacek

Darkness was upon the face of Willoughby. Darkness except for the red light of the flashing traffic signal in the center of town, at the intersection of State Highways 21 and 36. At 5:00 A.M. on that day in April, each flash of the traffic signal threw a reddish cast onto the four buildings that anchored the intersection—anchored, indeed, the town of Willoughby itself: Perry's Grocery and Feedstore, Town Hall, the Baptist church, and the Crossroads Cafe.

At that hour, on that day in April, the town was quiet and still; quiet except for the humming of the refrigerator compressors behind the grocery and the cafe; still except for the shambling of a raccoon as it crossed the vacant lot beside Town Hall.

Shortly before 5:30 A.M., Juanita Greer approached the intersection from the east on Highway 21. She slowed just enough to downshift her Toyota, then—with only a token glance left and right—passed under the flashing red light and turned right into the gravel parking lot of the Crossroads Cafe. She wasn't about to come to a full stop at an empty intersection in a sleeping town. The cafe would open for breakfast in thirty minutes. She had eggs to break and coffee to make.

Eight miles from the flashing red light in Willoughby, darkness also was upon the face of Balaam Gimble.

Shortly before 5:30 A.M., Balaam Gimble was awakened by crows cawing reveille in the treetops around his cabin. He lay on his back and listened. Nights were still cool in April, but Balaam had slept with the window beside his bed raised an inch so that he could hear the outdoor sounds. Between the caws, he heard a woodpecker hammering in the distance, a squirrel fussing nearer, and a cowbell tinkling nearer still.

As the tinkling of the cowbell grew louder, Balaam rolled onto his side and, in the darkness, could just make out the two big eyes now staring in at him at the window, the black nose now pressed against the screen.

"Hey, fella. Don't push that screen in. Gimme a minute."

Balaam Gimble threw back the blanket and unfolded out of bed, feeling the cold of the bare stone floor on his bare feet. He switched on the overhead light and walked to the kitchen window.

At the Crossroads Cafe, Juanita Greer unlocked the back door of the cafe, stepped into the back room, and switched on the overhead fluorescent lights. One fluorescent tube flickered and died, but the others lighted up in unison with a suddenness that, as always, made her squint as they revealed surfaces of stainless steel, Formica, and Naugahyde. As Juanita proceeded by rote to prepare the cafe for the breakfast rush, her shoulders sagged a bit when she reflected that this was as rested as she would feel all day. She heard a faint rumble from the east while she whipped eggs in a bowl, unaware that she long ago had internalized the cadence of the traffic sounds. The faint rumble was a tractor-trailer truck entering town. She heard it decelerate at the railroad crossing, clatter over the tracks, and accelerate. Ten seconds later she heard the truck—louder now—again decelerate, downshift, and stop at the flashing red light just outside the cafe. She heard the flatulence of air brakes. Then she heard the groan of the engine and transmission rising in pitch through first gear as the truck struggled to overcome inertia, a short pause in acceleration to shift to second gear as the truck passed her cafe, another slow rise in pitch, another shift; by then the truck was beyond the city limits sign at the western edge of town.

Willoughby was a three-gear town.

Balaam Gimble stood at the window of the kitchen area of his one-room cabin, the low morning sunlight casting the reflection of his face onto the window pane. As usual, his eyeglasses needed cleaning; as usual, he did not notice. His hair was sandy and straight, receding in front and usually in need of a trim elsewhere. The face had a hint of sadness in the eyes, but there also was the hint of a latent grin in the set of the mouth. When he smiled, which he did more often when alone than when in the company of others, two vertical curved creases—one at each corner of his mouth—seemed to enclose his smile in parentheses.

Like most men who work outdoors, Balaam Gimble had squint lines radiating from the outer corners of his eyes; the palms of his hands were rough; his fingernails were chipped. His arms and face were very tanned, but his body below the neck and four inches above each elbow was as pale as a shut-in's.

At the Crossroads Cafe, as waitress Brandi Renee Miller arrived at 5:40 (ten minutes late) to help Juanita open, the flashing red light flashed on. In a town with a part-time mayor, a part-time police chief, and a City Hall open only three days a week, the flashing red light was the most visible symbol of municipal order. It was the town's gatekeeper. Day or night, whether big or small, whether traveling across town or across country, every vehicle had to stop and pay momentary obeisance to the light.

At 6:00 A.M., Juanita unlocked the front door and turned the "OPEN/CLOSED" sign to "OPEN." Below that sign was another sign on which were handpainted three lines of print, the retailer's haiku of negativity:

> No Third-Party Checks.
> No Shoes, No Shirt, No Service.
> Don't Ask For Credit.

By then, the sun was rising above the treetops, painting the town first in monochrome, then in faint colors, and finally in bright colors. Before the sun had risen completely over the treetops on the horizon, it had humbled the flashing red light to the rank of second-brightest light in town.

The flashing red light also was the town's timekeeper, flashing once a second day and night. It flashed three hundred and forty-seven times from the moment when Juanita unlocked the front door until the moment when her first customer came in to the cafe. J. D. Vernon always looked as if he had just swaggered in off the cover of *Soldier of Fortune* magazine. He was a big man, at fifty-two still tall and broad shouldered, his hair still thick and dark, his eyes still not in need of glasses. As usual, that morning he had dressed in a camouflage outfit and hunting boots, even though he was making a trip just to town. Vernon lived on twelve hundred acres across from Balaam Gimble's two hundred acres. In rural Texas, hunting is a tradition for many, but J. D. Vernon hunted more than most. He hunted, in season and out of season, with rifle and scope, bow and arrow, and even black-powder muzzleloader. He stocked his deer feeders year around. He trapped. He tracked with hounds. He went on organized "shoots" at game ranches. The den of his ranch-style house was a glass-eyed tribute to taxidermy.

"Just bacon, ham, eggs, biscuits, hash browns, and waffles, Juanita. I'm travelin' light." Vernon had come in to wait for Earl Perry to open the grocery and feedstore across the street. Vernon needed twenty sacks of cattle supplement, ten sacks of horse feed, and no sacks of deer corn.

When Juanita brought his breakfast, Vernon said, "It's the damnedest thing, Juanita. I just checked a couple of my deer feeders on the way in, and they've barely been touched. I hardly ever have to fill them, and I hardly ever see any deer tracks at them. Just coon tracks and such. Where are all the damned deer? I haven't killed one in weeks. And those feeders always smell as rank as hell."

Juanita bit her lip until she had turned away to return to the kitchen. Only then did she smile. J. D. Vernon and Balaam Gimble were at war. Everyone in town knew that. Everyone except J. D. Vernon. In a town with precious few secrets, it was notable that no one had ever told Vernon that Balaam had been sabotaging his deer feeders for years.

Just after sunrise, Balaam walked out the door of his cabin into the fenced yard that he called his "compound." He could see maybe two hundred feet into the woods before the trees and brush became impenetrable. By May, after the trees and brush had leafed out, he would be able to see at best fifty feet into the woods. He scanned the trees until he located the fussing squirrel, who was twitching its tail in alarm or irritation, Balaam was not sure which. He looked at the shadows under the trees. They were still. No breeze.

A well-traveled ten-speed bicycle leaned against the trunk of one tree, as if weary. As Balaam walked the bicycle toward the gate of his compound, the tinkling of the cowbell followed him. Balaam stopped and gently scratched the two long, erect ears. "Get back now, okay? I'll be back in a minute."

Balaam nosed the bike through the gate and then closed the gate behind him. He coasted down the narrow dirt driveway through the loose sand toward the dirt road. The driveway curved through a thicket, tree branches on both sides reaching out into the driveway. At his mailbox he turned right onto the road. Tall and thin and loose-jointed, as he bent over the handlebars and pedaled, Balaam Gimble appeared to have more than the standard-issue two hundred and six bones: a ten-speed Ichabod Crane.

It was a pleasant ride. Post oaks and blackjack oaks were leafing out, hurrying to catch up with the cedars, which had stayed green all winter. Willow trees bowed over the stock ponds and dropped their tassels like offerings onto the surface of the water. Where bordering trees threw shadows onto the road, the air was noticeably cooler. The only sounds were the crunching of Balaam's tires on the dirt surface and the clicking of his chain as he freewheeled down the occasional slopes. The road passed through woods or pastures on both sides. In one pasture, a few crows and cattle egrets mingled, black and white, like living chess pieces.

Balaam did not see another human being, did not see a human structure until he had ridden a half-mile and was alongside a clearing in the woods of his neighbor, J. D. Vernon. In the clearing, raised five feet off the ground by a tripod of iron pipes, was a fifty-five-gallon steel drum. This was the nearest of Vernon's six deer feeders. Like the other five, this feeder contained dried corn that a timer mechanism dispersed at regular intervals. In theory, this dispersal conditioned deer to feed there. Each feeder was within easy rifle range of a deer blind—an elevated wooden hut where hunters hid and waited for deer to approach.

Balaam stopped and laid the bicycle over in the bar ditch. He

7

walked to the barbed-wire fence and listened for cars approaching on the road. "Nope," he said aloud to himself. Satisfied, he took off his boots and crossed the fence. Then, walking in his socks and staying on grass and fallen leaves to avoid leaving footprints, he moved toward the deer feeder.

When he reached the feeder, he saw the tracks of raccoons, possums, and birds, but very few deer tracks.

Good. All was as it should be.

Then, listening once more for approaching cars, Balaam Gimble unbuttoned his jeans and urinated at the base of the deer feeder.

This was a ritual for Balaam. Ever since he had discovered that the scent of human urine will repel deer, he had been urinating at J. D. Vernon's feeders. Balaam Gimble had long ago dedicated his kidneys to the proposition that deer are entitled to die of old age.

His pulse always registered a spike of irrational fear as he stood there, vulnerable, within range of the deer blind. No one was in the deer blind at the moment, of course, and it's not that he feared that Vernon would shoot him if he ever caught him befouling his deer feeders. But Vernon was a lot cozier than Balaam was with local law enforcement, and Balaam knew that Vernon would have the county and the Constitution on his side in a case of malicious urination.

While Balaam stood there, he multi-tasked—making the world safer for deer, and running a mental finger down his "to do" list:

> get rocks for flowerbed wall;
> clean cemetery;
> fix Imogene Ratliff's screen door;
> and fix Mazelle Henderson's garbage disposer.

Balaam was a self-employed handyman. His income was seldom better than break-even, but the work suited him. And he got along with his boss. Like the skill set of most rural men, Balaam's was manual. Such men know how to file a chain-saw chain so that it will cut straight; how to paint without leaving brushstrokes; how to use a high-lift jack to pull fence posts; how to use a come-along to pull a car out of a ditch; how to pull a strand of barbed wire so tight between posts that when plucked it will twang like a banjo string.

So Balaam did odd jobs for people in and around Willoughby—

doing minor plumbing, electrical and carpentry work, cleaning out garages, lending a hand to work cattle or get crops in. But otherwise Balaam did not get involved in church or community affairs. Everyone knew of him, most liked him, but few could say they really knew him.

In Willoughby, the flashing red light continued to flash away the seconds. By the time Earl Perry came in to the cafe, it had flashed one thousand, eight hundred and thirty-four more times. Perry was mayor of Willoughby, but his income came from his grocery and feedstore. Certainly Earl Perry could not say that he really knew Balaam Gimble, even though once a week or so Balaam came in to Perry's store to buy bachelor staples (Tater Tots, fish sticks, pickle loaf, Mountain Dew), even though Perry and Balaam both were fifty-six, both were native sons of Willoughby, and both had gone to Vietnam—Balaam after high school and Perry after junior college two years later.

"Hidy, Earl," J. D. Vernon said as Perry sat down opposite him in the booth. In a small-town cafe occupied by only one other customer, it would have seemed rude for Perry to sit by himself. "When you get a chance, I need some feed."

"You heard about Jimmy Green, I guess." Perry was preoccupied. He was speaking as Earl Perry the mayor, not as Earl Perry the merchant. He could not be concerned at the moment with mundane matters of grain. "Jimmy's moving to Amarillo to take a job."

"Ama-*rill*-o? Has he ever been in Amarillo in the winter?"

"Forty thousand a year will buy a lot of thermal underwear."

Impressed, J. D. Vernon emitted a two-note whistle. "Ewwww-eeee." Perry heard neither "ewwww" nor "eeee." He was busy feeling betrayed. Willoughby—what was left of it—was *his* town. Every time someone moved *in* to town or opened a business, he felt an inch taller. Every time someone moved *out* of town or closed a business, he felt an inch shorter. After six years in office, Mayor Perry felt as if he could limbo under a lizard.

Before 9:00 A.M., other merchants would come into the cafe before opening their downtown businesses.

Lawton Parker arrived at 8:35. Lawton ran the hardware store. But he ran it more like a museum. Lawton regarded each item in stock as a relic of great personal value, an artifact not easily replaced and only grudgingly parted with. He had managed to hold on to some items—handles for hand plows, lantern wicks, flit guns, brace and bit sets, cast-iron stove lids, glass household fuses, lead-based paint—until there was no longer a demand for them. Some of the price tags on his stock were more than twenty years old. He wanted to be able to just stand there amid all of the nuts and bolts and pliers and C-clamps and varnish cans and sandpaper sheets and butterfly hinges, lord of all he surveyed. Thus he applauded Balaam Gimble's practice of pulling nails out of used lumber, straightening them with a hammer, and reusing both nails and lumber. To Lawton, that meant just more nails that he did not have to part with.

Rudy Janacek arrived at 8:39. Rudy owned Janacek's Tractor Repair and Auto Parts next to the boarded-up bookstore. Balaam Gimble sometimes helped Rudy when he got behind in his repair work. Two or three times a week Rudy came in to the cafe in the morning and again in the afternoon on his way home. Ostensibly, he came in to eat. But there was method in his meatloaf: He also came in to stare at waitress Brandi Renee, whom he found to be almost painfully desirable. When she worked the cash register, he would look at her over the top of his menu, nostrils slightly flared, eyes narrowed, jaw clenched. When she waited tables, he would watch her—the muscles of her tanned calves flexing as she walked, her button nose crinkling as she bestowed smiles upon customers. But when she came to *his* table, his secret guilt would not let him look at her at close range. He would stare down at his plate and mumble, mentally undressing his mashed potatoes. Afterward, he would drive straight home to his wife, Donna Jean, in that amorous state that men achieve when their hormones have reached critical mass.

At J. D. Vernon's deer feeder, Balaam buttoned up, his mission accomplished, and thumped the side of the feeder so that kernels of corn trickled down through the dispenser into the shallow puddle and began to "marinate." Then he retraced his steps to the fence, put his boots on, and began pedaling home. Just as he passed the point where his property began, he noticed that one of his "no hunting" signs had been shot at. Again. There was a round puckered hole in the metal sign just above where Balaam had handpainted "goddam" between the factory-painted "no" and "hunting."

Back at his cabin, Balaam fried an omelet. He took his plate out to the front porch and set it on a wooden cable spool that served as a table. Then he went to a nearby galvanized trash can and with a coffee can scooped up one pound of dried corn. He poured the corn into an upturned hubcap on the ground by the porch.

"Breakfast is served."

At the sound of the corn spilling into the hubcap, the tinkling cow-bell was at his side and followed him to the porch.

"Uh-uh now, Stilts. Get back. You know you don't like eggs. Go eat your corn."

As Balaam chewed and swallowed, he watched Stilts chew and swallow, watched each mouthful of corn slide down the long, slender throat.

Stilts was a whitetailed buck.

Stilts had been a newborn spotted fawn when Balaam had found him four years earlier, huddled hidden in underbrush near the body of a doe. The doe had been shot, probably with her fawn nearby. When Balaam had found Stilts, the fawn had been too frightened to run, too frightened even to escape from the fire ants that were by then starting to crawl on him. Balaam had taken the fawn in and bottle-fed and handraised him. Stilts now weighed almost as much as Balaam and was only slightly less domesticated.

Balaam had always suspected that the doe had been shot by J. D. Vernon, who did not hesitate to cross property lines when hunting. But Balaam had never confronted Vernon with his suspicion. The two men, although technically neighbors, had little need—and less inclination— to speak to each other.

At the Crossroads Cafe, Juanita was frying omelets of her own. By the time her husband, Richard, who came in to work at 2:00 P.M., closed up at 10:00 P.M. that night, perhaps one hundred of Willoughby's five hundred residents would have been in the cafe. The Crossroads Cafe was the social center of town, where people met to visit over breakfast, where high school couples went after football games and rodeos, where men ate a last decent meal before going on fishing trips, where birthdays were celebrated and small-town deals consummated.

If the Crossroads Cafe was the social center, the Baptist church was, of course, the spiritual center. Located diagonally across the intersection from the cafe, it was a large but plain wooden building, its clapboards and trim painted white and green, respectively, by volunteers from its congregation. Its steeple, just taller than the oak trees that shaded the church on two sides, reached up toward heaven; its never-locked double doors reached out toward sinners. Most people in town who were inclined toward religion attended the Baptist church. In a less-central part of town two converted houses served as makeshift churches for fringe (that is, non-Baptist) denominations.

Willoughby, like every community, large or small, had certain social roles that someone filled, even if only by default. Every community has, for example, its richest, poorest, meanest, most powerful, most respected, and prettiest. Small towns merely have a smaller pool from which to draw the title holders. In Willoughby, the title of most respected was held by the Reverend Thomas Finch of the Baptist church. He was respected for his ever-onward Christian soldiership, his inspiring sermons, and his strict literal interpretation of the Bible, although when it came to Ecclesiastes 3:4 ("a time to weep and a time to laugh, a time to mourn and a time to dance"), he would compress his already thin lips and tsk-tsk: "However, I would remind those people who insist that there is a time to dance that just down the road Austin has many fine Presbyterian and Episcopal churches."

The title of most powerful was held by Earl Perry, mostly because as mayor he was the august head of municipal government but also because, as owner of the only grocery store in town, he controlled Willoughby's supply of Blue Bell ice cream and *People* magazine.

The title of prettiest was held by waitress Brandi Renee Miller. Brandi Renee was Willoughby's resident "pretty little thing." At nineteen, she was young, attractive, and well on her way to becoming totally self-absorbed. She was the queen of every rodeo, the throb of every heart, the toast of testosterone. Although men worshipped at her size-five sneakers, predictably some women in Willoughby begrudged Brandi Renee her unlined face, her varicose-veinless legs, and her impudent body not yet a slave to cruel gravity. Juanita Greer herself referred to Brandi Renee—with equal parts envy and sarcasm—as "Her Highness." But some women were more charitable. In fact, Donna Jean Janacek—who was Rudy's wife of thirteen years and was well aware of why her husband came home two or three times a week "in the mood for, well, you-know-what"—said, "Brandi Renee is all that keeps this marriage together."

The title of oddest, if such titles had been formally given in Willoughby, surely would have been given to the man eating an omelet over a wooden cable spool that morning: Balaam Gimble, straightener of nails, befouler of deer feeders. "Balaam, he does have his ways" or "Balaam, he's, well, you know . . ." or "Bless his heart, Balaam . . .," people in town would say. Usually, such sentences were left unfinished out of kindness.

Balaam's "ways" were usually overlooked in part because he had a sort of seniority over most residents of Willoughby: The Gimble name was one of the oldest in the area. The Gimbles had never been prominent, never well-to-do. Just there. Always there. There in the summer like the rattle of the cicada in the oak trees. There in the winter like the ice on the stock ponds. The Willoughby cemetery had a Gimble section. A detailed map of the county showed a Gimble Creek and a Gimble's Knob. Slanting skeletons of a couple of pioneer Gimble farmhouses could still be found settling into dignified decrepitude in the Johnson grass and sunflowers along back roads.

Willoughby had been settled by migrants, mostly from Kentucky and Tennessee, in the 1850s. Shortly thereafter, Balaam's great-great-grandfather, migrating from Mississippi, had homesteaded one thousand acres of raw land that were, in those days, a bumpy buckboard ride from Willoughby. Through the years, his children and his children's children had lived on the family land, spreading out to give each other room as they built their own homes. But because each generation had always been more in need of money than elbow room, only three hundred of the original one thousand acres had remained by the time the land had passed to Balaam's parents, Henry and Bessie. Henry and Bessie had sold off another one hundred acres and sold more than half the mineral rights to the remaining two hundred acres before Balaam had inherited the land.

Balaam was the last Gimble in the Willoughby area.

Balaam's "compound" covered only two of those two hundred acres. It was situated a quarter-mile off the county road, hidden from view by a curtain of oaks, cedars, yaupons, and grapevines. Within his compound, all that was not covered by trees and brush was covered by what Balaam called his "stuff."

It is a cardinal commandment of rural life: You do not discard stuff until you have wrung every drop of usefulness from it. If something might, by some stretch of the imagination, be useful in the future, you stow it someplace (probably some place where you won't be able to find it when you do need it).

A corollary of that commandment is: Your stuff will expand to fill the space available.

Certainly Balaam's had. Encroaching on Balaam's cabin on all sides was a labyrinth of stuff: storage sheds, stacks of lumber, spools of wire, rolls of tubing, rolls of insulation, and coils of rope; pairs of sawhorses supported lengths of rebar and chain, iron pipe, PVC pipe, fence posts, angle iron, corrugated sheet metal, and railroad ties. There were plywood tables covered edge to edge with plastic potting trays filled with tiny springs, cotter pins, half-moon keys, C-clips, and hammer handle wedges. There were coffee cans, some empty, some containing fasteners and nails and hinges and grommets and even shards of flint and unusual rocks that he had found. There were even containers that contained smaller containers. There were doodads stacked on top of doohickeys next to thingamajigs. An old telephone booth. Half a motorcycle. The marquee from Willoughby's long-closed movie theater, still advertising a Humphrey Bogart movie. There were stacks of cinder blocks, piles of bricks, columns of five-gallon plastic buckets nested one inside the other, and towers of stacked milk crates leaning like plastic Pisas.

The rest of Balaam's land was, as he put it, "woods and weeds." That was by design. He had no interest in farming or ranching. This attitude—*heresy*, some might have said—also raised Willoughby eyebrows. One thousand acres of good farmland and five generations of Gimbles had been winnowed down to two hundred acres of neglect and one man who had "TREASURE OF SIERRA MADRE" in his yard in twelve-inch plastic letters.

At 12:17 on that day in April, Beverly Faulk, who owned the antiques store, walked in to the Crossroads Cafe for lunch. She looked about for an empty booth and saw Liz Traynor, the Baptist church pianist, sitting at a booth behind Earl Perry. Liz had been out of town for a weekend visiting her daughter in Tulsa, and thus Beverly and Liz had not seen each other in all of twelve days.

"Liz! Where *have* you been, Hon?" Beverly called over the clink of knives and forks against china and the babel of conversation. "I haven't seen you in *ages*."

"Beverly Faulk! Come *here*, Darlin'. Sit down. No, wait. I can't let you sit down without gettin' a hug first."

At 12:17, while Beverly Faulk and Liz Traynor were—as Balaam would have put it—"carryin' on," Balaam had gotten—again, as he would have put it—his "pecker in a pinch." Less figuratively, he had gotten his shovel in a crack. Balaam was at work on the first item on his "to do" list: gathering stones to build a wall for his flowerbed. His source of stones was a limestone ridge at the far end of his property. Balaam had been inserting his shovel blade into crevices in the limestone, then standing on the blade with both feet to force it down for better leverage as he pried stones loose. But now he had bitten off more than his shovel could chew. The shovel blade was wedged tightly. He could not free it by wiggling the handle from side to side. And when he pulled back on the shovel handle, he could tell that the handle would break before the limestone did.

By 12:19, Beverly and Liz had unclenched, Beverly had seated herself and ordered, and the two women had settled in to visiting. Thus it was that Mayor Perry, in the booth behind them, could not help overhearing Beverly when she said to Liz, "I guess you heard that Flora is giving up and closing that little pottery shop of hers."

Had anyone present been inclined to count, when the mayor heard the word "closing," his forkful of green beans stopped between plate and mouth for a full three count of Willoughby's flashing red light.

By 12:19, Balaam knew that to free his shovel he would have to use the rock bar—a five-foot-long iron rod with a wide, chisel-like tip. Balaam raised the rock bar over his head and rammed it down onto the crevice beside the shovel head. A few chips flew off, but the shovel remained wedged. He would have to keep ramming until he got the tip of the rock bar far enough into the crevice to use the bar as a lever.

At the Crossroads Cafe just before 1:00 P.M., Mayor Perry sat in his booth as the lunch crowd thinned. He idly plowed the food on his plate with his fork and wished a wish that he had repeated so often that it had become his municipal mantra: He wished that something—*anything*—would happen to reverse Willoughby's fortunes.

At the limestone ridge just before 1:00 P.M., after several attempts to free his shovel, Balaam was out of breath, and his arms were aching; the limestone had not broken a sweat. For Balaam, it was becoming personal. He took off his glasses, adjusted his work gloves, planted his feet, raised the rock bar as high as he could over his head, and slammed it down into the crevice with all the might he could muster.

❧2❧

"I hear that Balaam and Ray Dean were doing something or other out at his place. Something about rotten eggs and a half-dozen brunettes."
———Euell Liddy

In the instant that Balaam Gimble's rock bar made contact with the limestone, Balaam Gimble's brain was far busier than it liked to be on a weekend: From each side, the ears were telling it that the rock bar had dealt the crevice a solid blow; from below, the knees were telling it that they had fallen hard to the ground; the cheeks were telling it that they had been hit by an uprush of hot, moist air; the nose was telling it that the hot, moist air smelled like rotten eggs; and the eyes were telling it that the rock bar had just disappeared into the ground.

As Balaam knelt, he turned his head and buried his nose in the sleeve of his shirt. When he turned back, the hot, moist air and the odor had dissipated somewhat. He stared at the ragged two-inch hole in the ground with awe and repugnance, as if he had lanced a boil on the butt of the planet. Then his right knee spoke up. He stood and found that when he had fallen to his knees, the impact had torn his jeans and bruised his kneecap, which was throbbing.

He placed his gloves one atop the other on the ground and used them to cushion his right knee as he knelt to look into the hole. He could not see more than a few inches. So he dropped a pebble into the hole and listened.

Silence for a half-second, then a plunk.

He dropped another pebble.

Half-second . . . plunk.

"Water," he said aloud.

He estimated how far a pebble would fall in a half-second. Maybe ten feet or more. So there was ten feet or more of cavity down there.

A cave.

The little boy that remained in fifty-six-year-old Balaam Gimble picked up his sledge hammer and began to pound away at the hole, each blow sending a shower of chips flying. By 2:00 P.M., the hole was large enough to allow a thin shaft of sunlight onto the dark surface of the water. By 3:00 P.M., he had widened the hole enough that a man could pass through. The limestone was more than a foot thick. Balaam knew that he had to go down there. But Balaam also knew that he was going to need help.

He drove back to his cabin and phoned Ray Dean Briley. Ray Dean farmed six hundred acres on the other side of Willoughby. Most men around Willoughby had a kinship with ranching and farming, even if they lived and worked in town. To them the work was a heritage that was akin to genetics in its hold on them. To them the long hours and hard work—spent mending fences, pulling stumps, feeding, fertilizing, plowing, harvesting, transporting stock to market, moving stock from one pasture to another, bouncing along pastures in pickups—were soothing, self-defining, almost transcendental. The plowed field and the grazed pasture—these were for such men a zen garden.

Such work allowed such men to be left alone, to be independent of bosses and bureaucrats. A man never had to read an interoffice memo in a pasture. A man never had to stand in a line, find a parking space, receive a performance review, fill out a form, or "press one to repeat this menu" in a corn field.

Ray Dean Briley was such a man. He was forty-seven, had dark curly hair, dark eyes, and an enthusiastic attitude. He also had a winch on his pickup. After Ray Dean arrived at Balaam's limestone ridge, he had to experience the same sense of discovery that Balaam had. He lay down and put his head into the hole and smelled the rotten egg odor and felt the moist heat. He dropped pebbles into the hole and listened to the plunks. He shouted into the hole and heard the reverberation.

18

"Damn, Balaam," Ray Dean said as he stood up and dusted himself off. "That's a new one on me. There's caves south of here, closer to the Hill Country, but I never heard of any up here."

"Nope."

Ray Dean moved his pickup closer to the hole, positioning the winch while Balaam took off his socks and boots, tucked a flashlight inside his belt, and sat on the edge of the hole.

"Ready?" Ray Dean asked.

"Okay."

As soon as Balaam slid off the edge of the hole and was hanging suspended from the winch cable, Ray Dean switched on the winch and watched Balaam disappear as the cable played out. Balaam felt a tingle of panic as first his feet, then his legs began to sink into the hot water, even though he doubted that the water was deep. Just as the water was rising above his waist, he felt solid rock under his feet.

"Okay," Balaam shouted. Ray Dean switched off the winch.

"What do you see?" Ray Dean was looking down from the hole. When Balaam looked up, he saw only a silhouette as the sunlight behind Ray Dean formed a halo around his head.

"You look like an angel, Ray Dean."

"Tell that to my wife."

Balaam switched on his flashlight and slowly turned in a circle. He saw that the cave was not large—maybe fifteen feet across. It was shaped roughly like an inverted bowl, with the ceiling sloping out and down at the edges where it met the floor. Only in the middle could a person stand straight. In the center of the cave was the pool of water; around the pool was a ledge of limestone that was wide enough to sit on.

"All the rock down here is coated with something that looks like petrified meringue. Like one of Juanita's pies—sorta gray and frothy."

"Mineral deposits, you reckon?"

"I guess. I don't see any real—what are they called?—stalactites or stalagmites. Just lots of points about the size of Hershey Kisses."

The water was hot—about bath water temperature. But the air in the cave was not uncomfortably hot. And the odor had lessened, or maybe Balaam was just getting used to it. He began slowly wading around, exploring, feeling the limestone floor with his bare feet. The

19

floor was fairly level and smooth. Just when Balaam thought that his feet had mapped the floor, he stubbed his toe.

"Dam-*nation!*" Balaam almost plunged the flashlight into the water as he instinctively tried to keep his balance on one foot.

"What? What is it?"

"I found the rock bar."

"Oh." It was an "oh" of disappointment, as in "Oh. I was hoping you'd found pirate treasure."

Balaam waited a few seconds until he could put his weight on the stubbed foot, then, with his other foot, he lifted one end of the rock bar high enough to grab it and fastened it to the end of the cable. Ray Dean reeled it up.

Balaam called up to Ray Dean, "Find me a leaf up there."

"A *leaf?* What kind of leaf?"

"Any kind. I want to see something."

Ray Dean plucked a leaf from a nearby live oak and let it flutter down to Balaam. Balaam placed the leaf flat on the surface of the water in the center of the pool. As Balaam watched closely, the leaf began to sail toward the edge of the pool.

"This water is moving," Balaam announced. "Slow. But it's moving."

"Damn" was the reply from on high.

Balaam knew that Ray Dean was eager to have his turn, so he told Ray Dean to reel him up. Then Balaam manned the winch and lowered Ray Dean—fully clothed—through the hole.

"God J. O'Mighty," Ray Dean said as he reached the bottom. The awe in his voice reverberated. "Send me down a bottle of sangria and a six-pack of brunettes. This thing is a friggin' hot tub!"

Balaam laughed. "Funny—you sure as shootin' don't *sound* like an angel."

In the water, Ray Dean stripped down to his shorts. He tied his clothes around the end of the cable and told Balaam to reel it up. When Balaam saw the clothes surface on the end of cable, he called down, "Are you buck naked down there?"

"Not quite. I'm saving that for the brunettes."

Balaam heard an exaggerated "pa-tooey."

"Did you taste this stuff, Balaam?"

"No way. This cave might have been a dinosaur latrine."

"It's salty. And maybe the rotten egg smell is sulfur."

"You hope."

"This is *so* neat." Then Ray Dean cackled madly and began splashing. He completely submerged himself in the water, kicking and thrashing and hollering just to hear his voice reverberate.

The evening star was shining by the time Ray Dean let Balaam reel him up. Ray Dean put on his wet jeans, and the two men leaned back against a fender of the pickup in the darkness and discussed the hole, like two disembodied voices. Every time Ray Dean took a drag on his cigarette, the tip glowed in the dark like a firefly.

"Reckon where the water comes from? And why is it hot?"

"Beats me. Must be a spring somewhere. Somewhere hot."

A moment of silence followed.

"What are you going to do with it, Balaam?"

"Do with it? What do you mean, 'do with it'? It's a cave. A hole in the ground. Not much you *can* do with it."

"But, Balaam, I mean, a *cave*. It's *got* to be good for something. It must have a use of *some* kind."

Balaam could think of no uses, and all the uses that Ray Dean could think of at the moment involved brunettes in one way or another.

That night, after Ray Dean and his winch had gone, Balaam sat on his porch, listening as the rural night shift came on duty: About 8:00 P.M., across the road, coyotes began to howl and then to yip with excitement as they gathered to hunt. A mourning dove called to its mate. From somewhere in the woods came the four-note call of a chuck-will's-widow, the first that Balaam had heard that spring.

Soon the coolness of the night drove him inside. Before Balaam went to bed, he took two aspirin for the pain in the knee that he had banged. As he lay there in the dark, waiting for the aspirin to take effect and replaying the day's events at the cave, he noticed that the pulse in his knee was throbbing in time with the lullaby of the chuck-will's-widow.

⋇3⋇

*"Did you know that Balaam has had that old pickup of his twenty years?
Helen Riesel says he apparently plans to drive it to heaven when he dies.
I told her he might wanna think about washing it first."*
——Mary Lou Wyatt

Balaam was awakened the next morning by the sound of Stilts nudging his hubcap along the ground with his nose.

"Breakfast in two minutes," Balaam called through the open window.

Because the previous day's working hours had been lost to finding and exploring the cave, Balaam had not gotten around to his paying work. After breakfast, he loaded tools and supplies into the bed of his pickup, which was parked just outside the compound fence. Balaam drove a Frankenford—a 1980 Ford pickup that was kept alive past its natural lifespan by the transplantation of parts from donor pickups: The hood, the right door, the back bumper, the bench seat, and several engine parts had come from wrecked Fords at salvage yards.

He got behind the wheel, turned the ignition switch to "on," shifted the transmission into first gear, and let the pickup roll quietly down the driveway, slowly picking up speed. At just the right place, he popped the clutch and let the engine lurch to life. He had decided long ago that "there's no use in wearing out a starter when you've got all this gravity lying around for free."

As Balaam drove in to town, he stopped at another of J. D. Vernon's deer feeders to let his kidneys pay their respects. Then he drove on to the Willoughby cemetery. Balaam was unofficial caretaker of the cemetery, located on the edge of town. He tried to get by twice a month to dispose of wilted flowers on the graves, spray weeds, mow, and trim around the upright tombstones, of which there were many in a cemetery that old. He always began his work in the Gimble section, which was located in the oldest part of the cemetery and set off by a crumbling concrete curb. There were seventeen Gimble tombstones, including those of his parents, grandparents, great-grandparents, and older brother Salathiel.

Balaam's and Salathiel's biblical names had been no fluke. Balaam's siblings had been named Salathiel, Solomon, Thomas, and Mary. Each time their mother, Bessie, had gotten pregnant, she had done two things: She had developed strange food cravings, and she had scoured the Bible for names to inflict upon her babe-to-be. With the firstborn, it had been laundry detergent and "Salathiel." With the second, it had been clay and "Solomon." With the third, it had been starch and "Thomas." With the fourth and fifth, it had been ice cubes and saltine crackers and "Mary" and "Balaam."

Growing up, Balaam had had to endure the inevitable jokes about "Balaam's ass" from his peers. But at least he and Salathiel had not been given names that a mother could expect a child to live up to. For example, there was Balaam's brother, Solomon. Was Solomon Gimble wise? Certainly. As wise as a man with three divorces, a suspended driver's license, and an addiction to horse racing could be. Then there was Balaam's sister, Mary Gimble. Was Mary Gimble virginal? Absolutely. Right up until Halloween night of her junior year in high school. And how about brother Thomas Gimble? Was he doubting? Not at all. When Mary had told Thomas, on the day after that Halloween night, that she had been out until 3:00 A.M. "carving jack-o-lanterns," he had believed every word she had said.

Salathiel had taken after their mother. Religious. He had been born in 1937 and again in 1981. But he had died only once—in 1994. His was the only Gimble tombstone that was flush with the ground—a small marble rectangle with unfinished edges. As Balaam tidied the Gimble section of the cemetery, he took a whisk broom from his back pocket and flicked dirt and grass clippings out of the recessed lettering. With his fingernail he scraped off a dried bird dropping.

"There you go, Salathiel. Good as new," he said to the tombstone.

Balaam stood up and moved his eyes across all those Gimble names. Seventeen people. He had been at the bedside when some, such as his father, had died; Balaam and his mother and other family members had stood around Henry's bed, linked hand in hand with Henry's clutching claw of a hand, as if their pitiful human lifeline could somehow keep him from slipping beyond their grasp. Others, like his grandparents, were just a few faded sepia memories to Balaam. Still others, like his great-grandparents, had always been only names and dates carved on stone totems above the words "Asleep in the Arms of Jesus."

Only one unused plot remained in the Gimble section of the Willoughby cemetery. It was reserved for one Balaam Gimble. Balaam looked down. He was standing on it.

After Balaam had mowed and was trimming the rest of the cemetery, he saw Charley Griggs at the other side of the cemetery. Charley was seventy-six and had been a widower for ten years. His wife's name had been Iola, but he had always called her "Mama," even though they had had no children. Every year on the anniversary of her death, Charley placed flowers on her grave. Balaam shut off the weed trimmer and walked over to say hello. As he came up behind Charley, he noticed that Charley had placed his flowers at the grave of Iola's sister Betty, who was buried next to Iola.

"Charley, that's Betty's grave, ain't it?"

Charley turned to squint at Balaam, then turned back and squinted at the two graves. He walked between them, bent over, and squinted left and right.

"Hell. How could I do that? Damn it. Mama always used to think I was a little too fond of Betty. What's she gonna think *now?*"

Balaam chuckled. "She's gonna think just what I think, Charley: that you've lost your good glasses again, haven't you?"

Charley shook his head woefully. "Oh, Balaam, I've even lost the glasses that I wear to *find* my good glasses."

Charley moved his flowers to the correct grave, mumbling what was probably an apology to Mama. Balaam said, "You be careful getting back home" as Charley shuffled away down the walkway toward the little gravel parking lot. Charley's and Balaam's pickups were parked next to each other beside a large oak tree. Both pickups were dark in color, but Balaam's was a Ford, Charley's a Chevy. Balaam watched Charley open the door of the Ford and climb in. Balaam mentally ticked off the seconds as he envisioned Charley trying to fit his Chevy key into the Ford ignition switch. Then he watched Charley climb out of Balaam's pickup and shuffle around to his own and get in. Balaam saw the tailpipe cough gray smoke, then watched Charley's pickup move slowly out of the parking lot. If a pickup could shuffle, Charley's was shuffling as it headed toward the highway.

After Balaam finished at the cemetery, he drove a few blocks farther in to town. First he stopped at Imogene Ratliff's. Imogene was a large woman, given to wearing bright yellow dresses and experimenting—with mixed results—with her hair rinse. On that day, she looked like a school bus with blue highlights. The frame of her wooden screen door had begun to sag, causing the door to stick in the upper left side. Balaam added a corner brace and a turnbuckle to keep the frame square, then painted the door edge and the doorway where they had rubbed. He charged Imogene three dollars.

Then he drove four blocks over and one block down to Mazelle Henderson's home. When Mazelle's grandson, age four, came to visit her, he was fond of putting coins down her kitchen sink drain when no one was watching. Mazelle usually discovered his latest deposit when she turned on the garbage disposer later and heard it try to make change.

It didn't take Balaam long, using a flexible magnetic rod, to fish three quarters and a dime out of the disposer's grinding chamber. While he was in the kitchen working and Mazelle was in the living room watching one of her "stories" on TV, he noticed that her faucet was dripping. So he ground the valve seats and replaced the washers. That's the way it is with these old folks on fixed incomes, Balaam knew. For every one repair they can pay for, there were ten more they can't pay for. Balaam knew that Mazelle's Social Security check was all she had, that each day she went to Town Hall for the subsidized lunch for senior citizens. Balaam, too, would have no pension after he grew too old to work. He wondered if, like Mazelle and others he knew, he would have to buy store brands to save a few cents, have to clip coupons, have to seriously consider whether to pay the electric bill promptly or to let it ride as long as he could. He was not sure that he could live more frugally than he already did.

When Mazelle asked Balaam how much she owed him, he said, "Don't worry about it, Mazelle. I can get money lots of places, but there's only one place where I can get one of your pecan pies. Just save me one next time you bake."

Back home that evening, Balaam again sat on his porch past dusk. Now and then Stilts appeared from amid the rows of clutter, as if to check in. Each time, Stilts would walk up to Balaam and lower his head to have his ears rubbed. Then he would disappear among the shadows of the trees and the rows of clutter. After Balaam went inside to go to bed, he had already opened the aspirin bottle and shaken two out into the palm of his hand before he realized that the pain in his knee, although still there, was less noticeable, despite the fact that he had aggravated it when he had "banged the fire out of it" while working on Mazelle's sink.

He put the two aspirin back into the bottle.

Balaam lay awake for a while, listening to the night sounds: the calling of night birds, the tinkling of the cowbell, the popping of the tin roof as it cooled and contracted. As Balaam Gimble fell asleep on that night in April, he was too tired to notice that the pulse in his knee no longer throbbed in time with the lullaby of the chuck-will's-widow.

❧ 4 ❧

"Nanetta told me that son of hers gets paid to think up the names for lipstick colors. But aren't all lipsticks red?"

——Cecil Bell

Two hours away in Houston, as David Wilson tried to fall asleep on that night in April, he noticed that the pulse in his temples was throbbing in time with the booming bass beat of the stereo next door. David Wilson had a headache. A the-teenager-next-door-is-throwing-a-party headache. He took a bottle of aspirin off the night stand, shook out two, swallowed, and chased them with a glass of water and a mild curse.

His neighbors—the parents, anyway—were away for the night, and their teenage daughter had stayed home, apparently—judging from the racket—having received a grant to collect and catalogue the acoustic signatures of puberty. Even with his windows closed, David Wilson could hear, in addition to the music, the giggling trysts outside in the shadows between the two houses, the occasional shattering of glass, the slamming of doors, the screeching of tires in the street, and the issuing of offers to "whip your ass, dude."

Despite the juvenile apocalypse next door, David's home was a nice townhouse on a nice street in a nice suburb. Such "nices" befit his position as a senior copywriter at one of Houston's most lucrative ad agencies, Adams, Hawkins, & Jenrette. Trafficking in words—the right words for the right clients—for thirty years had provided him with a country club membership that he never used and a portfolio of mutual funds that should, in his declining years, keep the wolf from the door, if not off the porch altogether.

David Wilson was *the* ad copywriter for the Ms.-tique Cosmetics account. The president of Ms.-tique, Claudia Curtis, thought that David was God's gift to adjectives. Through the years, she had attributed much of the success of Ms.-tique Cosmetics to David's ad copy, especially the names that he came up with for her lipsticks, eye shadows, and nail polishes. In fact, she put so much faith in his nose for names that she insisted that his copy not be edited by his superiors at Adams, Hawkins, & Jenrette. She did not want his copy to be, as she put it, "monkeyed with by some putz with a red pencil." David's copy went straight to her.

The Ms.-tique Cosmetics account was big enough that AH&J let her have her way.

Claudia Curtis believed that David came up with each name for her products after engaging in intense communion with each color sample for the new lipstick, eye shadow, or nail polish. In truth, David thought up the names almost arbitrarily, sometimes with barely a glance at the samples. He had learned years ago that the name need not have much in common with the color. Indeed, the name need not so much as hint at the color. Connotation and imagery were everything.

Alliteration always worked, he had found: Midnight Mauve, French Fantasy, Reckless Red.

Suggestion—naughty but nice—also worked: Candy Kisses, Rendezvous, Amorous, Stolen Moments, Afternoon Delight, Breathless.

Such names, David was well aware, just as easily could be the titles of soft-porn movies.

The work paid his bills, but it did not feed his soul. No one sets out after college to make the naming of lipsticks and nail polishes a life's work. Few children, when asked what they want to be when they grow up, answer with, "I want to be a writer whose prose makes women favor one brand of eye shadow over another." But there he was. For that reason, David Wilson had created what he thought of as his "cyanide file"—a list of cosmetics names so outrageous and in such poor taste that submitting them to Claudia Curtis would surely get him fired. Just having the list gave him great comfort. Sometimes he took it out of its locked desk drawer and read it. Then back into the drawer it went to be ready in case the day should come when it would be called upon to put David Wilson out of his misery.

Earlier that night, David had talked with his mother, Nanetta, on the phone, again suggesting that she sell that big old house in Willoughby and move down to Houston, perhaps into a small apartment near him. After David's father had died, Nanetta had moved to Willoughby to care for her elderly Aunt Mimi and had remained in Mimi's house after her death. Nanetta was seventy-three now, and although she was in good health, her mind—especially her memory—was not as sharp. Lately she had begun to ask David when Doodles, her terrier, was due his shots. David refrained from reminding her that Doodles had been dead for three years.

David knew that Willoughby didn't have a doctor, and he had little confidence in the nearest hospital. As Nanetta had gotten older, he had encouraged her to drive less. Toward that end, he now made the drive to Willoughby every other Friday after work and brought her back to Houston to see a movie or a play, eat at a nice restaurant, maybe strafe the malls on a few shopping sorties. He kept his spare bedroom set aside for her. It gave her something to dust away from home.

On that night in April, David listened to—he swore he could *feel*—the relentless dull thumping of the bass next door: *boom* ba *boom* ba *boom* ba.

"God," he said to himself, "it's like living in 'The Telltale Heart.'"

He picked up his bedroom phone and dialed. An adolescent male voice answered.

"Hello. This is Mr. Wilson next door." He had to raise his voice to be heard. "May I speak with Jennifer? . . . Jennifer Hastings. She lives there. . . . No, *Hastings*, as in the Battle of . . . oh, never mind. Look, she's about five-foot-six or so, long blond hair, one of those nose rings, I think. . . . Well, yes, I guess she does sound cute. Would you please just go find her for me?"

The boy who had answered the phone must have set the receiver down next to the kitchen sink. David could hear water splashing. Then he heard a "Hello?"

"Jennifer? Jennifer, this is Mr. Wilson next door. Jennifer, about the music . . . no, Jennifer, I do *not* want to request a song. . . . No, I don't believe I have ever heard of that particular band. . . . Yes, I'm sure you do own every CD they've ever made. Jennifer, I'd appreciate it if you'd turn down the music a bit. It's very loud over here. No, Jennifer, I did not tell that young man that I think you're cute. I was merely describing you so that he could . . . no, I don't mean you're *not* cute, Jennifer. Certainly you *are* cute, but please don't think that I meant . . ."

David saw that this conversation would take no prisoners.

"Look, Jennifer, just try to keep the noise down, okay? Thank you, dear. . . . Uh, Jennifer, I didn't mean anything by 'dear.' It's just a . . . oh, good night, uh, Ms. Hastings."

A few seconds after he hung up the phone, David heard the bass boom diminish by a few decibels. Within three minutes, it was as loud as ever.

A half-hour later, David was in bed but still awake when the first police car arrived next door. Through a slit in his drapes he saw the car's flashing light. He realized—gratefully, almost giddily—that sleep would surely come soon now. David Wilson's last fuzzy thought that night was that the color of the police car's flashing light was Reckless Red.

❧ 5 ❧

*"You know, you could lie down and take a nap in most streets of
this town and never get run over. That's no way to live!"*
———Earl Perry

At the flashing red light in Willoughby, Mayor Earl Perry sat in his
usual booth in the Crossroads Cafe on Monday morning and
stirred his coffee. Demographically, Earl Perry was representative of
Willoughby and, indeed, of most small Texas towns: white, Protestant,
over fifty, and born locally. Even those residents of Willoughby who
did leave town, perhaps after high school to take jobs in Waco or
Houston or Dallas, often moved back in twenty or thirty years to care
for aging parents or to look after homes or farms left behind by the
death of a parent. Each year more of the town's population was fifty
or older—the no-longer-a-baby boomers. One group of a half-dozen
or so such men was known affectionately as "the Boys." The Boys were
anything but. Average age: seventy-one. Average number of original
teeth: twenty-two. Willis Pinkston, Joe Adair, Charley Griggs, Lon "Big
Un" Petteway, and others of the Boys gathered daily on a bench in front
of the bank to watch the world of Willoughby go by and to comment
on what they saw—a Greek chorus in gimme caps.

Few people in town were rich, few were poor. Most ailments were
those that came from working hard or growing old. Stress, like wealth
and poverty, was rare. Willoughby was an ulcer-free zone.

Earl Perry looked out the window of the cafe. The parking lot contained more pickups than cars. Some of the pickups had stock trailers hitched behind them. Most had beds filled with the miscellany of farming and ranching: rolls of fencing, post-hole diggers, come-alongs, ropes, chain saws, water jugs, truck and tractor parts, vetting supplies, feed sacks both full and empty.

Willoughby men were a physical genus—accustomed to manual labor all their lives—and seldom went to bed anything but exhausted. For these men, indoors was where you go when it gets too dark to work.

Willoughby women were less physical, but they played many roles. In the same morning, a Willoughby woman might be called upon to take the crust off a sandwich with a knife, a splinter out of a finger with a needle, and the head off a rattlesnake with a hoe. Earl Perry nodded to Birdie Wagstaff, who had taken a seat at a table across the cafe. He knew for a fact that Birdie, like other Willoughby women, had nursed runt calves, midwifed colts, bandaged bleeding hands and feet, spoiled her grandchildren, spanked her children, and outlived her husband.

Residents were a homogeneous group. They were conservative, sharing core values. Rain in the spring, air conditioning in the summer, and football in the fall: These were the holy trinity of rural Texas. Even their differences were so slight as to reflect their similarities: education—tenth grade or twelfth; service—Korea or Vietnam; pickup—Chevy or Ford; tractor—John Deere or Kubota; cattle—Hereford or Angus; crop—corn or wheat; music—Hank Williams (Sr. or Jr.).

Culturally, Willoughby's orbit was well outside the gravitational pull of large cities such as Houston, Dallas, and Austin. Residents seldom found need to go to those cities. On Friday nights, most young people who were old enough to drive headed to Waco, moths drawn to the bright lights. In Waco they could misbehave, well beyond the range of Willoughby's social radar.

Neither fad nor social upheaval shook the bedrock of Willoughby's status quo. For the most part, Willoughby was vaguely aware of—but little affected by—the sexual revolution, the women's movement, and the technology revolution. Through the years, residents reacted to such tumults much as they would to the Middle East peace process or the Russian space program: "It's none of our affair."

Earl Perry looked out the window at the flashing red light. There were no cars at the intersection. From the light, Willoughby's downtown extended one block in each direction along Highways 21 and 36. In that cross-shaped area were a dozen small businesses. There were also six empty buildings and four vacant lots.

Downtown Willoughby had not always been so meager. During its salad days, eighty years earlier, when oil had made people rich overnight and cotton had kept them that way, the town had had a population of three thousand and many fine homes. Trains had provided freight and passenger service. The town had had several oil company offices, a cotton gin, a sawmill, a brickyard, two hotels, a daily newspaper, a doctor, an undertaker, a law office, a drugstore, a dry goods store, two banks, three schools (two white, one colored), four churches, and, depending on whom you asked, zero or four whorehouses.

Balaam Gimble's grandfather had farmed cotton on the family land back then. In fact, a horse and wagon belonging to him had brought in the first wagonload of cotton to Willoughby's new gin in the 1920s. The bank was being built at the time, and to tie the two momentous events together, civic leaders had embedded the shoes worn by that horse in the concrete of the sidewalk as it was being poured in front of the bank. Balaam only vaguely remembered his grandfather, did not remember the horse at all, but he knew the family story well, and now, each time he went downtown, he paused to plant both of his feet momentarily on those two horseshoes for luck.

Gradually the oil and the cotton had played out. By 1940, people had begun moving away from Willoughby, businesses had begun to close. Now the trains barely slowed when passing through town. There was not a single unit of lodging, and Willoughby children had to travel fifteen miles to attend schools in a larger town.

But here and there a bit of the prosperity of those years could still be seen. There remained a few big homes that had been built in the 1920s as showcases. Nanetta Wilson lived in such a home. It had belonged to her Aunt Mimi, who had married an oilman in 1922. He had built for Mimi a high, wide, and handsome two-story monument to ostentation, complete with a wraparound porch supported by fluted columns on the first story, a wide railed balcony on the second story, a chimney on each side, and a widow's walk on the roof. It looked less like a house than a riverboat. Nanetta lived there alone these days, dusting and polishing. Someday the house would belong to Nanetta's son, David, if he wanted it, which she very much doubted. Balaam Gimble mowed her lawn, did odd jobs for her, tried to keep the big house afloat. Often, after Balaam had settled up with her and gone, Nanetta discovered that he had repaired more than he had been asked to or been paid for.

From where Earl Perry sat in the Crossroads Cafe that morning, he could see reminders of Willoughby's better days along two short stretches of downtown. Perry's grocery and feedstore, City Hall, and the bank at one end, and the newspaper office, the boarded-up Mexican restaurant, and Town Hall at the other end stood shoulder to shoulder, each sharing a sidewall with its neighbor in row-house fashion. Along their facades, ornate fanlights, brickwork, limestone cornices, and other flourishes bespoke a time when Willoughby had money.

Town Hall was housed in the former dry goods store building. It had a seating capacity of forty folding chairs—about twice the number usually needed—and was used for community meetings, senior citizens lunches, elections, and charity events. City Hall was housed in the former drugstore building, a narrow storefront that was barely more conspicuous than a speakeasy. The office of the town's biweekly newspaper, the *Willoughby Bee*, was housed in the former law office building. The *Bee*, published by sisters Anita and Rosalee Taft, was four pages of news that everyone already knew days before the paper was published. In Willoughby, news spread by word of mouth: over neighbors' fences, at bank teller windows, in the post office lobby, and, of course, in cafe booths.

Like every small-town grapevine, Willoughby's grapevine employed its own version of the journalist's traditional five *W*'s: "Who?," "What?," "When?," "Where?," and "Why, don't that beat all?!" The good, the bad, and the juicy spread fast. For example, if Mary Lou Wyatt's daughter Becky came home from junior college for the weekend with her ears pierced, word would spread from one end of town to the other in three hours (maybe two, if Becky came home with anything besides her ears pierced).

Word that Balaam Gimble had found a cave on his property had spread with only moderate rapidity. Most residents classified the cave as interesting but of no aesthetic or practical value, much like watch pockets on pants or Imogene Ratliff's latest hair color.

The pace of life in Willoughby, seldom feverish even downtown, was even less animated beyond downtown. Along Highway 21, just three blocks from the cafe and the flashing red light, bantam roosters and their harems of hens browsed in the grassy bar ditches beside the road. In the summer, along Highway 36, just two blocks from the flashing red light, women wore straw hats and tended backyard gardens, always growing more than they could eat or can or give away. So they placed in their front yards handpainted signs advertising fresh tomatoes, okra, squash, peaches, and cantaloupe for sale. The produce was always stacked in neat pyramids on card tables for maximum curb appeal; the word *cantaloupe* was never spelled the same way twice.

Older residents living along the two highways waved to every vehicle that passed as they sat on their front porches. Their homes reflected Willoughby's architectural anarchy—mobile homes next to grand Victorian homes next to small businesses next to cows grazing in side lots. There were unpainted shotgun houses along one side of the railroad track and neat little prairie-style houses on the other side, their front yards decorated with beds of irises accented by wagon wheels, antique farm implements, and sun-bleached cow skulls.

As Perry finished his coffee that morning, Ray Dean Briley came in to the cafe, waved or nodded to a few faces, and sat down opposite him.

"Hidy, Earl. We need rain."

"Hidy, Ray Dean. 'Deed we do. How's the bursitis?"

Weather and health were the surest of small-town small-talk starters.

Ray Dean rotated his left arm at the shoulder. "You know, it's a bit better today. This morning I had to raise——."

But Perry had already stopped listening. The fact that Ray Dean Briley's bursitis was a bit better was, to Mayor Earl Perry, like the Middle East peace process or the Russian space program: It was none of his affair.

⁂ 6 ⁂

*"Dad points to his left side and says his liver hurts. I told him the doctor
says a person's liver is located on the* right *side. So Dad says, 'Well,
then, Buster, my liver's on the wrong side. No wonder it hurts.'"*
———Little Un Petteway

At 5:00 P.M. on that Monday afternoon, rush hour, technically, was
under way. But not one vehicle had passed through Willoughby's
main intersection in almost a minute—fifty-four flashes of the flashing
red light, to be precise.

By 5:45, however, the first five of perhaps twenty cars and pickups
converged on the intersection, all bound for a Town Hall meeting. This
was Willoughby's attempt at a traffic jam.

For most people who were driving to the meeting, the trip was very
short. Indeed, those people who had gathered at the Crossroads Cafe
just across the street to eat supper first could have simply walked over
to Town Hall. But Mayor Perry encouraged everyone to drive to Town
Hall meetings and City Council meetings because a full parking lot
looked more impressive, gave the town the illusion of being robust. On
this Friday, he parked in the vacant lot next to Town Hall and walked
around to the front of the building to unlock the door. As he walked,
he saw, a few blocks in the distance, the town's water tower. The sight
of the tower always made Mayor Perry flinch mentally. In 1939, after
the tower had been erected, the man who had been painting the town's

name in big, bold letters on the side of the tower had drunk his lunch one day, fallen off the tower, and had broken his neck after completing just the first four letters of "Willoughby." By 1939, the town had been in decline, and no one had ever been hired to finish the lettering. Now, sometimes the few travelers who stopped while passing through assumed that the town's name was "Will."

Every few years some of the local kids would get rowdy, climb the tower, paint a slash through the "Will" with whitewash, and paint "Won't" beside it.

To Mayor Perry, that pretty well summed up Willoughby's state of the union.

And that was why he had called the Town Hall meeting: to discuss Willoughby's inert economy.

Most of the regulars were in attendance.

Juanita Greer was there, dark haired and perpetually tired. Her husband, Richard, was minding the cafe. To cover all the business hours of a "mom and pop" cafe, the two worked different shifts, seeing each other only when her shift ended and his began. At home, they were seldom awake at the same time. Juanita and Richard had been married almost seven years, but Juanita said she had figured out that they had been married actually just three years based on how many waking hours they had shared. The cafe was their only child.

Dewayne Petteway was there. Dewayne ran the two-pump gas station next to the cafe. "Dewayne" was the name on his birth certificate, but most residents of Willoughby would have had to think a moment to recall his Christian name. To everyone, he was "Little Un." He was the son of Lon "Big Un" Petteway, who by the age of fourteen had weighed two hundred and twenty pounds and had stood six-foot-three. It was inevitable that any baby born to a father nicknamed "Big Un" would be nicknamed "Little Un." Little Un was now forty-four years old and at two hundred and thirty pounds outweighed his father, but the nickname lived on.

A delegation of the Boys also was in attendance.

Charley Griggs was there, having found his good glasses soon after he had returned home from the cemetery.

Willis and Jessie Pinkston were there. Both were getting along in years but in good health, except for Willis's psoriasis. Jessie was a big woman. She entered Town Hall like a full-rigged sailing ship and immediately docked at a folding chair to catch her breath. Jessie was one of those women on whom every small town depends: a volunteer. She volunteered for everything: charity events, church socials, senior citizens lunches, the Founders Day parade. Willis was a feisty little stob of a man with eyes as hard as knot holes. He had worked thirty-seven years as an electrician, wiring everything from businesses to barns. The rest of the Boys liked to say that Willis had been shocked so many times that he glowed in the dark. If wife Jessie was around to hear that crack, she would always counter that Willis did *not* glow in the dark and that she should know—she'd been there enough times. To which Willis would always counter with, "Well, maybe you just ain't found the switch yet, woman." Then everyone would laugh. It was vaudeville, Willoughby style.

And Big Un Petteway was there, wearing his faded blue overalls. The buttons on his chest looked like brass nipples.

As people arrived, the room filled with pre-meeting small talk.

"I saw that boy of yours at the bank. He's looking more like his daddy every day."

"You gonna have any okra this year?"

"I had two calves get out last week under the fence where it always washes out."

Big Un, of course, was talking about the only two things that he ever talked about: rainfall and his liver. Rainfall was a passion among all those whose rural livelihoods depended on it. But with Big Un rainfall bordered on an obsession. He had lived through the Texas droughts of the 1950s, when the ground had cracked and stock ponds had evaporated and cattle and crops alike had died of thirst. He had learned to revel in rain. He kept a rainfall log in his den just as other people might keep a wedding album or a family Bible. When rain fell, he would stop what he was doing to watch it, to listen to it, to smell it. He would phone people where he knew it was not raining, hold the receiver out his back door, and make them listen to "his" rain.

He had a way of putting any topic of conversation, even global issues, into the context of Willoughby rainfall. Once in a while, just to see Big Un bust his buttons, the rest of the Boys would spike his rain gauge. During a rain shower, one of the Boys would phone Big Un to distract him, and another of the Boys would drive by his house and pour water into his rain gauge, adding an inch or two to the rain that was falling. Then they'd all wait for Big Un to brag.

Big Un's other passion was his liver. He was convinced, despite the consistent findings of medical science to the contrary, that his liver was on the fritz. He wanted an operation but could not afford it. To humor him, Little Un had promised that if he could save enough money from the gas station, he would treat Big Un to an organ transplant of his choice.

The Taft sisters—Rosalee and Anita—were there, of course, to cover the meeting for the *Bee* and to supply the after-meeting punch and cookies. With the *Bee*'s intimate reader base, Rosalee and Anita kept the newspaper's content local and its style informal. The paper identified people by first name only ("If you want to help with the charity catfish dinner, call Jessie or Betty"). Rosalee handled the front page, typically devoted to hard news: Town Hall meetings, church socials, local genealogy, recipes, reader-written reminiscences of the old swimming hole or the old ice cream parlor. Anita wrote her "Dribs and Drabs" inside column, which was devoted to the microminutiae of small-town life. If someone had a new hairdo, if someone broke a bone, if someone had out-of-town kin visiting, if someone's dog had a litter of six puppies, Anita mentioned it. Seven puppies or more, Rosalee took the story away from Anita and put it on page one.

At 6:00 P.M., Mayor Perry took his place behind the podium, and everyone was seated. "Thank you all for coming. First, an announcement. Don't forget that the Lions Club Women's Auxiliary is having a fund-raising spaghetti dinner at seven next Thursday night. Jessie, would you like to add anything to that?"

Jessie Pinkston weighed anchor, stood, and turned to face the audience. "I just want to remind everyone that the spaghetti dinner is 'bring your own sauce.'"

"Thank you, Jessie. Does anyone have any other announcements?"

Big Un Petteway raised his hand.

"Big Un," the mayor said, recognizing Big Un with a nod and suspecting what was coming.

"I got one and six-tenths of an inch of rain out at my place on Friday."

Sitting behind him, Willis Pinkston and Joe Adair elbowed each other. One inch of that total had fallen from Joe Adair's water bottle, not the sky.

"That's terrific, Big Un. You can't put a price on rain, nosiree."

Mayor Perry shuffled some papers and cleared his throat, a guttural segue to the real order of business. "Now, tonight I want us to discuss Willoughby's economy. I know that everyone has lived here long enough to know that Willoughby was a thriving town years ago. I know we can't bring back the days of oil and cotton, but there must be something we can do to promote this town, to get it noticed."

Mayor Perry paused and looked at the faces in the room. He was not encouraged.

"In our city budget we have a little dab of money set aside to conduct a public relations campaign—a modest one—to attract new businesses and new residents. But we need ideas. We need a hook, something to set us apart from other towns, to give Willoughby an identity. Something we can put on billboards at the city limits, maybe even on postcards and souvenirs. Now here's one idea I had. Lots of towns call themselves 'the Texas Capital of This' or the 'Texas Capital of That': barbecue, wine, sausage, wildflowers, spinach, crepe myrtle, fossils. All sorts of stuff. It works for them. What would work for Willoughby? What have we got a lot of that we could capitalize on? Help me out here, people. Fill in the blank: Willoughby—the _____ Capital of Texas."

Mayor Perry scanned the faces expectantly. From somewhere in the back, a voice said, in a half-whisper and only half in jest: "Dust."

After a few titters, a wave of collective self-pity swept the room. In rapid succession came:

"Brucellosis."

"Tick."

"Grassbur."

"Welfare."

"Unemployment."

Mayor Perry put on a politician's plastic smile and let the cut-ups laugh themselves out. He looked up at a bit of flaking paint on the room's stamped metal ceiling. After a few seconds, he restored order by rapping his gavel on the podium, which anyone familiar with parliamentary procedure would have recognized as just a glass paperweight and a card table.

"Okay. Okay. Very funny. But that's my point, y'all. We need something to brag about so that negative things like that are *not* the first things that we—or anyone else—think of when our town is mentioned. Any ideas?"

Mayor Perry looked around the room at the faces, some still grinning and shaking their heads woefully.

Charley Griggs spoke up. "But *what*, Earl? We don't raise more or better cattle than any other town. We don't grow more or better corn or wheat or sorghum or pecans or any other crop than any other town."

"Well, that's true, Charley, but surely . . ."

"And the hunting around here sure isn't good enough to mention," J. D. Vernon interrupted from deep inside his camouflage outfit.

"And we don't have a lake or a river or a mountain," Cecil Bell said. "We aren't on the interstate. There's no industry. No one famous is from here."

Councilman Bill Moorehead, seated on the front row, spoke up as if to refute the latter negative: "Now hold on. Remember Audie Murphy? War hero, movie star. Well, he had a cousin that lived here for a spell. I never met the cousin. But I had a cousin that did."

Mayor Perry summoned all the tact at his command. "Real good, Bill," he said while trying to visualize a billboard reading "Willoughby—the Audie Murphy Cousin Capital of Texas."

The rest of the meeting was equally unproductive. Those present seemed to be able to suggest only what Willoughby *couldn't* be, not what Willoughby *could* be. Mayor Perry adjourned by asking everyone present to "keep thinking about it."

Mayor Perry was discouraged by this first summit conference on the Willoughby economy. But he remained undaunted. Mayor Earl Perry had a dream for his town. It was a specific dream and a modest dream, as dreams go. It was a dream that he had never shared with another Willoughby soul. At those private moments when he thought of his dream—took it out and coddled and petted it—he liked to recall a line of poetry, one of the few that he still remembered, from old Miss Louise Pool's high school English class: "Ah, but a man's reach should exceed his grasp, or what's a heaven for?"

After punch and cookies, as Perry was leaving the room, Vada Hoover approached him. "Earl, have you ever walked across my yard barefoot? How about 'Willoughby—the Fire Ant Capital of Texas'?"

As he watched Vada walk out the door laughing, Mayor Earl Perry reminded himself: Of course, the eternal truths of poetry just may not apply in a place like Willoughby.

❖ 7 ❖

*"My Willis just disappeared from the back yard today, like a UFO
had snatched him up into the sky. Well, when he comes home, he'd better have
either a good explanation or a whole helluva lotta frequent flier miles."*
——————Jessie Pinkston

Six days after Balaam Gimble and Ray Dean Briley explored Balaam's
cave, Ray Dean did a lot of driving. Two members of the Boys—
Charley Griggs and Big Un Petteway—were mildly mystified as they sat
on their bench in front of the bank a half-block from the flashing red
light and saw Ray Dean's pickup pass through the intersection three
times before noon.

Just before 9:00 A.M., they recognized Ray Dean's pickup as it passed
by traveling south. They did not notice the fourteen-foot aluminum
extension ladder in the bed of the pickup.

Less than five minutes later, they saw the pickup coming back.
When the pickup stopped at the light, they recognized Willis Pinkston
in the passenger seat. They had been waiting for Willis to join them on
their bench. Earlier that morning Willis had phoned Big Un to say that
he would be along "directly" after he had hung out the wash to dry. So
Charley and Big Un expected the pickup to turn toward them, but
instead it turned onto Highway 21 and headed east out of town, in the
direction of Balaam's property.

Just before 11:00 A.M., they saw the pickup return from the east and stop at the flashing red light. This time they could see Ray Dean in the driver's seat. Big Un waved, but Ray Dean seemed not to notice. Again, Charley and Big Un expected the pickup to turn toward them, maybe deliver Willis unto them so they could find out what was going on. But the pickup continued west, in the direction of Waco.

Ray Dean Briley's pickup did not return from the direction of Waco until after 5:00 P.M. By then Charley and Big Un had gone off duty and returned to their homes. But as the pickup stopped at the flashing red light, across the street in Mayor Perry's store, Perry had just rung up Liz Traynor's groceries and was bagging them when he happened to look out the front window. Perry recognized Ray Dean's pickup and then recognized Willis as the passenger. Perry could see that Willis was asleep, his chin almost touching his chest. Perry could see that Willis was wearing his sweat-stained old Purina Feeds gimme cap—the one that Willis kept rescuing from the trash can each time Jessie tried to throw it away.

What Perry could not see was that Willis had his right foot in a bucket of water.

⋇ 8 ⋇

"Juanita doesn't take any guff. If Jesus and the twelve disciples came in to the cafe for the Last Supper, she'd ask if they had a reservation."
——Richard Greer

On Sunday, Balaam's phone rang. The conversation was brief.
Balaam: "Hello?"
Caller: "Balaam? Ray Dean. Meet me at the cafe in an hour."
Dial tone.

Balaam suspected that he was supposed to be intrigued. But he was closer to annoyed. Nonetheless, he had a couple of jobs to do in town, so he loaded his pickup with tools and supplies, gave Stilts's ears a goodbye rub, and climbed behind the wheel. He let his pickup coast down the driveway to the point where he always popped the clutch to start the engine.

On Sundays, every business in Willoughby was closed except the cafe and Little Un Petteway's gas station. At 11:30, many people in town were in church, thus the cafe was thinly populated when Balaam walked in. That would change soon. Sunday at noon was the cafe's busiest time of the week. Both Greers—Juanita and Richard—worked the Sunday lunch rush.

Balaam sat down at his usual booth. Before the foam rubber of the seat cushion had even stopped sighing, Ray Dean Briley came in. He was carrying a plastic one-gallon milk jug.

In mild weather, the Baptist church across the intersection kept its front doors open during services. Thus when Ray Dean opened the cafe door, Balaam could hear a few bars of a hymn as the congregation sang:

> I love to tell the sto-ry,
> 'Twill be my theme in glo-ry . . .

Ray Dean sat down at the booth opposite Balaam, putting the jug under the table without saying a word about it. Juanita brought them menus. On the menus for Sundays, the bread and rolls were called "manna." Featured desserts were angel food cake and divinity.

As Juanita stood over them she looked closely at Balaam, reached over, and lifted his glasses off his head. She held them up to the light. "I swear, Balaam . . ."

The lenses of his glasses were a debris field of fingerprints, sweat streaks, dust, an eyelash, a strand of spider silk, and a splatter of what she could only hope was only mud.

Juanita wiped the lenses clean on her apron and put the glasses back onto Balaam's head. Balaam thanked her sheepishly.

Balaam could tell that Ray Dean seemed anxious, but Balaam was not going to prod him. While Juanita took their orders, Ray Dean kept looking toward the front door. Each time the door opened, Ray Dean looked expectant. Each time the door opened, a few bars of a hymn leaked in:

> There is pow'r, pow'r, won-der work-ing pow'r
> In the pre-cious blood of the Lamb.

Like many men of rural Texas, Balaam and Ray Dean had been raised on the Baptist hymnal, and even though neither man had set a backslider's foot in a church in years, both still knew the hymns by heart. Even after the cafe door closed and the singing could no longer be heard, the two men filled chinks in their small talk by humming the hymn, each man at his own tempo and in his own key.

After Juanita walked back to the kitchen to give their orders to Richard, Balaam saw Ray Dean's expression brighten. Balaam turned toward the door and saw Willis Pinkston walk in. Willis quickly found their faces and joined them. Ray Dean slid over so that Willis sat on the outside of the booth, opposite Balaam.

Ray Dean was still acting oddly, Balaam thought. Worked up about something.

"Okay," Ray Dean said in preamble. "Balaam, Willis has something to show you. Go ahead, Willis."

Taking his cue, Willis swiveled his legs out from under the table, coaxed his right foot up onto his left knee, slipped off his shoe, peeled off his sock, and with some effort hoisted his bare foot onto the edge of the table top.

Ray Dean the impresario pointed at Willis's bare foot and said, with triumph, "Whataya think of *that*?"

Balaam could not resist. He swung his own feet out from under the table, bent over, slipped off both boots, peeled off both socks, pointed his bare feet straight out away from the booth, and said with mock one-upmanship, "Hell, y'all, I got *two* of those."

From the cash register, Juanita had watched this exhibition in disbelief. She hurried over to the booth, her sunny-side-down disposition evident. She hissed, sotto voce, "Balaam Gimble and Willis Pinkston. You old fools. What are you doing? Put your shoes back on. Get that foot off that table. God knows where it's been. You want the health department to shut me down? I swear."

Juanita was at least twenty years their junior, but they took her scolding in silence, like chastened schoolboys. Willis and Balaam reshod themselves.

His moment of drama trampled on, Ray Dean regrouped after Juanita left their table. "Okay," he said, lowering his voice and bending slightly toward Balaam. "Let me back up a bit. I was at my sister's in Corsicana the other night. They've got cable TV, and she had us watching the Travel Channel. Well, there was some show about Baden-Baden. That's a place in Germany. They got hot mineral springs there that go back to the old Roman times. People still go there from all over to soak in the water and get healthy. Supposed to be good for all sorts of problems."

Balaam looked blankly at Ray Dean.

Ray Dean was not going to be denied his enthusiasm. Much of his life as a farmer was plodding routine: hours spent plowing, fertilizing, irrigating, harvesting, hauling. He countered that monotony with an active imagination, a touch of the dramatic, and an abiding interest in other people's lives. Thus Ray Dean's ears, like radar dishes, had immediately detected the words of the TV show's narrator and relayed them directly to the "Aha!" lobe of Ray Dean's brain. Ray Dean Briley had begun to wonder if there was more to Balaam's funny-smelling cave water than plain old H, 2, and oh.

"After I saw that show, I realized that the bursitis in my shoulder seemed to be better after I was in that cave water." To demonstrate, Ray Dean raised his left arm over his head and rotated it freely. "Just coincidence? Maybe so, maybe no. So Thursday I took Willis out to your place and got a bucket full for him to soak his foot in. You know about his psoriasis."

Now it was Balaam's turn to "Aha!" Hence Willis the foot flasher. Balaam gave Willis what he hoped was a sympathetic—yet manly—nod.

"Then me and Willis went up to Waco. There's a lab in Waco that analyzes water. I figured any water that smells and tastes like that of yours has to have something in it. Willis soaked his foot in the bucket of water the entire trip. Well, the guy at the lab said a test would take a couple of days. Hell, I didn't want to wait that long. I asked if they offered express service and put a fifty-dollar bill on the counter. This guy slipped Mr. Grant into his shirt pocket and told us to come back just before closing."

"You paid fifty dollars to get water from *my* cave analyzed?"

Balaam didn't know if Ray Dean had been generous or just nosy.

"Don't worry about that right now. Here." Ray Dean took a sheet of paper from his wallet, unfolded it, and handed it to Balaam. The sheet contained two columns: a list of minerals and beside each mineral a number. Balaam could not even pronounce some of the names.

"Those numbers are the milligrams of mineral per liter, the guy said. He told me that the water's mineral content is similar to that of some commercial hot springs." Ray Dean looked at Balaam to see if he grasped the significance. "Like Baden-Baden."

Ray Dean could tell that Balaam still was not getting it.

"That water of yours has iron and potash and zinc and manganese and other minerals in it. Just chock full of them. It's even got lithium. You know what lithium is, don't you? That's the stuff they put in automotive lubricants, watch batteries, and depressed people."

Willis had been quiet since Juanita's reprimand. Now he spoke up. "Balaam, you know how bad I've had the psoriasis on my foot. Itched like fire. Nothing seemed to help. Well, after soaking my foot in that water, it's better. Not as itchy, not as red and scaly. You saw it."

But Balaam's brain was still several revelations behind.

"You rode all the way to Waco and back with your foot in a bucket of water?"

"Sure did. It felt pretty good. Especially when the water was still nice and warm."

Balaam looked at Willis and wondered if Willis had been soaking the wrong end of his body. But Balaam also remembered noticing how quickly his own bruised knee had healed. And that had occurred after he, too, had sloshed around in the cave.

Balaam was still catching up.

"You were out at my place?" he said, looking now at Ray Dean. "Why didn't you come up to the cabin?"

"I didn't want to get your hopes up until I was sure."

"Hopes up? About what?"

"About the cave. About the water being good for something. Well, it *is*. Balaam, you could make money off that water. People would pay to drink it, to take baths in it. Easy money."

Balaam looked out the window toward the church. Every time Balaam saw the church he remembered when his mother, Bessie, would sit in the same wooden pew each Sunday with her five children beside her. Bessie would arrange them from youngest to oldest—Mary to Salathiel—in stair-step fashion, like Russian *matryoshka* dolls.

"Easy money," Balaam repeated to himself. He tried to be optimistic, to be excited, but his native Calvinism pulled him back from the brink of enthusiasm.

"Have you drunk any of that water, Balaam?" Ray Dean asked.

"No. I haven't even been back down to the cave."

"Well, here."

Ray Dean lifted the plastic milk jug from below the table, unscrewed the lid, and handed the jug to Balaam. Balaam took a swallow, held the water in his mouth a few seconds before swallowing, and politely passed the jug to Willis, who took a mouthful and passed the jug to Ray Dean, who also took a drink and passed the jug back to Balaam.

"Boy, that's salty," Balaam said, taking another swallow and passing the jug to Willis.

Balaam belched softly.

"And fizzy."

"That's the bicarbonate, the guy at the lab said. Just like in soda pop. He said the rotten egg smell comes from the sulfates and the salty taste from . . ."

Before Ray Dean could get to the various salts in the water, Juanita reappeared at their table, her face contorted. A fist of a face. "Okay," she said through her teeth. "First you're in here barefoot, and now you're passing around a jug!? Does this look like the set of "Hee-Haw?" Put that jug away. And before you even ask, when the time comes—and I can see now that it *will* come—when one of you marries his own sister, no sir, you may *not* have the reception in *my* cafe!"

Ray Dean tried to soothe her. "It's just water, Juanita. Honest." He held the jug up for her to sniff. She wrinkled her nose. "If that's water," she said, "you're better off with moonshine" and walked away.

"We'd better skedaddle," Balaam said. "She's mad enough to spit."

The three men left an extra big tip as an offering of atonement to Juanita.

In the parking lot, Ray Dean repeated his belief that Balaam could make money from his cave. Balaam took a toothpick from behind his ear and sucked on it. "I don't know, Ray Dean. I just can't see people paying money for that stuff. But either way, I owe you fifty bucks."

"Tell you what. Just give me fifty gallons of that mineral water, and I'll call it square."

Balaam laughed. "Deal. Come and get it." Balaam turned to Willis. "You and those feet of yours can start wearing sandals now."

As the men separated and walked to their pickups just at noon, they could hear the invitation being sung at the church.

On-ly trust him, on-ly trust him, on-ly trust him now
· · ·

Balaam hummed along softly.

That afternoon, as Balaam drove home after completing his odd jobs in town, he stopped at one of J. D. Vernon's deer feeders. There he relieved himself of several ounces of mineral water chock full of iron and potash and zinc and manganese and lithium. He contemplated the spreading puddle at his feet and said, "I reckon Ray Dean was right. That stuff is good for something after all."

❖ 9 ❖

"If Nanetta would just let a little dust collect on her floor
now and then, it might have broken her fall."
———Roberta Reeves

B y the time Balaam returned home that Sunday afternoon, word of
the mineral water was already spreading through Willoughby. Willis
had, understandably, told wife Jessie about the results of the grand foot-
in-bucket experiment. Jessie had told their neighbor, Mrs. Maddox.
That was at about 5:20 Sunday afternoon. By nine that night, in conversations over coffee and pie at the Crossroads Cafe and in small talk
after the evening service at the Baptist church, the words *zinc* and *manganese* and *lithium* were being bandied about far more than was the norm
in a town without a periodic table.

On Monday morning, Balaam set out on his bicycle to pay his
respects to one of J. D. Vernon's deer feeders. As he pedaled, he passed
a large oak tree, now leafing out as it had each spring of his life. The
sight of that tree always triggered the same thought in Balaam: That
road and the land it passed through looked as they had when he had
been a child, probably as they had when his father had been a child.
The road was still unpaved, there were still no homes or businesses in
sight. Perhaps the cottontail rabbit that darted across the road ahead of
Balaam was a descendant of rabbits that his uncles had hunted.
Perhaps the square-bud daisies blooming in the bar ditch on his right

were the great-great-great-grandseedlings of daisies that his grand-mother had picked. And the "neighborhood" still sounded as it had when Balaam had been a child. Quiet. No sounds except overhead, where a hawk wheeled and screeched, as if God were dragging a finger-nail down the blue chalkboard of the sky.

When Balaam reached the stretch of road where it passed nearest the cave, a movement in that direction caught his eye. When he turned his head, he saw a ghost dancing in his field. It was actually only a gray column of water vapor rising from the mouth of the cave, merely the result of the warm air from the cave rising to meet the cool morning air above ground, but to Balaam, who was still not accustomed to the pres-ence of the cave, the sight was eerie. He braked to a halt and stared. An occasional breeze caused the column of vapor to bob and sway jerkily. A ghost on puppet strings.

And then, as he stood in the road staring, a human head suddenly appeared low in the column of vapor. It was a woman's head. And it was followed quickly by a woman's torso. A woman's bare torso. A very startled Balaam Gimble and a very naked Nanetta Wilson stared at each other for less than a second before Nanetta disappeared down the hole with a swirl and a short scream. It was like Groundhog Day at a nudist camp.

Balaam dismounted from his bicycle and walked to the fence, grabbed the top strand of barbed wire with both hands and leaned for-ward to project his voice. "Uh, good morning, Nanetta. Gonna be a pretty day." He tried to use his best matter-of-fact, I-didn't-just-see-you-naked tone of voice.

"Oh, Balaam. I am so embarrassed," the mouth of the cave said. "I came up to cool off a bit. It does get muggy down here. I didn't think I'd see a soul way out here. I hope I didn't offend you."

"Never you mind, Nanetta. I'm sorry I spooked you." Balaam crossed the fence and raised his voice. "Nanetta, I'm walking toward the cave so we don't have to shout. But I won't look in, I promise."

"All right."

Balaam stopped within a few feet of the cave. The top of an alu-minum ladder protruded from the mouth of the cave. "Nanetta, here I am," Balaam said to the hole.

"I'm getting dressed," the hole said.

Balaam saw no clothes in sight and reasoned that Nanetta must have disrobed in the cave on the ledge around the pool of water.

"Are you okay down there? Where's your car? How'd you get out here?"

"I hope you don't mind," the hole said. Nanetta's words ricocheted off the limestone. "I heard about your little cave and how the water helped Ray Dean Briley's bursitis. And Willis's psoriasis. I wanted to try it for my joints. I could find your place but wasn't sure I could find the cave. So Ray Dean offered to drop me off. He had an errand to run. He brought his ladder and set it up so I could get down to the water."

After Nanetta had dressed, Balaam held the ladder steady while she climbed up. Her polyester pants and blouse were sticking to her body, her big Q-tip of gray-blue hair was damp and matted. By then, the sun had warmed the morning air; the ghost of Balaam's cave was gone.

"That's a lovely experience," Nanetta said, tucking in her blouse. "Very soothing. You can just feel the old joints limber up."

Shortly after Nanetta resurfaced, Ray Dean arrived. After Ray Dean and Balaam had walked Nanetta to Ray Dean's pickup and gotten her buckled in, Balaam asked Ray Dean to help him "check the ladder." Ray Dean understood that to be code for "Let's have a word in private." As soon as they were out of earshot, Ray Dean pre-empted Balaam: "I swear, Balaam, I didn't tell anyone about the water. Musta been Willis. Nanetta called me last night and wanted to know all about it. Said she sure would like to have a dip in the water for her stiff joints and did I think you'd mind. I said no but that she probably shouldn't come out here on her own. I offered to stay here with her while she went down in the cave, but she insisted she'd be okay on her own. You know Nanetta—independent as a mule with a government pension."

After Ray Dean and Nanetta had gone, Balaam got onto his bicycle and hurried on to the deer feeder that had been his original destination one hour and one naked old lady earlier. On his way back to his cabin, he passed a car parked where Ray Dean had parked earlier. Balaam recognized the car as Jack Stanley's Chevy. Jack was nowhere in sight. Must be in the cave. Two in one day, Balaam marveled. Balaam kept pedaling toward home, not even slowing down. He had seen enough for one day.

Two days later, Balaam saw another car parked by the road near the cave as he passed by on his way elsewhere. He was surprised. He would never have bet that three people would visit the cave in one week. What he didn't know—because his cabin and the cave were separated by a half-mile of woods—was that during that week, *six* people had visited the cave.

But only one person was a "regular." One week after Nanetta's first visit, Balaam was driving home from town when he saw her car parked by the road near the cave. Then he saw Nanetta herself; she was trying to get through the barbed-wire fence from the bar ditch to the field. She was fully clothed, Balaam was relieved to see. In fact, she was wearing a full skirt and trying to slip between two strands of barbed wire. Balaam called to her. "Nanetta, hold on. You're gonna snag that dress."

Sure enough, by the time Balaam parked his pickup and reached her, Nanetta had snagged the hem of her skirt on the bottom strand and the back of her blouse on the top strand. Balaam freed her clothing and then held the bottom strand down with his foot and the top strand up with his hand so that she could pass through.

"Thank you, Balaam," Nanetta said as she straightened herself. "That fence didn't want to let go of me."

"Back for another dip, are you?"

"If you don't mind, Balaam."

"Not at all, Nanetta. But you shouldn't be out here alone going up and down that ladder. At least let me steady it for you until you get down there."

Nanetta agreed to this. After Nanetta was safely in the cave, Balaam called down to her, "If you're sure you'll be okay, I'll leave you alone. I'll prop two fence wires apart with a branch so you can get through later. But when you leave, honk your horn so I'll know you got off okay."

Again, Nanetta agreed, although Balaam could tell that she thought he was being an old woman about it all.

Back at his cabin, Balaam suddenly realized that he was not even sure that he could hear a horn from the cave. He puttered about the compound, his ears alert. About an hour later, he was relieved to hear, faintly, two long honks. Even Stilts lifted his head and swiveled his ears in the direction of the unfamiliar sound.

Nanetta Wilson was as close as Willoughby came to having a trend-setter. She was perhaps less small town in her outlook, perhaps better traveled than most in town. She was adventuresome, curious, and young at heart. She had been the first woman in town to wear panty-hose, the first person in town to own a cordless phone, the first to exercise by power walking, which she often did up and down her side-walk while wearing pantyhose and talking on her cordless phone.

So it was no surprise that she was the first to "take the waters" at Balaam's cave, as she put it. In the two weeks after Balaam first inter-rupted her there, she went back three times. At the end of that period, Nanetta Wilson was prepared to testify that "taking the waters" indeed made her joints less stiff. Soon after her fourth visit to the cave, she was giving a progress report to her neighbor, Roberta Reeves. Like Nanetta, Roberta was a widow in her seventies. Most mornings the two had coffee and "something sweet" in Nanetta's parlor, with its high ceiling and ornate drapes and carved mantelpiece populated by photos of her son David, her parents, her Aunt Mimi, and her late husband, L. T.

On a morning in the first week of May, as the two women sat in her parlor, which she kept only slightly less sterile than an operating room, Nanetta said, "Really. I do think it's working, Roberta. I've taken the waters four times. I feel more limber. Let me show you."

Nanetta went into her kitchen and returned with a dust mop to the center of the parlor. As Roberta watched, Nanetta positioned both hands on the handle of the dust mop and held it upright and away from her body, as if it were a dance partner. "Watch. Just like Fred and Ginger." Then, with a flourish, Nanetta began to dance the dust mop across the parlor floor, stepping in time to the beat as she softly sang, in a wistful voice.

> The way you wear your hat . . .
> The way you sip your tea . . .

Roberta Reeves looked on with delight, the palms of her hands pressed together in a frozen clap.

> The memory of all *that*, . . .
> No, no, they can't take that away from———.

On the word "me," Nanetta attempted a dip. She had intended only a shallow dip, but as she leaned back, her foot slipped on the polished hardwood floor. She lost her balance and fell.

Fred the dust mop was uninjured. Fred's partner, however, broke her hip.

❖10❖

*"Beverly knows she doesn't need to go getting married again.
She already has two ex-husbands—one on each side of town.
Where would she put Number Three?"*

—Juanita Greer

As David Wilson drove home from work on Houston's 610 Loop, he was adrift in the doldrums of his fifties, divorced and childless. Lately he had begun to suspect that he was never going to grow up to be a buccaneer. He stared at the back end of a freight truck in front of him as the speedometer needle of his little red roadster quivered on the cusp of forty and then dipped into the doldrums of its thirties. He reminded himself: a buccaneer would pull out and pass. So he checked his rear-view mirror, signaled, and accelerated into the fast lane. After he got into the fast lane, he decided that the gap between the freight truck and the car in front of it was too small; he slowed, signaled, and pulled back in behind the truck. He reminded himself: but an ad agency copywriter wouldn't.

As the cell phone on his passenger seat began to beep, David was thinking that the day had not been a good one. He had not slept well. *Beep.* At work, he had snapped at an innocuous young intern. *Beep.* He had gotten a stain on his tie at lunch. *Beep.* And now he was stuck in traffic at afternoon rush hour. *Beep.* He picked up the phone while thinking that he very much needed to get home without anything else going wrong.

When he heard the sterile, bloodless tone of the voice on the phone, the barely suppressed sense of doom in David Wilson the child was instantly alerted. It was a hospital voice. His mother was dead. He didn't have to hear more than "Mr. Wilson? This is St. Joseph's Hospital in Waco. Your moth——." He *knew*. In his mind, he had drilled for this phone call for years. How it had happened did not matter—car wreck, heart attack, small-town boredom—his mother was dead.

With that innate anticipation of the worst, the rest of the caller's sentence, "——er has broken her hip," came as good news. David Wilson was actually relieved. He wanted to rush into the nearest bar and shout, "Hey, everybody! My mother broke her hip! Drinks on me!"

Instead, he changed directions and drove north to Waco, reaching the hospital in three hours. A young uniformed woman at a nurses station directed him to his mother's room. He knew she would look terrible, and she did. She was pale, small. And sedated. His first thought was irrational: He realized that he could not remember ever seeing his mother asleep before.

In a few minutes, Nanetta's doctor pushed the door open, introduced himself, and with a matter-of-fact professionalism that David found both off-putting and reassuring gave David the details. David knew that in his agitated state of mind he would not remember accurately, so he took notes: ". . . X rays good, given age . . . surgery tomorrow 8 A.M. . . . set bone w/screws . . . should mend well . . . stay 10 days min . . . convalesce rehab. center . . . home with nursing supervision, phys. therapy. First walker, then cane. If all well, most or complete mobility 4–6 mos."

David stopped taking notes when the doctor began talking about the risk of complications, the percent of women Nanetta's age who break a hip and then suffer depression, enter a nursing home and never leave, or even die. David knew that he could remember those details.

When David stepped out into the hall to collect his thoughts, two women approached him. He did not recognize Roberta Reeves and Beverly Faulk, although he had met Roberta before. Nanetta had moved to Willoughby from Houston after David had been grown and gone, and he had spent little time in Willoughby. These days, on his every-other-weekend shuttles to Willoughby to take his mother back to

Houston, David always ran on his own set of trolley tracks: He took the shortest route to Nanetta's house, turned around in her driveway, took the same route back to Houston. He had never been in most of Willoughby's businesses or down most of its streets or met most of its people.

When Nanetta had fallen, Roberta told David, she had phoned 911 and then Beverly. The two women had followed the ambulance to the hospital. David thanked them and asked how it had happened. As Roberta described the scene that had taken place in Nanetta's parlor, David rolled his eyes and shook his head. When they went back into Nanetta's room, she was still serenely unconscious. David was exhausted and realized that he would use his time more wisely by getting a few hours of sleep in a motel than by staring at an unconscious woman. Before they left Nanetta's room, David bent over her small face and kissed her forehead. As he turned to the door, Nanetta fluttered her eyelids and, without waking, began to mumble-sing.

The way you wear your hat . . .

David, Beverly, and Roberta stopped and looked back at Nanetta, who slept on.

The way you sip your tea . . .

David looked at Beverly and Roberta and began to laugh, releasing a gush of pent-up emotion. Beverly and Roberta stared at him for a second and then followed suit.

Beverly Faulk returned to the hospital the next morning to stand vigil during Nanetta's surgery. When Beverly saw David in the waiting area and smiled in recognition, David at first did not recognize her. But he was glad to share the duty of fretting. The surgery went well, and in the afternoon Nanetta was conscious enough to recognize them both and to ask if she was in Houston and if any of the department stores had any "good ads" in the newspaper.

When Nanetta drifted off again, David said to Beverly, "I don't know about you, but I need to get out of this death-and-disinfectant atmosphere for a few minutes. Want to go get a bite to eat?"

In the hospital parking lot, when Beverly saw David's low-slung sports car, she wished she'd brought along a shoehorn. And worn a longer skirt.

As they drove, David tried to think of non-Nanetta subjects to think about and talk about. "'Beverly.' That's an Indian word for 'beaver,' isn't it?"

Beverly, who was tired, narrowed her eyes. She did not know this man. She was not sure if he was being vulgar or showing off his education. She felt like telling him that she had been named for her grandmother, who had butchered hogs, broken horses, and plucked chickens but had, Beverly was quite sure, never gnawed down a tree, thank you very much.

But she didn't.

Settled in a restaurant on the edge of the hospital district, Beverly said, "She'll be fine."

"I guess. Mrs. Reeves said Mother has been going out to some cave to bathe in some kind of mineral water?"

Beverly told David what she had heard on the grapevine about Balaam's water.

"I'm starting to worry about her judgment. I don't know how much longer she'll be able to live by herself in that big old house. Even if she makes a full recovery from this."

"I'm sure that when I'm seventy-something I'll be trying just as hard to outrun old age."

Beverly Faulk was, like David, fiftyish. She was still, as she put it, "presentable," her hair still brown, her figure still within five—well, okay, *ten*—pounds of her high school prom dress. She was settled in her singlehood, having long ago fished out the limited dating pool of a small town with a static population. Her two ex-husbands—Jeeter and Donny—were on better terms with each other than with her. She sometimes saw them having coffee together at the Crossroads Cafe.

She was not thinking it, but had she been asked, she might have admitted that, on the other hand, she could enjoy the company of a clean, respectful, mature man with whom to share a trip to the outlet stores in Hillsboro or a tour of estate sales to scout for antiques.

As they talked lightly, David thought: "She probably goes to outlet stores and estate sales." He found estate sales to be a bit ghoulish: a lot of strangers pawing through the recently dead's personal belongings amid the medicine bottles and half-squeezed ointment tubes.

On the drive back to the hospital, Beverly asked, "Have you made arrangements for Nanetta?"

"I'm getting there. I called my boss last night and took some vacation time. I'll stay at Mother's house and commute to the hospital while she's there and whatever sort of rehab place she needs and then after she gets to go home. She'll need some kind of visiting nurse or therapist, too."

"Boy howdy, that'll be a change of pace for you. Willoughby, I mean. We're a pretty quiet little town. I have an antiques store, but business is always slow. So if you need any help, just holler. Nanetta is one of our dearest little old ladies, but she may be a handful if she can't get around like she wants to."

Beverly wondered if David would even be able to take Nanetta home in that little sports car. She turned to confirm that the car had not even a rumor of a back seat. Tucked in the space behind the driver's seat, she saw a pair of binoculars. "A big-city peeping Tom?" she wondered. But while she was jumping to conclusions, in midleap she saw beside the binoculars a copy of *Peterson's Field Guide to the Birds of Texas.*

"Oh," she said, as in "whoa." "Are you a bird-watcher?"

David was grateful to have another non-Nanetta subject to talk about. "Yeah. In theory, at least. I don't find much time these days."

Beverly reached for the book, flipped to the front, and scanned the lifetime checklist of birds sighted.

"You've been busy. Hey, you've seen a painted bunting. Male or female?"

"Both. A pair came to a feeder I had."

"You must be living right. I've never seen any. Just pictures. The little boys are so colorful. They remind me of parrots trapped in a sparrow's body."

David laughed in appreciation of the description.

Looking at the empty checkboxes, Beverly said, "But you've never seen a great blue heron?"

"Never have." David said as he shifted gears and looked for landmarks along the street. He did not know Waco and was following his mental trail of bread crumbs back to the hospital.

"Shoot, we have those around Willoughby. I see one now and then on a stock tank. They're huge. When they spread those wings and lift out of the water, it's a sight to see."

Beverly saw the hospital appear on their right. "Willoughby is not big enough to have a birding club, of course. But I used to go out with Mrs. Burleson. But she's not able to get around much anymore." Beverly refrained from explaining that Mrs. Burleson wasn't able to get around much anymore because she had broken her hip and had been confined to a nursing home by her son.

David said, "I keep my binoculars and *Peterson* in the car, but it seems I'm always in a rush to get from home to work or work to home. I don't find much time anymore."

"Time is one thing we do have in Willoughby. Tell you what, when you get your mom squared away, stop by the store someday about closing time, and we'll go watch us some birds." Beverly made the offer with an "I mean it if you want to, but if you don't want to, I didn't mean it" attitude.

David turned in to the hospital parking lot and drove down the row where Beverly's car was parked. As she got out, he said, "I might just do that."

To his own surprise, David realized that he really might.

David Wilson was about to jump his trolley tracks.

❧11❧

"Brenda Morrison's girl and that Yancey boy were out riding around last night and ended up in Balaam's cave. Seems the Yancey boy lost one of his socks. I reckon Brenda's girl lost a mite more than that."
——Luann Dawson

During the eleven days that Nanetta was in the hospital, four more Willoughby residents came to Balaam's cave. During the thirteen days that Nanetta was in a rehabilitation center, nine more came to the cave. A few people phoned first or drove up to Balaam's cabin to ask permission to visit the cave. Balaam appreciated their courtesy, but he normally did not receive many phone calls or visitors, and he liked it that way. Adele Watson had phoned while Balaam had been, as he had been sorely tempted to point out to her, "on the throne." Jenny Thorensen, with her three-year-old son Todd, had driven up while Balaam had been welding in his workshop. Todd had seen Stilts and had wanted to get out of the car and pet him, but when Todd had seen Balaam step out of his workshop wearing a full-face welding mask and holding a blue-flamed acetylene torch, Todd had begun to cry. So the next day, when Glenda Bratcher, Willoughby's part-time city secretary, had phoned Balaam to ask if she could come "borrow" a couple of gallons, Balaam said, "Glenda, you can have all the water you want if you'll do me just one favor. Tell everybody that there's no need to ask me first. Just go on down there. But be careful. If anyone gets hurt, I don't have insurance. And if they sue me, all they'll find in my pockets is lint."

Just in case Glenda didn't get the word out on the Willoughby grapevine fast enough, Balaam devised an even more efficient method of cutting down on annoying phone calls: He unplugged his phone.

Balaam had to admit that he had been wrong: People *were* interested in that smelly, funny-tasting water. Pilgrims to the cave were generally of two types: soakers and sippers. Soakers came to bathe in the hot water, bringing their tired, their poor, their huddled masses of muscles. Rancher Kenny Jacobs was one such soaker. He came out to soak whatever part of his body had most recently been kicked by a cow or stepped on by a horse. Sippers came to drink the water, seeking relief of an internal ill—indigestion, irregularity, vague "twinges." Big Un Petteway was a sipper. He began coming out once a week to fill a five-gallon jug and take it home, where he drank a quart a day for his wrong-sided liver.

Were the water's effects real, or were they imagined? Probably the answer is "yes." The medicinal value of some minerals in the water had been known for years, as had the therapeutic value of bathing in hot water. But as word of the water's positive effects spread, the power of suggestion no doubt contributed: People expected to notice results, and so they did. The effects of the water would have been difficult to measure scientifically. For example, when people heard that the water contained lithium, some began to drink it hoping to get a lift in mood. Among them was George Noblett, who began drinking the water in mid-April. By mid-May he was indeed smiling more. Ah, but shortly after he had begun drinking the water, his ex-wife had met an office supply salesman in a nightclub in Arlington, had gotten engaged in the Tunnel of Love at Six Flags Over Texas after a whirlwind courtship, and, in a spasm of generosity, had released George from his child support obligation to their son, Wesley. Thus it would be difficult to determine how much of George's smile was attributable to Balaam's water and how much was attributable to poor lighting.

By the end of May, the cave had developed a life of its own. Spontaneously, without benefit of meetings or memos, Balaam's Cave (by now a recognized local landmark and thus spoken of with a capital C) had developed its own culture.

First, cooperation came to Balaam's Cave. Ray Dean Briley, who had proprietary feelings about the cave, came out one day for his first post-discovery soak. Before he left, he anchored the feet of his ladder to the limestone ledge next to the pool with lag bolts to make it more stable. Balaam was grateful: less chance of someone getting hurt.

Soon after, Cliff Gholson came out to see what all the fuss was about and decided he'd like to take a dip. But the pool was occupied at the time by three young women from the Baptist church. Cliff was not in a waiting mood, but he also was not going to get into the pool with "three giggly girls." He tipped his cowboy hat to the hole and snorted, "No thanks, ladies. No Japanese hoochie coochie bathhouse for *me*." Cliff, a retired plumber, drove back to his home in town, rummaged around in his garage, and in less than a hour came back to the cave with the bed of his pickup filled with hardware. The three women in the cave could only hear sounds from above as Cliff engaged in some process that seemed to involve considerable tinkering, grunting, and cursing.

"Excuse me, ladies. Man at work," came Cliff's mischief-laced voice from on high as the women watched one end of a long black hose suddenly appear in the mouth of the cave and descend toward them into the water. They edged away from it as it penetrated the middle of the pool. Then the women heard the sound of a gasoline engine start and saw the black hose twitch and the surface of the water around it begin to stir slightly.

While Cliff's gasoline-powered pump was filling his old cast-iron claw-foot bathtub with water from the cave, there in Balaam's field Cliff stripped down to his bathing trunks. He called down to the women in the cave, "Now you gals stay away from the end of that hose while it's sucking water. Don't want you to go to choir practice with a hickey!" And then, cackling smugly, Cliff hopped into his own private hot tub. He was still wearing his cowboy hat.

Within days, two more old bathtubs and a galvanized horse trough appeared, contributed by anonymous donors and lined up neatly beside Cliff's bathtub and pump.

Before, Balaam had not been able to hear most activity at the cave because of the half-mile of woods that separated his cabin and the cave. But now, depending on weather conditions, Balaam could hear the sound of the pump engine when someone ran it to drain and refill a tub. The sound was alien to Balaam. He was not used to hearing any human sound other than J. D. Vernon's gunfire and the occasional passing pickup or tractor. He did not welcome the new sound, but he did not forbid use of the pump, telling himself, "If this is as bad as it gets . . ."

But with these cow pasture accoutrements, more pilgrims came to Balaam's Cave. A month after Balaam had discovered the cave, each time he passed it, usually someone was there. He often recognized the vehicle (usually a pickup) parked at the road. Sometimes he recognized someone's bald head or blue bouffant bobbing above one or more of the bathtubs.

Balaam's Cave was becoming Lourdes with mud flaps.

After cooperation came to Balaam's Cave, etiquette came. Nanetta Wilson unwittingly had set a precedent: The cave itself came to be zoned "clothing optional." Out of sight of the public above ground, bathers could wear as much or as little as others in the cave with them would stand for. But above ground, in the bathtubs, bathers were expected to wear swimwear.

The three bathtubs were reserved for bathing in, the horse trough for drinking from. One day, a metal dipper showed up, chained to a handle of the trough. Another day, a stack of paper cups showed up. Because the water in the cave was flowing and thus being refreshed constantly, few people minded drinking water from the pool that others used as a hot tub.

And finally—perhaps inevitably—after cooperation and etiquette came to Balaam's Cave, sin came. On a Friday night late in May, Balaam sat on his porch enjoying the mild weather. Days were longer now. The air smelled like spring. There was no single scent he could identify. Rather, it was a potpourri of scents whose bouquet occurs only in the country and only in the spring: plowed earth, cut hay, decaying leaves, damp wood, wildflowers, cow manure. He heard the insect orchestra rehearsing for the summer concert season—mostly crickets and katydids in the strings section and June bugs in the percussion section, banging into the screen door and the porch floor as they buzzed around an outdoor light mounted above the door. He heard, in the woods to his left, a treefrog talking with a treefrog in the woods to his right. Then, off to the east, perhaps a mile away, he heard the faint sound of a car on the dirt road. Within two minutes, the car passed his mailbox, going at least fifty, Balaam estimated, its muffler even louder than its stereo, but not by much. "Damned kids," Balaam said. The car was traveling in the direction of the cave. He thought little of it at the time, although he had noticed an increase in traffic on the road since the cave "went public." This, too, Balaam did not welcome, but he was still convinced that the cave was just a fad.

The next morning, Balaam went down to the cave to conduct what had become one of his irregular inspection tours to be sure that nothing had been stolen or damaged, to see that the pump engine had gasoline and that nobody had fallen and "cracked his fool head open." Inside the cave, on the limestone ledge of the pool, he saw an empty wine bottle, a pizza carton, and one sock. Floating in the water, he saw two spent condoms. As he climbed up the ladder to go find a tree branch with which to fish the condoms out, Balaam was indignant: It's bad enough to litter a man's property; it's even worse to have more fun on a man's property than *he* has!

❧12❧

*"I reminded David that the key to finding Balaam's place
is to turn left at Walter Ridgely's German shepherd."*
———Nanetta Wilson

D avid Wilson braked and downshifted when he saw "the second
mailbox on the left after the dip in the road." He had been dispatched by his mother to fetch some of Balaam's mineral spring water.
Nanetta had been back home four days, able to get around now with a
walker. In her condition, she could not go out to the cave to "take the
waters," but she could drink the water. It might help her heal faster, she
said.

Her first days back home were proving to be a period of adjustment
for Nanetta and David. She fluctuated between refusing to acknowledge her limitations and wallowing in her helplessness. In addition, the
two had not lived under the same roof in more than thirty years.
Because there was a bathroom on the first floor, David had set up his
mother downstairs and had taken the upstairs for himself—on
Nanetta's stipulation that he keep his area dusted and "picked up."
Roberta Reeves next door and Beverly Faulk were looking in on her; a
therapist was coming out from Waco regularly.

David's first trip to Balaam's property had been immediately pre-
ceded by David's first trip to Willoughby's only grocery store. David
had become mired in the checkout line while the cashier, Earl Perry's

daughter Earline, gabbed with the two shoppers ahead of him. In Houston, cashiers and shoppers did not "do" gab. As he had stood there, trying to make his point by occasionally sighing audibly, he thought, "If I was a lemming standing in a line at a cliff, I would be in the sea by now. If I was a two-ton lump of steel on a General Motors assembly line, I would be a Camaro by now."

His drive into the country had gone more quickly. As David had neared an intersection of two unpaved roads, a large dog had appeared from under the porch of a wood-framed house on the corner and raced out into the road toward his car, barking and snapping at the tires. As instructed by his mother, David turned left. Sure enough, as he accelerated out of range of the ground-to-Goodyear missile, the name painted on the mailbox was "Ridgely."

Still following his mother's directions, after a dip in the road farther along, David had found Balaam's mailbox. Now he looked at the rutted, overgrown driveway and decided to leave his low-slung sports car at the road. He grabbed his two empty gallon milk jugs and began walking up the driveway.

As David neared Balaam's compound, he heard a man's voice: "Do that tomorrow, I reckon," followed in a few seconds by "Nope. One trip ought to do."

David wondered if Balaam had a visitor. He didn't want to startle them, and he certainly didn't want to be mistaken for a trespasser. David stopped walking and decided to announce his presence before he got any closer.

But David Wilson already had announced his presence: Before David could call out, Balaam heard Stilts the watchdeer snort in alarm, saw Stilts look toward the driveway with his ears pointed, then stamp a front paw, lift and spread his tail, and retreat behind the cabin. Thus Balaam was already walking toward the gate when David called out, "Mr. Gimble?"

"Coming." Balaam picked his way through the clutter in his compound, reaching the gate just as David did.

"'Mr. Gimble' was my daddy. He's in the cemetery if you have any business with him. My name is Balaam."

"I'm David Wilson, Nanetta Wilson's son." David offered his hand over the gate.

Balaam shook David's hand and looked closer at his face.

"Sure. Nanetta's boy. We've met, but it's been a while. How is she doing?"

"She's home now, getting used to a walker. But the doctor is encouraged." David did not remember meeting Balaam.

"I went by to take care of her yard the other day, but no one was home. Mrs. Reeves next door told me what had happened. Poor thing."

"She wanted me to ask if she can have some of your mineral water to drink. She got some from Mr. Petteway, but she drank it all. Hell, I think she's watering her plants with it, too."

"Hop in the truck. I'll show you where the cave is."

David had to pull hard on the pickup's passenger door to open it. After he was seated, he acted nonchalant as Balaam depressed the clutch pedal and let the pickup begin to roll silently down the driveway. When Balaam popped the clutch and the engine lurched to life, David said, "That's a neat trick."

"That's why I still have the original starter in this truck. Twenty-two years old. Old enough to vote."

Balaam looked over at David. "Democrat, of course," he said with a wink in his voice.

When Balaam saw David's car parked at the road, he said, "Good thing you didn't try to drive that thing up to the gate. You'll tear the bottom out on these back roads."

As they picked up speed on the dirt road, dust and exhaust smoke swirled up from between David's feet. He looked down and saw holes rusted in the floorboard. In less than a minute, Balaam parked the pickup and pointed to his right. "Just beyond that fence a ways."

As they walked toward the fence, David looked for a gate and saw none. He had no experience negotiating barbed-wire fences. He said to himself, "Not much call for that when you're brandin' mascara and ropin' adjectives." He saw that there were only two options: squeeze between two strands or go over the top strand. Without waiting to see how Balaam did it, David bellied up to the barbed wire and chose to go over the top. He pushed down on the top strand with one hand, lifted one leg over, and promptly got the crotch of his pants caught on a barb.

David's eyes widened, and he stood perfectly still.

"You're the second Wilson that's got stuck on this fence lately."

"My mother. This is mean stuff. Must have been invented by someone a lot taller in the saddle than I am."

Balaam pushed the top strand down farther, allowing David to free himself and lift his other leg over the fence. At the cave, David looked down the mouth into the darkness, then looked at the ladder.

"My mother was going up and down this ladder into a hole in the ground?"

"That's right. And she's not the only one. Beats anything I ever saw."

David looked at Cliff Gholson's pump and the three bathtubs and horse trough. "Is the water really good for anything?"

"I don't know for sure. I don't put much stock in it myself, but people keep coming out."

David waited above as Balaam went down the ladder to fill the two jugs.

During their short errand, David had heard Balaam make comments—"blooming early this year," "need a new one, I guess." Then David remembered the conversation that he had thought he was interrupting when he had walked up Balaam's driveway. Now David understood that at such times Balaam was not engaging in dialogue. It was monologue. Balaam was, in his solitariness, used to thinking out loud. But now Balaam stopped where the road crossed a creek and looked down out the driver's window. "This little creek doesn't look like much now."

This time, David sensed, Balaam was talking to him.

"But when we were kids, it was deep enough in places that we could swim in it. We used to swing on the mustang grapevines that grew over the creek there and drop into the water. Sometimes on hot summer days I can still hear the splashes." Then Balaam drove on.

When they returned to the compound, Balaam parked the pickup just outside the gate and said, "Come on in and sit a spell."

On the porch, Balaam motioned David toward a lawn chair.

"Want a beer or coffee?"

"Coffee, thanks. Cream and sugar, if you have it."

After Balaam had been in the cabin a minute, David heard Balaam's voice: "Y'all get out of there now! Scat. Damned sugar ants."

David yelled into the house: "Make that a beer instead."

When Balaam returned to the porch, he handed David a beer and then, from amid the clutter in the yard, dragged an old bucket seat up onto the porch. "Out of a seventy-seven Dodge," he said as he sat down.

David looked out—without gawking, he hoped—at the expanse of clutter. His first thought was, "This place needs a tornado to come through and straighten things up. Or my mother."

At the far edge of the clutter, all he could see was woods.

"Mother said you have a pet deer?"

Balaam whistled. From around the corner of the cabin Stilts approached and slowly walked up onto the porch to Balaam, keeping an eye on David.

"I found this guy in the woods when he was a baby and raised him. Bottle-fed him goat's milk, but he still got the scours something awful. Didn't you, Bub?"

Stilts pushed against Balaam's arm with his nose until Balaam rubbed his ears.

"Does he stay in your . . . yard?"

"He could jump over the fence easy, but I've never seen him do it. But he will wander out the gate if I leave it open. So I have to be careful. Most people around here would look at him and see just a half a freezer of venison."

"I guess there's a lot of hunting out here?"

"Way too much to suit me. Starting with that son of a bitch over there," Balaam nodded his head southward. "J. D. Vernon. No, I take that back. He'd have to take a self-improvement course to rise to the level of son of a bitch."

David clung to an outsider's neutrality and did not reply. David had never been that close to a deer, not even in a zoo. The big, dark eyes were what David would have to describe as—his mental thesaurus failed him—"soulful." He leaned forward to look closer at Stilts's coat. He looked down at Stilts's forelegs, which seemed to be all bone, no muscle. The hooves were black and splayed.

"He's a beautiful animal."

"Shhh. He's already stuck up enough. Aren't you, Toot?" Balaam put his arm around Stilts's neck and squeezed in roughhouse fashion.

Then Balaam got up and walked around the corner of the cabin.

He came back carrying a coffee can full of corn. "Hold out your hand." Balaam poured corn into David's upturned palm.

"Hold your hand out to him."

Tentatively, Stilts approached David and began to eat. As Stilts buried his muzzle in the corn, David could feel the fingertip dexterity of the deer's lips as they pulled in the kernels. When Stilts swallowed, David could see each mouthful of corn travel down the long throat.

"Hell, I've had dogs that weren't as good company as this guy," Balaam said. "Of course, he ain't much on fetching a stick. And he doesn't seem to see the sense in chasing a Frisbee. But we do have one game, don't we, boy?"

Balaam stood and walked to a nearby plywood table stacked with odds and ends. He picked up a square of foam rubber with a cord attached to it and put it on his head, pulling the cord snug under his chin to secure the foam rubber. Then he got down on his hands and knees. As he did so, Stilts, who had stopped eating from David's hand and was watching Balaam closely, lowered his head and walked toward Balaam until the tops of their heads met. Then man and deer, with boots and hooves dug in, began to push against each other. As David watched, first Stilts advanced and then Balaam and then Stilts again. A time or two, Stilts butted Balaam's head so firmly that, even though Balaam was braced, he was driven back a few inches. Then Stilts would stop his charge and wait for Balaam to recover. Then their heads would redock, and the game would continue. After a minute or so, Balaam lunged hard enough to push Stilts back a few inches, stood up quickly, and dusted off his knees.

"I keep his antlers trimmed back to nubs so is less attractive to the damned hunters. Still, the top of his head is bony, and he pushes pretty hard, so I rigged up this rubber bumper. Want to try it?"

David, thinking, "This will be something to tell 'em back at the office," took the foam rubber from Balaam and strapped it on. Then he got onto his hands and knees, put his head down, and braced himself. But not enough. Stilts butted David with enough force to push him backward off his knees and onto his heels, where he teetered gracelessly for an instant before falling over flat on his back. When the dust settled, most of it was on David's clothes.

Stilts seemed to understand that the game was over and stood back as David got up and dusted himself off.

Balaam was laughing so hard that he sloshed beer as he opened a second can and handed it to David. "I've learned the hard way not to get on my knees when he's around unless I have that rubber bumper on and am good and ready for him."

After David sat back down in the lawn chair, Stilts, magnanimous in victory, approached and offered to let David rub his ears. "Stilts KOs Wilson in round one, huh, fella?" As David rubbed, he could feel the contrast between the tough ear cartilage and the soft coat. He could also feel how hard Stilts's antler nubs were.

"So how do you like Willoughby so far?" Balaam asked.

"It's a change, I'll admit. For me. But your family has been here a long time, hasn't it?"

"I'm fifth generation. This land, what's left of it, belonged to my . . ." Here Balaam quickly counted "greats" on his fingers. "Great-great-grandparents. The town hasn't changed much since I was a kid. There were five hundred people living there then. If anything, there's a few less now. Just as well, probably."

"I wrote an out-of-town check at the grocery today and handed the girl my driver's license. She didn't even want to see it."

"Yeah. It's like that. The tellers at the bank know every customer by name. Most people in town don't lock their doors at night. And grownups keep other folks' young 'uns in line by hollerin' 'Don't make me call your ma.'"

David looked around and listened. He considered Willoughby to be quiet, but Balaam's place was a vacuum, a wooded bell jar.

"It must be awfully quiet out here. I can't hear a thing."

"Oh, you can hear lots of things if you listen." Balaam stopped talking and cocked his head a bit. David, taking the cue, listened.

"Hear that?"

David did not hear anything. "What?"

"*That* . . . Listen."

David now could hear—or thought he could hear—a faint, deep, rhythmic vowel sound. "Over there?"

Balaam nodded. "Bullfrog. He's on a stock tank a quarter-mile away. He's really testifying."

David thought of what he could hear a quarter-mile away in

Houston: a boom box, a gunshot, a siren.

About midway through their second beers, Balaam cocked his head again. "Hear that?"

Again, David heard nothing. At first. Then he heard a faint sound, as of a lawn mower.

"Someone's at the cave. That's the pump running."

"You know," David said, "people might pay for that mineral water of yours. You're just giving it away."

"That's what Ray Dean said. But I think this cave business will blow over. Folks get bored in a small town and look for something to get excited about. Besides, I'm no businessman."

Balaam listened to the faint drone of the pump. "I'd a whole lot rather listen to the bullfrog."

By the bottom of David's second beer, the sun was setting. David could see, to the west, shifting slivers of red through a treetop. Just at dusk, David heard a single howl in the woods that quickly multiplied to two and three and then too many howls to distinguish. As David listened, the howls melded into yips of excitement. David felt goose bumps rise on his arms.

When Balaam heard the first howl, he pointed in that direction with his left hand. After about two beats, he pointed with his right hand in a direction about ninety degrees west. When he did, as if responding to a conductor's baton, howls began in that direction.

"What time is it?" Balaam asked.

David darted his eyes at Balaam's wrists and saw no watch.

"Seven thirty."

"Two packs of coyotes call to each other and then meet up across the road to hunt every day about this time. It's something to hear, isn't it?"

By the time Balaam finished speaking, the coyotes had finished their ritual greeting. Now they were silent. Their hunt had begun.

David suddenly heard his own words: "Seven thirty."

"I'd better be getting back to Mother. No telling what she might get up to alone."

Balaam walked with David to the gate and handed him the two jugs of mineral water.

"Can you find your way back to town in the dark?"

"I think so. I can always roll down the window and listen for the sound of Mother dusting her walker."

Balaam laughed. "Come back if your mama needs more water." Stilts stood beside Balaam, nudging his leg with his nose. Balaam smiled his parenthetical smile. "Or if you want a rematch."

❧13❧

*"When Rudy comes home from the cafe, I can always tell how short Brandi
Renee's skirt was by how soon he starts nibbling my neck."*

———Donna Jean Janacek

Mayor Perry was the first merchant in town to begin selling
Balaam's mineral spring water. One afternoon he had driven out
to the cave and filled ten one-gallon milk jugs. At his store, he had
poured the water into forty one-quart Mason jars and displayed them
on the soft drinks shelf. Below the Mason jars, he had taped an index
card on which he had written "Balaam's mineral water $1."

On a Wednesday, Perry was restocking the canned vegetables aisle
when he saw Balaam walk in. Perry watched as Balaam walked through
the store. Sure enough, Perry saw Balaam start down the soft drinks
aisle. "Him and his damned Mountain Dew," Perry thought. Perry the
pragmatist operated on the premise that it's better to seek forgiveness
after than to seek permission before. Thus he had not asked Balaam for
permission to sell the water.

Perry moved quickly to head off Balaam before he reached the display of Mason jars. "Balaam," he said with the dispense-on-demand
charm of a man accustomed to campaigning for high elected office.
"Boy, have I got a surprise for you. A pleasant surprise." Perry pointed
toward the display of jars. Balaam, puzzled at first, looked closer. He
saw his name on the index card. He would not have used the descriptor

surreal, but the sight was just that to him. Other than in a few letters from relatives, some report cards, and an army draft notice, he had never seen his name in print, certainly not in public.

He stared at the index card. There was "Balaam Gimble" on the same shelf with Mr. Pibb and Dr Pepper.

Perry gushed on, trying to gauge Balaam's reaction. "It's just for the convenience of people in town. So they don't have to drive so far. The dollar, well, that's just sort of a freight charge."

Balaam could tell that Perry was shoveling a bushel of manure. Balaam could have felt taken advantage of, but he instead tried to put Perry at ease. "Earl, if you can get someone to pay you good money for that stuff, and you're willing to drive out to my place and pump it and haul it back, well, more power to you."

Perry was relieved. "It was going to be a surprise. I didn't want to tell you until after I saw that the water would sell. I was going to split the money with you fifty-fifty. I've sold ten jars. Here's five dollars." Perry pulled a wad of bills from his pants pocket, peeled off a five, and handed it to Balaam.

Balaam looked at the five-dollar bill. It was better than finding money in the street: He did not even have to bend over to pick it up.

That five dollars covered the cost of Balaam's meager purchases. As he walked toward the door, he said to Perry, "Earl, this is the first time I ever walked out of your store with as much money as I came in with. I thank you."

Balaam walked out feeling blessed. But Mayor Earl Perry felt twice as blessed as Balaam—he actually had sold *twenty* jars.

Perry had sold ten jars to Big Un Petteway and ten to David Wilson, shopping for Nanetta. David was glad to pay one dollar per quart to avoid having to drive out to the cave and negotiate the speed trap that was Walter Ridgely's German shepherd.

During the next few days, as other merchants learned that residents would pay for the convenience of being able to get the water in town and that Balaam was amenable, they quickly arranged the same fifty-fifty split with him: Little Un Petteway at the gas station, Beverly Faulk at the antiques store, even Lawton Parker at the hardware store, although Lawton deliberately priced the jars so high that no one would buy them and thus reduce his stock. The arrangement was different with Juanita

Greer at the Crossroads Cafe. Juanita—now cured of her former skepticism about the water—offered Balaam a barter deal that he gladly accepted: Juanita could sell all the water that the market would bear; in return, Balaam's weekly Sunday supper of a double cheeseburger and two slices of chocolate pie would be "on the house."

Balaam was willing to let the merchants do all the work of pumping the water, carting it into town, filling jars, collecting money, and divvying up with him every week or so. He wanted no part of all that. He did not want to get into the bottling business, and he felt comfortable with most any machine except an adding machine.

After two weeks, Balaam was surprised. He was surprised that people were willing to pay money for that funny-tasting water. And he was surprised by how quickly he was getting used to the concept of "making money by doin' diddly."

"Diddly" was becoming Balaam Gimble's favorite number.

To that point, Balaam's mineral water had been a purely local phenomenon. Then two random events occurred.

Euell Liddy's daughter drove down from Oklahoma City one weekend to visit; Euell mentioned the cave to her, and she wanted to go have a soak. She drove out to the cave, had a good long soak before driving back to Oklahoma, and enjoyed the experience so much that she told a co-worker about it the following Monday. That co-worker drove down the following weekend—having a flat tire on the dirt road to Balaam's property—took a dip in the cave, and went back to Oklahoma City with a gallon of the water for drinking.

Two days later, a couple driving from San Antonio to Dallas along the back roads of central Texas stopped for gas at Little Un Petteway's station. The husband and wife saw Little Un's display of Mason jars and asked about it. Little Un told them about Balaam's Cave and the reputed health benefits of the water. To the couple, this was their kind of "adventure tourism." They jotted down directions to the cave from Little Un and felt fortunate that they had the cave to themselves when they arrived because they had not packed swimwear. After a cozy hour in the cave, they drove back to Willoughby to reach the state highway, running over a broken beer bottle along the way.

Mayor Perry received these two pieces of intelligence from an unlikely agent: Rudy Janacek, who operated the tractor repair shop/auto parts store/state inspection station. After 5:00 P.M. on a Tuesday, Perry walked across the highway to the Crossroads Cafe to eat supper. Seeing Rudy alone at a booth, Perry sat down opposite him. As Perry sat down, Rudy was watching waitress Brandi Renee, who was wearing a short skirt. Rudy Janacek was in love with Brandi Renee's knees. He would gladly have divorced his wife and married either knee. He would have gladly converted to Mormonism if doing so would allow him to marry both knees.

Rudy forced himself to engage in small talk between glimpses of Brandi Renee as she shuttled between tables carrying plates and pitchers. "You know, Earl, this week I fixed flats for two people from out of town. A guy from Oklahoma City picked up a nail going out to Balaam's to try that mineral water. And then a couple from San Antone ran over a chunk of glass on their way *back* from the cave. Two flats in one week. The county ought to do something about that road out there."

Perry looked at Rudy as if seeing him for the first time since Perry had sat down. "Oklahoma City, you say? And San Antonio?" The mayor was talking more to himself than to Rudy. For a few seconds, Perry stared into the middle distance, oblivious as Brandi Renee walked her knees across his field of vision. Then, if Rudy had been more perceptive, he might have seen the lightbulb switch on in His Honor's hundred-watt soft white eyes.

"Rudy, this is *it*. The *big* it. Why didn't I see this?" The pupils of Perry's eyes glowed like filaments. He squirmed slightly and then leaned forward conspiratorially. "Rudy. Listen to this. Fill in the blank: 'Willoughby—the _____ Capital of Texas'!" Perry watched Rudy's face expectantly, waiting.

Rudy looked at Perry and suddenly felt panicky. He felt like he was back in school, being quizzed but totally unprepared. He gave Perry the first answer that came to mind.

". . . the Flat Tire Capital of Texas?"

❧14❧

*"When Daddy offered me a job in 'retail,' I didn't know
I'd be watching old people bathe in horse troughs. Gross."*
———Earline Perry

"Don't act the fool, Rudy," Mayor Perry said. But he was too excited to be frustrated. He rose from the booth and hurried out of the cafe without even ordering. He had to get to City Hall. As he waited impatiently to cross the highway at the intersection, the flashing red light flashed only four times as he thought of the people he needed to consult with. It flashed only two more times as he began to think of logistics, assets, and liabilities. By the time he reached City Hall and unlocked the door, Operation Salvation was taking shape in his municipal mind.

The next day Perry consulted with three people.

First he drove out to Balaam's cabin. After about twenty minutes of talk on the porch, the two men drove to the cave, where they stayed another ten minutes. After Perry left, Balaam Gimble knew what he had to do: "I'm gonna need to put in a good gate at that fence and tune the carburetor on that pump engine."

Then Perry drove to Nanetta Wilson's home to talk with David. Perry and David talked for almost an hour. After Perry left, David Wilson knew what he had to do: "I've got to make some phone calls and do some writing."

Lastly, Perry dropped by the cafe while Brandi Renee was on her morning break. They talked less than two minutes. After Perry left, Brandi Renee knew what she had to do. Taking off her apron and grabbing her purse, Brandi Renee hollered toward the kitchen, "Goin' to Waco, Juanita. I've got to shop for a new bikini!"

A week later, the Willoughby Town Hall meeting for the month of June was held. Mayor Perry stood behind his card table podium, smiling and nodding to more faces than he was accustomed to seeing at such meetings. Even Nanetta Wilson was present. She was now able to get around on an electric "personal mobility" scooter and had insisted on "driving" to the meeting. David had finally stopped trying to persuade her to let him drive her in her car and had walked along beside her as she rode her scooter along sidewalks and side streets the six blocks to Town Hall. She had driven the scooter up the sidewalk ramp and right into Town Hall.

In front of Perry, a five-gallon crock and a stack of plastic cups were arranged on top of the card table. Behind Perry was a chalkboard with a bedsheet draped over it.

When everyone was seated and still (Nanetta had some difficulty parallel parking and almost sent Rosalee Taft's foot to the paint and body shop), Mayor Perry began. "Thank you for coming. I think you'll be glad you did. I'm real excited today to tell you about plans for a campaign to promote Willoughby. As you probably know, a couple of months ago Balaam Gimble found a little cave out at his place that has a hot spring in it. Water from that spring contains several health-promoting minerals. Many of you have been out to soak in the water, some of you drink it regularly now. Lately even people from out of town have been showing interest in the water. Locally, several of you have come to believe that the water indeed does promote health."

"Amen," called out Big Un Petteway, patting his wrong-sided liver.

"Ditto," added Willis Pinkston, holding his right foot out into the aisle and wiggling it.

Nanetta Wilson tooted her scooter horn as an endorsement.

"As you also know, for months we've been trying to think of a hook, something to give our town an identity, to put us on the map. Well, I think we've found it." Perry turned to the chalkboard, paused to savor the moment, and with a flourish pulled away the bedsheet.

Written in large letters on the chalkboard was "Willoughby—the Hot-Dam Mineral Water Capital of Texas."

Willoughby's new claim to fame was met first with whispers, then with applause and cheers, even some mild foot stomping, although avid hunter J. D. Vernon, wearing his customary camouflage outfit, was careful not to stomp his left boot, in which was concealed a .22-caliber pistol ("because you never know when you might see something move").

Mayor Perry continued, heartened by the response. "And there's more. As you may know, David Wilson," Perry nodded at David, "is staying in town while his mother, Nanetta, convalesces." Another nod at Nanetta, who was parked beside David. "David is in advertising in Houston, and I asked him for some ideas. Well, I think he has come up with a couple of keepers. How's this for the name of the spring-fed mineral water that Willoughby is going to be the capital of? Are you ready?" Perry paused for effect. "'Bounce, the Lone Star Wonder Water.' Hold on. Wait. There's more. David came up with this slogan to go with Bounce: 'Put our spring in your step.' Is that not great? Bounce . . . spring . . . step. Get it?" Perry scanned the faces in the audience, gauging reaction. When he saw Pat Yandell raise his eyebrows and drop his jaw in delight, Perry knew they had a winner. Pat, Perry was pretty sure, moved his lips when he read a stop sign.

The applause and remarks of approval, modest at first, quickly increased as more people in the audience "got it." Nanetta honked her horn with motherly pride. David Wilson lowered his head slightly and said to himself, "I can't take her *anywhere*."

Perry continued, reveling in the enthusiasm. "Balaam could not be here tonight," he said, knowing that most present would understand that as code for "Balaam just didn't *want* to be here tonight."

"But he and I have had some very productive talks, and we've reached an arrangement that I think will be win-win for Balaam and our town. Merchants in town can continue to sell the water under their existing arrangements with Balaam. But so we can promote our town as the 'Hot-Dam Mineral Water Capital of Texas,' Balaam has agreed to allow visitors access to the cave during business hours seven days a week. But please don't be going up to his house and bothering him. We will provide someone—possibly a college student—to be at the cave during business hours to handle the money, keep the place neat, and generally look after things. People will pay a small fee to soak in the water or drink it. Money received at the cave will go to Balaam; the municipality of Willoughby will receive no money directly. But the entire town of Willoughby stands to profit considerably by the increase in tourism that can come from being known as," Perry turned and tapped the chalkboard, "'the Hot-Dam Mineral Water Capital of Texas.' For every dollar that tourists spend on water, they may spend five, ten, or even twenty dollars in town—at the gas station, in our shops, at the cafe.

"And let me offer a word to the wise, people," Perry's voice assumed the tone of a man capable of looking into the future. "This town has not had any form of lodging in thirty years. But if this promotion takes off like it could, Willoughby might just have a need for a bed-and-breakfast or two."

A buzz of wonderment swept the room.

"Just something to keep in mind. Before I forget, there's one other person who has contributed to all this in a very important but unrecognized way. Back in April, after Balaam found the cave, it was Ray Dean Briley who first noticed that his bursitis seemed to get better after he had been in the water. He got curious about the water and had a mineral analysis done. We certainly owe Ray Dean a big hand for that."

Ray Dean, sitting in the front row with his wife, Charlene, lifted his gimme cap modestly in acknowledgment of the applause and a couple of pats on the back. Charlene squeezed his knee.

"And there's more to our campaign," Perry said, reclaiming the floor. "David has suggested that Willoughby get a 'Web site' to promote itself and its new title on the Internet. Now I know that many of us, maybe most of us, don't have computers and aren't on the Internet. But that's the future, they tell me. So David has arranged with a company in Waco to 'build' us a Web site. I won't tell you all the details until it's ready. You'll be able to see it at the computer at City Hall.

"There will be a few more surprises in the days ahead. Be watching for them. Folks, that's about it. This could mean big things for Willoughby. Before we adjourn, we have here on the table a crock of Balaam's spring-fed mineral water, now known as Bounce, the Lone Star Wonder Water. There are enough cups for everyone. Please join me in a toast."

With help from Jessie Pinkston, the Taft sisters, and a couple of other women volunteers, a plastic cup of Bounce was distributed to each person present. Mayor Perry raised his cup and proclaimed, "To Willoughby, the Hot-Dam Mineral Water Capital of Texas!"

As Perry swallowed, he hoped he was the only one who thought the water tasted terrible.

After the toast, Mayor Perry eagerly received congratulations on the new campaign. Even David Wilson found himself being thanked for his contribution. His time in the limelight was cut short as Nanetta scootered out the front door of Town Hall, tooting her horn to clear the path.

During the remainder of June, Operation Salvation progressed quickly. Rosalee and Anita Taft added "Willoughby—the Hot-Dam Mineral Water Capital of Texas" to the masthead of the *Bee*. The Web site was designed and "up" and soon receiving what David called "hits." The Web site's pages included the mineral analysis of the water, a map locating Willoughby in Texas, a list of town merchants, photos of a few of the town's finer old homes and "charming rural scenes," some endorsements of the water by "satisfied users," and, of course, photos of the cave interior, featuring Brandi Renee, luxuriating in the pool in her new bikini. As Willoughby's resident "pretty little thing," she had been the only person Perry had considered for the photos.

The flurry of attention made Brandi Renee only more self-absorbed. She became even less motivated to pursue a career in waitressing. After all, that was no job for a "model." And that, she told herself, is what you call a woman who is chosen to appear in photographs because of her great beauty. A model. And a model can become anything, even the wife—better yet, the *ex*-wife—of a fabulously wealthy man. Her heart swelled with Texas patriotism as she realized how fortunate she was to live in a community property state.

When Rudy Janacek heard that the Willoughby Web site featured photos of Brandi Renee in a bikini, he immediately went to City Hall on the pretext of making sure that his name was spelled correctly on the merchants page. He was not familiar with personal computers or the Internet, so Glenda Bratcher, Willoughby's part-time city secretary, logged on and loaded the Willoughby home page for him. But she was busy with city business, so she showed Rudy how to use the mouse to navigate through the pages and left him on his own. It took Rudy a few moments to get the hang of "that little plastic clicky doohickey" and the "little pointy cusser thing on the TV screen," but suddenly there on the screen appeared Brandi Renee. She was indeed wearing a bikini, leaning back against the edge of the pool. She was smiling at the camera just as she smiled at Rudy in his fantasies. Her bikini top was above the waterline. Her body from the midriff south was below the waterline, but Rudy thought he could make out her navel, her bikini bottom, and oh-my-God-her-knees in the water.

That evening after work, Rudy Janacek went home and engaged in a love-making session with his wife. Thus it was that Donna Jean Janacek, basking in the afterglow that inevitably follows three solid minutes of passion, was in an agreeable mood when Rudy cooed to her, "Honey, I think it's time we got a computer for the shop."

Mayor Perry appointed his daughter Earline, home from college for the summer, as custodian of the cave. A second-hand metal desk was placed in the shade of a live oak tree near the mouth of the cave. "That will be your office," Earl said to Earline. "You'll learn how to deal with the public and handle money and be responsible. It will be good business training for you."

Merchants began selling maps to the cave for a dollar in addition to selling the water in Mason jars that now bore the printed label "Bounce, the Lone Star Wonder Water."

Mazelle Henderson was the first "private citizen" in town to begin selling Bounce. On a picnic table in her front yard on Highway 21, she displayed a few jars alongside vegetables from her back yard garden, some jars of homemade chow-chow, and some gourds that she had grown, dried, and painted to resemble, she claimed, the cast of "Gunsmoke."

New "Welcome to Willoughby, the Hot-Dam Mineral Water Capital of Texas" signs were erected at the four highway entrances to town, featuring a closeup of Brandi Renee smiling hugely and holding a Mason jar of Bounce. After the signs were erected, Mayor Perry spent an hour one morning just driving into town from all four directions and taking joy in the sight. He did not notice, but on two occasions as he made his rounds past the new signs, Brandi Renee was behind him in her car, making the same rounds, sharing the same joy.

Slowly, travelers began to notice the new signs and to stop to inquire. The town began to see a species long thought extinct in those parts: tourists. Not many at first, but Little Un Petteway did notice a slight increase in gasoline sales in the second half of June. Juanita and Richard Greer noticed more unfamiliar faces in the cafe. And someone with an out-of-state license plate stopped at Beverly Faulk's antiques store, asked directions to Balaam's Cave, and bought a twenty-five-dollar vase that Beverly had paid five dollars for at an estate sale.

Two weeks after the Town Hall meeting, at dusk one evening Mayor Perry stood at the front window of his store looking out at his town as darkness fell. How much better Willoughby's future looked now than after the Town Hall meeting in April. So much had happened. Fate had delivered unto Willoughby a recipe for economic revival: "Just add water," Perry thought, pleased with the phrase. Too bad that water was in a cave owned by a man who wasn't even a registered voter.

Still, Mayor Earl Perry felt optimistic. Above and to the right of the flashing red light at the intersection, the evening star had appeared. Perry saw it and, in his sanguine mood, tried to remember when he had last made a wish on that star. Many years ago, he was sure, probably some wish about a girl or money. He was far too old and far too jaded now to make such wishes. But as he locked up his store and left for the night, Perry conceded that if he were to make a wish on that star, he knew exactly what that wish would be.

❧15❧

"You could just tell there's no Mrs. Gimble. I didn't see a single doily."
——Delia Tibbets

Mayor Perry had approached Balaam about a "partnership" with the town when Balaam had been in a condition that was common in the kingdom of Gimble: He was broke. Thus, when Perry had assured Balaam that the town would promote and operate the cave and deliver all profits to him, Balaam had consented, although with some qualms. Balaam enjoyed his aloneness, he valued the serenity of his woods and weeds. And even though most of the time he could not, with his five senses, detect when people—many of them strangers now—were at the cave—on *his* land—nonetheless he *knew* they were there. And for him, it changed the land.

But Balaam still thought that interest in the water would evaporate. And for all he knew, the source of the water, wherever the hell it was, also might evaporate. Get while the getting is good, he told himself.

And the arrangement had worked well enough so far. During the second half of June and into July, people had come to the cave in increasing numbers. Each day Earline Perry sat behind her metal desk under the live oak tree near the cave and collected a small fee from visitors, started the pump to fill the tubs, distributed new color brochures touting "Willoughby, the Hot-Dam Mineral Water Capital of Texas," and in general was what the brochures called "the friendly, knowledgeable staff of Balaam's Cave." Once a week she brought Balaam a coffee can of money: $67 the first week, $121 the second, and $278 so far in July. To Balaam, that represented the income from a lot of odd jobs. At this rate, he realized, he would be able to pay his property taxes on time for once and avoid those pursed-lipped letters from the tax district. And surely he would not have to resort, as he had one year, to selling plasma in Waco to pay his August electric bill.

And overall, Balaam's Cave was running smoothly with little effort on his part. True, once in a while Earline would flood the pump engine while trying to start it, and Balaam would have to go help her, and once she came up to his cabin almost in tears because "Mr. Jarvis keeps traipsin' around with that big beer belly and those teeny little swim trunks."

Thus when Earline appeared at Balaam's compound one day in mid-July, Balaam suspected that either she had been "monkeyin' with that choke again" or Leroy Jarvis had been "struttin' his stuffin'."

But, no, Earline had come to ask a favor: She and her boyfriend wanted to go to the lake the next afternoon and could Balaam sit in for her just this once and not tell Daddy and she'd be ever so grateful, pretty please. Balaam had consented, but the next afternoon, after about two hours of sitting behind that metal desk in ninety-degree heat with only sporadic business, he had suddenly realized, "I may be sitting under a tree in a pasture just off a dirt road, but *this is a desk job!*"

"Nope," Balaam said. "Ain't gonna do it." He scribbled "pay what you want" on a square of cardboard, displayed the cardboard on the desk next to the coffee can "cash register," and went back to his cabin.

Two hours later, an old Buick the size of a barge slowly sailed up Balaam's driveway. The driver politely honked. Two short toots. As Balaam approached the car, three women got out and began stretching, obviously travel weary. Balaam saw three faces with a total of at least two hundred years of living embossed on them. The driver was the youngster of the three—a woman of about seventy. She was maybe five feet tall and one hundred and ten pounds. Balaam wondered how she steered and stopped that big car.

"We drove up from Austin to go to 'Balaam's Cave,' but there's no one there to take our money," the driver said.

Balaam was not sure that these pilgrims could get safely down and up the ladder. "I can do better than that. Let me follow you down to the cave and make sure you get situated okay."

The women were delighted. They began to answer questions that Balaam never intended to ask: The youngster was Delia, who still lived on her own in Austin. The two older women, Fran and Hester, were residents of an assisted-living center in Austin. They had heard about "the mineral water at Willoughby" and, with the help of Delia driving "the getaway car," had gone AWOL. "And here we are. We have our swimsuits on underneath, and we have old bones and tired muscles that are ready for their hot mineral bath."

As Delia and Hester talked, Balaam noticed that Fran, the oldest, had walked to the fence and was staring at Balaam's two acres of clutter. Her milky gray eyes were sparkling. "Ohhh," Fran said in a voice that was half croon, half croak. "This is our good luck. You're having a yard sale. Do you have any World's Fair spoons? I collect those. Or any snow scene paperweights? I love those. Oh, or any Currier and Ives collector plates?"

Balaam told her that he was not having a yard sale, but the fact did not seem to register with Fran.

"Is that an antique coal-oil lantern over there?" she asked, pointing over the fence. "How much do you want for it?"

Balaam politely told her that it was not for sale.

Somehow Balaam got Fran into the big Buick, and somehow Delia got the big Buick backed down Balaam's driveway without hitting a tree. Balaam followed them to the cave in his pickup. He opened the new gate at the fence so that they could drive as close as possible. "Wouldn't you rather use these tubs? It's a lot easier. No trouble to fill them with water straight from the cave."

"Oh, no," said Delia, dismissing the idea of such a shortcut. She obviously was the ringleader and did most of the talking. "We want the full experience. We want the cave."

Balaam held the ladder (and his breath) as the three women descended one after the other. Balaam stayed, busying himself with checking the gas and oil levels of the pump engine while the women removed their street clothes in the cave. He heard them settle sighing and giggling girlishly into the hot water.

"Don't worry about us," Delia called up to him. "We'll be fine."

Nonetheless, Balaam thought he'd better stay close. He killed the time by tightening the clamps on the pump hoses and scrubbing the three bathtubs and the horse trough. But after thirty minutes, he again found himself sitting at the desk and doing nothing. He walked to the mouth of the cave and called down, "Y'all, I'm going back home. If you need any help, one of you get up to your car and honk. I'll hear you."

Delia's voice assured him that they would be "just dandy."

Balaam returned to his cabin and got back to work tuning Betty Hall's lawn mower. But he was afraid to start the engine because he would not be able to hear a distress honk. Instead, he found himself listening closely. He can almost hear withered feet slipping, brittle bones breaking. Just past six o'clock, after a honkless hour had passed, he became concerned and drove back to the cave. The big Buick was still there. No one was in sight. He shouted "Hello?" No response. He walked to the mouth of the cave, leaned over, and looked in. There, in the middle of the pool, standing motionless back to back to back, were Delia, Fran, and Hester. They looked like three missionaries in a cannibal's kettle.

"Hello? Are you okay?"

Delia turned her face up to him. She had a weary, slightly wild-eyed look.

She said, in a weak voice, "Over there. It snarled at us."

"What snarled at you?"

"A possum. I think."

Balaam repressed a chuckle. "If there's a possum in there, I promise you he's more afraid of you than you are of him."

Balaam descended the ladder and stood on the limestone ledge beside the pool. His presence seemed to reassure the women but not completely. "Where is he?" Balaam asked.

"It was over there a few minutes ago," Delia said, nodding straight ahead of her. "Under those rocks. It keeps moving around, circling us. Hester is convinced it's a rat. A giant rat. She's terrified of rats."

At the word "rats," Hester whimpered. Balaam looked at her. She did indeed look terrified.

"It hissed at us," Delia said. "And it snarled. We saw its teeth. We tried to throw water on it. That just made it snarl more. It won't go

100

away. We've been afraid that if we try to get out of the water it would get us. We couldn't reach the ladder. Or even our clothes."

Balaam got down on his hands and knees and looked where Delia had nodded. Sure enough, there in the shadows among the crevices where the ceiling of the cave sloped down to the floor was a frightened possum, crouching motionless with its head twisted and its mouth open.

"This guy won't hurt you," Balaam said as he stood up. "He's just putting on a show. But let's get y'all out of here. I'll stand between you and Brer Possum until you can get out of the water and up the ladder. Don't worry about your clothes. I'll carry them up to keep them dry."

Delia and Fran, thus assured, got out of the water and climbed, dripping and drooping, up the ladder in their wet swimsuits. But Hester was still stricken with fear and had to be helped out of the water. She was trembling even though the cave was very warm. Balaam saw that she was in no condition to climb the ladder. He had to carry her up piggyback, which was possible only because she was so light.

"Must be built of bird bones," Balaam thought as he carried her.

Above ground, the three women continued to stand close together even as they stood in the warm, bright, possumless sunshine. Balaam fetched bath towels for them from a drawer in the desk under the tree. Delia helped Hester with her towel.

After they had patted themselves dry, Delia went to her car and took her watch from her purse. "Oh, my. It's after six. We had planned to get home before dark. We'll never make it now. I'm the only one of us who drives. But I don't drive at night. We'll have to get a motel room in Willoughby."

"I'm sorry, y'all," Balaam said. "There are no motels in town." About halfway through that second sentence, Balaam foresaw an ugly possibility. He paused a couple of seconds to give fate a chance to have mercy on him and provide an alternative. Two seconds passed. Then a third. Fate clearly was otherwise engaged. Reluctantly, Balaam said, "If you don't mind roughing it, I guess I can put you up for the night, and y'all can drive back in the morning."

"You wouldn't mind?" Delia said. "That would be a lifesaver. I really shouldn't drive at night. The headlights blind me, and I get confused. I end up driving on the shoulder about fifteen miles an hour."

Balaam smiled at the image. "Well, we don't want that. But won't they miss you where you live? Do you need to call anyone at the"— "Balaam almost said "rest home"—"place where you live?"

Fran said, "Oh, I'm sure the Gestapo already does miss us. Or at least our checkbooks. Let them fret. They'll take us back with open arms."

In his pickup, Balaam followed the big Buick back to his compound. Then the three women followed him as he threaded his way through his "stuff" to his cabin. Delia and Hester tried hard not to stare at the landscape of clutter. Balaam was glad that Stilts—shy around strangers—was staying out of sight. When Balaam reached the cabin, he found that Fran had wandered off. He found her browsing among the jumble of items stacked on a wooden table.

"How much for this?" she asked, holding up a 1957 Illinois auto license plate.

Balaam diplomatically ushered Fran back to the cabin, wondering why on earth she would want such a thing. It did not occur to Balaam that someone might wonder why on earth *he* would want such a thing.

Inside, Balaam pointed out his tiny bathroom and went to his kitchen area, where he found one teabag and two coffee mugs and a jelly jar that would have to serve as teacups. As he stretched the teabag to three servings, one at a time the women went into his bathroom to "do something with this hair" and change into their street clothes—stretch pants and loose-fitting blouses.

The women had taken the only real seating in the cabin—the couch—and were primly looking around the room when Balaam brought them their tea and pulled up a metal folding chair opposite them. Balaam noticed that Hester was rocking slightly and picking nervously at the loose skin on the back of her hands.

Balaam was not used to having overnight guests, to playing host. He tried to think of all the things he needed to ask and say and do. He had the tools and training to pull a transmission, cinch a saddle, and shingle a roof, but not to bunk three little old ladies overnight. What do they eat? How do they sleep? What do they need in the bathroom?

For starters, Balaam asked if they were hungry.

"No," Delia said, "we stopped at a Stuckey's on the way up. Mostly we're just tired, I think."

Balaam went into his bathroom, opened the drawer that served as his linen closet, and drafted every bedsheet and pillow into duty, including some that would not stand close inspection. As he turned toward the bathroom door, he reminded himself that at this late hour they were an hour away from a store that sold hairbrushes or denture adhesive or any sort of—Balaam stopped and looked at his face in the medicine cabinet mirror—"lady's products." Balaam had seen that expression before—on Hester's face in the cave during the Great Possum Siege. Then Balaam began to wonder about medicine. What if they are on medication and don't have it with them? He didn't know how to ask.

"Do any of you need anything from the medicine cabinet like . . . aspirin or . . . vitamins or . . ."

"Oh," Delia said, remembering. "It's time for one of my greens. I take two greens for my heart and a blue for my . . . well, I'm not sure what the blues are for. But I have them in my purse. Fran, do you have your reds?"

Fran rummaged through her handbag and held up a small plastic bottle and shook it to rattle the pills.

Hester said, "Well, I didn't bring my white ovals. But I can skip a night. I don't think they're doing me any good anyway."

Balaam was relieved. There was a good chance that all three women would be alive when they left in the morning.

"I don't have any spare toothbrushes," Balaam said. "Or any pajamas or anything like that."

Delia seemed to appreciate that the situation was as trying for Balaam as for them. "Don't you worry about us, Mr. Gimble. We'll be just fine. We wore comfortable clothes for the drive, and they'll get us through the night. It'll be like a slumber party!"

Despite their trauma, the women seemed pleased with their soak in the cave. Gradually, after chit-chatting about the cave and its brief history and the water's reputed effects, even Hester seemed to recover. Gradually she stopped picking at the back of her hands and began to take part in the conversation. "I feel like we went rock climbing and swimming and on safari all at once."

"And a yard sale, too!" called Fran, who was standing at Balaam's door and looking out at his treasures.

"It was very primitive," said Delia. "Very restful. Almost womb-like."

Night had fallen by the time Balaam had prepared the couch and bed as best he could. He said, "Y'all must be beat. I'm going to leave you alone. Make yourselves at home. Two of you can take the bed and one on the couch. I'll be comfortable on the porch," he lied. "Holler if you need anything. Good night and sorry about . . . everything."

After Balaam went outside, he walked out to the Buick and put the money that the women had paid him in the glove compartment. The interior of the car smelled like a sachet that as a child he had smelled in his grandmother's closet. Balaam used a mover's blanket and a folded sweater to fashion a pallet and pillow on the porch floor. The night was warm; he turned in wearing shorts and T-shirt. He listened to the wind in the trees and the crickets and heard Stilts's cowbell tinkle once from somewhere in the compound. Then the mosquitoes began to arrive. With each swat, Balaam thought of Earline and hoped that she had gotten sunburned at the lake. In a short while, the three women began to turn in. Through the open bedroom window, he could just make out two voices—Hester and Delia, he guessed.

Balaam didn't know how long he had been asleep when he was awakened by a sound. By the time he had identified the sound as the creak of the screen door opening, he heard Fran's thin voice: "Mr. Gimble, how much for this salt and pepper set?"

In the darkness, Balaam Gimble swatted another mosquito and tried to remember what life had been like before that day in April when he had opened Pandora's cave.

❧16❧

"Balaam was playing some scratchy old country-western record.
Personally, I thought the scratches were the best part."
——David Wilson

As David Wilson walked up Balaam's long driveway on a day in late July, the afternoon was hot and muggy. The heavy air seemed to cling to him like a woolen suit. When David was within sight of the cabin, he saw Balaam outside, among the clutter. Balaam was standing motionless and seemed to be pointing a finger at David. To David, Balaam's stance looked vaguely confrontational. David called out, "Balaam? It's David Wilson. Can I come up?"

Balaam said nothing. But still holding his body and his outstretched left arm motionless, he slowly lifted his right arm and motioned to David to approach. David, taking his cue from Balaam's behavior, approached but slowly. When he got closer, he could see a butterfly perched on Balaam's left index finger.

Balaam said in a soft voice, "This guy lit on my finger a couple of minutes ago, and I've been standing here waiting for him to fly. It's drinking the sweat."

The butterfly was a red admiral. David and Balaam watched as it jabbed its crooked proboscis at the damp surface of Balaam's finger. Now and then it folded and unfolded its wings.

"Reckon what that butterfly is thinking? Or if it even *can* think?"

Balaam asked, more to himself than to David. As Balaam spoke, the butterfly, perhaps not appreciating being talked about as if it were not even present, flapped away, hitching a ride with an itinerant breeze.

After Balaam had offered David a seat on the porch, asked about his mother, and brought him a beer, David said with a smile, "I understand you had a slumber party the other night."

"Oh, you heard about that."

"I get the impression that not much happens around Willoughby that people don't hear about."

"I'll bet that possum had a better night than I did. The next morning, after those little old ladies got back on the road, I caught him and let him go a good five miles away."

Balaam sat down on his bucket seat but immediately stood back up. "Hey, listen to this." Balaam's voice had the enthusiasm of a child who has brought a puppy to show-and-tell at school. On the wooden cable spool that served as a table sat a portable phonograph, a 78-rpm record on the turntable. At least fifty years old, David guessed. Balaam turned a switch, and the tone arm moved up, over, and down. When the music began—a twangy male vocalist and a fiddler competing with the scratches on the record—Balaam began to dance, sashaying off the porch and between two rows of clutter, moving with exaggerated pivots and slides and singing along.

> I met the girl I love
> In a town way down in Dixie.
> 'Neath the stars a-bove
> She was the sweet-est girl I ever did see.

David was slightly embarrassed. It seemed odd for one man to watch another man dance in such a setting. David also was slightly envious. His ex-wife had always complained because he would not dance with her. But David had always been too inhibited, too self-conscious to dance. (His ex-wife had worded it less charitably: "David, you've got a tempered steel rod up your butt.")

Balaam danced his way back onto the porch and sat down as the song ended. "I hadn't heard that song in twenty years. Maybe more. I've been playing it all day. This was my father's record player," Balaam said, patting the phonograph. "It hadn't worked in years, but I didn't know how to fix it, and I couldn't afford to get it fixed. And then last week, between the water that was sold in town and what Earline took in at the cave, I made more than two hundred dollars. So I thought, 'what the hell?' I took it to a little old-timey shop in Waco, and the guy fixed it right up. Even put a new needle in it. It's not worth what it cost to fix, but it's hard to find something to play 78s."

David had his opening. "Two hundred dollars. It's really taking off, isn't it? The water, I mean. People in town say they are doing more business because of tourists. The Web page is getting a lot of traffic. That's one reason I came out."

Balaam looked at David and waited.

"Well, it occurred to me the other day that the cave and the water might have some commercial value. I mean on a larger scale. I mentioned it to Earl Perry, and he asked me to pass the word along to you."

"You mean like a bottling company?"

"That. Maybe even develop the cave as a commercial property."

"Boy, I'll bet Perry wet his pants when you told him. He'd like to see Willoughby grow until it busts its britches."

"Yeah, he was pretty excited, I admit. Now, I don't know much about business, but I do think that the way the cave has caught on in the short time it has been promoted points to a larger potential. And that would mean more money for you."

Balaam spread his hands in his lap and stared at them a few seconds. "Well, I've been wrong about this thing at every turn. I didn't think there was a dime in it. I guess I oughta keep an open mind if someone is interested."

"I'll tell you what. Mother's going to need me to stay in Willoughby for the time being. So I'm going back to Houston this week to close up my house and arrange to do my work from Mother's by email and teleconferencing. While I'm down there, I'll make some calls. Maybe someone knows someone who knows someone."

About dusk, Stilts appeared and approached first Balaam and then David to have his ears rubbed. David had ministered to the left ear and was starting on the right when he saw a pinpoint of light blink against the dark backdrop of trees. He watched and soon saw a second blink.

"Lightning bugs?" he asked.

Balaam turned and looked in the direction that David was facing.

107

Mike Nichols

"Hey, sure enough. First ones I've seen this summer. Did you ever catch them as a kid?"

"In mayonnaise jars. All of us kids on the block."

David and Balaam continued to talk and to watch for the flashes of lightning bugs, as if the flashes were the dots and dashes of a Morse code that could spell out a past long forgotten. Soon, from about a half-mile to the south, came the overture howl of a coyote. When David heard the howl, he pointed ninety degrees to the west, anticipating a second chorus of howls. Sure enough, a second chorus rose from the direction he was pointing.

Balaam was impressed. "You'll make a country boy yet."

A minute later, from that same direction and distance, came a gunshot, followed a second later by another.

"God, I hate that sound. That's probably Vernon," Balaam said, "trying to pick off a coyote or two. I don't understand a man like that. Always wanting to see something die. Hell, I used to hunt. When I was twelve, I had a little single-shot .22. But I also wet the bed when I was four and cried in the dark when I was six. I outgrew all three."

David kept quiet and let Balaam have the floor. Night had fallen. To the right of Balaam's silhouetted head, David saw another lightning bug flash.

"People like Vernon call themselves 'sportsmen.' Hell, hunting the way they do it ain't a 'sport,' and those who do it ain't 'men.' If Vernon wants to be sporting, let him get naked, get down on all fours, and take on a ten-point buck with his bare hands during mating season."

Balaam laughed so loudly that he startled Stilts. "Now I'd pay to watch *that*." Balaam leaned forward and patted Stilts on the flank. "And I'd pay to get to visit Vernon in the hospital afterward."

Twenty-three lightning bug flashes later, David said he needed to be getting back to town. As David and Balaam walked between the rows of clutter toward the gate, Balaam again broke into song and dance.

> So, I held her in my arms
> And told her of her many charms,
> And I kissed her while the fiddles played 'Bonaparte's Retreat.'

Balaam's musical spasm passed as quickly as it had come. He said,

108

"Yeah, if you find some commercial guy who might be interested, I reckon I'd listen. But I don't want this cave situation getting out of hand. And I have no interest in selling the place. Hell, I'm just now getting the place in order."

David, following Balaam in the low light, stepped on an eight-inch conch shell that had fallen from its resting place atop a paint can that was resting atop an old TV set that was supported by a bundle of softball bats. David Wilson moved the conch shell aside with the toe of his shoe and wondered just what kind of "order" Balaam had in mind.

❧17❧

"Jesus turned water into wine. I'm quite content to turn it into money."
——Howard J. Liggett

David had been back to Houston only three times—and each time only briefly—since his mother's accident. On his fourth trip back—to close up his house and arrange to do his work for Adams, Hawkins, & Jenrette from Willoughby—for a few moments he suffered culture shock as he entered his own hometown. He found the pace more hurried than he remembered, the decibel level higher, and the people less pleasant than he remembered. He was chagrined to find that he lacked his usual confidence to drive aggressively on the 610 Loop. He got honked at for driving fifty-eight in the fast lane. David Wilson looked at his speedometer and wondered if his little red roadster suspected that it had been hot-wired by a gang of joyriding Amish.

He first stopped at his office, met with his boss, loaded his laptop with the files he would need, and grabbed his Rolodex. He also took from a locked desk drawer his "cyanide file." At his townhouse, David had no pets, no houseplants, only a lawn that needed regular care. That done, he began making phone calls to people higher up the business food chain. After two hours of dead ends, he reached a Houston entrepreneur who suggested that David contact "an old poker buddy of mine"—Howard J. Liggett of Colorado, head of the Aquavita Company, which operated upscale mineral spring resorts in several states. David thanked the entrepreneur for the lead and was taking the receiver from his ear to hang up when the entrepreneur said, "Hey, David?"

David put the phone back to his ear. "Yes?"

"More times than I care to remember, I've seen ol' Howard draw to an inside straight. And win."

When David phoned Howard J. Liggett at his flagship resort outside Denver (the receptionist answered with a bright "Aquavita Company. To your good health"), David told Liggett what he knew about the water and the cave. Liggett listened politely, asked a few questions, and suggested that David fax him the mineral analysis that Ray Dean Briley had had done.

Liggett received the fax that day, read it, and phoned David the next day. "The mineral content is interesting. If you'd like, send me a sample of the water." Liggett told David how to collect and package the sample and gave him Aquavita's FedEx account number.

David returned to Willoughby the next day and, without telling Balaam, went out to the cave and collected a water sample and sent it to Liggett. When Liggett received the sample, he poured a few ounces into a wine glass and held it up to the light. He swirled the water under his nose and smelled. Then he took a sip, inhaled through his teeth, and sloshed the water around in his mouth. He spit the water into his sink and noted the aftertaste. His palate was happy. And Howard J. Liggett had learned to trust his palate. He then sent the remainder of the sample to his own lab to be analyzed. Meanwhile, Liggett did his home-work: He ordered the most recent aerial photos and geological charts of the Willoughby area, studied a road map of central Texas, and acquired information on Texas public utility costs, tax rates, and real estate values of comparable rural tracts around Willoughby. Two days later, his lab's analysis was essentially identical to the original analysis.

Liggett phoned David at Nanetta's home and said the water from Balaam's Cave "might hold some promise commercially, but there are a lot of other variables." Liggett said he'd like to talk to Mr. Gimble about arranging to inspect the cave and the surrounding area. Liggett was careful to show only enough interest to ensure that David passed him along to Balaam.

David gave Balaam's phone number to Liggett, hung up, and immediately phoned Balaam to tell him to expect a call from Liggett. As he talked to Balaam, David hoped he was doing the right thing.

The next day Liggett phoned Balaam. After an exchange of pleasantries, Liggett said he'd be interested in seeing the cave in person "with some members of my development team."

Balaam was agreeable but made it clear that he was not interested in selling the entire property.

Liggett's voice was velveteen. "I understand, Mr. Gimble. It's your land to do with as you please. But surely it won't hurt for me to come down and take a look around, inspect the cave, sit down with you under a live oak tree"—Liggett had even brushed up on the flora and fauna of central Texas—"and drink a glass of that good mineral water of yours."

The two men agreed that Liggett would visit the cave in one week.

After Balaam hung up, he sat on his porch thinking. He reminded himself that he was in control. Liggett had the money, but Balaam had the deed. Then he thought: "That's a long drive just to have a glass of water." Then he reminded himself that Liggett would surely fly. Maybe even first class.

"First class. Think of that," Balaam said to Stilts, who was napping nearby.

After Howard J. Liggett hung up, he sat thinking behind his George III mahogany desk. Then he pressed his office intercom button. "Mrs. Loomis, I'll need to go down to Texas a week from today. I'll need the Lear."

Liggett switched off the intercom and thought a moment, counting the number of people and amount of equipment he'd need to take along. He pressed the intercom button again. "Correction, Mrs. Loomis: Make that the *big* jet."

❖18❖

"Maybe it was instant karma. I had bacon for breakfast."
——David Wilson

Two days before Howard J. Liggett was scheduled to inspect Balaam's Cave, at 8:00 A.M. David Wilson and Beverly Faulk threw their binoculars and bird books into her car and drove out of town, heading up the Brazos River valley. Because Beverly had been "looking in on" Nanetta during her convalescence, David and Beverly had seen each other briefly several times a week, but this was their first time spent alone and in a non-Nanetta setting. David had grown to feel comfortable around Beverly. She was attentive and patient with Nanetta, even when Nanetta was out of sorts. And Beverly did not have the sharp edge of the professional women whom David met in Houston, who could inflict a paper cut on the male psyche at ten paces.

As Beverly turned off a paved farm road onto a gravel county road, she said, "I'm surprised Balaam would even consider selling his place. In fact, I'm surprised he's even letting people come out to the cave, even if he makes money on the deal."

David said, "He says he doesn't have any plans to sell the place. But two hundred acres is a *lot* of land. There might be some way for Balaam to keep most of it and make a lot of money, if this Liggett guy likes what he sees."

Beverly looked at David. "I'll bet if you ask Balaam, he'd say two hundred acres isn't a lot of land. But I'll tell you one thing. This pro-motion of Willoughby as the 'Hot-Dam Mineral Water Capital' has made a difference in town. I can see it at my store. I hear it from others. Any kind of commercial deal could *really* help business."

Beverly drove to an isolated area of farmland broken by woods and brush where she had had good luck birding in the past. As they walked from the car to a neglected field, there wasn't even a barbed-wire fence for David to do battle with. They walked on into a wooded area of oak, cedar, and yaupon and stood in the shade looking and listening, their binoculars at rest. Soon a familiar call—a short, thin "chip"—came from their left. "Cardinal," David said. Then a "peet peet peet peet" from their right. David scanned the canopy with his binoculars. He focused on a small bird flitting from branch to branch. "Chickadee."

"What kind?"

David easily identified the dark, swept-back topknot. "Black-crested."

Beverly looked at David's check list. "Score one for David. All you've got here is 'plain' and 'tufted.' Not bad for a few minutes' work."

David soon lost sight of the chickadee and lowered his binoculars. He gazed dumbly at the foliage. David, whose work forced him to notice colors, had never seen so many shades of green—from the almost blackish green in the rough texture of tree trunks to the golden green of new leaves reflecting the sun high in the canopy. As he let his eyes unfocus, every leaf in his field of vision, near and far, became a dot, making the woods look as if it had been painted by a pointillist.

During the next hour, David and Beverly moved between the woods and the field and back again. Beverly spotted a loggerhead shrike and a Bell's vireo. David spotted a dickcissel and a Bewick's wren. To their mutual frustration, they both heard, but could never sight, a scarlet tanager.

"There's a big stock tank down this way," Beverly said, pointing south. "Want to go have a look? Maybe we'll see that great blue heron you've never seen."

The easiest route to the stock pond took them just a hundred yards or so from Beverly's car. While they trudged through the overgrown field, David noticed that Beverly scanned the ground as she walked. Beside a rotting tree stump, she stopped and knelt.

"Ever see one of these?"

David joined her, knelt, and saw that she was pointing to a brown, golf ball-sized growth with a tiny hole in its top center.

"What is it?"

"A devil's snuffbox. It's a fungus. Like a mushroom. Tap the side of it with your finger."

When David did so, from the hole shot a cloud of brown powder as fine as smoke.

"Those are spores. Millions of them. That's how it reproduces."

David tapped the devil's snuffbox again and watched the cloud of brown powder. "Now I can say I've had sex with a fungus. Twice."

"I hope you're not the tap-and-tell type."

"Touché!" David thought. He hadn't expected to find someone to verbally fence with in Willoughby.

They walked on together. Soon Beverly stopped and knelt beside a small plant with blue flowers. "These are erect dayflowers, but I call them the 'butterfly plant.' See? The two petals are shaped like butterfly wings, and these two stalks on the end between the wings look like the antennae. It's a morning flower. It'll fold up soon in this heat."

"It won't be alone." Indeed, to David it seemed that the temperature was rising one degree each minute. The drone of insects, the rattle of cicadas in the trees, and the heat were making David sleepy.

As they continued toward the stock pond, Beverly and David had drifted perhaps one hundred feet apart, following their separate lines of inquiry, when David heard a rustle nearby in a thicket of brush. He walked over to investigate and was surprised to find one, two, three black piglets, each a foot long, each adorable. He waved to Beverly and called out just loudly enough for her to hear, "Come here. The three little pigs!" David expected Beverly to respond with some joke about the Big Bad Wolf. Instead he heard:

"David!" Even in just two syllables, the tone of Beverly's voice got his attention. "Get away from there. Get back to the car as quick as you can." Beverly herself began walking quickly to the car. David, seeing that she was serious, began moving toward the car behind her, not understanding why. Beverly was closer to the car than David was and reached it just as a feral hog—black, bristly, and one hundred and forty pounds—charged out of the tall weeds toward David.

David began running, but his feet were slowed by the tall Johnson grass and thick trumpet vine. His binoculars, hanging from a strap around his neck, bounced up and hit him in the chin with each step. He jerked frantically on the strap to break it and threw the binoculars down. He ran through a swarm of gnats, inhaling several. The hog, although bulky and short legged, was agile and fast on her feet. She closed the distance between her and David to less than ten feet just as he reached Beverly's car. Beverly had begun honking her horn to try to scare the hog. David had to stop to pull open the passenger door, momentarily making himself a stationery target. Just as he was bending to get into the car, the hog nipped him on the right back pocket of his slacks.

David yelped. Beverly screamed. The hog grunted. The hog then backed off and milled around on David's side of the car in a frenzy for a few seconds. Then she grunted two more times, pivoted, and trotted back to her piglets.

David was arching his back against the back of the passenger seat to avoid having to sit down. His heart was dancing the four-chamber flamenco. Beverly saw blood dripping from the torn back pocket of David's slacks.

"Let me see how bad she got you."

In a small car, it was difficult—to say nothing of embarrassing—for David to show his right buttock to a person who was (1) a woman he didn't know very well and (2) sitting on his left. He had to twist around and face the rear window with his knees on the seat and the back of his head pressed up against the moonroof.

Beverly had to pat some of the blood off the wound with a handkerchief to see it. David winced with each pat. The hog had taken a chunk out of David's slacks, his undershorts, and his flesh. "I usually don't let a woman do this on a first date," David said as he spat out a gnat and hugged the headrest tightly. David instantly regretted the use of the word *date*, even in jest. But Beverly laughed, although her laughter was partly motivated by relief: The wound must hurt like hell, but it was not serious.

"You probably need stitches. We'd better get you to a hospital. We're as close to Waco as we are to the nearest doctor's office anyway. Is St. Joseph's okay—where your mother was?"

"Swell. Maybe the Wilson family can get a volume discount."

Beverly drove as fast as she safely could down the gravel road back to the paved farm road. As she talked, she kept her eyes on the road. "I should have warned you. There are hogs out here, and the sows can be mean when they have litters. You were lucky."

"This is lucky?" David asked through clenched teeth.

"People have been mauled pretty bad by hogs. If she'd gotten you down on the ground before you reached the car, I might be driving you to the morgue."

"Don't rule that out yet. God, this hurts. I didn't know a hog could move that fast."

"They're faster than you'd think. And very strong. And very intelligent."

"As my final wish, I want you to see to it that my obituary does not reveal the terrible truth: that I was savaged by the spawn of Wilbur and a Muppet."

Beverly laughed. "No problem. Because you weren't. These are feral hogs. They descended from domestic hogs, but they're wild as can be. Some males even have tusks."

As they drove, David could find only two comfortable positions: sitting with all his weight on his left buttock or kneeling on the seat facing backward with his head rubbing the moonroof. He could not endure either for very long at a time. Finally he said, "Can you open this moonroof?"

Beverly pressed a button, and the glass panel slid back. David straightened up, raising his head and shoulders above the roofline. He was looking backward as they sped up Highway 6 toward Waco. The wind whipping around his head was fierce; he felt as if he was being sucked from the car. But it helped David to take his mind off his pain.

Beverly was going seventy-five when her car crested a hill and registered on the radar gun of highway patrolman E. E. Lewis. As Beverly's car passed him, Lewis got a glimpse of a middle-aged man sticking out of the roof backward with an I'm-not-doing-this-for-the-fun-of-it expression on his face. Seventy-five, to patrolman Lewis, was a judgment call. But he switched on his light bar and pulled out in pursuit because, after fifteen years as a patrolman, Lewis had become a collector of highway stories—stories that begin with "But officer, I can explain . . ."

And this one, E. E. Lewis thought, had possibilities.

David, facing backward, saw the flashing lights of the patrol car before Beverly did.

"But officer, I can explain . . ." Beverly began when she had pulled over and rolled down her window. She explained the situation to patrolman Lewis while he looked past her at David, who wisely had assumed what he now thought of as his "half-assed" sitting position. Lewis ran a records check on Beverly. She was clean. Lewis saw that these were normal, middle-aged people, not nuts, not teenagers. The woman looked respectable. The man was in obvious pain, and patrolman Lewis knew real blood when he saw it.

He made up his mind. "Ms. Faulk, we're ten minutes out from Waco. Follow me to St. Joe. But, sir, keep your head inside the vehicle at all times."

"God, this hurts," David whined as Lewis walked back to his patrol car. "The man's got a gun. Do you think he'd shoot me if I ask nicely?"

Beverly always got a kick out of the way men channel pain into humor. Her first husband, Jeeter, had once snagged his thumb with a fish hook. While she had worked to free his thumb before he tipped over the boat and drowned them both, Jeeter had been hysterically funny. Looking back, Beverly counted those two minutes as among the best of their marriage.

Patrolman Lewis pulled ahead, and Beverly followed. David was grateful for the escort. But he was even more grateful that Lewis did not use his lights or siren. At the emergency room of St. Joseph's Hospital, patrolman E. E. Lewis handed Beverly and David off to the medical staff and returned—one story richer—to his beat on Highway 6.

Forty minutes later, a doctor finally examined David. As David lay on his left side on the narrow bed, he could not tell what the doctor was doing back there, but the pain of being examined by the doctor was not unlike that of being bitten by a feral hog. The doctor told David that because he had been bitten by a wild animal, he'd need to stay overnight while tests for disease were run. David protested, saying he needed to get back to Willoughby to care for his mother.

Beverly said, "Look, I'll go stay with Nanetta tonight and come back for you tomorrow."

120

As she left, David thanked her and said, "Remind me to buy stock in Beverly's Hospital Shuttle Service."

Beverly returned to the hospital the next morning, and David was sent home with a few stitches, a large dressing, and a couple of prescriptions. When Beverly delivered David to Nanetta's house, he was able to walk fairly comfortably but still could not sit comfortably in a "two-point position."

Word of his adventure, of course, spread quickly through town. A few people phoned, a few dropped by. David was surprised and touched; despite several weeks' residency, he considered himself an outsider. As David told his tale, his dignity got the better of him, and he referred to the affected part of his body as his "upper thigh." When Nanetta told the tale, of course, she referred to the affected part as "his butt."

Feral hog attacks always rated the front page of the *Willoughby Bee*, especially if the wound was (1) serious or (2) not serious but affecting a comical part of the body. That afternoon Nanetta and David were in her parlor—one with a mending hip, one with a mending "upper thigh"—when Rosalee Taft phoned to get the facts. Nanetta scootered to the telephone in the kitchen and answered. David could tell by overhearing Nanetta's side of the conversation what the call was about and listened and waited for Nanetta to call him to the phone to give Rosalee his stirring first-person account. David had even worked up some sound effects. But Nanetta felt fully qualified to deal with the media. Finally, when David realized that he was not going to be interviewed, he called to his mother, "Tell her I've got her headline: 'Pork Chop Bites Man.'"

Nanetta thought about that for a second and relayed the headline to Rosalee, adding under her voice:

"'On His Butt.'"

"I heard that!"

❖19❖

"They weren't much on talk. I asked one fella how he was doing.
He said, 'Oh, I can't complain.' And he never did. I kept waiting
for him to. Well, what kind of conversationalist is that?"
———Ray Dean Briley

At 11:43 A.M. the next morning, two identical black Chevy Suburbans with tinted windows, one behind the other, entered Willoughby from the west and paused at the flashing red light. In the Crossroads Cafe, Juanita Greer happened to look out the front window. "That might be him," she said to herself. To her, the two black Suburbans looked important, official, like a mini-motorcade.

Indeed it was "him." Howard J. Liggett, accompanied by several of "his people," had flown into Dallas-Fort Worth Airport on his corporate jet and had rented the two Suburbans—one for people, one for equipment. South of Waco he had phoned Balaam and Mayor Perry to give them his ETA. Liggett, riding in the front passenger seat of the lead car, had not even noticed the "Welcome to Willoughby, the Hot-Dam Mineral Water Capital of Texas" sign as his entourage had entered town. He did make note of the downtown area as his driver drove to City Hall, where Mayor Earl Perry was waiting. Ever since Perry had learned that a potential developer was coming to inspect Balaam's Cave, he had been anxious. He had never met a millionaire, much less a millionaire who could put Willoughby on the map even better than could a Web page, some signs, and a slogan. Liggett could be Willoughby's patron saint. As Liggett walked in the door, Mayor Perry wiped his hands on his slacks before offering his hand to Liggett. Liggett was dressed casually but expensively. Perry, who had worn a suit for the occasion, instantly felt foolishly overdressed. Perry looked at Liggett and saw a dynamic man of early middle age and slightly less than average height. Howard J. Liggett was a bottom liner. Numbers—net profits, stock prices, interest rates, overhead, tax brackets, return on investment—meant everything to him. Numbers were what motivated him, and he suspected that deep down numbers were what motivated most sane people: numbers that express amounts of money, years of age, frequency of sex, ideal weight, calories, days until the weekend.

Numerically, Howard J. Liggett was forty-one years old with a personal wealth of twenty-seven million dollars. He was sixty-four inches tall, wore a size-seven Gucci loafer, and had a size-forty-two ego.

After the handshake, Liggett invited Perry to accompany him to Balaam's property. Perry was delighted. He would be able to lobby Liggett during the drive. But as they drove, Liggett paid little attention to Perry's cheerleading ("good, honest, hard-working people . . . fair tax rates . . . business-friendly"), instead paying attention to the condition of the road and watching for eyesores.

Perry had given daughter Earline ("the friendly, knowledgeable staff" of Balaam's Cave) the day off, and Balaam had posted a sign reading "closed today" on the fence so that Liggett would not be disturbed. But Balaam had taken the liberty of inviting Ray Dean Briley and David Wilson to be present. David still felt a twinge with each step of his right leg when he walked, and he could not sit comfortably. He had cursed the stiff suspension of his little red roadster as he had driven out on the unpaved road.

The three men were waiting in the shade of the live oak tree near the cave. They heard the two Suburbans approaching a full minute before they arrived. Guided by Perry, Liggett's driver turned off the road through Balaam's makeshift gate. Liggett saw three men in the shade of a tree in a field. Also in the field, he saw the three bathtubs, the horse trough, and the metal desk under the live oak tree. "Our first eyesore," he said to himself.

Liggett instructed his driver to park in the shade of the tree.

Balaam, David, and Ray Dean stepped aside as they saw the Suburban turn in their direction. The equipment Suburban parked in the sun.

Liggett got out and introduced himself to Balaam. Balaam introduced Liggett to David and Ray Dean. Liggett did not introduce his people: the two drivers, a vice president of marketing, a building architect, a landscape architect, a photographer, a geologist, and two hydrologists.

The marketing VP, the photographer, and the two architects were there to look at the "big picture," to look for features that could be exploited and features that might require a "workaround": the practical and aesthetic aspects of the terrain, the vegetation, the cave, the location of the cave on the property, the location of the cave relative to the road and the wooded areas. The geologist and hydrologists were there to, as they put it, "do the real work": to make Balaam's Cave yield as many secrets as possible about itself and its water.

With the zest of a craftsman beginning a pleasant project, Liggett said to Balaam, "Well, if you don't mind, let's see this famous cave of yours." Balaam led him to the mouth of the cave and steadied the ladder as Liggett descended. Balaam followed. In midsummer the air in the cave was cooler than the air above ground, even though the water in the cave was hot. "Are there any other caves like this in this area?" Liggett asked Balaam, although he already knew the answer.

"Not that I know of. Nearest one is a hundred miles south."

Liggett walked around the pool, looking at the sloping ceiling, the dimensions of the cave. He knelt on the limestone ledge and swished his hand through the water. He also filled a small bottle with water, snapped a cap on it, and put it into his pocket. Before ascending, Liggett paused with one foot on the bottom rung of the ladder and looked around at the cave. "No one can decorate a room quite like Mother Nature."

Above ground, Liggett called over his marketing VP, removed the protective cellophane from two glass tumblers, and filled them with water from the bottle. As he had done in his office in Colorado with the sample that David had sent him, Liggett performed his four-S ritual: He sniffed, sipped, sloshed, and spit. "Hmm-mm. Heavy salts. A bit reminiscent of Tranquility Cove [a Liggett mineral spring resort], don't you think?" he said to the marketing VP, handing a tumbler to him.

The VP likewise sniffed, sipped, sloshed, and spit. "Definitely. And maybe just a hint of Hygeian Hills [another Liggett mineral spring resort]."

Balaam was standing not far away. He observed the ritual of Liggett and the other man. Balaam looked at the two dark, wet spots in the dust at their feet. Balaam did not know much about judging mineral spring water, but in his experience, spitting was not an expression of approval.

Balaam, with a studied casualness, then moseyed around to the back of the equipment Suburban and peeked in the open cargo doors. He saw, among equipment that he could not identify, a portable generator and a portable air compressor. Another piece of equipment that Balaam recognized was a large auger. As he stood looking in, first one and then another of Liggett's people said, "Excuse me" and began removing equipment from the back of the Suburban. Balaam moved out of their way a few yards. In a few minutes, three other of the men drove the equipment Suburban into Balaam's field about one thousand feet away. Balaam heard them start the compressor and watched them begin drilling with the auger.

Liggett walked up to Balaam. "Do you mind if my people take some core samples?" Liggett asked after they had already begun. "We'll fill in the holes as good as new."

The three men moved the Suburban to four other widely separated locations in the field and took more core samples. They then backed the Suburban up to the mouth of the cave, lowered the auger, and took a core sample down there.

No one near the cave could hear or be heard over the noise of the compressor and auger, so Balaam just stood under the live oak tree and watched. He had no idea about the other mysterious instruments and gadgets that these strangers were looking through and tapping with and reading from. Just high-tech divining rods, he assumed.

When the noise stopped, Balaam asked Liggett, "What are they looking for?"

"Well, I don't fully understand the technical parts of some of it myself. But I trust my people. You see, we know the mineral content of the water. We need to determine, as best we can, the source of that water and the volume of that water that we might expect that source to produce over time. We want to know the geology that is involved."

Balaam next watched one of the men—a geologist of some kind, he guessed—go down into the cave with a small pick and a metal carrying case. Balaam heard intermittent taps from the cave for about five minutes. When the man came back up, he was using more effort to carry the case.

About 3:00 P.M., Liggett's landscape architect drove the equipment Suburban up the road toward Balaam's cabin. Balaam watched him leave and wondered where he was going. The architect had been instructed by Liggett to have a quick look at the rest of the property. When the architect drove up Balaam's driveway and saw Balaam's compound, he did not even get out. On his clipboard he had a full sheet on which to describe his observations and recommendations. He wrote the single word "bulldoze," backed down the driveway, and returned to the cave.

Ray Dean Briley, a curious, outgoing sort, tried—with little success—to get involved in the activity. He introduced himself to Liggett's people one by one and tagged along with them as they went here and there and did this and that, asking them questions, telling them how his intuition had told him that the water was special. No one was interested. After one of the architects went down the ladder into the cave to "lose that Chatty Cathy farmer," Ray Dean joined David under the live oak. He picked a leaf off a low branch and chewed it. "Did you shake hands with any of those guys? Boy, you can tell that none of them's ever pulled a stump or dug a posthole. Hands soft as butter."

Discretely, David rubbed his own palms together. Pure Land O'Lakes.

Mayor Perry, after having lobbied Liggett to the best of his ability, turned his efforts on Balaam. "Isn't this something?" he said, sweeping his hand majestically. "Look at all this activity. You could end up on Easy Street, Balaam."

"Earl," Balaam said, making an effort to talk more evenly than he felt. "Even assuming he's interested, I'm not sure what kind of deal we could do. If he wants to haul water out of here to bottle and sell, that's one thing, maybe, but I don't want to sell this place. He knows that."

"Just keep an open mind, Balaam. That's how you make money."

Upon their arrival, Liggett and his people had been drenched in sweat within five minutes of leaving the air-conditioned Suburban. It was late July, and the afternoon temperature was in the high nineties. David, who was accustomed to the heat and humidity of Houston, suspected that to these people, accustomed to the Colorado mountain climate, Texas in summer must seem like one of the rings of Dante's Inferno—the ring reserved for gun nuts, pickup drivers, death row inmates, and people who use the word *y'all*.

During their entire time on the property, Liggett's people kept the lead Suburban's engine idling and its air conditioner running. Periodically they took breaks to sit in the Suburban and take refreshment from an ice chest stocked with soft drinks and bottled water. At other times, they loitered in the cave, out of the sun. Liggett himself soon began to spend most of his time in the Suburban. He had two reasons: (1) to stay cool and (2) to be able to consult privately with his people about their findings. The Suburban became his private office. He did not intend to do all the work and share his findings with Balaam Gimble only to have Gimble then realize what he was "sitting on" and proceed to "shop it around" to the highest bidder.

Which, Liggett readily conceded, is exactly what *he* would do if he were Gimble.

As the afternoon passed, while Balaam had little to do but stand under the live oak and watch, the scene around him looked more like an invasion than an inspection. Instead of guns and bayonets and grenades, the invaders had scientific instruments and clipboards and expressions of detached interest. They were brisk and efficient. They smelled of cologne and rental car interior.

David joined Balaam in the shade. "What do you think?"

Balaam felt like saying, "I think I'd like to cut a switch and chase them all back up to Colorado." But instead he said only, "I hope I'm not going to have to feed this army."

To Balaam, this was different from letting people he knew or even tourists come out to enjoy the cave. Balaam looked around at Liggett's people and wondered how things had gotten to this point. He had had that thought several times since he had found the cave on that day in April. Before that day, the electric co-op meter reader accounted for most of the visitors to Balaam's property. Now he looked around and counted ten strangers. Balaam realized that it was not a rational reaction, but he felt a bit panicky. He felt that he had lost control.

These people were acting like, well, like they owned the place.

By 4:00 P.M., Liggett's people were wrapping up their work. One by one, they packed their equipment and took their seats in the idling Suburban. Mayor Perry joined them. Liggett walked over to Balaam. "Well, this has been interesting," he said, shaking Balaam's hand. "This is a very serene corner of the world you have here. Thank you for your hospitality, Mr. Gimble. I'll think about it."

Liggett got into the lead Suburban, and Liggett's drivers pulled onto the road and headed back in the direction of the flashing red light in Willoughby. Balaam could not see Mayor Earl Perry riding in the lead car, but as the two cars picked up speed on the dirt road, stirring up a comet tail of dust behind them, Perry turned and looked back at Balaam.

Balaam watched the comet tail. "'Think about it'?" he said to himself. "Think about *what?*"

The suspense was intentional. Liggett already had made up his mind. He knew that he would make Balaam an offer for the property. He knew the amount of money he would offer. And he felt that he knew how many milliseconds would pass between the time he made the offer and the time Balaam Gimble said "Sold!"

But Howard J. Liggett had not become a millionaire by wearing his wallet on his sleeve.

❧20❧

"Bless his heart, Balaam really oughta sell that place of
his and move into town. Just not next to me."
——Anita Taft

Three days later, on the first Monday in August, Balaam was outside
in his compound, browsing through his stuff piled on his many
makeshift tables. He was looking for his ten-year-old pipe threader. He
needed his ten-year-old pipe threader to replumb the gas line to Frieda
Dunlap's twenty-year-old kitchen stove. Balaam knew that pipe
threader was somewhere on the west side of the cabin. Or maybe the
east. Then the phone rang. Balaam could not get inside to answer
before the fifth ring.

"Good morning, Mr. Gimble. How are you today?" The voice was
professional. Balaam at first thought it was a telemarketer. He was
bothered and about to launch into what he hoped would be a guilt-
inducing tirade about "that poor widow woman" and "gas leak" and
"explosion on *your* conscience." But before Balaam could get Frieda's
foot in the grave, the voice continued: "Howard Liggett getting back to
you. I won't waste your time or mine. We think we can use your cave
and your water as the centerpiece of a resort complex, and we'd like to
make you an offer for your property."

Balaam had been halfway hoping that he would never hear from
Liggett. "You mean for the whole two hundred acres?"

"That's right. I am prepared to offer you two hundred thousand dollars for your property. How does that sound?"

Balaam was mildly stunned. "Well, that's a good price, no doubt about it. But like I told you, Mr. Liggett, I'm not interested in selling this place. Now if you were interested in pumping the water out of the cave and bottling it, then maybe———."

"The Aquavita Company develops mineral spring resorts, Mr. Gimble; we don't run bottling plants. But please hear me out. I'm sure you are as aware as I am of the market value of comparable rural tracts in your area. About half what I am offering."

Balaam knew that Liggett was right.

"Mr. Gimble, you understand that with that much money you could buy twice as much land somewhere else. Probably in the same area. Keep the same friends, the same business contacts, still be near your town of Willoughby." Before Balaam could reply, Liggett pressed on. "Let me tell you what we have in mind. We would build a state-of-the-art mineral spring resort that would include deluxe accommodations for overnight guests, an upscale restaurant, Roman bath, spas, swimming pool, facilities for massage and aromatherapy, and other features, all nestled in a park-like environment with trees, fountains, ponds, and bike paths. We would call it 'the Waters at Willoughby.' I like that. The Waters at Willoughby. Nothing like it in the state of Texas. It would be the jewel in Willoughby's crown. Jobs, revenue, status."

Liggett was beginning to sound like a telemarketer again. But Balaam was amazed by what he heard.

"What do you say, Mr. Gimble?"

Balaam said to Liggett what Liggett had said to him as Liggett had driven away after inspecting the property: "I'll think about it."

Actually, Balaam did not think about it. He had already made up his mind. He went outside and sat on his porch. When Stilts walked up to have his ears rubbed, Balaam leaned forward and rubbed an ear with each hand. "Nope," Balaam said. "Gotta say 'no.'"

On Wednesday, Liggett phoned again to get Balaam's answer. When Balaam said, "I'm sorry, but I'm not interested in selling," Liggett said, "Very well. Would you consider three hundred thousand dollars? You would not get a fraction of that amount from anyone else on earth. But you have a natural resource that I can develop into something that would be a showcase for your town, for the entire county. I am willing to pay a premium for that."

"I'll think about it," Balaam said.

But he didn't.

On Friday, Liggett phoned again. When Balaam again said "no," Liggett was silent for a moment. "Mr. Gimble, I still think we can do business. How about three hundred thousand dollars and two acres?"

"You mean you buy just two acres around the cave?" *That* Balaam might actually consider.

Liggett chuckled. "No, Mr. Gimble. No, I mean that I think I could find a way for my company to develop the resort it envisions *and* reserve two acres of your land for you to remain on."

"You mean the two acres up here where my house is, right?"

"No, Mr. Gimble, that's too centrally located for our plans. But I do think we could reserve two acres for you at the opposite end of the property from the cave and our resort. We would, of course, deed you an easement to guarantee you access to the county road. And, Mr. Gimble, not only that, we could replace your existing home with a nice new home of comparable size."

Again Balaam said, "I'll think about it." And he did, but not for long. Balaam knew that he could not bear to live on just two acres of land and each day have to see what had become of the land that was now "next door."

On the following Monday, one week after Liggett made his first offer, he phoned again. Balaam again said "no." In Colorado, Howard J. Liggett tapped the nib of his Montblanc fountain pen on his notepad.

"Final offer. Five hundred thousand."

Balaam was not sure he heard correctly. Before he could reply, Liggett said, "I'll let you think about it. I'll phone on Wednesday."

By now both men knew the cycle.

And so, on and off for two days, Balaam thought about it, playing devil's advocate against himself. Having been self-employed and having straddled the poverty line for most of his adult life, Balaam had no pension and little savings. Thus he appreciated what a half-million dollars could mean to him: He could afford medical insurance. Homeowner's insurance. He could buy a newer used pickup. Shoot, he thought, realizing how accustomed he was to thinking meagerly, with that kind of money he could buy a *new* pickup, if he dared such extravagance. That much money would mean financial security for the rest of his life. But financial security at the considerable cost of giving up his homeland. Where would he live? The possibility that he could—or would—live anywhere else had never occurred to him. Balaam had meant what he said: "No" meant "no." He was not holding out for more money. He really did not want to sell. Of course, a half-million dollars—"*million,*" Balaam said aloud several times—would buy much more land elsewhere. But that land would be just that—elsewhere. Elsewhere, there would not be that tree stump near the old cattle guard that always reminded him of his brother Salathiel's last visit: Salathiel had sat on that stump to rest when he and Balaam had taken a walk during which little was said but much was understood. Elsewhere, there would not be that patch of Indian paintbrush that bloomed every spring near the old sheep pen, reminding him of his grandmother, who once had told him that all the lambs in her flock with any black wool were his personal lambs to care for. Elsewhere, there would be no concrete foundation footings overgrown by trumpet vine—all that remained of his childhood home—to remind him of the time, the time, the time. Balaam felt that Liggett was trying to rob him of his past—rob him while pointing a large-caliber checkbook at his head.

At the same time, Balaam found himself, against all reason, feeling a bit sorry for Liggett. Too bad, Balaam thought, that cave hadn't been found on someone else's land. Most people would be tickled to death to sell at Liggett's outrageous price. Ray Dean Briley, for example. Or Earl Perry. Or J. D. Vernon. "*Vernon!*" Balaam said. Vernon, Balaam knew, would sell his land at that price in a flash and move to some wide-open wilderness state like Idaho that had better hunting. That would have been a perfect arrangement. That way, Vernon would get rich, Howard J. Liggett would get his Waters at Willoughby, and Balaam would be left alone with his woods and weeds. Everyone would be happy.

Everyone except the wildlife in Idaho.

When Liggett phoned on Wednesday, Balaam again said "no."

"Very well, Mr. Gimble." But there was nothing "very well" about the tone of Liggett's voice. "Good day to you." Liggett hung up.

The dollars-and-cents side of Balaam's brain knew that the sentimental side of Balaam's brain was crazy for saying "no."

But overall, Balaam Gimble felt comfortable with crazy.

❧21❧

"Rudy just bought a computer for the shop. To keep up with inventory, he told me. Inventory?! All he's got is two shelves of dusty old tractor parts, a case of motor oil, and a girlie calendar."
————Donna Jean Janacek

During the ten days that Liggett and Balaam danced their long-distance two-step, residents of Willoughby anxiously followed each offer by Liggett, each refusal by Balaam. On the Monday that Liggett made his first offer, Liggett phoned Mayor Perry afterward. Ostensibly, Liggett phoned to tell Perry—"in strictest confidence"—about his plans to build the Waters at Willoughby resort and to reassure Perry that if the resort were indeed built, merchants would be able to continue to sell the mineral water, purchasing it from the resort at a discount. But Liggett had another motive. By telling Perry—who, he knew, would leak like a sieve—about the planned resort, Liggett hoped to enlist the residents of Willoughby as his personal army of persuasion to bring peer pressure to bear on Balaam. Indeed, soon Liggett's plans for the resort were an open secret, as were his increasingly larger offers and Balaam's increasingly incomprehensible refusals.

That Monday afternoon, inside his grocery store at the main intersection of town, Perry found it difficult to concentrate. At the cash register, he overcharged Jessie Pinkston sixty cents on a pound of carrots and gave Bill Stoner twenty dollars change for a ten. Outside his front window, each flash of the flashing red light ticked away the seconds as Perry awaited Balaam's decision.

On the Wednesday that Balaam turned down Liggett's first offer, Mayor Perry dropped in on Balaam. Ostensibly, "I just wanted to see how everything is going with the cave. Is Earline doing a good job? Any problems to report? You're getting a lot of business, I know. It's making a real difference in town, too. Everyone's doing more business."

Perry was talking like he was on the campaign stump. Balaam suspected that he had more on his mind, so Balaam just let him talk. Finally Perry's tone changed. "Balaam," Perry said, recrossing his legs and flicking a bug off his shirt sleeve as he sat on Balaam's porch, "just between you and me, I got a call from Howard Liggett. He told me he'd like to build a resort on your place and that he's offered you two hundred thousand."

"Yeah, he did. But this morning I told him I don't want to sell. And now he's offered three hundred thousand."

Perry took a deep breath, puffed out his cheeks, and exhaled slowly with a soft pneumatic "puhhh-h-h." Perry then reminded Balaam that it was within Balaam's power to make Willoughby the town it once was "when our grandparents lived here." He told Balaam that the resort would mean more jobs, more commerce, more people. "Balaam, you could make Willoughby a better place."

"Earl, are you talking better or just bigger?"

Perry was not going to be drawn into a debate in a nonelection year. He changed tack. "Okay, never mind Willoughby for the moment. Think of yourself. Three hundred thousand dollars. Balaam, I know where there's two hundred acres of good farmland with an old house on it for sale on the other side of Willoughby. Not twenty miles from here. Got a three-acre pond on it, stocked with catfish."

"It the old Adams place?"

"That's it. You could buy that place, still have a ton of money left over to retire, and spend the rest of your days fishing."

"Earl, I don't fish."

Earl Perry was beginning to feel Howard J. Liggett's frustration.

"Hell, Balaam, then don't put any bait on your hook!"

On the Friday that Liggett sweetened the pot by offering to let Balaam keep two acres and to build him a cottage, Rosalee and Anita Taft of the *Willoughby Bee* agreed that it had already been a big summer of news for the *Bee*. First had come the Fourth of July parade, with a record nine floats, counting Euell Liddy's riding mower. Then had come David Wilson's feral hog adventure. And now came potentially the biggest story of the past fifty years: A developer was prepared to build a fancy resort just outside Willoughby. Rosalee knew that the "negotiations" were front page news, even though Balaam so far had said "no." She tried to phone Liggett for an interview but was told that he was "unavailable." In all her years of conducting interviews for the *Bee*—from 4-H show blue-ribbon winners to fish-fry coordinators—Rosalee had never been told that a news source was "unavailable." Unbeknownst to Rosalee, Liggett had been "unavailable" only because he was playing golf with investors when she had phoned. But the unavailability of Liggett made Rosalee feel important. She boasted to Anita that she had been "stonewalled." Rosalee then phoned Balaam. Balaam saw no reason to be secretive, answered all of her questions about Liggett's offer and plans for the resort, but recited his litany: He was not interested in selling.

On the second Monday of the Liggett-Gimble negotiations, Liggett again phoned Perry. Perry told Liggett that he had spoken with Balaam and had pointed out to Balaam the reasons—both selfish and altru-istic—why he should accept Liggett's offer of three hundred thousand dollars and a cottage on two acres. "He'll come around. You'll see. He'll say 'yes,'" Perry said to Liggett without conviction. "He's a sen-sible, good man."

Perry then repeated, as if to reassure himself, "He's a sensible, good man."

"He said 'no.'"

"He's a crazy bastard."

Liggett then told Perry that he had just made Balaam his final offer—five hundred thousand dollars.

Perry's cheeks again became a deflating blowfish: "puhhh-h-h." He marveled that one man could have that much money to spend and that another man might turn it down. Perry's reaction reflected the two schools of thought that had developed in Willoughby:

> 1. Anyone who would turn down an offer like that would say "no" to *any* offer.
> 2. Every man has his price, and anyone with the determination and deep pockets of Howard J. Liggett will find that price.

Those who belonged to the first school were dreamers: willing to imagine all that the resort could mean to Willoughby but skeptical that it would ever come to be. Those who belonged to the second school—and there were not many at that stage—were doers: ready to spend some money now in order to be in a position to make even more money after the deal was made.

That evening, several dreamers gathered by chance at the Crossroads Cafe. The first to arrive was Perry. He was joined over the course of an hour by, among others, Lawton Parker, J. D. Vernon, Charley Griggs, Little Un Petteway, and D. B. Baxter, president of Willoughby's two-teller bank. Juanita Greer even joined them when she could find a moment to sit down. By 7:30, so many dreamers were present that they pushed two tables together to accommodate ten people.

They were talking about Liggett's final offer of a half-million dollars. Newcomers to the impromptu meeting typically reacted to the update with a whistle, a "damn," or a momentary loss of speech.

Little Un followed his "damn" with "Just for that rundown old place?"

"Believe me," Perry said, "people like Liggett don't waste money. If he's willing to pay that much, he knows he'll get it back. Those resorts charge plenty. They aren't for poor folk."

"Like us," Charley Griggs said, triggering scattered chuckles.

Perry remained somber. "The bad news is that I have talked to Balaam. He's still saying he's not interested in selling."

"But a half-million dollars," Baxter said, mentally calculating the interest that a bank would earn on a deposit of that amount.

Perry said, "I know. I reminded him it would mean no more living month to month, no more working from 'can' to 'can't.'"

A few eyebrows were raised at Perry's reference to working from sunrise, when you *can* see, until sunset, when you *can't* see. No one pre-

140

sent had ever known Balaam to apply himself that diligently.

Perry craned his neck and looked around the cafe. He leaned forward and lowered his voice. "I count three strangers in here right now. Used to be, I'd know every face in this cafe. In the last two weeks I've had people in the store from Oklahoma and Louisiana. I saw a Kansas license plate at Little Un's the other day. I almost took a picture of it. Y'all, that is the result of our promotion campaign."

There were nods and murmurs of agreement in Perry's audience.

"This resort would have a hundred times more impact. It would be the best of all worlds: We could remain the Hot-Dam Mineral Water Capital of Texas while Liggett does all the work, spends millions of dollars, and we just sit back and reap the benefits." As Perry spoke, his eyes moved around the two tables, looking directly at each face.

"While that resort was being built—over the course of months—where would those construction workers live and eat and shop? And after it was built, where would the permanent employees live? Where would they shop?" Perry did not wait for a reply. "I'll tell you where: in Willoughby, many of them. I don't have to remind you how long it has been since a new home was built in this town. And not all overnight guests at the resort would stay there. Remember what I said at the Town Hall meeting about bed-and-breakfasts. And it could mean new businesses. We all can think of retail businesses that we'd like to see this town get."

"Like a good steak restaurant," Lawton Parker said. He immediately realized where he was and turned to Juanita and said, "Uh, no offense, Juanita."

But Juanita was offended, at least mildly. "Hell, Lawton, do I come into your hardware store and say this town sure could use a nice big Home Depot?"

Lawton averted his eyes and stirred his tea.

"Or a Blockbuster Video," Little Un said.

"Or a good taxidermist," J. D. Vernon said, dressed in his customary camouflage outfit, which did little to render him invisible against a backdrop of Formica and stainless steel.

Then came a Babel of voices: "a barber shop," "a dry cleaner," "a pharmacy," "a Wal-Mart."

At the word "Wal-Mart," everyone at the two tables paused. A reverent hush fell. Dare they even dream it?

D. B. Baxter chose not to mention his own personal dream: He dreamed of an ATM for his bank. To him, an ATM was a status symbol. All the big banks had one.

Likewise, Mayor Earl Perry chose not to mention his dream. It was a dream for Willoughby, a specific dream and a modest dream, as dreams go. Many people would have laughed at its modest scope, he knew. For that reason he did not share it with the other dreamers that evening.

On the Wednesday that Balaam said "no" to a half-million dollars, Rudy Janacek had heard enough. It was just a matter of time, Rudy felt, before Balaam came to his senses and sold, the resort was built, and money started rolling in to Willoughby. Rudy dropped out of the dreamer school and enrolled as a freshman doer. Anticipating increased business for his tractor repair shop and auto parts store, Rudy bought a personal computer for his office. He told his wife, Donna Jean, that the computer would modernize his business, let him keep the books more efficiently, and help with inventory. In truth, he bought the computer so that he could view the photos of Brandi Renee on Willoughby's Web site. Rudy bought the computer from a store in Waco and paid the store's technician to set it up for him and connect him to the Internet. The technician showed Rudy how to log on, how to use a Web browser, and how to bookmark the new Willoughby home page. That put Rudy just four clicks away from Brandi Renee's knees.

"What else can I get on the Internet?" Rudy asked. "Is it like cable TV?"

"Well, sort of. There's everything you can imagine. News, sports, stock market quotes, chat rooms, shopping, discussion groups, pornography."

At the word "pornography," an observer might have attributed the slight flaring of Rudy's nostrils to some misfiring of a synapse or a nervous tic. Rudy tried to sound casual. "Pornography? No way, man."

"Oh, yeah, tons of it. A huge part of Internet traffic is porn."

"I don't believe you." Rudy was using his best tractor repairman's reverse psychology.

"Watch. All you have to do is—this is your Web browser,

remember?—use a search engine—this one is Yahoo!—and type in something like 'XXX,' 'sex,' 'erotica,' or something less formal." The technician typed in "boobs." Rudy watched the screen display change as a Web page loaded. The technician ran the cursor down a list of hyperlinks and clicked on one. Suddenly Rudy saw the image of a young woman in an advanced stage of nakedness. She was every bit as pretty as Brandi Renee. All over.

"See these?" the technician said, using the cursor to indicate other hyperlinks on the page. "Click on these, and they'll take you to more sites. You could never see them all."

The technician clicked on several more hyperlinks while Rudy stared at the screen. Rudy had been exposed to nothing racier than *Playboy* and one trip to a topless bar when he was nineteen. What he was seeing didn't seem possible. He felt that he could actually *hear* the FBI's unmarked cars speeding to Willoughby to arrest him.

"Is this legal?" he asked the technician. But the technician's answer didn't matter. Rudy Janacek was already too far gone. Rudy was hooked. He had a mouse on his back. In a matter of days, Rudy began to forget all about Brandi Renee. Soon, after closing his shop in the evenings, rather than go to the Crossroads Cafe to ogle her, he stayed at the shop, surfing porn. As the days passed, Brandi Renee, in her self-absorption, did not notice the increased absence of Rudy at the cafe, although as she walked from booth to booth, perhaps her knees felt a chilly breeze of abandonment.

On the Internet, Rudy Janacek discovered that he could find Brandi Renees of every shape, size, age, color, sexual orientation, and pixel count.

And they all had knees.

And he didn't have to tip.

❖22❖

"Can you imagine those three guys up there at that la-ti-da resort?
David will have to show Earl which fork to use,
and Earl will have to show Balaam what a fork is."
———Joyce Perry

Just before dawn on a morning during the second week in August, a
light rain had fallen on Willoughby, fallen like a benediction. Rain in
August was always welcome. It temporarily broke the oppressive heat,
it was a balm to crops that were burning in the fields, it raised the level
of lakes that were low and of stock ponds that were almost dry, their
edges just a pan of crusted, curling mud.

When rain fell in central Texas in August, people celebrated. Some
more than others: When the rain had begun to fall that morning, two of
the Boys—Charley Griggs and Willis Pinkston—had driven out to Big
Un Petteway's home and, seeing no lights on in the house yet, had
spiked his rain gauge with an extra inch of water. They had then
returned to their homes and waited. An hour later, after the rain had
passed, Big Un had read his gauge and had begun making phone calls
to compare totals.

"Charley? This is Big Un. How much rain you get at your place?"

"Half an inch, Big Un. What'd you get?"

"Hah! Inch and a half here."

"Boy howdy! Big Un, you must be living right."

Big Un dialed another number.

"Willis? This is Big Un. Did you get some of that rain?"

"Sure did. Just under a half-inch. You?"

"Inch and a half, Willis, inch and a half."

"I'd say that calls for a beer. You buying?"

"Damn right."

Charley and Willis had not had to pay for their own beer since the drought of '92.

That morning Balaam lay awake in bed and smelled the rain, the sweet scent of wet sand and wet mown hay. At such times, he pitied those who cannot see and cannot hear less than those who cannot smell. He listened to the rain on his tin roof. The sound always reminded him of the sizzle of eggs frying in a pan. When his phone rang, the sound was jarring.

"Good morning, Mr. Gimble." It was Howard J. Liggett. He sounded almost amiable. Balaam heard in his voice none of the curtness of their last phone conversation.

"Mr. Gimble, I appreciate a shrewd businessman. I'd like to think I'm one myself. And part of being a shrewd businessman is keeping lines of communication open. I want to do that. I'd also like to show you what the Waters at Willoughby could look like. I'd like you to be the special guest of myself and the Aquavita Company at our flagship mineral spring resort here just outside Denver. I have extended the same invitation to David Wilson and your Mayor Perry, and they tell me that they are looking forward to joining you on the trip. My jet would pick the three of you up at the airport in Waco. Tell me, Mr. Gimble, have you traveled much, ever been out of Texas?" Liggett asked, feigning interest.

"Once."

"Where did you go?"

"Vietnam."

"I think you'll like Colorado better."

❧ 23 ❧

*"After Mr. Gimble goes home tomorrow, Denise, I want him
to associate our resorts with the pleasantest memories possible.
Your job tonight is to 'associate' his brains out."*
———Howard J. Liggett

Earl Perry, David Wilson, and Balaam had driven to the Waco airport in Perry's car. Traveling north on Highway 6 had caused
David to relive the humiliation of his feral hog adventure. As Perry had
crested the hilltop where the highway patrolman had stopped Beverly,
David had asked Perry to slow down, even though Perry had been
going only sixty.

Balaam had flown very few times in his life and never in such a
small jet. But the flight had been mercifully short; Balaam had spent
most of the flight looking out his window and marveling as the flat-as-
a-floor terrain of the Texas Panhandle became the rumpled rug of the
Rockies.

Upon arriving at the resort, Perry, David, and Balaam were quickly
waved through reception. A young man wearing a name tag that read
"To your good health—SEAN" escorted them to their adjoining VIP
suites. "Your luggage will be brought shortly. Mr. Liggett will meet you
at 5:00 P.M. for a reception on the Vista Grande patio," Sean told them.
"You can rest a few minutes and freshen up. I'll be back at 4:55 to
escort you."

At the reception, they were greeted by Liggett, who introduced them to the resort manager, the chef, and a few well-dressed people whom Liggett called "some of our favorite regulars," including a state senator and a Broadway actress. Waiters served hors d'oeuvres, wine, and, of course, mineral water from the resort's spring. Balaam found the water to taste every bit as foul as his own. In a corner of the patio, a string quartet played, largely ignored. David recognized the piece as something by Brahms. Balaam listened to the quartet and thought it was a waste of perfectly good fiddles. He whispered to Perry, "I'll give you a dollar to request 'Orange Blossom Special.'"

Liggett noticed Balaam standing at the edge of the patio admiring the view of the mountains to the west.

"What do you think of our Colorado landscape, Mr. Gimble?"

"That's real handy to have those mountains so close. What—four or five miles?"

"More like forty, that particular range. But they do look much closer, don't they?"

"Is that really snow?"

"Oh, yes. It's a bit unusual in August, but it can happen at the higher elevations."

A waiter materialized to refill Balaam's glass.

"We're glad you could arrange to get away to visit us and let us show you around."

In fact, arrangements for all three men had been simple: David had asked Beverly Faulk and Mrs. Reeves next door to look in on Nanetta; Earl Perry had left his wife, Joyce, in charge of his store; Balaam had put out a two-day supply of corn for Stilts and urged him not to eat "the whole shebang" as soon as Balaam was out of sight.

Liggett had invited David Wilson and Earl Perry to accompany Balaam because he knew that it would not hurt to have two of Balaam's "own kind" on his side. Perry, of course, was almost as eager as Liggett was for Balaam to sell. But David made a point of staying neutral about Balaam's decision. As an outsider, David had no stake in the decision, although he had come to like Balaam and realized what that much money could mean to a man of Balaam's limited means.

After the reception, Liggett led them on a tour of the resort. They used golf carts to travel between buildings and around the grounds, which to Balaam seemed to cover many acres. The grounds were green and well tended, like a golf course. Balaam did not recognize some of the types of trees. The evergreens all looked like Christmas trees to him.

Liggett showed them the lobby, which they had seen only briefly upon arrival. It was a three-story glass atrium with marble floors, ferns, statuary, and a fountain in the center. In one corner was an open-faced enclosure containing lush vegetation and free-flying birds. Balaam watched a dove flit from the ground to a low branch. As Liggett led them away, Balaam said to David, "Wonder how long it would take J. D. Vernon to bag his limit in *there?*"

Some of the public areas were formal, with fluted columns, carpet, and gilded mirrors. Other areas were more rustic, with fireplaces, cedar paneling, and rugs. In the treatment rooms, most of the guests seemed to be half-clad and partaking of the water—sauna, indoor pool, whirlpool—or being ministered to by staff members in massage rooms, a manicure/pedicure room, a facial room, and an aromatherapy room. There was also a restaurant, a gift shop, a room called the Medicine Cabinet, a reading room, and there were at least two conference rooms. Staff members dressed in white and wore rubber-soled shoes. They seemed to glide along the corridor walls like cats.

Mayor Perry was enchanted by it all, even taking photos with a disposable camera. David noticed how spotless and tidy the resort was and wondered if Liggett had Nanetta come in twice a week to clean.

For dinner that evening, Balaam wore a suit that David had lent him. The slacks were two inches short, so he wore them two inches lower on his waist. Perry, David, and Balaam were seated at Liggett's table. David, knowing that Balaam might feel out of his element, sat next to him. Balaam indeed felt uncomfortable with the formality of the dinner. The dinnerware was laid out coldly and precisely like instruments on a surgeon's tray. He was afraid that he might drop or spill something. He scolded himself for not realizing that guests would probably not be eating Tater Tots off of paper plates with their fingers.

Waiters came and went silently. Ever since Balaam had arrived, people had been "doing for him": carrying his suitcase for him, opening doors for him, refilling his glass, offering him trays of little tidbits on crackers and toothpicks. Balaam was not used to being waited on hand

and foot or, as he put it, "hoof and mouth."

When waiters placed a whole lobster before each dinner guest, David looked at Balaam. Balaam was looking at the lobster on his plate with an expression more of dread than bon appetit.

David leaned toward Balaam and asked in a low voice, "Ever eaten lobster?"

"Never. I guess I'll just watch you and fake it."

David did not want Balaam to feel awkward. "Personally, I don't think they're worth the effort. I'm going to pass on mine."

"Then I will, too."

Relieved, Balaam "ate around" the lobster. But as he did, he felt as if it were staring at him, perhaps feeling rejected. Finally, while pretending to casually tidy up some morsels of food on his plate with his fork, Balaam speared two carrot slices and placed them over the lobster's eyes.

After dinner, Perry, David, and Balaam went their separate ways, David to have a sauna, Perry to have a dip in the whirlpool. Balaam holed up in his bedroom. Away from the formal setting of dinner, he was relaxed. He changed into jeans and a T-shirt and lay on his bed enjoying real luxury: watching TV and drinking a beer and eating a pimento cheese sandwich from the room's honor bar. At home, Balaam had only an antenna for local channels. On the resort's satellite TV system, he found a channel broadcasting old TV westerns. He was watching "Wagon Train" when he heard a soft knock on his door. He suspected that it was some resort employee come to "do for him."

"Come in."

It was Earl Perry, as excited as a schoolboy. "Hey, has your bathroom got one of those bidets? Mine has. I took a picture. Joyce will want to see that."

Perry sat in an arm chair and began watching TV with Balaam, occasionally commenting on features of the resort that he had been impressed by. During a lull in the "Wagon Train" plot, Perry said, keeping his eyes on the TV screen, "Balaam, I'm glad you took this trip. And a bit surprised. I hope it means you're keeping an open mind."

"Earl, mostly it means that back home lately it's been ninety degrees at night and a hundred and five in the daytime. My little window unit is running full-time, but the cabin is still ninety degrees. I reckon that's reason enough. Besides, it might be my only chance to see this part of the world."

Perry stayed in Balaam's bedroom during the remainder of "Wagon Train." And then "Bonanza." Halfway through "Have Gun Will Travel," Balaam began to wonder if Perry was ever going to go back to his own suite. Finally Balaam said, "Earl, if you're going to spend the night, hadn't we better ask our parents if it's okay first?" With mock enthusiasm, Balaam suddenly sat up, crossed his legs, and began bouncing on the bed. With a voice as childlike as he could muster, he said, "And if they say it's okay, I've got some neat-o comic books, and maybe later we can send David on a snipe hunt."

Balaam was still laughing and Paladin was pistol whipping a scoundrel as Earl Perry retired to his own suite, wondering when America had lost its respect for the office of mayor.

The next morning after breakfast, Perry, David, and Balaam were escorted to the executive conference room to view a presentation on the proposed Waters at Willoughby resort. A few other people were present. Balaam recognized some of the faces as Liggett's people who had inspected his property. When everyone was seated, Liggett addressed Balaam, David, and Perry. "We've taken the liberty of preparing a little presentation based on our plans for the hoped-for Waters at Willoughby. It's a virtual reality tour, using computer animation based on architects' renderings and photos and video taken when we toured your property, Mr. Gimble."

From speakers, music rose. On a large screen on the wall in front of them, various stock scenes of water—crashing surf, waterfall, dew drops on tropical leaves, even children playing in water gushing from a fire hydrant—appeared. The voice of a narrator began: "The surface of our home, planet Earth, is covered by more water than land. Our own human bodies are mostly water. Water is essential to existence. Water is the elixir of life. But not all waters are created equal. Many people believe that water that flows from certain springs that have just the right mineral content has health-giving properties. People have been using such springs for centuries."

The scene changed to show people in togas lounging at an ancient Roman bath.

"Such water has been shown to improve conditions such as psori-

asis, joint inflammation, and circulatory, nasal, and respiratory problems. Other people believe that treatments based on these waters can
provide increased vitality, memory, mental acuity, even better sleep."

The screen showed scenes of modern-day clients luxuriating in various resort water facilities.

"The resorts of the Aquavita Company provide these treatments in
a relaxing, refined atmosphere. But we provide more than treatment for
specific ailments; we provide a total sensory package. We pamper. We
are a guilty pleasure."

Balaam, David, and Perry watched the scene shift to a virtual version of Balaam's Cave. It was an accurate rendering, except that the
limestone ledge around the pool was sparkling. The music changed to
a plaintive traditional Native American melody on flute and tom-tom.
And then two Indians walked into view in the cave! Balaam, David, and
Perry shared a group gawk. The "brave" was wearing a loincloth and
beads, the "squaw" was wearing a short buckskin shift. Her hair was
braided. Their appearance and motion were very lifelike.

"Centuries ago," the narrator continued, "the Native Americans of
central Texas knew of a mineral spring located in a cave near what
would later become the town of Willoughby. Native Americans bathed
in the water of the spring and used the water in their sacred rituals,
believing the water to have healing powers of both a physical and spiritual nature. Today that same spring water is available to clients of the
Waters at Willoughby, an Aquavita Company resort."

"This Liggett guy is good," thought David, who in his years in
public relations had peddled his share of thirty-weight snake oil.

As the music changed to contemporary and soothing, the scene dis-
solved: It was still Balaam's Cave, but now a contemporary white man
and woman, straight from Central Casting, were soaking in the pool.
"Today the Waters at Willoughby resort has incorporated that sacred
cave, with its healthful spring water, into its breathtaking glass atrium.
We call the cave 'the Grotto of Good Health.'"

"This Liggett guy is *real* good," thought David.

As the narrator spoke, the perspective on screen zoomed up and
out through the mouth of Balaam's Cave. Suddenly the viewer was in
an atrium, much like that of the Colorado resort. The perspective
panned, even tilted upward to view the sky through the glass roof. In

the atrium, virtual people were moving about, all of them attractive and smiling.

"The Waters at Willoughby is a full-featured mineral spring water resort. Facilities and services include saunas, Roman baths, steam rooms, whirlpools, makeover rooms, mud packs, meditation, acupuncture, and massage. There are also conference facilities, a restaurant, and upscale overnight accommodations, including VIP suites. Our helpful, healthful staff members pamper clients with the Aquavita line of moisturizers, body gels, shampoos, lotions, bath crystals, and aromatherapy oils."

The screen showed quick scenes of each feature mentioned. Animated people lounged in whirlpools and saunas or mud baths or on massage tables, laughing and talking and sipping water or wine. Apparently the Waters at Willoughby would be very similar to Liggett's Colorado resort.

The screen then showed a bird's-eye virtual view of Balaam's entire property. The resort's driveway curved gently from an arched gateway at the county road through trees and shrubs and flowerbeds and green lawns to the main entry at the atrium. There was even a pond with a fountain. Balaam saw that large areas of woods—as well as his own cabin and compound—were completely gone to make way for the formal grounds, buildings, and parking lot. Other wooded areas were severely thinned out. Some of the remaining trees were "his," and some would be new transplants, he guessed.

The narrator continued, "The Waters at Willoughby is situated on two hundred acres of landscaped grounds, surrounded by a buffer zone of trees to create a cocoon of quiet and comfort for clients."

The presentation continued for a few more minutes, but Balaam lowered his eyes from the screen and stopped watching. To him, the images may as well have been of Hiroshima after the bomb.

After the presentation, Balaam was relieved that there had been no hard sell from Liggett. In fact, Liggett had not even raised the subject of buying Balaam's land. Mayor Perry was the one who was campaigning. As Perry and Balaam walked along a corridor, Perry waved his arm in an arc over his head like a rainbow and said, "Balaam, you could have that half-million dollars *and* live on two acres in a new home and have something like *this* next to you. What would you say to that, huh?"

Balaam started to say, "I'd say, 'There goes the neighborhood,'" but he held his tongue.

On the morning of Balaam's second and final day at the resort, Howard J. Liggett asked the personnel director if any of the masseuses on the staff were "of southern extraction." He was told that there were two: one from Alabama, one from Texas.

"Bring me the Texan."

Denise Lowry was twenty-two, charming, pretty, and petite. More important, she had a pronounced southern drawl that Liggett personally found displeasing. She was perfect.

"Tonight, Denise, you will be giving our three special guests from Texas their complimentary massages. We are particularly concerned with Mr. Gimble. I am negotiating with him to buy his property for our next resort. So far he is resisting. I'd like for you to lower his resistance. There's a thousand-dollar bonus for you if he agrees to sell before he leaves us in the morning."

Liggett looked closely at Denise Lowry's face to be sure she understood. He could tell by the way she wrinkled her nose that she did.

Denise was scheduled to give David, Perry, and Balaam their massages, thirty minutes apart, in their suites after dinner that evening. Balaam was to be her last massage of the night. She knocked on Balaam's door at 9:15 and rolled in her portable massage table. As Balaam watched her unfold and set up the table, he again felt out of his element. "Are we going to play Ping-Pong?" It was a nervous joke.

Denise laughed. "Uh-uh now. Paddling is extra." She laughed again. "Just kidding. Y'all are up from Texas, aren't you? I grew up in Winnsboro."

To Balaam, Denise's drawl was like a phone call from home. Still, he had never had a professional massage and did not know the procedure. "Here," Denise said, handing him a large white towel, "just go into your bathroom and undress and wrap this towel around your waist."

When Balaam came out of the bathroom wearing just the towel, he felt pale and shapeless and soft, like an oyster with legs.

"Just lie down on your stomach and put your face here in the face cradle."

As Denise began her friendly assault on his muscles, Balaam said,

"You know, ever since I got here, people have been 'doing' for me. I could get used to this, though. You've got strong hands. Did you milk cows back in Winnsboro?"

"I milk a lot of tight, tired muscles. Like yours. I can tell from a person's muscles how they work, if they live in town or not. If they work at a desk, if they walk a lot, et cetera. You live in the country, don't you? And you haven't been behind a desk a day in your little life, I'll bet. You work with your hands. And you work outside a lot, but you wear long pants even in summer."

As Denise massaged his shoulders, back, and legs, Balaam was having a hard time playing Watson to her Holmes. No woman in Willoughby smelled as good as this young woman did. No woman this young and this pretty had touched that much of his body in far too long.

"Well, Mr. Gimble," he heard her say far too soon, "we're all done with the back. You just turn right over now, and we'll do the front."

Balaam had dreaded hearing that for several minutes. His body was going to betray him. As Balaam turned over onto his back he blushed, which was no mean feat considering that his blood supply had redistributed itself in his body, and far more blood had gone south than north.

As Balaam turned over, Denise added, "Sometimes the front takes longer." She then flabbergasted him by removing the towel from his waist.

"Mercy me," Denise Lowry said sweetly, "sometimes a *lot* longer."

❧24❧

"Two bed-and-breakfasts?
Can this town stand that much charm?"
——David Wilson

The next morning, Balaam, David, and Earl Perry were flown back to Waco on Liggett's corporate jet. Balaam entered Texas air space at twenty-eight thousand feet, sublimely relaxed but with his resolve intact. There would be no Waters at Willoughby for Howard J. Liggett, no thousand-dollar bonus for Denise Lowry.

As Balaam, David, and Perry drove into Willoughby on Highway 21, in front of them five cars were backed up at the flashing red light. Balaam could not recall ever seeing more than two cars trunk to hood at the intersection. As Perry slowed to a stop, Balaam counted a total of ten cars backed up on the four sides of the intersection. The red light flashed twenty-three times before Perry's turn to cross came.

Liggett had given Perry a copy of the CD containing the presentation of the virtual Waters at Willoughby. Within an hour of returning to town, Perry was at City Hall, inviting others in town to watch it on the city's computer. Many of those who did so came away feeling inadequate to express their awe. Clearly, with its plush accommodations, with all that visible flesh, and with its emphasis on healing and health, the Waters at Willoughby would be at once decadent and clinical, like some wonderful bordello run by the Mayo brothers.

During the week after Balaam returned from Colorado, other tremors—of varying intensity—were registered on the social seismograph of Willoughby.

Hoping that the mineral spring that fed Balaam's Cave ran under his property, too, Foster Jergens, who farmed a hundred and fifty acres just north of Balaam, paid a water douser to come in from San Angelo. "If there's any of that spring on my place, you can bet I won't have to be asked twice to sell, nosiree," Foster said. But after two hours of traipsing back and forth across Foster's property holding a Y-shaped willow branch, all that the douser found was Foster's septic tank.

Capitalizing on the town's modest boom in tourism, Flora Vickers reopened her little pottery shop, which she had closed a few months earlier, and added gifts, postcards, and souvenirs. Her new line of merchandise was limited at first. Of course, she sold Mason jars of Bounce, the Lone Star Wonder Water, and maps to Balaam's Cave. She also stocked some small antiques that she had bought from Beverly Faulk. On her display shelves were genuine Texas souvenirs: oil well paperweights, miniature horned toads, armadillos, roadrunners, rattlesnakes, saddles, cowboy boots, and Longhorn steers. All made in China.

And Juanita Greer added a part-time waitress at the Crossroads Cafe. Her reasoning, she explained to husband Richard, was twofold: Business had picked up, largely because of out-of-town diners, and Brandi Renee had become almost useless as a waitress, having become consumed with her dream of becoming a model. While on duty, Brandi Renee had begun to strike poses that she saw on the covers of fashion magazines. She also had begun to imitate the way she saw fashion models move on catwalks.

One afternoon, Big Un Petteway and Ray Dean Briley came in to the cafe for a cup of coffee and a slice of pie. After they were seated, Big Un began talking about his wrong-sided liver, and Ray Dean began pretending to listen. As Brandi Renee took their orders, she tilted her chin up, turned her head to a three-quarter profile, and drooped her eyelids languidly. Ray Dean also noticed that her lower lip was protruding ("pooched out," as Ray Dean would later describe it). It was Brandi Renee's attempt at a sultry pout. Ray Dean wondered if she had a cold sore.

After Brandi Renee took their orders, she walked away, swiveling her hips and taking long, lingering steps, almost scuffing the toes of her sneakers on the floor.

"You know," Ray Dean said to Big Un as they watched Brandi Renee's odd ambulation, "she's a pretty little thing, no doubt about it, but if I had a calf that was acting that way, I'd have it wormed."

And then, suddenly, that weekend Willoughby became a police statistic. On Saturday, two out-of-towners leaving head-in parking spaces on opposite sides of the street downtown backed into each other. No one was injured, damage to the two cars was limited to a broken taillight lens and scratched paint. But statistically, as Willoughby's part-time police chief, William "Trot" Lyons, told all who would listen, it represented Willoughby's first traffic accident since 1979, when Lawton Parker, driving his first car with an automatic transmission, had shifted into "D" instead of "P" and lunged his car into Mazelle Henderson's chicken coop, puncturing Lawton's radiator, killing Mazelle's rooster, and making a widow of a hen named Debbie.

The day after the downtown fender bender, the Baptist church was forced to postpone its Sunday baptism ceremony because vandals had broken into the sanctuary the night before and had filled the baptismal font with Jell-O.

The Reverend Finch was almost too shaken to deliver his sermon. Trot, who had not arrested anyone in almost two years, was considering conducting a dragnet of known Methodists.

Two "incidents" in one week! Trot could hardly call that a crime wave. "But," he said to himself, "it's a start."

Eight miles from the epicenter of Willoughby, Balaam Gimble, too, detected tremors.

On Monday morning, Lilian Kreuter phoned. Lilian was forty-five, divorced, and had owned a small nursery in Willoughby before business had fallen off fifteen years earlier. Now, she told Balaam, she had decided to convert two spare bedrooms of her house into a bed-and-breakfast. Her house was almost as large and as grand as Nanetta Wilson's, one of the finest in town, and in a good location just one block from the main intersection. She wanted Balaam to come by and give her an estimate on the work.

"I asked myself, 'Why not a bed-and-breakfast?' After all, I already have the beds. And I can cook breakfast when I have to," she said to Balaam. "Beverly is going to find me some antiques to finish out the rooms with. But I need some ceiling fans added. I'll buy them if you'll install them. Need the carpet taken up in those two bedrooms so I can show off the hardwood floors. The little breakfast nook needs sprucing up with some paint. The guest bathroom ought to be retiled. Need some door knobs changed. Do you have any of those old-timey glass knobs?"

Balaam knew that he had a dozen of them in a coffee can, if he could find the coffee can.

"That's about it. No, wait. And can you do wallpaper?"

Balaam said, "Only if I can cover up my mistakes with wide molding."

"Fair enough. That's about it. No, wait. One bedroom has its own outside door. I need a new lock for that."

"Lilian, that's a big project, and I can always use the money, but I want you to understand that I don't plan to sell my place for that resort. I wouldn't want anything I do or don't do to figure in your plans."

"Balaam, I appreciate that. I do. And I admit that some of us think it would be the greatest thing ever if we got that resort. But things have picked up enough around here just with the new promotion and that cave of yours that I think I can make it work just based on that. You don't have any plans to close the cave or anything like that, do you?"

"No, Lilian."

And Balaam meant it, although sometimes he felt that the money he received from the mineral spring water and the cave came at a high price. Ever since he had refused to sell his land to Liggett, people in town had treated him differently. Some were mad at him and were less friendly. Some were actually friendlier, perhaps vaguely hoping that Balaam might be influenced by smiles and handshakes. A few people even told him outright that they hoped he'd change his mind and sell. Balaam understood that that was not an easy thing for them to say. Willoughby people valued their independence and respected the independence of others.

And the cave could be troublesome. The pump was ornery sometimes and needed his attention. Balaam recently had had to build a simple wooden changing booth to accommodate people who did not arrive at the cave wearing their swimwear beneath their street clothes. And now, at the height of summer, even though visitors still came to the cave, Earline had told Balaam that she was having to turn away business because few visitors wanted to soak in the three bathtubs in the shake-and-bake sunshine of August. Visitors wanted to soak in the cave, which was much cooler but had limited capacity. So Balaam had erected a wooden frame over the tubs and stretched a tarp over the frame to provide shade.

Then, five nights after Balaam had returned from Colorado, someone had pried open the locked drawers of the metal desk under the live oak tree, apparently looking for the day's receipts. Balaam repaired the drawers, but now each night he was riding his bike down to the cave to check on it. He had become, he lamented, a night watchman.

After his phone call from Lilian Kreuter, Balaam put a few tools and his tape measure into his pickup and headed to town. He stopped on his way to urinate at one of J. D. Vernon's deer feeders. In midstream, he heard a car approaching. Balaam, always paranoid about being discovered by Vernon on those missions of mercy, took cover behind a nearby bush and peeked over the top. BC (before the cave), Balaam could urinate at a deer feeder all day long and never have to worry about a passing vehicle. Balaam watched the car come into view—a silver minivan—and pass by in the direction of the cave. He saw a passenger lower a window and throw out a food wrapper and a drink cup. Balaam picked them up as he walked back to his pickup.

As he drove on to town, he ticked off other negatives that the cave had brought. But he also reminded himself that, because of the volume of visitors, he was about to make a rare deposit to his bank account. In town, Balaam parked and walked into the bank. While he stood in line at one of the two teller's windows, bank president D. B. Baxter, standing in the doorway of his office, saw Balaam across the lobby, and waved to him, smiling. Balaam was sure that Baxter now saw him as a dollar sign in blue jeans.

After Balaam had made his deposit and walked outside, he repeated his downtown ritual, pausing on the sidewalk in front of the bank to stand for just a second on the two embedded horseshoes, now worn smooth by eighty years of foot traffic, that had been worn by his grand-father's horse.

A block away, Lilian Kreuter was waiting impatiently. "Balaam," she said to him as soon as she met him at her front door. "I don't have much time. I need to get to the Sears in Waco to pick out some Laura Ashley 'Poppy Meadow' dust ruffles for the beds in the two bedrooms."

As Lilian was showing Balaam the work she needed done, her phone rang. While she was occupied, Balaam walked through the rooms, sizing up the project. It was a fine old house. High ceilings, wooden interior walls, a lot of millwork. When Lilian rejoined him in the hall, she was agitated. "That was Beverly. She just heard that Mary Lou is thinking about converting *her* house into a bed-and-breakfast!"

Mary Lou Wyatt was forty-three, married, and did not work outside the home. Her husband, Paul, earned a good living, so Lilian knew that a bed-and-breakfast would be just a lark for Mary Lou.

Lilian walked quickly past Balaam into one of the bedrooms. She turned in a circle, surveying it, her hands clasped on top of her head.

"Oh, this changes everything. Balaam, you've got to help me get my place ready before hers is. Promise me you will." Lilian was pleading.

"Well, Lilian, I'll give you all the time I can, but———."

"Mary Lou'll probably spend a lot of money." Lilian began rethinking her needs. "I'll upgrade the ceiling fans and the drapes. I guess I should add a wicker porch swing, too. The beds are iron. I'd better get brass. Or should I go with oak? I'd better pray about it. Damn her!"

Lilian looked at her watch. "Better get to Sears before Mary Lou does." She walked out her front door and down the front steps. Balaam stood on the porch as she got into her car and began backing down the driveway. "Look around all you need to," she called out her window, "and just leave the house unlocked. Gotta scoot."

"But what about———." But Lilian didn't hear him. She had already rolled up her window. Balaam watched her drive up the street and turn left out of sight.

The Great Willoughby Bed & Breakfast Race was on.

Balaam stood on Lilian's porch for a moment. All of his life, Willoughby had been content to mosey; to just make ends meet; to be anonymous. But lately, he could see, Willoughby was becoming ambitious. It wanted money. It wanted fame. It wanted, he shuddered, Laura Ashley "Poppy Meadow" dust ruffles.

tious. It wanted money. It wanted fame. It wanted, he shuddered, Laura Ashley "Poppy Meadow" dust ruffles.

Whatever the hell *that* was.

❧25❧

"Did he call me 'Moneypenny'? I think maybe there's a
'Bunny Denny' on the manicure staff."
———Mrs. Inez Loomis

Balaam was in his compound browsing through a table covered with coffee cans filled with treasures: bolts, washers, nuts, fuses, nails, cotter pins, wall sockets, grommets, even marbles. Balaam said to Stilts, who was noshing nearby at his hubcap of corn, "Now where was I the last time I saw that can?" Balaam stood among the rows of tables of clutter and the piles of lumber and sheet metal and iron pipe and tried to visualize a coffee can filled with glass door knobs.

Balaam pulled off the tarp covering another table of cans and jars and cigar boxes. He surveyed them quickly.

"Nope."

When the phone rang, Balaam hoped that it was not Lilian Kreuter. She had already phoned twice to ask if he had found those damned door knobs: "Because if you can't find them, Balaam," she had said, "I'll have to order them. I heard that Mary Lou is going to have antique skeleton key locksets on her doors, so I've just *got* to have those glass door knobs."

When Balaam picked up the receiver and heard Howard J. Liggett's voice, he wished it *was* Lilian Kreuter. After a wooden exchange of pleasantries, Liggett said, "I hope you enjoyed your massage with

Denise."

Balaam could tell by the elbow in Liggett's voice that he knew all about the massage. Perhaps had even put Denise up to it. Balaam was not naive enough to think that a woman Denise's age would voluntarily lavish that much personal attention on him. Balaam's initial reaction to Liggett's statement was a vague fear of some sort of blackmail. Then he reminded himself that he had done nothing illegal. It had just *felt* illegal.

Nonetheless, there was some apprehension in Balaam's reply. "It was okay."

"I'm sure it was. Well, what would you say if I told you I am willing to transfer Denise to the Waters at Willoughby, give you a lifetime VIP pass to the resort, and assign her as your personal masseuse?"

Balaam was relieved. Just another sales pitch. Liggett as pimp. When Balaam again said he was not interested in selling his land, Liggett hung up abruptly.

Howard J. Liggett was frustrated that both money *and* sex had failed to move Balaam. "Do these hillbilly Texans have *no* values?" he asked himself as he stood staring out his office window over the grounds of his flagship resort. And then, as many a frustrated man has done when faced with a project that requires the finesse of a jeweler's screwdriver, Howard J. Liggett picked up a sledge hammer.

"Mrs. Loomis, ask Ernie Ruiz to drop by my office," Liggett said to his office intercom.

Two years earlier, because of a couple of "worrisome details" on Ruiz's job application, Liggett had personally had to approve the hiring of Ruiz. "Still trying to find himself" had been the personnel director's assessment. Hell, Liggett had thought, when *he* was that age, he was trying to find his third million. And, Ruiz had admitted during his interview, at the age of nineteen he had done six months for being in the wrong place at the wrong time—the stockroom of an electronics store at 2:00 A.M.

But Liggett had taken a chance on Ruiz. And indeed Ruiz had developed into a good masseur. Clients seemed to like him; many asked for him by name. Ruiz had a good face, was trim, and his tan went well with the resort's white uniform. He looked younger than his twenty-four years. Liggett suspected that women clients tipped him well.

Five minutes after Liggett had buzzed Mrs. Loomis, Ernie Ruiz walked into Liggett's office.

"Close that door behind you, would you, Ernie?"

As Ruiz turned from the door to approach Liggett's desk, his eyes climbed up and down the dark wood-paneled walls, which had once been part of an eighteenth-century English manor house.

"Ernie, I need some help with a unique problem. Would you like to earn twenty-five thousand dollars for a few days' work and be promoted to head of the massage staff of a new Aquavita resort?"

For the second time that morning, Howard J. Liggett had asked a question that had had the opposite of his intended effect. Ernie Ruiz was wary. He wondered just exactly how many people Liggett wanted killed.

"I guess you're not talking about a deluxe massage, are you?"

Liggett smiled. "No . . . Well, in a way, yes. I'd like you to massage someone's frame of mind. You see, I'm trying to buy a piece of property in Texas. It has a very good mineral spring on it. But the owner, some dirt-poor rural type, won't sell. I need someone to go down there and conduct, shall we say, a 'covert campaign of persuasion.'"

"Cool," Ruiz thought. Liggett's choice of words conjured up visions of Ruiz going around spying and committing sabotage and playing dirty tricks.

"So, what would you want me to do?"

"Excellent. Basically, scare him; make him paranoid. Make Balaam Gimble think that someone local very much wants him to sell out. Hell, that makes perfect sense. Having our resort there would put money in the pockets of most people around him. They probably already hate him.

"But keep two points in mind." Liggett tapped his index finger on the top of his desk. Ruiz noticed how shiny the mahogany was. "First, use your imagination, but don't get too cute. Don't hurt anyone, especially Gimble. We want to make him sell, not make him mad. Those people down there all have guns."

"Not so cool," Ruiz thought. Liggett's choice of words conjured up visions of Ruiz resting in peace.

"Second, keep a low profile. It has to look like someone local is doing it. Don't do anything in any way that could be traced within five hundred miles of me or Aquavita. By Gimble or by the police or anyone else." Liggett looked hard at Ruiz, and his voice matched his look. "If anything you do comes back on me, it's your word against mine. The difference being that the police will look at you and then look at me and ask themselves, 'Which one is a pillar of the community, and which one has done time?'"

Now Ernie Ruiz understood why he had been selected.

"But the potential payoff for you is considerable. If you are careful, and if you can persuade Gimble to sell his land to me at the current offer, I'll make you head of the massage staff at the new resort after it is built. And pay you a twenty-five-thousand-dollar 'relocation fee.'"

It was decision time for Ernie Ruiz. He looked at Liggett. He felt jazzed. "I've always liked chili and the Dallas Cowboys," he said.

Finally, Liggett thought, someone who appreciates the value of money.

"Gimble lives alone out in the country. The nearest town is a place called Willoughby. I'll give you more details before you leave. Denise can handle your workload here. We'll get you on a plane this week."

Ruiz turned to leave and had almost reached the door when Liggett said, "And one more thing, Ernie." Ruiz stopped and turned. Liggett said, "Don't hurt my cave."

Ernie Ruiz, a young man to whom fantasy was no stranger, walked out of Liggett's office feeling deliciously capable and clandestine. The big man had entrusted him with a secret mission. Ruiz imagined that James Bond must feel much the same way when he walks out of M's office after having been given a dangerous assignment in Istanbul or Paris. As Ruiz walked past the desk of Liggett's executive secretary, he tossed her what he imagined to be a suave "Later, Moneypenny."

Mrs. Inez Loomis, grandmother of three, did not even look up from her *Redbook*.

❖ 26 ❖

"What a nice young man. Too bad about that shirt, though."
——Nanetta Wilson

Ernie Ruiz, Howard J. Liggett's masseur-turned-dirty trickster, flew into Dallas-Fort Worth Airport early on a Wednesday. He was excited, eager to throw himself into a role that he saw as part spy, part saboteur. To "fit in" with his concept of Texas, he rented the biggest GMC pickup available at the terminal's Hertz counter. He immediately loved sitting behind the wheel of the big truck—like being in the cockpit of a fighter jet—and feeling the power and hearing the deep beat of the engine. To further fit in, as he drove south out of Dallas he stopped at a K-Mart on the interstate to get outfitted: jeans and cowboy boots and a western shirt. The shirt had the traditional western cut— scalloped yoke front and back and scalloped pocket flaps with simulated pearl snaps—but its pattern was oddly floral, its colors oddly tropical, as if the shirt had been designed by the Marlboro Man after watching *South Pacific*.

Ruiz also bought some tools—gloves, bolt-cutters, pry bar, flashlight, red spray paint—and a country music CD for the pickup. He was back on the road by 11:00 A.M. When he stopped at a gas station at 1:00 P.M., he made a discovery that stripped some of the gloss off his fantasy: The temperature was one hundred and two. When he stepped out of the air-conditioned cab, the heat enveloped him like shrink wrap. He could feel the softened tar of the gas station pavement ooze under his boot soles when he walked from his pickup to the restroom.

An hour after, he left the interstate and drove east on Highway 21, another layer of gloss was stripped away: He was not familiar with small Texas towns, did not know how small they could be. As he entered Willoughby and made a quick survey, driving from city limit to city limit in all four directions and then meandering down side streets, he saw that it was a poor, shabby, tiny town. He was reminded of the miniature village on the model railroad layout that he had had as a boy—after his brother Jerry, while "playing army," had attacked it with a BB gun.

Ruiz saw little traffic and even less commerce in town. "I mean," Ruiz said to himself, "I've driven around for five minutes and still haven't seen a Starbucks."

He also had not seen a motel. He needed a "base of operations," as he put it. His mission might require a few days. But soon, after turning down a shaded residential street with some "better homes," he saw in a yard a wooden sign advertising "Chateau Willoughby—Bed & Breakfast." In smaller letters beneath was printed "Mary Lou Wyatt, hostess."

Mary Lou had won the Great Willoughby Bed & Breakfast Race. But she had just one guest bedroom ready, and it still smelled of fresh paint when she showed it to Ernie Ruiz. She then showed him the guest bathroom and the breakfast nook. The bedroom was air conditioned— that's all that mattered to him.

"I'll take it."

"Wonderful. Welcome to Chateau Willoughby. You're our very first guest. May we extend to y'all a big Texas 'howdy,'" she said, delivering her lines just as rehearsed. "How many nights will you be staying?"

Now it was Ruiz's turn to deliver his rehearsed lines. "Two, maybe more. I heard about this cave you have here and want to try the water." Liggett had suggested the cover: "You're just another tourist in town to have a healthful soak at the cave."

"Well," Mary Lou said, pleased to be able to show off her hospitality, "you can sample the water before you even go out to the cave: There's a complimentary jar of Bounce in your room." As she spoke, she found it difficult not to stare at his shirt. She had tried to find some wallpaper just like that for her second guest room.

After Ruiz got settled in his room, he drove over to a small cafe that he had seen at the town's main intersection. The cafe seemed clean enough, so he ordered a hamburger and fries. He assessed the waitress as cute but her walk as rather graceless. In fact, Brandi Renee had begun wearing three-inch heels on duty—"for modeling practice"—and had not yet mastered walking at high altitude. Waitressing in heels for eight hours made her legs tired and her feet sore. The combination made her surly. These days, by the end of a shift, if impatient diners asked her more than once where their food was, she was prone to ask them if they wanted their ranch dressing "on the side or over the top of your head."

Driving back to his room, Ruiz saw an old woman coming toward him on an electric scooter. She was driving right down the middle of the street, even though a sidewalk ran parallel. Ruiz stopped, rolled down his window, and waved to her. He wanted to double check something.

"Excuse me, ma'am. Can you tell me how to get to Mr. Gimble's place?"

Nanetta Wilson had to crane her neck to look up at the young man in the big pickup. He had to stretch his arm—covered by a sleeve that Nanetta could describe only as "festive"—down out of the window to hand her the map that Liggett had given him. Nanetta looked at the map, turned it sideways, then upside down, then right side up again. "Well, this is mostly right. But I can tell you some definite landmarks to look for." She then gave Ruiz her own set of directions, ending with "then turn left at Walter Ridgely's German shepherd. Keep on going until you hit a dip. After the dip, look for a mailbox on the left. The cave is just past that. Balaam's mailbox is just past that."

Ruiz thanked her and drove on to the Chateau Willoughby. He stayed in his room until well after dark. About 9:00 P.M., he drove through the flashing red light and east out of town, following Liggett's map and keeping in mind what the Scooter Lady had told him. After he turned off Highway 21 onto an unpaved county road, in the dark, the countryside took on a sameness that provided no reference points. Just trees and shadows along dirt roads with no street lights, no street signs, only an occasional mailbox with no name on it. But then at an unmarked intersection, a large dog ran out to his pickup, barking and

171

snapping. Ruiz honked to discourage the dog, but the dog seemed to interpret each honk as "here, boy." Ruiz turned left and accelerated out of range of the dog. While still going sixty, Ruiz hit a dip, causing his head to bounce up to the roof of the cab. A dog and a dip—the first two landmarks that the Scooter Lady had told him about. In a minute or so, he saw a mailbox on the left. He slowed down and leaned forward, staring down the beams of his headlights, watching for the second mailbox. A half-mile later he felt another dip—this one even more pronounced. "Or was *that* the dip she had referred to?" he wondered. He decided to count mailboxes from the first dip.

As soon as his headlights illuminated a second mailbox, he doused them and stopped. He waited for his eyes to adjust to the dim light cast by a sliver of moon. Then he drove ahead slowly and stopped at the foot of the driveway by the mailbox. There was no car in the driveway, no lights anywhere. He turned into the driveway—just two dirt ruts. He switched off his engine and sat a few minutes, watching and listening. He could not hear a sound except the chirping of crickets and the metallic popping of his engine compartment as it cooled. He could make out the dark outline of the small house beyond a fence. After ten minutes, he was satisfied. He slipped on his gloves, picked up a small bag, and got out of the pickup, quietly closing the door. He switched on his flashlight only long enough to pick out a path to the gate. He stood at the gate a minute. He considered aborting his mission right there and leaving. He could drive straight back to Dallas that night, he told himself, hole up in a nice hotel for a few days, and report to Liggett that he had tried, at great personal peril, to intimidate Balaam Gimble but had failed. But then Ruiz, firming his resolve, lifted the latch. The gate creaked as he swung it open. Ernie Ruiz had crossed his chain-link Rubicon.

He again switched on his flashlight only long enough to pick out a path to the front porch. On the porch, he again stood listening. Nothing. He knocked loudly on the door, ready to run back to the pickup at any sound. He listened. Nothing. He pulled open the screen door. It creaked almost as loudly as the gate had. He turned the door knob. The door was unlocked. Ruiz felt vaguely cheated: Breaking and entering without breaking was just, well, entering. The pry bar in his bag would go unused. He pushed the door open and stepped inside.

Each creak of the hinges sounded like the crack of an iceberg to him. He closed the door and again stood listening. More nothing. His heart was pounding. In the dark, he ran his hand along the wall just to the left of the doorway until he felt the light switch plate. He put his finger under the switch. He held his breath. He flipped the switch. The room appeared before him.

"Hey!" he shouted, although the word came out more meekly than he had planned. "*Hey!*" he shouted again, more forcefully. So far, so good. Then he went into the kitchen, hoping to find a back door. He opened the door so that he'd have an escape route if he heard anyone arrive at the front. He picked up a teacup from the dish rack and smashed it on the floor. Just to get in the mood. Pieces of china flew like shrapnel. Then he smashed another. And then a third. Then he opened a cabinet over the counter and smashed all the remaining teacups. On the counter, he saw a box of doughnuts. He popped one into his mouth, hooked three more with his finger, and went back into the living room.

Ernie Ruiz went about his work timidly at first, but soon his heart began to pound less wildly, and he grew into the role. He turned over a coffee table, spilling magazines and breaking a china platter. Using his pry bar, he smashed the glass of some pictures on the living room walls, watching as the glass shattered into a spider web of shards radiating out from the point of impact. Then he swept his forearm along the fireplace mantelpiece, knocking to the floor the usual mantelpiece knickknacks and framed photos. Ruiz was careful not to look at the people in the photos—he had to be objective, ruthless. This was a job—a job that could mean a lot of money and a promotion for him.

He went back into the kitchen and brought a short stack of saucers into the living room. He began throwing them at the stone fireplace. As he watched them smash, the pieces flying like sparks, he thought of his brother Jerry smashing his model railroad village with his BB gun. Ruiz found that the memory made him mad enough to throw harder.

After the last saucer, he opened the front door and listened. Then he took the can of spray paint from his bag. He shook it as he picked out the living room wall with the largest open area. Beginning at eye level, he sprayed "BALAAM GIMBLE GO AWAY" in red letters a foot high. He noticed that the adjacent feet of the double "A" in

"BALAAM" were touching; using his fingertips as an eraser, he wiped away the paint to create a space between them. Then he put the can back into his bag, grabbed the box of doughnuts, and walked to the front door. He realized that he was sweating and wiped his brow. He looked around the room with an artist's eye for composition. He walked over to the couch and tipped it onto its back. Then he turned out the light and hurried to his pickup. Not bad for fifteen minutes' work, he thought as he backed out of the driveway. Actually, he had been inside the house less than five minutes. Ernie Ruiz followed his landmarks back to Willoughby: mailbox, big dip, mailbox, little dip, barking dog, flashing red light, and "home." By the time he reached the Chateau Willoughby, it was 10:00 P.M. He expected to find the front door locked and to have to ring the bell to get in. But the door was not locked. In fact, Mary Lou Wyatt, who was sitting in the living room, saw him as he passed in the hallway and called out "good night" to him. She said nothing about the smudge of red on his forehead.

In his room, Ruiz turned on the little portable TV, but he was too excited to pay attention. He had executed his first dirty trick and gotten away with it. No one had seen him. He was pumped up. He was confident that Mr. Liggett would be pleased.

Mr. Liggett would have been even more pleased if Ruiz had vandalized the home of Balaam Gimble instead of the home of Balaam's nearest neighbor, the widow Wagstaff.

❧27❧

"First Jell-O in the baptismal font, and now stolen doughnuts.
Verily, Satan has a sweet tooth."
——Reverend Thomas Finch

Birdie Wagstaff had stayed to "visit" with friends after the Wednesday night service at the Baptist church and thus did not return home until 10:05.

At 10:06, Balaam's phone rang.

"Balaam, can you come over right now? Please." In her agitation, Birdie forgot to identify herself, but Balaam recognized her voice. She sounded terribly upset.

"What's wrong, Birdie?"

"Just come. Hurry. I don't want to be here alone."

Not knowing why he was needed or what he would find, Balaam took along his flashlight, a snake snare, and a baseball bat. He did not own a gun. It would take him almost two minutes to drive the mile to Birdie's. As he drove past the cave, he saw parked beside the road a nondescript compact car that he did not recognize. Ever since someone had rifled the metal desk under the live oak tree, he had been more suspicious of after-hours visitors at the cave. "Later," he said aloud and drove on to Birdie's.

The nondescript compact car belonged to Beverly Faulk. She and David Wilson had dropped by the cave after their second bird-watching outing. Late that afternoon, Beverly had driven them to an area of neglected farmland north of town. As they had gotten out of her car, David had scanned the field with his new binoculars and had said dubiously, "Do you promise me that this field is one hundred percent kosher?" Indeed, they had seen no feral hogs. They *had* seen a male black-chinned hummingbird at a trumpet vine, a scissor-tailed flycatcher on a fence, and a cliff swallow under a bridge over a creek.

Meanwhile, the education of David Wilson had continued apace. During their meanderings in the field, Beverly had paused to show him a low-spreading patch of "sleeping weed," running her finger down a row of fronds to demonstrate how they fold when touched. Then she had shown him a click beetle, placing it upside down in her palm so that David could see it click its hinged shell to spring itself into the air and land right side up. She also had shown him a gall—a golf ball-sized growth produced by an oak tree. She had taken a pocketknife out of her jeans pocket and cut the gall in half, showing David the tiny larva of a wasp curled in a cavity in the center. David had never known a woman who carried a pocketknife.

They had gotten a late start on their outing and, coming back into town after dark, had impulsively decided to make a detour out to the cave. Neither had been inside the cave before.

When Balaam arrived at Birdie Wagstaff's, she was still dressed in her "prayer meeting" clothes. She held the front door open for him, not saying a word as he walked past her through the doorway into the living room. There was not much for Birdie to say. The scene told Balaam all that she knew. In fact, of course, the scene told Balaam *more* than Birdie knew. When he saw "BALAAM GIMBLE GO AWAY" on the wall, a simple syllogism instantly formed in his mind.

Around here, most everybody knows where most everybody else lives.

Whoever did this apparently thinks I live here.

Therefore, whoever did this probably is not from around here.

This reasoning led Balaam in one direction: northwest to Colorado. But he pictured the wealthy, refined Liggett while looking at the heavy-handed, petty destruction in Birdie's living room. As suspects, Liggett and some local person seemed equally unlikely. This much Balaam felt sure of: This vandalism had something to do with the cave, with his refusal to sell his land. In fact, to Balaam, it suddenly seemed that everything that had happened in the last five months had been because of the cave.

Balaam looked around the room. He felt sick—for Birdie and for himself. "Birdie. I feel terrible about this. Somebody sure needs to have their britches busted. Is anything missing, or are things just torn up?"

"No, nothing's missing that I can tell. Just a box of doughnuts. There's not much to take. It's just knowing that someone was in here, some stranger. In my home, touching things, hurting things." Balaam knew that Birdie had to be in her seventies, but she was a tough, independent woman who still lived on the little farm that she and her late husband, Roy, had bought forty years earlier. Now, as Balaam looked at her, she seemed like a little old lady. She began picking up bits of debris from the living room floor—small framed photos from the mantelpiece, the tiny leg of a broken porcelain cat, even shards of broken saucers—and rubbing them with her fingers, as if to comfort them.

Balaam helped Birdie clean up the shards of glass and china and broken knickknacks in the living room, the smashed teacups in the kitchen, helped her right the couch, and promised to come back the next morning to repair the damage as best he could—remove the spray paint, fill and repaint some dents in the wallboard, cut new glass for the picture frames. He sat talking with her on the couch until she insisted that she was calm enough to be left alone. "This wouldn't have happened if I'd been home. This was some little cockroach who has to do his dirty work on the sly."

After Balaam returned to his pickup, as he backed out of the driveway he watched the windows of Birdie's small house. Every light in the house was switched on by the time he reached the county road.

In Balaam's Cave, David and Beverly had lit every candle that had been left there by previous pilgrims. They sat on the ledge of the pool with their bare feet in the water, watching the shadows dance and talking in the quiet voices that quiet places inspire.

"I can see why this place has caught on," David said. "It would be hard to find something like this in Houston."

"Of course, it would also be hard to get chased down by a feral hog in Houston."

David laughed softly. "But, you know, I'm coping without Houston better than I thought I would. It's amazing how much work you can get done when you don't have to commute and attend office meetings. I can get eight hours of work done in five and have the rest of the day to," David swished his toes through the hot water, "just soak my feet."

As they sat there amid the shadows and light, a bittersweet thought occurred to David—and in Beverly's mind a similar thought was only a few seconds behind his: How romantic such a setting would have been when they were twenty. Or even thirty. But between them, David and Beverly had three unsuccessful marriages. In midlife, each no longer felt that youthful angst to find out "where this relationship is going" or, indeed, to insist that it "go" anywhere in particular. For now, without ever discussing it, each felt comfortable enjoying the other as a toe-swishing birding buddy.

David leaned back on one elbow. "Did you ever read *Tom Sawyer*?"

"Oh, gee. It's been many moons ago." Then Beverly made the association. "Tom and Becky in the cave!"

David wished that he had a straw hat on his head and a corn cob pipe in his mouth. At least he was barefoot. "They were lost in the cave, and Tom saw Injun Joe appear from around a boulder, and they thought they were never going to be found and would starve to death down there. But then Tom found a hole in the cave and looked out and saw the blue of the Mississippi, and they were saved."

Beverly looked up at the mouth of Balaam's Cave. She saw only the black of the sky. "Wonder what became of Tom and Becky," she said wistfully. It was her way of keeping the topic alive. "I think," she said, "Becky probably grew up and had two bad marriages and lived all her life in that same sleepy little town, running the antiques store." She looked at David. "What about Tom?"

David leaned forward and looked down at his white feet in the water. "Tom had always planned to grow up to be a buccaneer and sail the Spanish Main. But somehow he got blown off course. He had one bad marriage and ended up in public relations, naming lipsticks and nail polishes and mascaras." David did some math in his head. "Let's see, Tom and Becky would have been grown about the time of the Civil War. During the war, popular colors for cosmetics probably would have been . . ." David pursed his lips and rocked back and forth on the ledge of the pool a few times. That peculiar waterwheel of his brain mill began to grind. "Well, first you'd have Harpers Ferry Cherry . . . oh, and John Brown, available in both light John Brown and dark John Brown . . . And, of course, O'Hara Scarlet . . ."

David was on a roll now. "Just like working on the Ms.-tique Cosmetics account," he thought. He continued to rattle off names—some admittedly better than others—as he bent to relight a candle that had gone out. He lit a match and held it to the wick. "Another popular color would be Eat Lead Red. That would go simply *mar*-velously, don't you know, with Gang Green."

Beverly's laughter ricocheted off the limestone. "Stop it. You're terrible." She splashed the surface of the pool with the soles of her feet. As she tilted her head back in delight, she saw the mouth of the cave again overhead. This time it was filled with the face of Injun Joe.

Beverly screamed, causing David to burn his fingertips with the match and utter a curse. Her scream and his curse blended and reverberated inside the cave. David followed Beverly's eyes upward to the mouth of the cave. It was Balaam, of course, the shadows cast by the candlelight exaggerating the features of his face.

"Sorry, y'all." He was embarrassed to have caused such a ruckus. "I didn't recognize your car. Just wanted to see who was down here."

Balaam told David and Beverly what he had seen at the widow Wagstaff's. Balaam did not want to intrude on David and Beverly and soon said "good night" and left. David and Beverly followed suit soon after, the whimsical spell of the cave and Tom and Becky broken by what had happened just down the road.

In Willoughby the next day, news of the vandalism spread. Some people, although regretting the injustice done to Birdie Wagstaff, secretly hoped that the spray-painted message would be heeded by its intended reader and that Balaam would sell his property to Liggett. But news of the vandalism had competition on the Willoughby grapevine. Early in the morning, an account of David and Beverly's tryst in Balaam's Cave began to spread. As the day wore on, the account mutated into two versions. By nightfall, the version popular among men was that David had coaxed Beverly out of her clothes and had had his caveman way with her three times in as many hours. By nightfall, the version popular among women was that by candlelight and on bended knee David had recited romantic poetry to Beverly. In truth, of course, David and Beverly had done no more than sit chastely on the ledge of the pool, fully clothed but for their bare feet. When Beverly had seen "Injun Joe" in the mouth of the cave and screamed, causing David to burn his fingers, David had recited the only poetry of the night.

"Hell's bells!"

❖28❖

"Well, maybe I would have realized it wasn't a man's house if that woman had had the decency to leave some pantyhose or a copy of Cosmo *or* Steel Magnolias *lying around in plain sight."*
——Ernie Ruiz

Balaam was asleep when his phone rang later that night. He turned over in bed, switched on a lamp on his night stand, and looked at the alarm clock: 1:20 A.M. After the earlier events of the night, he was afraid to not answer.

"Hello?"

Balaam heard nothing, not even breathing.

"Hello?"

After a few more seconds, Balaam hung up.

In his room at the Chateau Willoughby, Ernie Ruiz also hung up. He had been surfing the late shows on TV, still pumped up, and had decided to strike again. He had found Balaam's number in the little county phone book and had dialed.

Twenty minutes later, after Balaam had gotten back to sleep, his phone rang again. When he answered, he again heard only silence from the other end. He hung up. Normally he might have disregarded two such calls as wrong-number hangups or a prank. But not that night, not after what had happened at Birdie Wagstaff's.

Ernie Ruiz hung up and unmuted the volume on his TV. He had found *The Thomas Crown Affair* on an all-night channel and had settled on that.

Another twenty minutes later, Balaam's phone rang again. This time, after a few seconds of silence, he heard a man's voice in a forced whisper: "Did you get my message?"

Seizing his opportunity, Balaam said, "Okay, this is Balaam Gimble, if that's who you're wanting. I'm taking my phone off the hook until you get this out of your system. But you listen to me: You got the wrong house tonight. Don't you bother that poor old woman no more. Why'd you wanna do a jackass thing like that for? If you've got any business with me, you just speak up right now. And if you want to find me, I'm one mile east of where you were tonight."

Balaam listened for several seconds. He heard only silence. Then he hung up, unplugged his phone, and lay back down. He slept, but only fitfully.

At the Chateau Willoughby, Ernie Ruiz, too, hung up. His silence had been no act. He was stunned. The wrong house! He must have mis-counted mailboxes or something. He thought of how nervous he had been in that house, of the risk he had taken, of how exhilarated he had felt afterward. All that good work for nothing. He felt as if *he* had been victimized. Still, this Gimble guy had seen his little message and, as far as Ruiz knew, had no idea of his identity. So his first effort at intimida-tion had not been a total waste. But still . . .

Ernie Ruiz went back to watching TV, but his heart wasn't in Steve McQueen anymore. It was early yet, but so far this Gimble guy just did not sound very intimidated.

❧29❧

"You take a man away from his Misty, you gotta pay."
——Rudy Janacek

The next morning, by the time Balaam phoned Lilian Kreuter to ask if he could delay installing her ceiling fans for a couple of hours while he repaired the damage at Birdie Wagstaff's, Lilian already knew about the vandalism. Lilian was sympathetic but sounded distraught herself: She was trying to decide between a butter churn and a washboard as an accent in her bed-and-breakfast breakfast nook.

"I guess I'll just keep praying about it," she told Balaam.

When Birdie Wagstaff met Balaam at her front door, in the light of day she seemed more her former self, now more indignant than pitiful. While Balaam cut new glass for the picture frames, she busied herself by looking for any overlooked bits of debris on the floor. Then Balaam sanded off the spray-painted message and repainted the entire wall. "I think this will match pretty close when it dries."

Birdie was grateful. "Balaam, I'd offer you a cup of tea, but . . ." She looked at him with arched eyebrows and a thin, wry smile. Balaam knew that she would be all right.

Balaam did not tell her about the late-night phone calls.

In town, Lilian Kreuter was "just sick to death" because Mary Lou had opened her bed-and breakfast first. "She's already got a paying guest!" Lilian ranted as Balaam went about installing her ceiling fans. "And she took the best name, you know—'Chateau.' *I* wanted 'Chateau.' Now I have to settle for 'Maison.' Or maybe 'Casa.' Which do you think?"

Balaam was not listening.

"I'll pray about it."

It was late afternoon when Balaam returned home. He sat on the front porch with Stilts until dusk. Then he put on a dark T-shirt, packed two sandwiches, a Thermos bottle of coffee, a flashlight, and an aerosol can of insect repellent in a paper bag, and walked down his driveway. Almost at the foot of the driveway, he veered into the woods. Behind a screen of brush, he sat down and leaned back against the trunk of a tree. From that concealed vantage point he could see almost a half-mile down the road in the direction of Willoughby. He made himself comfortable and sprayed insect repellent over his head. After the spray settled, he poured a cup of coffee.

Then he waited.

Ernie Ruiz left the Chateau Willoughby after dark and drove east on Highway 21. On the unpaved county road, he turned left at the kamikaze German shepherd, noted first the small dip and then the big dip in the road, and began watching for what he now thought of as the Impostor House—Birdie Wagstaff's. When he saw it on his left, he looked at his odometer. Balaam Gimble had told him that his house was one mile farther. Ruiz was determined to do even more damage, leave an even stronger message, make up for the previous night's mistake.

At a half-mile, Ruiz slowed. At three-quarters of a mile, he doused his headlights and slowed even more. At eight-tenths of a mile, he saw the dim outline of a mailbox on the left. He parked his pickup and got out. He switched on his flashlight and walked the remaining distance to the mailbox. It was the only sign of human habitation he could see. There were no houses, no lights—just trees.

When he reached the mailbox, he continued up the dirt driveway. As soon as he saw a pickup parked ahead and beyond that a light shining in a window, he switched off his flashlight and hurried back to his pickup in the dark. He had no appetite for confrontation. He would wait for an opportunity: until he saw Balaam Gimble drive away or until Gimble had gone to sleep for the night.

Ruiz turned his pickup into Balaam's driveway, backed out, and—keeping his headlights off—retreated a half-mile down the road toward Willoughby. He pulled over and killed the engine and began to wait.

In the brush, Balaam heard a vehicle approach from the direction of Willoughby, watched its headlights appear at a distance. Then the headlights went out, and the vehicle stopped less than a quarter-mile away. Balaam heard the engine idle—a big pickup, judging from the sound. Then the engine stopped, and Balaam saw a flashlight beam begin wagging along the road toward his driveway. He watched the flashlight bob up his driveway, then back down at a faster pace. Balaam was concealed barely fifty feet from the driveway. He could hear the footsteps.

He watched the flashlight return to the vehicle, heard the engine start, heard the pickup turn around in his driveway and drive back in the direction of Willoughby—still with no headlights. But then Balaam saw two red taillights. As he watched, their brightness did not decrease. After they stayed on for a full minute, Balaam knew that the driver had stopped and had parked with his foot resting on the brake pedal.

In his pickup, Ernie Ruiz kept his eye on the driver's side mirror, watching the road behind him in the direction of Balaam Gimble's driveway. But he soon felt too conspicuous, too vulnerable sitting in the pickup on the road. After his eyes adjusted to the near-darkness, he got out and looked around. There was nothing he could do to hide the pickup, but he could at least take cover in the trees. Then he saw the dark outline of two small structures across the road. With his flashlight, he picked his way across an open field to them. He had no idea what they were: One was a steel drum supported five feet off the ground by three steel pipes. As Ruiz stood inspecting it, he noticed a rank odor. He walked over to the other structure, maybe two hundred feet away. It was a wooden hut on stilts, even higher off the ground. On each side, it appeared to have hinged shutters. A short wooden ladder led up to a small door on one side. Ruiz climbed up and into the hut. It was furnished with more cobwebs than suited his taste, but he knew that it would be a perfect vantage point from which to watch Balaam Gimble's driveway. He pushed open the wooden shutter covering a window.

A half-mile away, Balaam was pouring his last cup of coffee from his Thermos when he saw the courtesy light switch on in the stranger's pickup and saw a flashlight beam begin to bob from the pickup across the road and into a field. Balaam knew that country well: The stranger was headed toward one of J. D. Vernon's deer blinds.

Sure enough, as Balaam squinted into the darkness, he saw the flashlight beam waggle upward as the stranger climbed into the deer blind. The beam disappeared, then reappeared as the stranger opened one of the blind's windows. Then the beam disappeared again.

In the little wooden hut on stilts, Ruiz sat on the floor and watched the darkness in the direction of Balaam Gimble's driveway. The night was hot, with no breeze, and the hut felt like a steam cabinet. He passed the time by sweating and swatting mosquitoes. Then he made up a guessing game—What's That I Feel Crawling on Me *Now*? He had no idea what kind of spiders and scorpions and snakes might be tenants in the hut, but he didn't dare turn on his flashlight each time he felt something crawling on him. So he just sat and waited for the bite or the sting that would inject venom into his bloodstream, paralyzing his central nervous system until he died—died with his K-Mart boots on.

After Balaam saw the stranger's flashlight settle into the deer blind, he stood and walked up his driveway to his pickup. He switched on the headlights, coasted down the driveway, popped the clutch, and drove down the road, parking his pickup behind the stranger's big GMC. Balaam first wrote down the license plate number. Then he got out and checked the passenger side door. It was unlocked. So was the glove compartment. In it, Balaam found some Hertz car rental paperwork bearing the name "Ernesto D. Ruiz." Mr. Ernesto D. Ruiz listed his residence as Golden, Colorado. Normally, Balaam might have been inclined to call that a coincidence and give Howard J. Liggett the benefit of the doubt. But Balaam was running short on benefit of the doubt just then. He hadn't gotten much sleep the night before.

Ernie Ruiz suddenly saw headlights appear at the foot of Balaam Gimble's driveway and turn onto the road. "He's leaving," Ruiz thought. "This is my chance." Ruiz suddenly felt himself coming out of the funk he had fallen into after his mistake at the Impostor House. But then Ruiz saw the headlights slow as they neared the stretch of road where he had parked his own pickup. As he watched, the headlights stopped immediately behind his pickup, illuminating the back of it. Then he saw the headlights go out and heard the engine stop. Then he saw the courtesy light come on in Balaam Gimble's pickup. Gimble was getting out. Ruiz patted his jeans pocket. At least he had not left his keys in the pickup. Then he saw the courtesy light came on in his own pickup. But he had neglected to lock the damned thing.

Ernie Ruiz's funk was back.

Balaam crossed the road and began walking across Vernon's field. He knew the lay of the land so well that soon after crossing Vernon's fence he turned off his flashlight. He could see the dim outlines of the deer feeder and the deer blind. He first stopped at the deer feeder to urinate at its base. He then began slowly walking toward the deer blind.

Ernie Ruiz's funk quickly blossomed into near panic as he watched the beam of a flashlight cross the road from his pickup and begin to cross the field toward him. Then the flashlight beam disappeared, and Ruiz had nothing to track but sounds. He could not hear footsteps, but he could hear the soft swishing of someone walking through tall grass—the same sound he had made when he had crossed the field.

Ruiz was baffled and frightened. "What is he doing out there?" Ruiz asked himself. "Could he possibly know I'm in here? Is he armed?" Ruiz heard the swishing stop. After several seconds, the swishing started again and gradually grew louder. "He's coming this way!" Ruiz realized. As he listened to the swishing grow ever louder— he could hear it very close now—he berated himself for agreeing to take part in such an insane scheme. And then Ruiz heard the swishing stop—directly beneath him. Gimble was standing under the hut! Ruiz felt helpless. Trapped. He was close to tears. He began to wonder, morbidly, what the next few seconds would bring. A severe beating? A cowhiding? Do they still fight duels in the South? What's delaying that deadly insect bite that he had been expecting any second?

In the darkness, Balaam Gimble stood still for several seconds. His head was only about three feet below the floor of the deer blind. Then he looked up at the deer blind and casually drawled, "You doin' all right tonight?"

Then he turned and walked away.

In the hut, Ruiz felt his skin prickle when he heard the voice from below, heard it in spite of the pounding of his own pulse in his ears. He also heard the swishing as it began and gradually grew fainter. "What does it all mean?" he asked himself. Why had he been spared? Was Gimble toying with him?

Back at the road, Balaam spent less than a minute at Ernesto D. Ruiz's big GMC. Then he turned his own pickup around and drove home.

Dumfounded, Ruiz stared into the darkness at the road. He saw the courtesy light in his pickup come on, saw a flashlight beam dart about, and heard two metallic sounds as if something had been opened and closed. Then he heard an engine start and saw the headlights of Balaam Gimble's pickup turn around and move down the road toward Gimble's driveway. Ruiz watched the pickup's taillights disappear among the trees.

Ernie Ruiz sat in the wooden hut several minutes, wondering. He wanted out of that hut and out of that field, but he was reluctant to go back to his pickup. But he had no choice. When he left the hut and walked back to his pickup, daring to use his flashlight, he found nothing disturbed. Then he inserted his key in the ignition switch and turned it. The engine cranked but would not start. Ruiz knew nothing about engines, but this one had never even hesitated to start before. As he listened to the engine crank impotently, he knew that Balaam Gimble had done something—Gimble had sabotaged the saboteur.

Ruiz got out of the pickup. Only minutes earlier, in that hut, when he had realized that Balaam Gimble was standing right under him, he had braced himself for a bullet to rip through him from bottom to top. He had truly thought he was going to die. Now he had to make other plans.

He would have to walk back to Willoughby. The road was dark and quiet. As he walked, he used his flashlight sparingly to conserve the batteries. He hoped that a car might come along and offer him a ride into town. But then with a chill he asked himself: "What if that car turned out to be Balaam Gimble's pickup?"

Ernie Ruiz was working on a good case of paranoia. "How did Gimble know I was in that hut?" he asked himself. "Why did he just walk up to me and not *do* anything? Has he somehow connected me to the message I left on the old lady's wall? How compromised am I now that he can identify my pickup?"

Ruiz walked on, pondering. When he came to the Impostor House, he looked straight ahead and walked quickly past. Thirty minutes later, as he trudged up the slope of the second dip in the road, he remembered what lay just ahead—that damned overachieving German shepherd. Ruiz braced for an attack as he neared the house. But the dog did not appear. Walter Ridgely's German shepherd was inside the house. Walter Ridgely, on the other hand, was sitting on his front porch steps, smoking a cigarette because his wife would not let him smoke in the house.

As Ruiz hurried past the house, Walter Ridgely saw him and hollered "howdy."

Ruiz, in his paranoia, was startled. He did not reply to the voice. He began to run—as well as he could in cowboy boots that were now rubbing blisters on his heels—and didn't slow to a walk until he was out of sight of the house. Withering heat, killer German shepherds, people saying "howdy" without provocation: "What kind of place is this?" Ruiz asked himself.

It was midnight by the time he limped into the Chateau Willoughby. Again, the house was not locked. In his room, he pried off his boots, undressed, and walked into the bathroom to shower. His legs were tired. His feet were sore. His heels were blistered. The blisters complemented the mosquito bite welts on his arms. He looked at his face in the bathroom mirror. It was coated with road dust. He looked like he was wearing makeup. Ernie Ruiz did not recall ever seeing James Bond wearing makeup.

After showering, Ruiz found only one towing service listed in the

Willoughby phone book—both a business number and a home number. It was past midnight, but he had to get that pickup off the road. He dialed Rudy Janacek's home number.

When Rudy Janacek's phone rang, he was having sex with his wife but thinking about porn that he had seen on the Internet earlier that day. Rudy was not pleased to be interrupted right in the middle of a twenty-year-old blonde named Misty ("junior, UCLA, interests: dancing, partying; favorite position: whatever"). The caller said his pickup would not start, provided an approximate location, and asked that it be towed in that night. Rudy consented, but he added ten dollars to his usual after-hours road service fee.

Balaam Gimble sat on his porch late into the night, listening. Just before 1:00 A.M., he heard something big approach and stop a half-mile down the road. Rudy Janacek's tow truck, Balaam guessed. Faintly, Balaam could hear an occasional clang of metal and whir of hydraulics as Rudy secured Ernesto D. Ruiz's pickup and towed it away. As Balaam listened to the big tow truck rumble through the gears back toward Willoughby, he took another sip of beer and set the can down on the wooden cable spool, right next to the GMC spark plug wires.

❧30❧

*"Have you seen the way that poor fella is walking?
We oughta fix him up with Brandi Renee."*
———Mary Lou Wyatt

At 8:00 A.M., Mary Lou Wyatt noticed her guest's limp as he came in to the breakfast nook for coffee and orange juice and biscuits and gravy. When she asked him about "the hitch in your giddyup," Ernie Ruiz told her that his pickup had broken down in the country and that he had had to walk back to town in new boots.

"Bless your heart, son. You need to go soak those feet of yours at Balaam's Cave."

The irony was not lost on Ernie Ruiz.

At 8:05 A.M., the phone rang at Rudy Janacek's garage.

"Rudy, this is Balaam. Say, did you tow a GMC pickup off my road last night?"

"Sure did."

"Did you see the owner?"

"No. He just called and told me where the truck was and asked me to tow it ASAP. He said he'd bring me the keys this morning, but I haven't seen him yet."

"It probably needs spark plug wires, doesn't it?"

"How'd you know?"

"Lucky guess. Rudy, I think I've got some plug wires that will fit that truck, and I'll bring them to you as soon as I hang up. But if the guy comes in, I want you to stall him, tell him it'll take a couple of days to get the parts in."

"Sure thing, Balaam." Rudy could tell that something was going on, but he didn't have time to play games. He had a Kubota valve job waiting in the garage and twins named "Yvette" and "Yvonne" waiting on his computer screen.

Balaam drove in to town and went straight to the small auto parts store that Rudy operated in front of his garage. He handed the plug wires to Rudy before 8:30. Rudy set them on his counter while he cracked open a roll of pennies into the cash register. As far as Balaam knew, Ernesto D. Ruiz had never seen his face. So Balaam waited in the store.

After breakfast, Ruiz walked—in constant pain—the few blocks to Rudy Janacek's garage and parts store. Ernie Ruiz was losing his enthusiasm for his mission and wanted to bring it to a conclusion, successful or not. As he approached the parts store, he noticed the only vehicle in the parking lot—a Ford pickup. He noticed it only because it was so old and multicolored. He did not recognize it as the pickup that he had seen in Balaam Gimble's driveway the previous night.

Balaam turned when he heard the front door of the parts store open. He saw a young man limp in and approach Rudy at the counter.

"Here are the keys to that truck you towed in last night. Do you know what's wrong with it?"

"Sure. No spark plug wires."

"Oh."

The spark plug wires were still sitting on the counter where Rudy had placed them, right in front of Ruiz. Ruiz did not know a spark plug wire from barbed wire.

"Reckon where they got to?" Rudy asked with a straight face, looking down at the plug wires.

"I don't know. I guess some teenagers must have stolen them."

"Darned kids. Well, I don't have those particular plug wires in stock. I'll have to order them out of Waco. Might take a day or two."

"Two days?" This was a major setback to Ruiz. "Can't you get them any faster? I need that truck."

From the motor oil aisle, Balaam studied Ernesto D. Ruiz. "Just a kid," Balaam said to himself. "Probably needs a belt applied to his backside." But Balaam had found that if you just wait, eventually people like that will apply a belt to their backside themselves.

Sometimes they use their own belt.

Sometimes their pants fall down in the process.

Pretending to check to see if he could obtain the parts sooner, Rudy stepped into his little office for a moment. Balaam took that opportunity to sidle up to Ernesto D. Ruiz. Balaam stood beside him, picked up the plug wires, and turned them in his hand, as if examining them.

"That's a long ol' walk back to town, ain't it?" Balaam drawled casually and smiled his little parenthetical smile.

That voice! Ruiz knew that voice. That voice, those words, and the tone with which they were spoken normally would hold terror for few people. But for Ernie Ruiz, they meant that the predator had again been surprised by the prey. A half-strangled yelp escaped from Ruiz's mouth. As his head turned involuntarily toward Balaam, his feet were already turning to hobble out the door.

Rudy Janacek came back into the parts store just as his front door was banging closed. He saw Ruiz hobble-running across the parking lot. Ruiz had already passed Balaam's Frankenford and was gaining on the Dumpster.

Rudy shook his head. "Rush, rush, rush."

As Ruiz hobble-ran he checked over his shoulder every few seconds and soon realized that no one was chasing him. He slowed to a gimpy walk and returned to the Chateau Willoughby. He pulled off his boots and stayed in his room, now and then peeking through the curtains, watching TV, and thinking. Now this Gimble guy could recognize both his pickup *and* his face. Gimble seemed to always know where Ruiz was. Ruiz felt like a decidedly unsecret agent. And something else nagged at him: This Gimble guy had had him at a disadvantage twice now—at the wooden hut and at the mechanic's. And yet Gimble had not laid a hand on him. Is that any way to fight? What is that hillbilly pacifist, Ruiz wondered angrily—some kind of goddamned Hopalong Gandhi?

Limpalong Ruiz knew that he had to do something, do it soon, do it big.

He ventured out only once the rest of the day—to Earl Perry's grocery store. When Ruiz walked in, Perry thought it was unusual that the stranger was barefoot. When Ruiz placed his purchases on the checkout counter, Perry did not think it was unusual that the stranger was buying a can of lighter fluid and a box of kitchen matches.

❧31❧

"I wonder if John D. Rockefeller started out with just a claw-foot bathtub."
—————Cliff Gholson

D uring Ernie Ruiz's first three days in Willoughby, he was not aware, of course, of other human dramas playing out around him.

On the Wednesday that he arrived, Flora Vickers, who had reopened her pottery shop and added gifts and souvenirs to take advantage of Willoughby's increased tourism, noticed that an antique calendar clock that she had for sale was beginning to run fast. Ever since she had bought it from Beverly Faulk, it had been accurate. At eleven that morning, the clock dial had read "11:00, Wednesday, August 26," which agreed with Flora's watch. But at 2:15, it read "7:21." And by the time she closed her shop that day at 6:00 P.M., the clock dial read "9:27, Thursday, August 27." Flora decided that she would talk with Beverly about it the next day.

Beverly Faulk had quickly become the chief supplier of antique furnishings for the bed-and-breakfasts being rushed into service by Mary Lou Wyatt and Lilian Kreuter. If Beverly could not supply the antiques from her own store, she tried to locate them at other dealers: butter churns, picture frames made of weathered barn lumber, crocks, washboards, coal-oil lanterns, milk cans, patchwork quilts, spurs, tin types—anything that said "old and charming."

Mary Lou and Lilian both felt that they simply could not operate bed-and-breakfasts without antique cast-iron claw-foot bathtubs in the guest bathrooms. They needed a total of four. But Beverly had been able to locate only two. She agreed to sell one to Mary Lou and one to Lilian at the same price. Then she remembered that Cliff Gholson had taken a claw-foot bathtub out to Balaam's Cave. Beverly told Mary Lou and Lilian. Both women phoned Balaam to ask if the tub was for sale. Balaam told both women that it was not his to sell, that it belonged to Cliff. Mary Lou was the first to phone Cliff. She offered to trade him two modern steel bathtubs for "that rusty, chipped ol' claw-foot contraption of yours." Cliff told her he had no use for two bathtubs. "I'm a big man, Mary Lou, but I can't take but one bath at a time."

Mary Lou then offered him twenty-five dollars for the bathtub. Cliff said he'd think about it. He then sat back and waited for Lilian to phone him. The bidding war began.

That Wednesday was the seventh wedding anniversary of Juanita and Richard Greer. Juanita and Richard had been able to save some money—again, because of increased business at the cafe—and had been discussing expanding the cafe: adding a banquet room or an outdoor dining area. "Or at least let's replace that old deep fryer," Juanita had said. "I swear, sometimes I put a fillet into that thing, and it comes out with freezer burn!"

Unbeknownst to Juanita, Richard had just used the money in their "cafe kitty" to buy a fishing boat from a young man in Waco who wanted to sell it after he and his girlfriend, Lorraine, had split up. Richard had intended the boat as a surprise "we've earned it" anniversary extravagance for himself and Juanita. Granted, he knew that Juanita did not enjoy fishing, but he thought that she might learn to enjoy the boating aspect.

At two that afternoon, Richard relieved Juanita at the cafe. When Juanita drove home, she saw a big boat on a big trailer in their little driveway. Juanita squeezed her car in beside the boat, got out, and walked around it. It had an obscenely large outboard motor, a windshield, and "Sweet Miss Lorraine" printed on each side of the bow.

Juanita refrained from phoning Richard at the cafe to ask him about the boat. But when Richard came home that night, Juanita was waiting up for him. She had a few questions, the first of which was "Did you buy that boat with our cafe money?" and the last of which was "Well, we may as well start getting some use out that damned boat—why don't you just sleep in it tonight?"

By Thursday, the calendar clock in Flora Vickers's shop was ticking ever faster. It seemed to be suffering heart palpitations. Flora phoned Beverly Faulk to tell her that it was running fast. "It now reads 'Saturday, August 29.'" Beverly was puzzled, said the clock had been accurate for months, and suggested that perhaps Flora had overwound the clock a tad or "fiddled with the regulator lever." Beverly also said that having an antique clock repaired could be expensive. Flora took offense and accused Beverly of blaming her for breaking a clock that was probably defective when she bought it *and* of trying to stick her with the repair bill.

That morning, Lilian Kreuter, hearing that Mary Lou Wyatt had offered Cliff Gholson twenty-five dollars for his claw-foot bathtub, offered him fifty dollars. By noon, Mary Lou had offered seventy-five.

That afternoon, when Mary Lou heard that Juanita had thrown Richard out, she phoned him at the cafe and offered to let him stay in her second guest bedroom—"it's almost finished"—at half rate. "Until you two kids work things out."

Richard accepted. When he relieved Juanita at the cafe at two o'clock, she was still angry. Indeed, with the passage of time, she became more, not less, angry. Each hour she seemed to think of another reason why Richard's unilateral decision was selfish. That night after work, before Richard checked into the Chateau Willoughby, he went by their home to try to talk to Juanita. In the driveway, he paused to admire the boat. It was a beaut, from "Sweet Miss Lorraine" on the bow back to "Mercury" on the outboard. As he walked from the driveway to the front porch, Juanita appeared at the door and began throwing out his belongings—clothes, handtools, bowling ball, fishing rods, CDs, his Zane Grey paperbacks. Richard was not sure if she was throwing them *to* him or *at* him. When *Riders of the Purple Sage* clipped his left ear, Richard felt that he had his answer.

On Friday, Beverly Faulk walked over to Flora Vickers's shop to try to make peace. Flora saw Beverly crossing the street in her direction. Flora locked her front door, pulled the shade down over the door glass, and stood lurking behind the door. Beverly saw the shade go down and was puzzled. When she reached the door, she turned the knob. It was locked. She knocked, then tried the door knob again. Then, looking through the slit between the bottom of the shade and the door frame, she saw Flora's ankles. "Look, Flora," Beverly called through the door, "let me try to find someone who can fix that little clock, and we'll split the cost."

Flora snapped, "I'm sorry, but I don't care to pay to fix a clock I didn't break—a clock, by the way, that now reads 'Monday, August 31.' I am closed on Mondays."

Frustrated, Beverly turned and walked away. Flora unlocked the door, jerked it open, and yelled at Beverly, "Come back tomorrow, which by then will probably be Christmas Day. *I am also closed on Christmas Day!*"

At that moment, Mrs. Rachel Nesbitt and her five-year-old son, Kevin, from Austin, were approaching Flora's gift shop and had stopped to look in the shop window. When Kevin heard Flora's outburst, he turned to his mother and asked, "Mommy, is tomorrow Christmas?"

The look that Mrs. Rachel Nesbitt gave Flora Vickers was not in keeping with the spirit of the holidays.

When Lilian Kreuter heard that Mary Lou Wyatt had topped her bid on the claw-foot bathtub and now had *two* paying bed-and-breakfast guests—the stranger from out of town and Richard Greer—she was frantic. Balaam had been working on Lilian's rooms, and one was marginally ready, if the guest did not mind that Balaam had pulled up only half the carpet in the bedroom and had replaced only half the tile in the guest bathroom.

Lilian knew that there was no time to pray about it. First she phoned Richard Greer and offered him a room for twenty-five dollars a night less than he was paying Mary Lou. Richard agreed to move from Mary Lou's to Lilian's and to stay "just until Juanita cools down."

Then Lilian phoned Cliff Gholson and topped Mary Lou's bid by twenty-five dollars. "As of now, you're the higher bidder," Cliff told Lilian. "If Mary Lou doesn't up the ante, that tub is yours."

Lilian Kreuter hung up her phone feeling that she had won two moral victories. She felt capable. Decisive. She was determined to make her bed-and-breakfast a success. And if she had to spend too much and earn too little and go broke in the process, well, so be it.

That night after closing the cafe, before going to Lilian's, Richard again went by his home to try to reason with Juanita. But Juanita had been thinking. She had one more question to ask Richard. As he began walking from his car in the driveway to the front porch, she stepped out the door, pointed at the boat, and screamed: "And just who the *hell* is 'Lorraine'?!"

❧32❧

"My dog is going to miss that fella, whoever he was."
——Walter Ridgely

On Saturday morning just before noon, Balaam secured the gate to his compound with a chain and padlock, rubbed Stilts's ears over the gate, and said, "I'll be back before dark." Then he drove in to town to work on Lilian Kreuter's rooms. At 12:17, Balaam paused at the flashing red light in Willoughby.

At 12:17, Ernie Ruiz was eating lunch at the Crossroads Cafe. He noticed that the cute waitress was walking in her high heels not much better than he was walking in his boots. Ruiz then looked out the cafe window. He saw a multicolored old pickup at the flashing red light and remembered it from the mechanic's parking lot the previous day. In his panic, he had gotten only a glimpse of Balaam's face, but the face he now saw in the pickup window, even at that distance, made his pulse quicken. Trusting that instinct, Ruiz left a twenty on his table and hurried out the cafe door, keeping the pickup in sight as it passed through the intersection. Ruiz trotted limping and wincing after the pickup. He lost sight of it as it turned left onto a residential street. But at the corner, Ruiz peeked around a shrub and saw the pickup parked in front of a big house in the next block. He watched Balaam Gimble carrying tools and what appeared to be building materials from the pickup into the house.

"He looks like he's going to be there a while," Ruiz told himself. "This is my chance. This time I *know* he's not home." After the previous two nighttime debacles, Ruiz could hardly do worse during the daytime.

Ruiz then hobble-trotted—"Why," he asked himself, "didn't I pack a pair of sensible shoes?"—to Rudy Janacek's garage to see if his pickup had been repaired. Rudy continued to stall, saying that the Waco parts supplier had sent out the wrong spark plug wires, that now the pickup would not be ready before Monday.

Ruiz told Rudy that he had some important errands to run locally. "Can you let me have a loaner? Anything. Just as long as it runs. Just for an hour or so."

Rudy didn't fully understand what was going on between Balaam and this stranger except that Balaam apparently didn't want the stranger to leave town right away. "Sorry. Everything I've got now is down. Even the tow truck. Relining the brakes."

"But you must have *some*thing."

"Honest. All I got that's runnin' right now is a riding lawn mower."

"A riding lawn . . . Are you sh———," Ruiz swallowed his frustration. He couldn't let this opportunity pass just for lack of transportation. "Surely one of those———." But as Ruiz looked at the side lot at the collection of crippled cars, trucks, and tractors, he suspected that a riding lawn mower might be his best bet.

"Let me see it." Ernie Ruiz's voice was lined with black crepe.

Rudy knew that the stranger couldn't leave town on a riding mower. So he walked him outside to a bright green mower with small tires and a small steering wheel.

Ruiz looked at it skeptically. "How many miles will this thing go on a tank of gas?"

"Well, if all you're doing is riding it and not mowing, I'd say twenty miles or so."

Ruiz knew that should get him to Balaam Gimble's cabin and back. "How fast will it go?"

"Oh, I got this little dickens hummin' now—it'll do eight, ten miles an hour."

Ruiz thought, "That's an hour out and an hour back."

Ruiz looked at the mower. His window of opportunity was getting smaller each minute. "It'll have to do," he said. "Show me how to run it."

Rudy looked at the stranger as if he were a freak in a carnival side show. "Step right this way! Marvel at the amazing one-headed Mower Boy!"

"You really want to use a riding mower to get around town? Shoot, you could walk almost as fast."

"Maybe you could. Not me. I've got bad feet. Real bad feet. Look, just let me have the mower for a few hours, okay?"

Rudy gave the stranger a quick course in how to start the engine, and how to use the foot and hand controls. "This," Rudy said, pointing to a lever, "engages the blade. Unless you're going to do some mowing, leave it like it is."

Ernie Ruiz climbed into the seat and started the engine as he had been shown. He put the mower in gear and slowly drove an inelegant figure-eight around the parking lot to get the feel of it. Then he straightened the wheels, accelerated, and putt-putted out onto the street, staying close to the curb. He felt sublimely foolish, but at least he was on wheels again, albeit eight-inch wheels, and not on foot.

Rudy went back inside to his office to phone Balaam but, of course, got no answer.

Ernie Ruiz drove at full throttle back to the Chateau Willoughby, where he retrieved his bag of tools, the can of lighter fluid, and the box of kitchen matches. Then he floorboarded the mower to within a block of the house where he had just seen Balaam Gimble, left the mower idling, and hobble-trotted to the corner. He again peeked around the shrub and saw that Balaam's pickup was still there. He could even hear the sound of a power saw coming from inside the house.

Ruiz returned to the mower and drove back the way he had come. A block later, before he reached the highway that he would follow out of town, he saw the Scooter Lady coming toward him on the street. As Nanetta Wilson passed him she smiled, tooted her little horn, and gave him a "thumbs up" sign. "God," Ruiz said to himself, "to that old lady, we're two of a kind. Maybe she wants to drag race." He tried not to think of how it had come to this, step by step, setback by setback, in just four days.

On Highway 21, Ruiz kept to the shoulder as traffic whizzed by him. Now and then a passing tractor-trailer truck whipped road grit into his face and forced him to steer against the slipstream. Ruiz was certain that people were laughing at him. "Going out to burn down a man's house on a lawn mower!" he could imagine them saying. Actually, a few people waved to him in a friendly fashion, but most people took no notice of him, including David Wilson and Beverly Faulk, who passed him as they drove out of town on their third bird-watching outing. Oh, perhaps they did see a rather sour-faced young man on a riding lawn mower two miles from the nearest patch of St. Augustine, but the sight did not register with them. They had towhees and titmice on their minds.

As Ruiz poked along, he indulged in more self-pity. "Here goes James Bond, superspy," he thought. "He battles international arch villains. He makes love to beautiful women. He mows lawns on the weekends for spending money." A week earlier, Ruiz had been in Denver, far from this heat and humiliation, wearing smart clothes, rubbing people the right way, and receiving big tips for it. Ruiz had lived all of his life in cities, had no experience with the country. He did not care for the country, he had concluded. Everything was too far from everything else. It was too slow and backward and too quiet and—he flicked off something with legs that had just landed on his face—too full of insects.

"Burn down a man's house?" he repeated to himself. Yes, that was his plan. Do something dramatic, get back to Denver that weekend with something big to report to Mr. Liggett. The way Ruiz saw it, that Gimble guy, without his house, would have even less reason not to sell his land, even more need for money. Ruiz now knew where Gimble's house was, he knew that Gimble was not at that house, he had plenty of daylight and no witnesses.

This time, it felt right.

Two miles out of Willoughby, just past a bar named "Rusty's Bar F Tavern," Ruiz turned south off Highway 21 onto a county road. He knew the way well by now. The mower could barely go fast enough to raise dust on the dirt road. Ahead, Ruiz saw the house where he had to turn left. Then Ruiz felt the "uh-oh" lobe of his brain twitch. Sure enough—even earlier than before—Walter Ridgely's German shepherd ran out snapping and barking. Ruiz knew that he was vulnerable on the mower—low to the ground, exposed, unable to outrun the dog. Just before the dog reached him, Ruiz remembered something that the mechanic had told him. He grabbed the lever that engaged the mower blade and released it. Instantly the mower began spewing gravel and raising a cloud of dust. Ruiz could hear gravel hitting the metal under-carriage of the mower. He began to choke on the dust, but as he looked back, he saw that the dog had stopped chasing him and veered away.

"Just like a James Bond smoke screen," Ruiz thought triumphantly. After he was well away from the dog, Ruiz disengaged the mower blade and began spitting to clear the dust from his mouth. As he passed the Impostor House and then the wooden hut on stilts—symbols of his failure-so-far—Ruiz realized that the mower engine was so loud that he could not hear a vehicle approach from behind. The mower had no mirrors. Ruiz asked himself, "What will I do if Gimble returns from town while I'm creeping down this road?" He had no answer.

About an hour after he left Willoughby, Ernie Ruiz saw Balaam Gimble's mailbox ahead. He turned into the dirt driveway, drove all the way up to the gate, and killed the engine. His ears rang after the drone of the engine stopped. Sweat was dripping from his brow into his eyes, and he knew that his face must be—again—covered with dust. He saw the chain and padlock on the gate. He could have simply climbed over the gate to get into the compound. Instead he tugged roughly on the gate until the loose hinges pulled out of the gate post. He stepped past the gate and left it dangling from the chain and padlock.

Inside the gate, Ruiz stood staring at Balaam's cabin and compound. To Ruiz, it was a hovel wrapped in a junkyard inside a disaster area. It was hillbilly heaven. "Oh, no," he said to himself, "*this* man doesn't need fistfuls of Liggett money. Not much he doesn't. Burning this place down is doing the old bastard a favor."

But the cabin was a disappointment to Ruiz. Because it was made of stone with a metal roof, there was not much to set fire to. Just the contents. On the other hand, the compound was a conflagration-in-waiting. Stacks of lumber and other combustibles everywhere. Ruiz decided to first start a small test fire to see how the lighter fluid would behave. He was not an experienced arsonist. While he was looking around for a good place to pour the lighter fluid, he heard a tapping sound, as if someone was lightly hammering metal. He froze, his heart pounding. The tapping stopped. He relaxed and continued browsing through the clutter. In a few seconds, the tapping resumed. Ruiz froze again. The tapping stopped. Ruiz did not realize that he was hearing the tapping only when the wind blew: On the other side of the cabin, wind was causing a washtub hanging on a hook to tap against a wooden crate.

Then Ruiz heard what sounded like a wheezy snort from behind him in a nearby thicket. A distinct snort. From a living thing, he was sure. He spun around but could see nothing but brush and tables of junk. A squirrel? A raccoon? He had no idea what they sound like. Maybe they snort, for all he knew.

Increasingly uneasy, Ernie Ruiz hurried about his task. He saw a stack of old plywood sheets. The top sheet's plies were warped and separating, and it looked like it would burn well. As he was squirting lighter fluid onto the plywood, he heard a pop from the direction of the cabin. Again he jumped. Then he heard another pop. He did not recognize the sound of the roof popping as the panels of sheet metal expanded in the heat of the sun.

Then Ruiz heard a snort again, this time from a different location—not behind him this time, more to his side. "Squirrel or raccoon," he repeated to himself, but with less conviction and more anxiety.

As he was watching to see if the lighter fluid would soak in or evaporate or what, he heard a third snort—from somewhere in front of him this time and louder, definitely louder.

The snorts were coming from Stilts, of course, who had retreated, white flagtail raised in alarm, when Ruiz had arrived. Alert to danger, Stilts had maneuvered around the compound, keeping an eye on the stranger while gradually narrowing the distance between them.

Ruiz's anxiety graduated to paranoia. *Why won't this place shut up?!* When he tried to strike a match he fumbled with the box, spilling matches to the ground. He got down onto his hands and knees and began picking them up. Stilts lowered his flagtail as he watched the stranger assume the familiar "let's have a game of headbutt" position.

What happened next lasted less than two seconds. Ernie Ruiz, who wanted only to please his boss and make some money, was unconscious before his head hit the ground.

As Ruiz was on his hands and knees picking up matches he heard a rustle, a metallic tinkling sound, and a short burst of galloping. By the time he could look up to see some kind of crazed demon beast with big black eyes, Stilts was only five feet away and closing fast. While Ruiz was still in mid-gasp, Stilts butted him hard on his uncushioned forehead, lifting him off his knees and propelling him over into a patch of weeds. Ruiz lay on his back, the toes of his K-Mart boots pointing up and slightly out. If the soles of his boots had been hands on a clock, Ernie Ruiz was out cold at ten minutes of two.

As David Wilson and Beverly Faulk drove back to Willoughby on Highway 21, they were hot and tired and thirsty. But their bird-watching outing had been pleasant. And for once, David had not been injured— no bitten backside, no burned fingers. As they approached Rusty's Bar F Tavern on the way into town, Beverly suggested that they stop for a beer. When she turned in to the gravel parking lot, David looked at the building with doubt. The Bar F Tavern was just a tin-skinned Quonset hut. A honky tonk, at best, David could see. But when they walked in and sat down at a table, the air conditioning, although turned up to a frugal eighty degrees, felt good.

David and Beverly were reliving their outing, debating good naturedly whether one particular bird they had seen was a Cassin's finch or a house finch. Beverly was defending her pro-Cassin's position when David saw her look past him and heard her voice change. Her expression changed from carefree to annoyed. David turned in his chair and saw a man standing inside the doorway. Beverly leaned across the table. "That's Jeeter, my first ex. The divorce still sticks in his craw."

Jeeter saw Beverly and David. Jeeter grunted an acknowledgment at her, glared at him. Then he walked to a table across the room from them, sat, and ordered a beer. Judging from the way Ex One was walking, David suspected that this was not his first refueling of the afternoon. After David and Beverly had rebuilt their conversation, Ex One continued to order beers and stare at them.

When Ernie Ruiz regained consciousness, his size-six and three-fourths head had a size-seven and three-eighths headache. He gingerly got to his feet, dizzy and wary that "the beast" might still be out there lurking, preparing to maul him again. Ruiz did not know how long he had been unconscious. He looked at the plywood; it was dry, no sign of the lighter fluid. It had evaporated. "How long does that take?" he wondered. Minutes? Hours? He panicked to think that Balaam Gimble might return home at any moment. Ruiz would be caught red handed. "What do they do to trespassing arsonists in Texas?" he wondered. Sic Beelzebub's Bambi on them, apparently. Ruiz scooped up the spilled matches, grabbed the lighter fluid can, picked his way quickly through the rows of clutter in the compound, and practically leaped over the dangling gate. The mower took an eternity (about four seconds) to start. As he was chugging at full throttle down the dirt road, he again wondered what he would do if he saw Balaam Gimble driving home in his direction.

But the six miles of dirt road passed uneventfully. Passing Walter Ridgely's house, Ruiz again engaged his mower's dust screen—the superspy's secret weapon—to keep the dog away, and he was feeling less vulnerable by the time he reached Highway 21. Just two more miles to town. Ruiz was whizzing toward Willoughby at a full ten miles an hour when he suddenly became aware of the *other* reason why riding lawn mowers are not used more often as getaway cars: They have a very limited range. The little engine coughed a few times, sputtered, and died. Out of gas. Ruiz lurched forward in the seat, trying to keep the mower going by sheer body English. But it silently coasted to a stop on the shoulder of the highway. Ernie Ruiz closed his eyes. He leaned forward to rest his head on the steering wheel, but his forehead hurt too much. He could feel a whimper welling up inside. He fought it down—something that he had done far too often in the last four days. When he opened his eyes, he saw the sign at Rusty's Bar F Tavern less than a quarter-mile ahead.

Ruiz picked up his bag of tools and began limping toward the tavern. He was sweating through his shirt by the time he got inside. He limped past a middle-aged man and woman and sat down at a table behind them. His wet shirt felt cool against his skin when it pressed against the vinyl back of the chair. Ruiz ordered a beer ("shaken, not stirred," he said to himself bitterly).

Rusty brought the beer, and Ruiz lightly rolled the label of the cold bottle across his tender forehead. *Oh, that hurts so good.* He paid no attention when the man at a table across the room got up and walked rather unevenly past him and on toward the table of the middle-aged man and woman.

Ex One stood between David and Beverly at their table, swaying gently in a Bud breeze. He looked down at David. "Who the hell are you?" It was more accusation than question. Beverly was determined to ignore Ex One. She looked at David and locked his eyes to hers, willing him not to respond in kind.

"I said, 'Who the hell are you?'"

David, who insisted in believing that most volatile situations can be disarmed with politeness, slowly stood, smiled at Ex One, and held out his hand. "I'm David. And you are . . ."

"Pissed off."

Ex One pushed David with both hands, propelling him backward. Behind David, Ernie Ruiz had risen almost to his feet to get out of the way when David stumbled back into him. David's momentum took him and Ruiz to the concrete floor, the difference being that Ruiz broke David's fall, whereas only the concrete floor broke Ruiz's fall. For the second time in an hour, Ruiz was flat on his back. The impact with the floor knocked the breath out of him and caused him to bite his lower lip.

Rusty hurried around from behind the bar and ushered Ex One outside. "Jeeter, you beat all I ever saw."

As Beverly helped David up and back into his chair, he said, "Beverly, I think I'm going to have to stop going bird-watching with you. It's just too dangerous."

Beverly smiled sympathetically. "Bless your heart. But you were lucky. My *other* ex is the mean one."

Beverly turned to apologize to the fallen stranger, but he was gone.

Ernie Ruiz had decided that outside was a good place for his aching feet, his tender forehead, his bleeding lip, and the rest of his body. By "outside" he meant "Colorado." He limped out the door and into the parking lot, where Rusty was standing by while Ex One was being unwell.

Ruiz hobbled past them and onto the shoulder of the highway. He stuck out his thumb. He was not going to travel one more foot on his feet.

The first vehicle to stop was a tractor-trailer truck traveling west. When Ruiz hurried around to the driver's side of the cab and looked up, the trucker asked, "Where you headed?"

"Anywhere but here. The neareth big airport." His lip was swelling.

"I'm going up to Oklahoma City."

"You go near the Dallath airport?"

"Maybe twenty, thirty miles."

"Leth do it," Ruiz said.

Ruiz went back around to the passenger door, hoisted up his bag of tools, and climbed up after them. He did not ask the trucker to stop in Willoughby so that he could collect the rest of his belongings at the Chateau Willoughby. To hell with them. To hell with the rented pickup. To hell with the riding lawn mower. To hell with the twenty-five thousand dollars.

As the truck paused at Willoughby's flashing red light and then groaned through the gears toward the western edge of town, Ruiz sat slumped against the passenger door, feeling his body serenade him with pain: His two feet were throbbing one duet, his forehead and lip another duet. He tried to find a good thought to cling to. This was the best that he could come up with: "Surely to *God* I have just survived the worst day that I will ever have in my life."

Almost twenty-four hours would pass before Ernie Ruiz discovered that the patch of weeds that Beelzebub's Bambi had headbutted him backward into was poison oak.

❧33❧

"I'm just glad I'll never grow up to be a middle-aged man. Gross!"
——Earline Perry

When Balaam returned home that afternoon after working at Lilian Kreuter's and saw his gate dangling from its chain and padlock, his first thought was of Stilts. He began calling as soon as he got out of the pickup, surprised by the anxiety that he heard in his voice in the very first "Stilts? Hey, boy!"

He walked quickly through the compound calling, then stopping to listen and watch, then calling again. Balaam filled a coffee can with dried corn and began shaking it to lure Stilts out if he was still within earshot. He walked the two-acre compound from edge to edge, looking in thickets of brush and among his "stuff" where Stilts might be concealed if he was "down," although Stilts had seldom been sick. Balaam then went back to the gate, still shaking the coffee can, and looked for deer hoofprints in the driveway. But, of course, when he had driven up the driveway his tire tracks had obliterated the record of any recent comings and goings—such as by a deer or a riding lawn mower—that could have been read in the soft sand. On the ground just inside the gate, he saw deer hoofprints, but Stilts had stood at the gate as Balaam had left for town earlier that day, so those prints meant nothing. And Balaam knew that he would find no hoofprints on the ground in the woods, which was covered year around with a mulch of leaves from the previous autumn.

Balaam naturally suspected that Ernie Ruiz had somehow found a way to get out to his place and had torn down the gate, although Balaam found no other signs of vandalism, nothing missing or damaged. But blame could wait. Balaam's immediate and overriding concern was to find Stilts, who knew little of the world beyond the compound. Balaam went into the cabin to phone his two nearest neighbors. He asked Birdie Wagstaff to please notify him if she saw—or heard—Stilts. Birdie had met Stilts before, knew that he wore a cowbell. Balaam did not tell Birdie that he suspected that the same person who had vandalized her house had torn down his gate. Balaam then dialed J. D. Vernon's phone number. Balaam needed to reach Vernon for two reasons: to ask Vernon, and his wife, Marlene, to please watch for Stilts and to ask Vernon *please* not to harm a buck with a cowbell and no antlers. But no one answered the phone at the Vernon home.

Balaam then drove down to the cave. He saw only three cars parked at the road. That was a low number lately. But by now it was after 4:00 P.M., and the late afternoon temperature in August kept away all but the most heat-hardy pilgrims. Balaam saw Earline Perry, "the friendly, knowledgeable staff" of Balaam's Cave, sitting at her desk under the live oak tree, fanning herself with a paperback book.

"He's been at it again, Mr. Gimble," Earline said even before Balaam had reached the tree's shade. Those days, when Earline said "he," she usually meant Leroy Jarvis, who had begun to abuse the "clothing optional" policy in the cave. Leroy would wait until he was in the waist-high water before slipping off his one-size-does-not-fit-all swim trunks. But then sporadically he would surprise others in the pool with him by lunging straight up and shouting, "Owww! Crawdad bit me!"

"He's a pasty, pudgy little man, Mr. Gimble. Who does he think wants to look at him?" Earline asked rhetorically. "There were two couples from San Antonio in the cave this morning. Then Mr. Jarvis showed up and went down there. I knew what was coming. Sure enough, the two couples left about five minutes later. One woman said she was no prude and that she had been in hot tubs before and even been to California, but she didn't drive all the way up here to be flashed by no Pillsbury Doughboy."

212

"I'll talk to him, Earline."

Earline was surprised that Balaam did not even smile at the woman's tirade.

"Earline, I need your help. Stilts has gotten out, and there's no telling where he might be. Would you watch for him down here? As far as I know, he's still got his bell on."

"Oh, no," Earline said with genuine concern. She had become fond of Stilts and enjoyed seeing him when she brought Balaam the weekly receipts from the cave. Stilts had grown accustomed to her and would let her rub his ears. She took out of the desk the spiral notebook that served as her ledger, tore out a blank sheet, and handed Balaam her felt-tip pen. He wrote "Lost Deer with Cow Bell. Tell Earline" in large letters and tacked the sheet to a fencepost by the road as he left.

Balaam drove back to his cabin and continued calling to Stilts. Then he began walking without direction through the woods beyond the compound, calling and rattling the coffee can of corn. He believed that Stilts would not wander far, and he trusted in the deer's sharp senses, including the sense of home. He paused to listen. All he heard was the euphoric jabbering of a mockingbird. Now and then a breeze blew through the treetops; at such times the woods sounded—and even looked—as if it were breathing, inhaling as the treetops swayed first in the direction of the breeze and then exhaling as the treetops relaxed after the breeze passed.

After seven o'clock, Balaam went back to the compound and called out just in case Stilts had returned. At dusk, Balaam began walking along the county road, rattling the coffee can and listening. Once he thought he heard—from the woods on Vernon's side of the road—a sound that might have been a cowbell. He strained for a full minute to hear it again, to home in on its direction and distance. But he didn't hear the sound again and walked on.

After sunset, a half-moon rose. It had just cleared the trees down the road in front of Balaam when the silhouette of a deer suddenly ran out of the brush on his left and bounded across the road, over the fence, and into the woods. Man had startled deer; deer had startled man. Balaam enjoyed only an instant of hope: As soon as the deer took its second silent stride, Balaam knew that it was not wearing a cowbell. There were wild deer in that sparsely populated area, of course, although not as many as there had been ten or even five years earlier. Balaam often saw them crossing the road in ones, twos, or even threes, their flagtails flying at full mast. And he could tell when wild deer came near the compound because at such times Stilts acted differently—fractious.

About 10:00 P.M., the cadence of Balaam's walk and the sound of his boots crunching on the gravel of the road began to remind Balaam of the sound of Stilts chewing his corn. Balaam knew that it was time to stop for the night.

At the compound, he removed the chain and padlock from the gate and moved the gate to one side, leaving the gateway wide open in case Stilts came back during the night. Balaam scattered a trail of corn from the gateway into the compound toward the cabin. Then he sat in the dark in his lawn chair on the front porch, the can of corn on the floor beside him.

Sometime after midnight, Balaam Gimble fell asleep in his chair while listening for the sound of a cowbell or hooves on dry leaves.

❧34❧

"I understand that J. D. had gone out to mend a fence.
Ranch work can be dangerous."
————Sheriff Sam Kirby

By the next morning, David Wilson had heard through the Willoughby grapevine that Stilts was missing. He phoned Balaam to offer to help search but received no answer. So he drove out to Balaam's. As David was about to park at Balaam's mailbox and walk up the driveway, he saw someone walking along the road almost a half-mile ahead. He drove down and pulled alongside Balaam, who was rattling his coffee can of dried corn as he walked.

"No luck yet?"

"Nope. How'd you hear?"

David chuckled. "You know. The usual."

"I'm going up to Vernon's to tell them that Stilts is loose."

"Get in, and we can both look along the way."

Balaam bent over and folded himself into the little red roadster. "I feel like I'm in a roller skate," Balaam said, looking out the window and down at how close he was to the road.

"Costs a lot more to repair, though."

"About a half-mile up here," Balaam said. He had never had a quarrel with Marlene Vernon but dreaded having to talk to Vernon face to face, especially to ask for help.

Just after 9:00 A.M., David turned into a winding asphalt driveway leading to a brick ranch-style house. In front of the garage, Balaam saw a car but not Vernon's pickup. David waited in his car while Balaam went to the front porch and rang the bell. Marlene Vernon told Balaam that her husband had gone out about twenty minutes earlier to mend a stretch of fence.

Just after 9:00 A.M., as J. D. Vernon mended his fence he did not even notice the little red roadster as it drove by. He was working about a quarter-mile off the road. It was one of the few stretches of fence on his property that he had not updated with steel posts. He straightened from nailing a staple into a cedar post and wiped sweat from his face. When he took his forearm from across his eyes, he saw a deer standing perhaps six hundred feet across the pasture at the edge of a woods. Vernon had a 30-06 rifle in his pickup with a new scope that he had not sighted in. He walked slowly to the pickup, keeping his eyes on the deer. He took the rifle from the gun rack and moved slowly back along the fence. The deer had not moved. As Vernon aimed at the neck, the deer was within rifle range but too distant for Vernon to see or hear a cowbell.

Stilts did not hear the crack of the rifle before the bullet slammed him sideways and down. He scrambled to get up, staggered a few steps into the woods, fell back onto his haunches, and collapsed, legs flailing, head arching back, teeth bared in a rictus, cowbell ringing wildly. He thrashed a few seconds, bleated weakly, shuddered, and then the cowbell was quiet.

As Mrs. Vernon and Balaam talked on her porch, they heard a shot fired. Balaam could tell that the shot had come from somewhere on the western part of Vernon's property. He walked quickly to David's car. "She said he's down near where that shot came from, gate five."

"Where's that?"

"Back toward my place, the way we came."

David turned around in the driveway and drove back the way they had come. Balaam looked out his window and was silent.

Vernon walked quickly across the field and just into the edge of the woods to the fallen deer. When he saw the cowbell and collar, he knew that it was Balaam Gimble's pet. Vernon's only reaction was annoyance. "What the hell was it doing over here?" he wondered. "That's what happens when you try to make a damned pet out of a wild animal."

Vernon found the entry wound in the left shoulder and made a mental note that the scope was a tad off. But the deer was dead or near enough. No need for a second shot. Vernon leaned the rifle upright against a tree trunk just to the rear of the fallen deer.

As David drove, Balaam leaned across the console and began tapping the horn button, one second on, one second off. Balaam wanted to distract Vernon, to get him to stop shooting at whatever he had shot at.

"Pull in here," Balaam said and pointed when they reached a galvanized panel gate with a "5" painted on it. Balaam continued to honk the horn as David turned off the engine.

At the edge of the woods, J. D. Vernon heard the blaring of the horn and said to himself, "Who the hell is making all that rac——?"

Between the first and last syllables of the word "racket," J. D. Vernon, age fifty-two, tall and broad shouldered, stepped off the curb into the intersection of Grim Reaper Avenue and Rube Goldberg Boulevard. Three elements—carelessness, a honking horn, and the involuntary muscle contraction of a dying animal with strong hind legs—joined to act as fate, although each element was, by itself, impotent. Vernon had neglected to engage the safety on his rifle before he had leaned it against the tree trunk. When Balaam began honking David's horn, Vernon, irritated, turned his back on the deer and took three steps to his left, just forward of a tree stump, to gain a better view of the road. As death shut down the systems of Stilts's body, his right hind leg jerked backward, kicking the butt of the rifle and knocking the rifle sideways onto the tree stump with enough force to discharge, sending a bullet along a trajectory that Vernon only a second earlier had stepped into. The bullet entered Vernon's back at an upward angle between the shoulder blades. The impact pitched his body forward, and he collapsed to his knees and then crumpled onto his side, his body jackknifed at the waist, his arms akimbo, as graceless as if he had been thrown from a speeding car. The bullet hole in the back of his cus-

217

tomary camouflage outfit was no bigger than a fingertip.

David and Balaam heard the second shot as they were getting out of David's car. "Over there," Balaam said, pointing toward the woods. Balaam began shouting as he walked: "Hey! . . . Hello? . . . Vernon? Hey!" In the pasture, along a fence, he saw Vernon's pickup. "Why don't you check over that way," Balaam said to David, pointing toward the woods. Balaam walked to Vernon's pickup and began honking that horn. David walked on.

David Wilson had never seen dead people except at hospitals and funeral homes. What he saw among the leafy green trees under a blue sky as birds sang seemed surreal. He felt dizzy and had to turn away and stare at the ground. He opened his mouth to call out to Balaam but had no voice. He began walking toward Vernon's pickup, where Balaam was still honking the horn.

Balaam stopped honking when David was seventy-five feet away. Balaam knew. David's face told him. Balaam had seen that face on a hundred men in Vietnam—men who had seen too much. The color-less face, the blank stare, as if they were unconsciously mimicking the dead faces they had seen.

Balaam ran past David into the woods, ran just to get it over with. By the time David caught up with him, Balaam was sitting cross legged with Stilts's head cradled in his lap, holding the slack jaw closed with one hand, rubbing the ears with his other hand.

To David Wilson the scene looked like a kind of strange *Pietà*.

"Can you help me carry him back home?" Balaam did not look up.

"Balaam," David said softly. "I don't think we'd better move anything." David was not sure that Balaam comprehended that there was a dead man lying less than ten feet away. Balaam had stepped over Vernon's body as if it were a fallen log.

"We've got to call the sheriff or someone, Balaam. And someone has to tell his wife."

"Who? . . . Oh . . . yeah." Balaam said, his voice on auto answer.

"I've got a cell phone in the car. I'll be right back." Of the four warm bodies at the scene, David was best qualified to take charge only by default. He felt profoundly unequipped to deal with the situation. He had never been at the scene of violent, sudden death, never seen so much blood, never had to notify or deal with medical and law enforcement personnel, never had to try to comfort someone in such circumstances.

David turned and began walking to his car. After a few steps, he looked back. Balaam sat with his back to the road, his head bent over Stilts's head, his shoulders heaving gently.

At his little red roadster, David dialed 911. He answered the questions he was asked as best he could, and gave the best directions he could. He then phoned Nanetta but told her only that he would be home late.

"Have y'all found Balaam's deer yet?"

"Not yet." David tried with great effort to make his voice sound normal.

When David walked back to the woods, Balaam was still sitting with his back to the road, still cross-legged with Stilts's head in his lap, his head still bent, his shoulders still heaving gently.

As David approached, he tried not to look at the body of Vernon. "I dialed 911," David said to Balaam's back. "They're sending out the sheriff or someone. And the paramedics. They'll look for my car at the road. They said they'd take care of telling his wife." David was very relieved to have avoided that task.

David tried to think of something to say. "As soon as I get the chance," he said to Balaam's back, "I think I'm going to have a good cry, too. I could tell you I know how much Stilts meant to you, but I don't. No one does. I had a dog when I was———." David realized he was babbling and shut up. His eyes felt irritated. Profoundly dry. He could not remember when he had last blinked. He walked between the two bodies and stood in front of Balaam.

Balaam lifted his head. David looked at his face. Balaam was laughing even as he cried.

"I know that I'll never know everything about how this happened." Balaam nodded toward Vernon's body. "It'll be called an 'accident.' And it was. I know that. But if you were to just walk up here and see this, it sure looks like this little guy decided to fight back and take that son of a bitch down with him. That's how I am going to think of this. One final game of headbutt." Balaam's left hand was wrapped around Stilts's ear. Balaam's breath caught as he inhaled. His nose and eyes were running. He looked down. "Fought him to a draw, didn't you, boy." Balaam began to cry again.

David sat down with his back against a tree trunk to the side of Balaam, facing away from Vernon's body. David didn't know how to "be there," but at the same time give Balaam some space.

"It's perfect, isn't it?" Balaam said, looking over at David. "Just perfect." Balaam had begun to cry-laugh again. "Do you reckon there just might be a God after all?"

"If there is," David Wilson thought, looking at the tableau around him, "he's fair to a fault."

❖35❖

*"David Wilson claims that my poor little bed-and-breakfast
was used as a criminal hideout. I don't know whether
to deny it or include it in my Yellow Pages ad."*

———Mary Lou Wyatt

Just after 10:00 A.M., Sheriff Sam Kirby arrived. A few minutes later, two paramedics arrived in a lights-laden van, but, of course, J. D. Vernon was beyond resuscitation. Kirby asked David and Balaam some questions.

"Has anything here been moved?"

"When did you hear the first shot? The second shot? How long after that did you reach the body? Where do y'all live?"

"You say the deer was your pet?"

Kirby then examined the scene, walking around, shaking his head now and then: the barrel of the rifle resting across the top of the tree stump, the butt of the rifle resting on the ground near the hind feet of the deer, the safety not engaged, the upward trajectory indicated by the low entry wound and high exit wound, the fact that two shots were heard by witnesses.

"Hunting accident, all right," Kirby said to no one in particular. "Ol' J. D. just plumb got careless."

The paramedics loaded Vernon's body into their van and left to take it to the morgue at the county hospital. Kirby then drove to the Vernon home to notify Mrs. Vernon. David and Balaam stayed behind with the body of Stilts.

David knew that Mrs. Vernon would need some support. He phoned Beverly Faulk and told her what had happened. Within an hour, three women who were not in church that morning drove out to be with Mrs. Vernon. Following custom and without consulting each other, each woman brought along a covered dish to sustain mourners who would gather at the Vernon home in the next few days.

All three women took potato salad.

After the women arrived, Kirby returned to Balaam and David, preferring a bloody accident scene to a distraught widow. He allowed David to drive Balaam back to his place to get Balaam's pickup. Balaam and David returned, backed up as close to the scene as they could, and carried Stilts's body on a tarp to the bed of the pickup.

After they returned to Balaam's compound, David tried to persuade Balaam to come back to Willoughby with him. "You don't want to be out here alone tonight."

Balaam declined. "I'll be okay. I'll bury him tomorrow. I could use some help then if you don't mind."

After David left, Balaam went into his tool shed, picked out a shovel, and walked into the woods.

The next morning, David Wilson made a bemusing discovery: While making a deposit for his mother at the bank, he found himself holding up the modest line of fellow customers by gabbing idly with the teller—something that he had detested in others when he had come to town less than six months earlier.

David then walked over to the post office. In line ahead of him were Mary Lou Wyatt and Jessie Pinkston. David found himself listening in as Mary Lou unburdened herself about her missing guest: "I haven't seen him since Saturday morning. He just disappeared without a 'goodbye,' a 'thank you,' or a 'kiss my foot,'" she said, punctuating "kiss my foot" with a sideways thrust of her hips on each word.

"He was nice enough, I guess, but he kept late hours. He came back one night with red paint on his forehead. I was afraid he was in some kind of cult, like one of those Hindus. Never even signed my guestbook—and he was my very first guest. All his personal items and his clothes are still in his room. Even that beautiful cowboy-tropical shirt. I'll tell you one thing: If that young man doesn't come back soon, that shirt is *mine*."

David's curiosity was piqued. He interrupted to ask Mary Lou on what night her guest had come back with red paint on his forehead. Neither woman was at all offended that David had obviously been eavesdropping.

"That was Wednesday night. I remember because it was the night Juanita went home and found that boat in their driveway and threw Richard out of the house. If you ask me, any man who would buy . . ."

David tuned out and began to think.

As David drove out to Balaam's, he stopped at Birdie Wagstaff's. When she opened her front door, he introduced himself as Nanetta Wilson's son and said he was sure sorry to hear that someone had vandalized her home—and mistakenly, at that. She asked him in and showed him where the damage had been done.

"What color was the paint that was used?"

"Red."

"Bingo!" David thought. "You know, Mrs. Wagstaff, just between you and me, I think the guy who did that was staying at Mary Lou Wyatt's bed-and-breakfast."

He then told Birdie what Mary Lou had told Jessie Pinkston.

He had just committed gossip.

The Willoughbyization of David Wilson was almost complete.

David then drove on to Balaam's. As he walked up the driveway, he looked away from the bed of Balaam's pickup, away from the tarp tucked around the sad shape beneath it.

Balaam's face was drawn; he seemed glad to see David. But David was disappointed that Balaam was not galvanized by his theory that the Wagstaff vandal had been staying at Mary Lou Wyatt's.

"I figured he was staying somewhere in town," Balaam said as they sat on the front porch. "He was on foot at Rudy's."

"You've seen him?"

"Oh, yeah. Mr. Ruiz and me have had two or three meetings, of a sort," Balaam said with a wry smile.

"You know his name? You've *met*?" David stared at Balaam.

Only the vandalism at Birdie Wagstaff's was common knowledge in Willoughby. Beyond that, Balaam had told no one what he knew or suspected about Ernie Ruiz. Balaam put his boots up on the wooden cable wheel and proceeded to tell David everything, including the latest update from Rudy Janacek—that Ruiz had borrowed a riding mower on Saturday afternoon and that Rudy had later found it abandoned on Highway 21 near Rusty's Bar F Tavern.

David was flabbergasted. How could such a small town hold so much intrigue? "You think Liggett is desperate enough to put someone up to that?" David tried to reconcile what Balaam had just told him with the VIP treatment they had received in Colorado.

"I imagine he'd call it 'determined,'" Balaam said.

"If you don't mind my asking, why were you so, well, gentle with this Ruiz guy?"

Again the wry smile. "I think sometimes you need to pick your fights."

Balaam stood. "Come on. Let's make a couple of phone calls." Balaam went into the cabin.

David followed. He had never been in the cabin before. It was small and simple but clean enough.

Balaam stretched the phone cord from the bedroom area to the couch and sat down. "Let's start with Mary Lou."

Mary Lou Wyatt was agitated when she answered her phone—Birdie Wagstaff had already phoned to tell her David's theory.

"No, Mary Lou, I don't think that makes you an accessory to a crime. Say, can you describe your guest for me? . . . Yeah . . . Yeah. Tell me this: Did he ever walk with a limp? . . . Was that Friday morning? . . . That's him, all right, Mary Lou. And you haven't seen him since Saturday morning?"

After Balaam hung up, David said, "Did you say 'limp'?"

"Yeah. After I pulled his plug wires, I guess he had to walk back to Mary Lou's. He was limping pretty bad the next day at Rudy's."

"What's he look like?"

"Just a kid. Twenty, not much older. Dark hair. Not tall, not short. Nice enough face."

David felt the small world of Willoughby shrinking by the minute.

"I gave him a fat lip," David announced with a touch of dramatics.

Now it was Balaam's turn to stare at David.

"Well, in a way." David then told Balaam of his experience in Rusty's Bar F Tavern on Saturday afternoon. He wrapped up with, "I wish I could tell you I flattened him on purpose, but it was just the domino effect: Surly ex-husband pushes cosmetics ad copywriter, who falls on millionaire's limping, bumbling henchman."

"Well, for whatever reason, he's been quiet ever since. Tell you what, let's make one more call."

Balaam took a card out of his wallet and dialed the number of Howard J. Liggett's flagship resort in Colorado.

"Aquavita Company. To your good health."

"Ernesto Ruiz, please."

"Sir, we have an *Ernie* Ruiz. Would you like me to transfer you?"

"Please."

"Massage. To your good health."

"Is Ernie Ruiz in?"

"Sir, he's with a client right now. Would you like to leave a message?"

"No. No message."

Balaam hung up and looked at David. "He's busy right now. So that tells us two things: Ruiz does work for Liggett, and he's back in Colorado." Balaam put the phone back on his nightstand.

"And you saw Ruiz at Rusty's, within two miles of here, on Saturday—the afternoon the gate was torn down. The gate was up when I left before noon and down when I got home after three. Now, I made C's in arithmetic, but two miles and four hours is proof enough for me."

"Based on what you've told me, I'd say so."

Balaam was silent for a minute. "He may not have meant the end result, but because of him, I have to do what I have to do right now." Balaam stood. "I can't put this off forever. I dug a hole yesterday. Right under the tree where I found him as a fawn. He was such a little guy. Trembly. Easy to carry home. He'll be a bit heavier to carry back. We'll have to walk."

It was a half-mile hike carrying a full-grown buck by the edges of a tarp. Balaam and David had to stop several times to rest.

Balaam didn't say much as they buried the deer. Stilts's cowbell had tinkled when they lowered the body into the grave. David had looked obliquely at Balaam's face but could not read it.

As they walked back to the cabin, Balaam said, "You remember that fancy virtual tour of the Waters at Willoughby that Liggett showed us? According to that, if I'd sold this place, that grave back there would become a parking lot."

As they sat on the porch and rested, both men were quiet for a while. Then Balaam said, "In the mornings, when the sun comes up over those trees over there, the light would shine through his ears and turn them just as pink as could be."

David didn't reply. After several moments, he said, "You know, people actually study grief. Psychologists say that grieving people go through five stages."

Balaam looked at his boots. There was still blood on them from sitting cross-legged on the ground holding Stilts's head. He stood, went back inside the cabin, and returned with two cans. He tossed one to David. Balaam sat down.

"I reckon I'm at the beer stage."

❧36❧

"When a fella says to you, 'That horse of yours is worthless.
Please let me buy him,' that fella is talking out both sides of the bridle."
———Harvey Burkett

By the time Ernie Ruiz reported to Howard J. Liggett in Colorado on Monday, he had had a lot of time to think about how he could put the best possible spin on his time spent in Texas. He had thought about it while riding up to Dallas in the cab of the big tractor-trailer truck, while waiting in the airport terminal, while flying back to Denver.

When Ruiz stood before Liggett in his office, it was a fairy-tale account that he told: He had vandalized the correct house, had painted "BALAAM GIMBLE GO AWAY" on the correct wall, had made some intimidating late-night phone calls, had set a couple of small fires in the Gimble compound.

Liggett listened, tapping the top of his desk with his fountain pen. "And do you think you scared him; do you think he will sell?"

"Hard to say, sir." Ruiz knew better than to make promises that that crazy old bastard would not keep.

Liggett looked hard at Ruiz. Ruiz walked with a slight limp, had a bruise on his forehead, ugly blisters on his arms, and a slightly swollen lip.

"You seem to be somewhat the worse for wear."

Ruiz did not want to tell Liggett that he had been worked over by a pair of tight cowboy boots, headbutted by a deer into a patch of poison oak, and knocked down in a fight between two other men.

"All in the line of duty, sir," Ruiz said, trying hard not to rake his fingernails down his itching arms.

"I see. I trust you kept a low profile and were discreet—no one knows who you were or where you're from?"

"I was the Invisible Man, sir."

"Very good. Welcome back. I hope your little campaign brings rewards to both of us."

But as Ruiz left the office, Liggett was not optimistic. In fact, just in case Ruiz's campaign proved to be unsuccessful, while Ruiz had been in Texas, Liggett had devised yet another angle of attack: When money, sex, and intimidation fail, fall back on the law.

For Balaam Gimble, the other Gucci was about to drop.

Liggett had commissioned a title search of Balaam's property and had learned that in the 1950s, Balaam's parents, always in need of money, had sold sixty percent of the mineral rights to their property to an oil speculator. They had retained the remaining forty percent. The sixty percent had since been inherited by a great-nephew of the speculator.

After Ruiz returned to his station in the massage department, Liggett phoned the great-nephew, Harvey Burkett, a native Texan who recently had been transferred to New Jersey.

"Mr. Burkett, I believe you own sixty percent of the mineral rights to a small property down in Texas—the old Henry Gimble property outside the town of Willoughby. The other forty percent is owned by the current landowner, a son named Balaam Gimble. Now, there is very little oil or gas production in that area these days, and, as you know, the cost of exploration is prohibitive, but for purely speculative reasons I am willing to make you a generous offer for your sixty percent of the mineral rights."

From the earpiece of his phone, Howard J. Liggett again heard that Texas drawl, which he was coming to find so very irritating.

"Ah'm listenin'."

❖37❖

"I hunted with J. D. lots of times. He was all man, let me tell you,
from his head down to his toes. Well, okay, damn it, down to his ankles."
——Big Un Petteway

On Monday morning, family members from out of town began to
arrive at the Vernon home. As did friends from Willoughby. As
Balaam puttered around his compound trying to stay occupied, he
could hear the cars as they passed by on the road. Many of the friends
from Willoughby brought offerings of food to sustain those gathered
during their time of bereavement. By noon, the counters in Marlene
Vernon's kitchen were stacked two covered dishes deep with fried
chicken, casseroles, meatloaf, rolls, pies, and more potato salad.

At 4:00 P.M., Marlene and Vernon's sister drove into Waco to arrange
for the funeral and burial. Vernon had been born in Waco, still had
family there, would be buried there. When Marlene returned home late
that night, she found an ice chest that had been left on her front porch.
Taped to the lid of the chest was a sympathy card. Inside the chest were
two more Tupperware containers of potato salad.

Twenty miles away, medical examiner Dr. Theo Cantwell and his assistant returned from lunch at 1:00 P.M. and walked into the small morgue
housed in the basement of the county hospital. The next body on their
schedule was J. D. Vernon's. Prior to conducting the medical examina-

tion, they removed the hunting boots and hunting socks from Vernon's body. As they did so, they looked at each other with some surprise. When they removed the camouflage trousers, they again looked at each other with surprise. Because the details they observed had no bearing on the cause of death, the details were noted in Cantwell's handwritten personal notes as "irregularities observed in deceased" but not entered in his official report.

But as Cantwell conducted his examination of the body, he idly wondered if Vernon had applied the nail polish to his toes before or after he had put on his camouflage outfit. Cantwell also wondered how a man as large as Vernon had found women's silk bikini panties in his size.

The rest of the examination was routine: The sheriff's report and an examination of the body clearly indicated death caused by massive internal trauma from a high-powered bullet fired at close range. Cantwell ruled J. D. Vernon's death an accident.

At 3:00 P.M., Vernon's body was taken to a funeral home in Waco to be prepared for viewing the next day.

By 5:00 P.M., word of those "irregularities" leaked to a reporter for the county weekly newspaper, who leaked word to Rosalee Taft of the *Willoughby Bee*. From Rosalee, word spread, off the record, as quickly as if she had made it her banner story: J. D. Vernon—the quintessential man's man—had died with more than his boots on.

As word spread across town, reaction varied. At the Crossroads Cafe, if waitress Brandi Renee had been interested enough to listen, she would have heard, as she wobbled from table to table, booth to booth, that among men the reaction ranged from "That's a damned lie" to "I think I'm going to be sick." Among women, there was less shock. "Men lead secret lives," Juanita Greer said with a shrug. "You never really know what they're thinking. Personally, I consider that one of life's greatest blessings."

David Wilson, as an outsider less affected by Vernon's death, wondered what shade of nail polish Vernon had been wearing.

David said to his mother as they sat in her parlor, "I'd say, with his complexion, Petal Pink."

When Balaam Gimble heard the rumor, he laid out the suit that David had lent him for the trip to Colorado and then opened his little county phone book and called selected residents of Willoughby.

The first three hung up on him.

The fourth threatened to "call the law."

The fifth, Beverly Faulk, understanding what Balaam was going through, said, "Well, Balaam . . . I guess so. When do you want it?"

"Wednesday morning."

"Okay. I'll have it at the store. In a sack."

After Balaam thanked her and hung up, Beverly wrinkled her brow and said to herself, "Don't men mourn in the strangest ways?"

❧38❧

"It was the first time I ever conducted a funeral and felt the need for a Kevlar pulpit."
——Reverend Thomas Finch

On Wednesday morning about eleven o'clock, Balaam Gimble put on David's suit and tie. As he inspected the tie, wondering if a brown spot was a stain or part of the pattern, he realized that that was the second time in only a month that he had worn a suit. Before that, he had gone probably five years without having to get "all duded up." Then he phoned David Wilson.

"You said I should get away from here for a while. I'm ready now. Wanna go with me?"

"Well, sure. I guess. Where are we going? How long will we be gone? Do I need to bring anything?" Spontaneity was not David Wilson's strongest trait.

"Just up the road a piece. Be gone about three hours. I'll pick you up at noon. You dress purty now, okay?"

At 11:30, Balaam passed his vegetable garden as he walked to his pickup. The leaves of his plants were wilted in the heat—"limp as wash rags." He bent and spoke to them. "I know it's hot, y'all. But hang in there. Fall's coming."

Balaam counted four cars parked near the cave as he passed. In town, he stopped at Beverly Faulk's antiques store. When Beverly saw

Balaam enter, she walked behind her check-out counter, reached down to a shelf under the cash register, and handed him a brown paper sack.

"Here you go."

"Thanks, Beverly."

As Balaam walked out her door, Beverly asked herself two questions. The second question was, "Why is he wearing a suit?"

Balaam drove on to Nanetta's. David opened the front door and saw Balaam wearing David's suit. "We're not going back to Colorado, are we?"

"Gonna take a little spin up to Waco."

David was mildly stunned. "You're going to attend Vernon's funeral?"

"Just the burial. The fun starts at 1:30."

David didn't like the sound of that second sentence. He was apprehensive about accompanying Balaam to the burial of a man who was at the top of Balaam's enemies list. Would Balaam make a scene? But David decided to give Balaam the benefit of the doubt—he was a friend in need, and the experience might be therapeutic for him, provide some kind of closure.

Balaam's pickup was not air conditioned, and David was sweating well before they reached the interstate highway. David removed his coat, loosened his tie, and watched I-35 pass by below through the holes rusted in the floorboard.

Vernon was to be buried in the cemetery's Beautiful Dreamer section. Balaam turned into the gated entry and followed the signs past row after row of tombstones. He pulled over on a narrow asphalt lane behind a line of parked vehicles. Among them were several Broncos and Explorers and other rugged vehicles. These belonged to men who had hunted with Vernon—men from Willoughby, from elsewhere in the state, and even from out of state.

Balaam and David walked across the lane to a portable canvas canopy. At the front of the canopy was a closed bronze casket suspended over an open grave that was framed by Astroturf. Beneath the canopy were two dozen or so people, some standing, some sitting on a few rows of metal folding chairs. On the front row sat members of the Vernon family. Marlene was the only one whom Balaam recognized.

Balaam and David were a few minutes early. David anchored himself just inside the edge of the canopy near the back and kept an eye on Balaam. Balaam just milled around looking suitably somber. He greeted a few residents of Willoughby, all of whom were surprised to see him in attendance.

Balaam overheard the woeful exchanges between small groups of men he did not know.

"The NRA has lost a good friend," he overheard one man say.

"J. D. was never too busy, too tired, too sick, or too drunk to shoot something. He'll be missed," he overheard a second man say.

Balaam overheard no reference, however oblique, to the medical examiner's revelation of the previous day.

Just before the burial service began, Balaam returned to where David was standing. "I overheard someone who was at the funeral. Vernon is being buried wearing a camouflage outfit. What a surprise. And in the casket beside him is his favorite deer rifle. I hope the safety is on. If that son of a bitch gets shot again, he might come back to life."

In spite of the setting, David had to tighten his stomach muscles to keep from laughing.

The Reverend Finch of Willoughby's Baptist church delivered a short eulogy. David listened and felt a bead of sweat trickling down his back. Balaam listened and tried to reconcile what he heard with the man he had lived near for years. As Finch intoned, Balaam heard a mockingbird singing somewhere. He could hear traffic on the interstate. A faint breeze rippled the scalloped fringe of the canopy.

After the Reverend Finch closed the service with an "amen," everyone stood. David and Balaam watched as Vernon's fellow hunters began to respectfully file by the casket over the open grave. David was surprised when Balaam said, "Come on."

Balaam led David to the back of the line of men filing past the grave. Some, as they paused at the casket, tossed spent shotgun shells or bullet casings into the grave. Another dropped a duck call; another, a hunting license; a third, a bottle of deer-attracting scent. One mourner dropped in a compass to guide Vernon to the Great Hunting Lease Beyond.

Balaam was closely observing this ritual. He whispered to David, "That compass doesn't need but one direction on it—south."

Balaam made sure that he and David were always at the back of the line. When other men joined the line after them, Balaam moved himself and David to the back of the line. Balaam also kept David in line ahead of him, so that Balaam was always the last person in line. When David's turn came, he quickly moved on past the casket. Balaam was now a line of one. When he reached the center of the grave, he turned facing the casket and paused respectfully, his head bowed. No one, including David, saw Beverly Faulk's black lace brassiere drop from the inside pocket of the borrowed suit coat and fall into the grave.

On the drive back to Willoughby, David said, "Balaam, I'll be honest with you. I was afraid you might do something back there at the cemetery. You know, 'act ugly,' as Mother would say."

"David," Balaam said, sounding stung by the mere suggestion. "A man has died. That's no time to cut didoes."

David looked closely at Balaam's face. It was inscrutable. Balaam kept his eyes on the road and began to softly sing a hymn that he had learned as a child:

> O, some-times the shad-ows are deep,
> And rough seems the path to the goal.

Balaam dropped David off at Nanetta's, declined an invitation to come in, and drove toward home. On his county road, he stopped and walked across a familiar field to one of J. D. Vernon's deer feeders. It was the deer feeder closest to the deer blind that Ernie Ruiz had hidden in one very long week earlier. As Balaam stood there in the late afternoon sun, he began to sing softly again:

> And sor-rows, some-times how they sweep
> Like tem-pests down o-ver the soul.

Then Balaam unbuttoned his fly and urinated at the base of the feeder. "Stilts," Balaam Gimble said softly, "the good work will go on."

❧39❧

*"When Mr. Liggett asked to see Ernie 'on the double,'
he was not using the 'To your good health' tone of voice."*
——Mrs. Inez Loomis

Balaam had just taken off David's suit and draped the coat and pants over a hanger when his phone rang. He picked up the phone as he hung the hanger on a nail on the wall. He knew that voice by now. Before Howard J. Liggett could finish his wooden "How are you today?" Balaam "lit into him."

"Well, well. I just watched 'em bury one son of a bitch, and now here's the other one. Now you listen, you———."

"Mr. Gim———." Liggett tried to interrupt, but like a ship under steam, Balaam had momentum that could not be stopped quickly. The *S.S. Gimble* sailed on.

"I'll never be able to prove it, and you'll never admit it, but that little pissant of yours—and I know his name, it's Ernie Ruiz, and I know he works for you, and I know what he looks like, and I know where he was staying, and I know what he was driving, it was a GMC pickup, and I've got the license number *and* the spark plug wires—was around here causing trouble last week." Balaam was pacing the floor in his boxer shorts. "He vandalized an old woman's house, thinking it was mine and trying to scare me into selling, I guess. And then he tore down my gate. Well, because of him my pet deer is dead and so is a man. The man wasn't worth much, in my opinion, but that deer was worth ten of Ernie Ruiz and fifteen of J. D. Vernon and twenty of *you*."

Balaam hung up and sat down, shaking.

Liggett listened with displeasure, even slight alarm, to these revelations. He knew that he would have to conduct a more detailed debriefing of Ernie Ruiz. At that point, a man with less audacity than Liggett would not have pressed his advantage—he would have been glad to have the chance to back off, cut his losses, and avoid further provoking someone who could bring, at best, bad publicity and questions from law enforcement. But as Liggett's old poker buddy had told David Wilson weeks earlier, Howard J. Liggett was not afraid to draw to an inside straight.

Liggett redialed, knowing he had to get Balaam Gimble's attention before he hung up again.

"Hello, partner."

Balaam did not hang up. He just held the receiver to his ear, his heart still pounding.

"First, Mr. Gimble, let me assure you that I know nothing about the allegations you make. There surely is some mistake. But let me say how sorry I am to hear about the loss of your pet."

Balaam disregarded Liggett's predictable response; Balaam was waiting—with trepidation—to hear more about "partner."

"But I do have some good news for you. You and I are going to be partners. In a way, at least. 'Partners' in the sense that we both could make a lot of money from your property, and you won't have to sell a single acre. You won't have to move one inch. In fact, you won't have to do a thing, won't have to spend a dime. I'll spend all the money, take all the risk, and, if we get lucky, you just cash your royalty checks. I have recently acquired the outstanding sixty percent of the mineral rights to your——."

As soon as Balaam heard the words "mineral rights," he felt the same panic, the same sinking feeling in his gut that he had felt when he had come home and had seen his gate dangling. Balaam knew that Liggett had won. Killed his pet *and* taken his land. Why, Balaam asked himself, hadn't he just sold his land before everything got so crazy? Why had he thought he could hold out against power and money?

Liggett continued to talk, but Balaam heard only fragments: "When we toured your property, my people did some 'additional testing.' They advise me that there is an acceptable likelihood of oil, with that area's history of production. I intend very soon to hire an exploration company to explore for oil and gas on your property. The company I have in mind is very experienced. They will be as considerate as they can of you and the environment. And they tell me that residents adjust to the sound of the drilling and pumping and the presence of exploration crews . . . eventually."

Balaam felt naive for not having seen this coming. Liggett was right, of course: Oil and gas were produced in the area. In fact, a well was in production just over two miles from Balaam's cabin. He could hear the pump sometimes—more than two miles away!—"like some god-damned flub-dubbing iron heart that never stopped." Balaam had seen rural land like his that had been subjected to oil exploration and drilling and production. It was rendered uninhabitable to any man with a majority of his five senses intact: crews of roughnecks mowing down trees, constructing roads, erecting derricks, drilling wells, installing pumps and pipelines. Balaam realized that Liggett had, in effect, given him a choice: (1) sell his land to Liggett for the resort or (2) keep the land and watch Liggett rend it into Balaam's personal vision of hell.

Liggett, Balaam knew, was taking advantage of the duality of property ownership: Ownership of surface rights to a property and ownership of mineral rights below the surface of that same property are separate. Balaam owned the surface rights and forty percent of the mineral rights. Now Liggett had told Balaam that he had bought the remaining sixty percent. Balaam knew that Liggett could explore for oil and gas, and Balaam as landowner would have no legal right to stop him. Liggett did not even need to acquire the majority percentage of the mineral rights to be able to come onto Balaam's land and drill. He could have acquired just one percent, but, of course, he would then have received only one percent of any royalties after footing one hundred percent of the cost of exploring, drilling, and producing. With a sixty-forty split, Liggett would have to give Balaam forty cents of every dollar of profit.

As Balaam stood there, he realized that he was pressing the receiver against his ear so hard that it hurt. He refocused his attention; Liggett was still talking: "Despite my acquisition of the outstanding mineral rights, my offer to buy your land outright for my resort still stands. So, you see, we both have more options than ever before. However, due to the extra expense of acquiring the mineral rights, I must now revert to my original offer for your two hundred acres: two hundred thousand dollars."

Liggett paused for a two-tap count of his Montblanc fountain pen on his desk top. For a moment, as his lips pressed together tightly, his mouth resembled a scar.

"I'll let you think about your options."

Balaam did not reply. Dazed, he placed the receiver on the cradle and sat down, his body slumped and heavy and inert, like a tow sack of grain. In Vietnam, Balaam had served in a demolition squad. He had seen men—men he knew, men he liked—blown to bits and had vomited, he had been so afraid for his own life that he had sweated, had felt the hair rise on his neck, had peed in his pants, but he had never cried, not once.

As Balaam sat there in his boxer shorts and socks, Howard J. Liggett for the second time in a week was able to accomplish what the North Vietnamese had never been able to accomplish in twelve months.

❧ 40 ❧

"That's the dirtiest dirty trick of all—resorting to something perfectly legal."
———David Wilson

"He can't do that!" David Wilson said, staring at Balaam as they sat on Balaam's front porch late the next afternoon.

"Sure he can," Balaam said with bitter matter-of-factness that bordered on resignation. "Happens all the time. Some folks get it even worse: They own a piece of land but don't own any of the mineral rights and wake up one morning to find an oil well in their yard pumping money into someone else's pocket."

"But he can't be allowed to get away with this." David was outraged. "He broke the law. At least he put someone up to breaking the law. Look at all that has happened because of him. I mean, in a way you can trace Stilts's death—and J. D. Vernon's, of course—to Liggett."

"Sure I can. But I can't prove it. Wouldn't undo anything if I could."

Balaam listened to a chickadee scolding in a nearby tree.

Of course, David also felt guilty, felt responsible for helping to set in motion a chain of events that had led to such catastrophes. Never mind that David's intervention had also led to a nice supplement to Balaam's income. "Sometimes I think of how different things would be if I'd gotten a busy signal back when I first called Liggett to ask if he'd be interested. You know far better than I do how different things would be right now."

Balaam thought a moment. "Well, if you want to look at it that way, if I'd just left my shovel stuck in that limestone instead of pounding away at it with a rock bar back in April, you wouldn't be living in Willoughby with a mother with a broken hip and getting knocked down by ex-husbands and bitten on the butt by wild hogs."

David and Balaam looked at each other, pointed a finger, and said, with timing that was only about one syllable out of unison, "This is all *your* fault!"

Both men laughed more than they had in days.

"Upper thigh," David corrected.

Balaam didn't respond. The moment had passed. Balaam lapsed into silence.

"You've had one hell of a week," David said quietly, looking out across the compound.

"I don't even recognize my own life anymore. I can't control what happens in it."

Balaam tossed a few kernels of dried corn to a squirrel who had approached within ten feet.

"I've got two choices, one about as bad as the other. I can sell out and leave, or I can sit tight and watch this place be occupied by an army of roughnecks and machinery making enough racket to rattle your teeth. Either way the place gets torn up. And I can tell you this much for sure: They would *not* start exploring away off on the other side of the property. No, they'd be up as close to my house as they could get."

"Can he take the mineral water?"

"Not a drop. Groundwater isn't considered a mineral asset like oil and gas. So he has to drill for oil to get me to sell so he can get at the water, which is what he wanted in the first place."

"Couldn't you just wait him out, let them explore until he gives up and goes away? And if they *did* find oil, you'd get forty percent of the profits."

"Some people would do that. Maybe a lot of people would. They'd say, 'Sure, come on in here, you bastard, and I'll put up with it until you strike oil and make me rich, and then I'll move up to Colorado right next door to you and raise goats in my front yard.'"

Balaam tossed more corn toward the squirrel, who had inched forward and was looking at him.

"But I'm all give out. I want it to be over. Besides, how much profit are we talking about? Might be a lot, might not. People hear 'oil well' and think millions of dollars. You don't hear about all the wells that don't pay a dime."

"Isn't exploring for oil awfully expensive?"

"To you or me? Unbelievably. But you know what kind of money he's got. Look at all the money he's tried to throw at me. Now he's spent the money to buy up the rest of the mineral rights, and he'd spend even more money to drill just to get me to sell out. And it's more than that now, I reckon." In his cupped hand, Balaam shook a few kernels of corn like dice. "Liggett's not used to people saying 'no' to him and his money. He's used to winning, to getting his own way. I think after all this rigamarole he just wants to beat me."

Balaam looked over at the hubcap that had been Stilts's dinner plate. Above the treetops, clouds clabbered in the western sky.

"And I wish I coulda beat *him*."

❧41❧

"Balaam never even showed up today. If I can't get my rooms finished, how can I get a criminal of my own?"
———Lilian Kreuter

When Balaam's phone rang four days later, he just listened to the first six rings, his mind made up not to answer. It seemed to him that no good came from answering the phone. But after nine rings, Balaam gave in and picked up the receiver, albeit with apprehension. He was relieved to hear a woman's voice.

"Balaam, this is Lilian. I need you to hurry and finish my two little rooms. I've *got* to get this house ready to open. Yesterday I had to turn away a couple from Amarillo. They wanted to use my bed-and-breakfast as a base to explore estate sales in central Texas. You know, so many old folks die in the August heat. *Four* nights they wanted to stay! But they went to Mary Lou's instead. She put them in the room where that young man from Colorado stayed. She has starting calling it the 'Outlaw Suite.' Well, la-ti-da!"

Balaam rolled his eyes.

"Now, Balaam, Juanita has let Richard move back in, so his room here is empty. Can you come over today and do some work? The sooner I get the Maison Willoughby open for business—that's the name I've decided on, unless I go with 'Casa Willoughby'; I'm still praying about it—the sooner I can get a guest who is colorful or shady or maybe even sinister, in a polite sort of way. Balaam," Lilian was almost whining now, "I want an Outlaw Suite, too!"

Balaam told Lilian that he'd "be along directly." He loaded his pickup and left before noon, counting five cars parked along the road near the cave as he passed. The day before, Earline Perry had brought him a hundred and eighty-seven dollars in receipts from the cave for the previous week.

In town, Balaam stopped at the flashing red light and then drove straight rather than turn to go to Lilian's. Six miles on the other side of town, he turned onto a county road and drove another three miles. He stopped when he saw a sign advertising "FOR SALE 200+ AC" posted at a culvert. It was the old Adams place. Balaam had driven along that road before, knew roughly the layout and nature of the acreage and house but, of course, had never looked at them as a potential home. The land was mostly flat and open—farmland with few trees except along fence lines. The wood-framed house was small and old but, Balaam felt, would do for his needs. But the house was only three hundred feet off the road and in plain sight of anyone driving by. Balaam knew that he would feel that he had to put on pants just to work in his garden.

Balaam turned his pickup around in the dirt driveway next to the sign and drove back into town.

At the flashing red light, he turned right toward the bank, intending to perform a new ritual—make a small deposit—and an old ritual—stand for a moment on his grandfather's horse's two shoes embedded in the sidewalk. But while Balaam was still at the intersection, he heard a jackhammer. Jackhammers were not part of the normal soundscape of Willoughby. When Balaam neared his usual parking space in front of the bank, he found two pickups parked across it, their tailgates angled toward the front of the bank. Two men were removing the sidewalk— one man breaking it up with a jackhammer; the other man lugging the jagged chunks of concrete to the beds of the two pickups. Balaam took the next parking space he could find and walked back to the bank. The first thing that he noticed was that the section of sidewalk containing the two horseshoes had already been broken up and removed and replaced by a temporary boardwalk. The second thing that he noticed was that the bench that members of the Boys usually sat on in front of the bank was gone. Balaam looked down the block and saw the bench in front of City Hall. On it sat Big Un Petteway, Willis Pinkston, and Charley Griggs. Balaam walked down to them. The volume of the jackhammer was only slightly diminished where they sat. Conversation was futile, so when Balaam approached, Big Un, Willis, and Charley just waved to him and began mimicking—Balaam suspected that they had been practicing on passersby—the poses of the "see no evil-hear no evil-speak no evil" monkeys.

When the jackhammer operator shut down briefly to help the other man carry an especially heavy chunk of concrete to the pickups, Balaam had a chance to find out what was going on.

"We've been evicted, Balaam," Speak No Evil Big Un said with a rueful laugh. "Cast out of Eden. They're sprucing up the bank. Gonna get a new sidewalk. New awning. Even gonna add an A-T-*Em* machine. Big doin's."

Balaam excused himself and walked away before they could ask him "if it's true what we heard." He assumed that word of Liggett's mineral rights checkmate had already gotten around town. Maybe Liggett had told Mayor Perry. Maybe David had told Nanetta or Beverly, and thus word had spread. It didn't matter. Judging from the "sprucing up" under way, bank president D. B. Baxter felt certain that Willoughby was going to receive a shot in the arm—a shot of oil or a shot of mineral water. Either way, it meant more business for the bank. And it meant that D. B. Baxter was going to get his dreamed-of ATM.

Balaam left the Boys east of Eden and walked back to the two pickups that contained the sidewalk rubble. He turned over several chunks of concrete in the pickup beds before he found the horseshoes, now split apart in two separate chunks. Balaam stood there looking at the horseshoes a moment. They had been undisturbed almost eighty years. They had been there all his life and most of his parents' life. They had been there when businesses up and down the street had come and gone. The sidewalk that held them had become cracked and uneven, but the shoes had endured.

"Nope," Balaam said. He made up his mind. Balaam would not have used the same words, but an incubus had been lifted from his chest.

The jackhammer restarted as Balaam got back into his pickup.

Rather than drive on to Lilian Kreuter's, he drove back home, not stopping even to pay his respects at one of the late J. D. Vernon's deer feeders. In his cabin, Balaam took a business card from his wallet, sat down by his phone, and dialed.

After his call had been transferred, in a controlled, even voice, Balaam spoke into the mouthpiece. "I've reconsidered your offer. I'll sell."

"Fine, Mr. Gimble, fine. Excellent. You've made the right decision." Then Howard J. Liggett's voice became less cordial, more businesslike. "You do recall that my latest offer was my original offer: two hundred thousand dollars for the entire two hundred acres?"

"I understand that."

"Fine."

"There's just one thing I'd like to ask," Balaam said.

"Certainly," Liggett said warily, his jubilation suddenly on hold.

"That resort of yours is going to be a mighty big deal to everyone around here. It would mean a lot to our mayor and our town if we could mark the event by holding a little ceremony down here when we sign the papers."

Liggett, feeling both relieved and magnanimous in his crushing victory, said, "I think we can arrange that. The Waters at Willoughby will certainly be the jewel in Willoughby's crown. Where should we have our little ceremony?"

"I was thinking that Town Hall would be good. It holds a lot of people and would be indoors out of the heat."

"Town Hall it is, then. And as to a date?"

"How about noon two weeks from today?"

Liggett looked at his calendar and pretended to check for open dates. No prior commitment would interfere with this appointment. "I think I can get the legal work expedited. Today is the seventh. Two weeks would be the twenty-first at noon."

"September 21 at noon," Balaam repeated, writing down the date and time.

"Very good, Mr. Gimble. Someone from my staff will contact you in a day or two to go over some details." Liggett was cordial again. "And I'll see you in Willoughby in two weeks."

To which Balaam replied, with equal cordiality, "Okey dokey."

As Liggett hung up the phone, he was confident that at last it was all over. The land—with its mineral spring—was his. And at the low-ball price. Ernie Ruiz's blundering had not cost him anything. Balaam Gimble was a beaten man. Still, a tiny worm of uncertainty squirmed in Howard J. Liggett's mind: Do beaten men—even Texans—he asked himself, use the words "okey dokey"?

❖42❖

"Imagine not only red, but also yellow and green!
It would be like having a rainbow for a traffic cop."
——Earl Perry

After Howard J. Liggett buzzed Mrs. Loomis and told her that he'd need the "little jet" in two weeks—early on the twenty-first—he phoned Mayor Perry to tell him that Balaam had finally agreed to sell his property and that Balaam had even asked that the initial papers be signed at a "little ceremony" in Willoughby. Perry was too elated by the first revelation to be surprised by the second. Balaam Gimble had at last come to his senses and was no longer standing between Willoughby and prosperity!

Perry immediately phoned Balaam to thank him "on behalf of the town of Willoughby." Balaam was not very talkative, saying only, "Earl, I'm just plumb give out. I asked Liggett to come down to sign the papers. Why don't you get the details from him." Later that day, Balaam had essentially the same message for Rosalee Taft when she phoned him for an interview. Rosalee and Anita were suddenly faced with publishing an issue of the *Bee* that would have coverage of *two* major events. The event that would symbolize Willoughby's future would be held on the twenty-first. That would coincide nicely—if busily—with the event that would symbolize Willoughby's past: The annual Founders Day parade was held each September on the seventeenth to commemorate the town's beginnings and its history.

During the two weeks after September 7, almost everything that the people of Willoughby would say and do would center around those two events.

Most people in and around Willoughby were excited about the town's new prosperity, although, in truth, at least two, from their professional perspectives, foresaw other ramifications. To part-time Police Chief William "Trot" Lyons, the new resort would mean more people, and more people would mean more crime. To the Reverend Thomas Finch of the Baptist church, more people would mean more sin. But, both men reasoned, keeping a happy thought, crime and sin are going to happen anyway, so they might as well happen in Willoughby, where the two men could keep an eye on them.

And a few other residents who had no direct economic stake "bitched and moaned" that Willoughby "just isn't the same anymore." For example, those locals who two months earlier had been able to have a soak in Balaam's Cave in privacy now often had to wait their turn or share the cave with "folks from Oklahoma and Arkansas and other places up north."

On the morning of September 8, Willis Pinkston sat with Big Un Petteway and Joe Adair on their bench-in-exile down the block from the bank, where the new sidewalk had still not been poured. Willis still went out to the cave regularly to soak his feet. "You know," Willis said, swatting at a fly, "I went out to the cave yesterday, and there were two people already in there, a man and a woman, just had their pants rolled up, sitting on the edge with their feet in the water. Well, I didn't know those people from Adam. Never seen them before. So I just turned around and came back home. A man reaches a certain age when he doesn't want to soak his feet in the company of strangers. He wants to be around feet he knows, feet he has grown up with, feet he goes to church with."

"You got that right," Joe said. "Before all this rigamarole about mineral water and resorts started, I never had to wait to get a booth at the cafe. I never had to wait in line at Little Un's to get gas. I used to know every face in town. I don't no more."

Conversely, new faces in town were as welcome as little faces of Washington and Lincoln and Hamilton to those residents who cheered

Willoughby's new prosperity, chief among them being, of course, Mayor Perry. He awoke that morning feeling that a heavy yoke of angst had been lifted from his neck. His town, already the newly self-anointed Hot-Dam Mineral Water Capital of Texas, would soon—perhaps eighteen months, Liggett had told him—be able to boast of the Waters at Willoughby. And Liggett had assured him that merchants would still be allowed to buy the water from the resort at a discount to sell. "The Waters at Willoughby." Perry was smitten with the name. He had already begun to say the words: "The Waters at Willoughby," experimenting with diction and emphasis. "The *Wa*-ters at Will-ough-by. The Wa-ters at *Will*-ough-by."

"Yes, that's it," he decided early on: emphasis on the *Will*. "Welcome to *Will*oughby, y'all, home of the Waters at *Will*oughby," he enunciated with a sweeping gesture of his arm and a bow of his head, welcoming an imaginary group of well-dressed clientele.

Two days later, on the tenth of the month, Cliff Gholson cashed in on his own personal adventure in capitalism. Bidding between Mary Lou Wyatt and Lilian Kreuter for Cliff's coveted claw-foot bathtub had continued to climb beyond the limits set by good judgment. Cliff knew that Beverly Faulk had already sold one claw-foot tub each to Mary Lou and Lilian—and at a much lower price. Cliff began to fear that Beverly would locate another tub at a lower price and that his two-bidder auction would "go to smash." So Cliff decided to take the sure money. When he stopped the bidding, Mary Lou had the high bid of four hundred and twenty-five dollars. She had won.

"Mary Lou has won. Again," Lilian said on the phone to Charlene Briley, wife of Ray Dean. Lilian was desolate as she recited her litany of woe: Mary Lou had taken the best name for a bed-and-breakfast, she had opened hers first, she had snagged the first customer (and a customer who was a suspected criminal, at that), and now she had won the claw-foot tub.

Charlene listened patiently, occasionally clucking a "tsk-tsk-tsk" or saying, "You're being tested, girl."

"And what's worse, Charlene, I can't get Balaam to do anything. He's just stopped coming in to work on my rooms. When I phone him, half the time he doesn't answer. When he does answer, he has some excuse. I'll never get my poor little bed-and-breakfast open."

"You're being tested, Lilian, I tell you that's what it is."

As Lilian mourned for her unfinished bed-and-breakfast, a few blocks away Rudy Janacek had saddled up his mouse and was conducting his daily roundup of cyberflesh. Like other merchants, Rudy Janacek was getting more business because of Willoughby's modest boom: Now and then a tourist needed a flat tire fixed or bought a quart of oil, and those in town who directly profited from Willoughby's upturn were more willing than they otherwise would have been to have auto repairs done. But Rudy's increase in business did not mean an increase in profit for him because a repair job that once took him an hour nowadays took him ninety minutes because of the time he devoted to surfing the Internet. He had yet to use his new computer for the avowed purposes of bookkeeping and inventory. In fact, that morning Rudy had just discovered Web sites featuring images of young women posing with motorcycles: standing beside motorcycles, caressing motorcycles, but mostly sitting astraddle motorcycles. All that skin, all that horsepower awakened in Rudy Janacek something that was primitive and powerful and smelled faintly of perfume and engine sludge. Such images were a happy marriage of his two loves in life: gas engines and naked women. And such images caused Rudy to remember an ancient Triumph motorcycle that had been sitting on his side lot for years, unclaimed by the owner after a minor repair. Never mind that it would no longer start or pass inspection and that the gas tank was rusted and tires were rotted. Rudy put down his mouse and went outside to the Triumph. He pulled the Johnson grass from between the wheel spokes and swept away the cobwebs and wasp nests. Then he hosed down the motorcycle. Suddenly, in the sunshine, the paint regained some of its gloss, the chrome again shined. Then he rubbed the leather seat with a lanolin hand lotion. It regained some of its suppleness.

That evening after work, Rudy rolled the motorcycle up a two-by-eight plank onto the bed of his pickup and hauled it home. He offloaded the motorcycle, rolled it into his garage, and turned on the overhead light. Rudy Janacek looked at the big Triumph. His nostrils flared.

That night, Rudy and his wife, Donna Jean, had a conversation that began in bed with Rudy asking, casually, "Do we still have that old Polaroid camera your mother gave us one Christmas?" The conversation ended several minutes later in the garage with Donna Jean asking, less casually, "Well, okay. . . . But won't I stick to the leather?"

The following day, four days after Balaam and Liggett had "set the date," anyone watching the intersection at the flashing red light just before 10:00 A.M. would have seen a white Lexus pause and then proceed quietly, smoothly—like a prairie breeze with cruise control—to Willoughby's downtown area. Anyone watching Willoughby's downtown area—as Joe Adair, Big Un Petteway, and Willis Pinkston happened to be—would have seen the driver hitch the Lexus to the curb in front of City Hall and step out onto the asphalt of the street, still soft even in mid-September.

"Stranger in town," Big Un said on their bench, expressing the conclusion of all three men as they watched the middle-aged woman adjust her tailored suit and walk purposefully into City Hall. Of course, strangers were not all that unusual in Willoughby since it had become the Hot-Dam Mineral Water Capital of Texas. But Joe, Big Un, and Willis could tell that this stranger was different. "This one," Big Un said, "isn't in town for the water. Nosiree."

The stranger stayed in City Hall a few minutes and then walked to the bank, where she again stayed a few minutes. Then she walked to the Crossroads Cafe, where she stayed more than an hour. Mostly she just sat in a booth and stirred her tea and listened, overhearing conversations, although she introduced herself to a person now and then when the moment seemed right. As she left the cafe, she handed her business card to Juanita at the cash register. "I hear that this town might be needing my services."

Juanita looked at the card:

> Judy Ann Giles
> Real estate agent
> Waco, Texas

Below those lines was this line in italics:

> *Because they just ain't makin' any more land, Hon*

255

Little Un Petteway had begun looking in the Waco phone book for a real estate agent as soon as he had heard that the fancy resort was going to be built after all. He owned a couple of vacant lots next to his gas station and realized that they might suddenly have some value with the expected influx of people to first build and then staff the resort. Judy Ann Giles had been the first agent to return his call.

By the time she drove back to Waco at the end of the day, Judy Ann Giles had listed for sale not only Little Un's two lots, but also two other lots and a house. And she was not done.

That same day, Cliff Gholson drove out to Balaam's Cave to fetch the prized claw-foot bathtub and deliver it to Mary Lou. He drove up to Balaam's compound to ask Balaam to help him load the tub, but Balaam's pickup was not in the driveway. Cliff turned around and drove down to the cave. The tub was unoccupied, so he drained the mineral water out of it, and he and Earline manhandled it into the bed of his pickup.

"I guess the cave will be shutting down soon anyway, now that Mr. Liggett is going to buy this place," Earline said.

In town, Cliff and Mary Lou's husband, Paul, slid the tub out of the bed of Cliff's pickup onto the Wyatts' driveway and prepared to lug it into the house.

"Just set it there beside the driveway for the time being, y'all," Mary Lou said.

Paul set down his end of the tub, straightened, and looked at her. "You think guests are going to take a bath in the front yard?" he asked.

"Just never you mind," Mary Lou said. She then handed Cliff a check for four hundred and twenty-five dollars.

The following morning, Judy Ann Giles returned to Willoughby prepared to stay a few days and "do some business." She took a room at the only place available—the Chateau Willoughby. When Lilian Kreuter heard that Mary Lou had snagged yet another guest because Lilian's own rooms were still not ready, the news was one more nail in her cross to bear.

"That real estate lady could have been staying with *me!*" Lilian whined that afternoon to Glenda Bratcher at the cafe. "Do you know how much the good word from a real estate agent could be worth in free advertising? But no. Balaam has just disappeared off the face of the earth. I guess he figures he doesn't need to work anymore now that he'll be getting all that money for his land. I told him that if he didn't finish what he started and pronto, I'd get someone else to. Well, he said that would probably be a good idea and that I didn't owe him anything!"

Glenda pursed her lips and shook her head sympathetically.

"Believe me, Glenda, I have prayed about this and prayed about this. Charlene said I'm being tested. Well, believe me, if I'd known I was going to be tested, I'd have studied harder."

By September 13, two days after Judy Ann Giles had driven into town, the number of "for sale" signs on houses and lots in Willoughby had doubled, the asking price of houses and lots had tripled. Suddenly more people realized that they could have an economic stake in Willoughby's new prosperity. The Taft sisters, who owned the boarded-up bookstore next to Rudy's garage, immediately listed it with Giles. Euell Liddy listed one acre just inside the city limits that he kept a few cows on. It was carried on the city tax roll with a value of two thousand dollars. He had told Giles, "If you can get me four, I'd take it."

"I think I can get you eight," she had said.

"Let's do 'er," Euell had said.

Six hours after the "for sale" sign went up, Charley Griggs offered Euell seven thousand, and Euell accepted. Charley left the "for sale" sign right where it was and began asking ten thousand for the same acre.

Word of Willoughby's instant real estate boom spread rapidly to Joe Adair and Willis Pinkston. Twenty years earlier, they had gone halvsies on a small wood-framed house near downtown. They had bought it for just five thousand dollars with the intention of becoming landlords. "Easy money, Joe," Willis had said at the time. "Just cash that rent check every month. And just one rule for renters: No pay, no stay."

But they had never followed through with their plan to rent the house. Each year they just paid the property taxes as the paint on the house faded, and the rats gnawed the insulation of the wiring, and tree roots in the front yard buckled the sidewalk.

But now, with the sudden flurry of real estate activity, Joe saw their chance to get out from under the taxes and turn a profit. That morning, before he joined Big Un and Willis on their bench, he talked with Judy Ann Giles. She told him that with Willoughby "about to get hotter'n a pistol," she could get them twenty thousand dollars for their little house. Later, Joe told Willis what she had said. Joe wanted to begin asking for twenty but to settle for fifteen. Willis was willing to sell but wanted to hold off on listing the house to see if prices would go up even more in the weeks to come. "There's not even anyone ready to move to town yet. Let's bide our time."

Joe and Willis debated the issue until both men suddenly remembered why they had never followed through with their plan to rent the house after they had bought it—they had never been able to agree on anything. Joe had wanted to divide the house into duplex units; Willis had not. Joe had wanted to install central air conditioning; Willis had wanted to "just chunk in a couple of window units and be done with it. No reason for renters to live like the governor."

As they sat on their bench-in-exile that afternoon, Willis was adamant. "Come on, Joe," he said. "Look what happened to Euell. He thought too small. You gotta think big. This week twenty, but next month maybe thirty. Half of thirty is a sweet fifteen each."

But Joe Adair was not a chance taker. "Yeah, and next month, maybe squat, Willis," he said testily. "And you know what half of squat is."

Joe was beginning to relive his frustration of twenty years ago. "Or maybe you don't," he added with more sarcasm than he felt. He knew he'd said too much as soon as he said it, but he did not take back his words.

Willis was offended. He turned away and stared across the street. Joe looked at Willis and worked his jaw a bit, but nothing came out of his mouth. Then he, too, turned and stared across the street. Big Un sat between Joe and Willis, unaccustomed to rancor among the Boys. He waited a moment, expecting a reconciliation. Then, outvoted, he joined the majority and stared across the street.

Down the street at the Crossroads Cafe, Juanita Greer had troubles of her own. She still hurt because Richard had spent all the money in their "cafe kitty" to buy that fishing boat without consulting her. "He hasn't even put the damned thing in the water since he dragged it home," she told Brandi Renee. With effort, Juanita was transforming her hurt into anger, which she found easier to live with. Each morning her anger subsided as she had to channel her energy into running the cafe, but each afternoon when she drove home from work and saw the boat sitting in the driveway, she became angry all over again. Although Richard and Juanita were living under the same roof again, at home and at the cafe, her exchanges with him were robotic.

"You feed the dog?"

"Yeah."

"That leg on table five is loose again."

"Okay."

Juanita was also frustrated by Brandi Renee's waitressing, which was approaching a cosmic level of uselessness. Juanita could fire her, of course, but she grudgingly acknowledged that a certain percentage of the cafe's male customers came in as much for the "scenery" as for the chicken-fried steak or pecan pie.

And then there was the increase in business, mostly accounted for by out-of-towners. Juanita had come to realize that out-of-towners were harder to please, more impatient, more impolite: "This is not the way they make it in Dallas." "Where's my order?" "You call *this* 'presentation'?"

Juanita wiped her hands on her apron and walked into the cafe's women's restroom, where she found Brandi Renee striking poses in front of the mirror. Brandi Renee was going to ride on a float in the Founders Day parade and was practicing a crowd-pleasing pout.

"Brandi, I just saw a van pull into the parking lot. Please, please, *please* get back out there."

Between her domestic upheaval and increased stress at the cafe, Juanita had begun to suffer frequent heartburn. After Brandi Renee gave the mirror a final pout and wobbled out of the restroom, Juanita snapped open her purse and took out a roll of Tums. She popped one tablet into her mouth, chewed it, and chased it with a Dixie cup of water from the lavatory tap. Through the thin walls of the restroom, she heard Brandi Renee's voice: "Sir, pitching a conniption fit won't get your garden-fresh vegetables out of their can any faster."

As Juanita left the restroom, she looked at her face in the mirror.

She snapped her purse closed and knew that it was only a matter of time before she began mainlining antacid tablets from a Pez dispenser.

On the following day, the fourteenth, when Juanita drove home from the cafe and saw the fishing boat in the driveway, mocking her, she had a horrible thought: The cafe needed to expand to keep up with business. But now there was no money for that. What if the cafe could not accommodate all the new business, and someone opened a competing cafe in town?

That thought made her madder than ever at Richard. When he came home from work that night, she threw him out again. This time he landed at his brother's home in San Antonio. He did not come in to work at the cafe the next afternoon.

"Fine," Juanita the cafe owner said to herself at 3:00 P.M. on the fifteenth when Richard had not showed up for work. "If that's all this cafe means to him. This cafe—our *baby*." Juanita the wife pulled a Kleenex and a roll of Tums from her purse. She blotted her eyes while chewing a Tums. Then she marched outside to the front of the cafe and bought a copy of the Waco newspaper from a rack. She read the "job wanted" classified ads, made a few phone calls, and hired a man with short-order cook experience. The new cook showed up for work promptly the next day, the sixteenth—the eve of the Founders Day parade. The new cook and Brandi Renee didn't get along from the start, so Juanita liked him immediately.

As the new cook began his first shift that afternoon, Mayor Perry sat in the cafe with Lawton Parker. Lawton looked out the window at the cars at the intersection. "You know, Earl," Lawton said, "there are days when this town is just about that close," Lawton held his index finger and thumb an inch apart, "to having a traffic problem."

"You really think so?" Perry said wistfully, completely missing Lawton's point. To people like Perry, people like Lawton—and Balaam—were obstructionists, blinkered old mossbacks. Perry followed Lawton's gaze out the window toward the intersection. As he looked at the intersection, he became wistful, as he often did lately. He had already seen that dreams can come true: Banker D. B. Baxter had gotten his dream ATM machine. A traffic problem—Perry had begun to informally monitor traffic flow at the intersection through his storefront window as he worked the cash register—was exactly what Willoughby needed in order for *his* dream—his secret dream of dreams—to come true. Yes, the honorable Earl Perry, mayor of the municipality of Willoughby, Texas, hoped to convince the state highway department that there was just cause to replace Willoughby's flashing red traffic light with *a full, four-way, three-color traffic signal.*

Reluctantly, Earl Perry looked back at Lawton Parker. Lawton owned the only hardware store in a twenty-mile radius, and his wares were much in demand of late. But there were three drawbacks to shopping at Lawton Parker's hardware store: (1) his stock was limited, (2) his stock was outdated, and (3) he didn't want to sell any of it.

Lawton preferred to be more of a curator than a merchant. He was happy to putter around his store all day, keeping his displays and stock in perfect order, all the cans of WD-40 facing the front, all the saws with their teeth pointing in the same direction, the contents of the dozens of bins of nuts and bolts and washers all pure and uncorrupted.

Lawton complained to his wife, Catherine, at home that evening. "People come in there and pick up a bolt from the half-inch stove bolt bin, decide they don't want it, and put it back in the five-eighths carriage bolt bin! I've seen 'em do it time after time. They take a slot screwdriver off the wall hook and put it back on the Phillips hook. Is it any wonder the world is full of chaos?" he said, slapping his hand on the armrest of his reclining chair.

Catherine had been listening to Lawton "go on about that store" for most of the thirty years he had owned it. She was always supportive, responding to his complaints about the latest transgressions by customers as if he were describing atrocities of the Spanish Inquisition.

"A stove bolt in the carriage bolt bin? Some folks weren't raised right," Catherine said.

Lawton usually tried to talk people out of their purchases, telling them that they could find the same item at a better price at Home Depot or Lowe's in Waco. Sometimes he outright lied: "I don't have one of those." "That one's broken." "I'm holding that one on layaway for somebody."

Lawton fidgeted in his recliner. "A man gets attached to a box of nails or a set of drill bits or a gallon of lead-based paint after he's had 'em in the store for twenty or twenty-five years."

"I know, dear, I know," Catherine said, nodding her head. Lawton was technically retired now; he and Catherine could manage without his limited income from the store. But she knew that he loved being among his doodads and thingamajigs. She suspected that it was, as she'd heard an expert say on "Oprah," "a guy thing."

Lately, people had been pestering Lawton "something fierce," wanting to buy his doodads and thingamajigs. First Paul Wyatt had been in wanting this and that as he worked on that bed-and-breakfast of Mary Lou's. Then Balaam had begun coming in for first one thing and then the other for Lilian's bed-and-breakfast. Now people wanted to fix up and sell old houses and vacant lots that they hadn't touched in years. On top of that, Jessie Pinkston and others working on the Founders Day parade floats were coming in and wanting to buy rolls of chicken wire and paint brushes and other of Lawton's heirlooms.

"If business at the store gets any better," Lawton Parker said to Catherine, foreboding in his voice, "I'm going to have to close it."

Just down the street from Lawton's hardware store, despite Big Un's well-intentioned, if awkward, attempts at diplomacy, Joe Adair and Willis Pinkston were still not talking to each other. Joe and Willis had showed up at their bench-in-exile that morning but just sat there sulking, Joe on one side of Big Un, Willis on the other side. Each would talk only to Big Un, the man in the middle.

Big Un tried to start a conversation by telling Joe and Willis that if his son, Little Un, could sell his two vacant lots for the asking price, Big Un might get his new liver.

"Can I count on you two to read my rain gauge for me while I'm in the hospital?"

Joe and Willis just grunted.

About 3:00 P.M., a concrete mixer truck arrived in front of the bank down the block and began pouring the new sidewalk. The three men watched the concrete sluice down the chute, watched four workers in rubber boots use shovels to distribute the concrete along the wooden form. When the mixer's drum stopped rotating for a moment, Big Un stood up to stretch. He put an index finger into a belt loop on each side and hitched up his pants, which were always in danger of falling down because his belt was three notches too loose. Hoping to break the ten-sion, he said, "Anybody want to go scratch our initials in wet cement?"

No reply.

Big Un sat back down between Joe and Willis and glanced at each man. Joe and Willis stared straight ahead, jaws set. As the concrete mixer's drum began rotating again, Big Un said loudly, "Why do I feel like the peanut butter between two slices of pride?"

Against the churning of the concrete mixer, neither slice of pride heard a word that the peanut butter said.

❧43❧

"Hey! Where'd everybody go?"
——Nanetta Wilson

In the relative coolness of morning on September 17, in the parking
lot of the Baptist church, Pegasus was in his can, Lucas Elisha was in
front of his log cabin, the Conductor had his lantern-waving arm lim-
bered up, Queen Cotton was in her bale, even the Mermaid finally had
her tail fins "just right."

And Jessie Pinkston saw that it was good.

"I do believe this is going to be the best one ever," Jessie said to
Vada Hoover as they walked among the Founders Day parade floats,
conducting a last-minute inspection. For the past several days, Jessie
had supervised a small group of volunteers—mostly women and a few
husbands—as they had prepared the half-dozen floats. Of course,
because the parade each year consisted of, for the most part, the same
floats, the same participants, the same route, that year's parade had not
required much preparation. Most floats had been merely rolled out of
the barns and garages where they had been stored for the past year and
towed to the church parking lot that morning. The floats were small-
town simple: for color, some bright crepe paper bunting, a few small
arrangements of flowers from the prettier yards. The major displays
were made of a simple framework of chicken wire, plywood, and
papier-mache and mounted on flat-bed utility trailers drawn by tractors.

The theme, of course, was the town's past, although enforcement of that theme was less than rigid. Jessie had even asked David Wilson if he'd like to be in the parade in that "cute little car of yours," but he had declined. David's mother, Nanetta, however, had readily agreed to be parade marshal, leading the procession in her electric personal mobility scooter. Its top speed of five miles per hour would assure that even a parade measuring only two hundred feet from end to end would take a full minute to pass a given point.

For the third year running, Little Un Petteway would portray the town's namesake and first mayor: Lucas Elisha Willoughby. Lucas Elisha had been among the town's original settlers in the 1850s. No one knew what he had looked like, so each year the person who portrayed him was free to interpret his bearing and appearance. In the first parade in 1901, he had looked vaguely Lincolnesque, with a full, dark beard. Over the course of subsequent years, he had been aloof and outgoing, animated and immobile. He had worn coonskin cap, top hat, cowboy hat, and once, after a barnstormer had thrilled area residents in 1919, goggles and a scarf. Sometimes those who portrayed Lucas Elisha did so in a way that, perhaps unconsciously, reflected the times. In 1944, during FDR's third term, Lucas Elisha had sported a jutting chin and a cigarette holder. And once, in the late 1960s, Lucas Elisha was seen—to the dismay of conservative Willoughby adults—to flash the peace sign. Afterward the parade committee had voted, in emergency session, to never again allow Lucas Elisha Willoughby to be portrayed by someone from the liberal wing of the high school drama class.

The Lucas Elisha display consisted of the half-scale facade of a log cabin made of papier-mache. Little Un's role was to stand in front of the log cabin and look suitably pioneer.

Symbolizing the town's cotton-growing heritage was Earl Perry's wife, Joyce. She wore an oversized rectangular cardboard box from the Perry grocery store. It had a hole cut in top for her head and a hole cut at each side for her arms. Volunteers had hot-glued hundreds of cotton balls to the outside of the box to make it look like a cotton bale.

As the august head of municipal government, Mayor Perry would ride on horseback behind Nanetta's scooter. He was not an accomplished equestrian, but Cecil Bell, who always provided any horses needed for the parade, had trotted out a gentle old mare that, Cecil said privately, "even a politician couldn't rile."

A fifty-five-gallon steel drum with a stylized rendering of the Mobil Oil Pegasus red flying horse trademark painted on its side represented a one-quart can of motor oil, symbolizing the town's petroleum heritage. Standing in the drum (on a plastic milk crate) was Jason Riesel, age eight, grandson of Helen Riesel. Ever since Jason had seen his first Founders Day parade at age five, he had wanted to be "that red horsey guy."

The display symbolizing the railroad was a plywood backdrop cut in the silhouette of a locomotive and painted black and silver. Charley Griggs stood in front of it wearing blue overalls and swinging a kerosene lantern.

And, of course, the tractors in the parade did double duty, pulling the floats and symbolizing the town's farming heritage.

There was one new float—the Balaam's Cave float. At first, there had been a flurry of talk among Jessie and her volunteers about creating a float to honor Howard J. Liggett as a kind of modern-day patron saint of Willoughby. Granted, rumors persisted around town that Liggett had dispatched that young man—the one who had stayed at Mary Lou's—to cause trouble, but because the town's collective memory was short and forgiving, many people were willing to dismiss such rumors as a misunderstanding. But in the end, Jessie had decreed that instead a float would be created to acknowledge Balaam's Cave—in its own way the source of Willoughby's new prosperity. Jessie's volunteers had borrowed another flat-bed utility trailer, drafted another tractor and driver, and fashioned a chicken wire-and-papier-mache backdrop that was supposed to look like the limestone interior of the cave in cutaway view. The dome of the cave arched over a plastic children's wading pool. Obscuring the wading pool from parade viewers was a facade of plywood painted blue and cut to simulate choppy waves.

Brandi Renee, as the town's "pretty little thing," was the only choice to play the mermaid of Balaam's Cave. On her human half, she wore a bikini top covered with glitter and simulated seaweed. On her fish half, she had been wrapped from waist to ankles in swaths made from cut-up plastic trash bags that had been sprayed green. On her feet, she wore rubber swim fins, sprayed gold.

The wading pool, although not visible to the crowd, was filled with water because Jessie thought it would be "darling" if Brandi Renee would sit at the edge of the pool and playfully flick water toward the crowd with her tail fins.

At 8:30, as the mayor and his horse and the tractors and their floats maneuvered around the parking lot to get into their parade order, Nanetta drove around between them on her scooter, tooting her horn, having a great time, and generally being a nuisance.

At 8:45, Jessie and all other volunteers not actually appearing in the parade left the staging area and walked over to join the crowd downtown, where a block of the main street had been closed to serve as the official viewing area. At nine o'clock, Nanetta tooted her horn, gave a "forward" motion with her arm, and drove her scooter regally onto Maddox Street. First Mayor Perry and then the floats followed her—very, very slowly—in single file.

Because the parade wended along several residential streets before reaching downtown, many residents chose to simply sit on their front porches—where several of them would have been anyway—and watch the parade pass. As the parade turned onto Fuller Street, Euell Liddy came out his front door wearing his old army uniform and began marching alongside the Lucas Elisha float. As the parade turned onto Bidecker Street, Eugene "String" Blevins got off his porch swing and, with his banjo, joined the procession. He walked along beside Euell playing the only song he knew: "Red River Valley."

When Nanetta neared the downtown area, she began to toot her horn again. Cheers and applause greeted her on both sides of the street. On her handlebars, she had mounted small American and Texas flags; her scooter lacked the speed to cause the flags to even flutter.

As the parade moved farther into downtown, those on the floats knew that it was "show time." With increased enthusiasm, Mayor Perry waved his borrowed cowboy hat astride his borrowed horse, Charley Griggs called out "All aboard," "String" Blevins strummed, Euell Liddy saluted, Jason Riesel jumped up and down in his drum, Little Un Petteway and Joyce Perry smiled, and Brandi Renee, on the final float, flicked her tail fins and pouted alluringly.

From somewhere in the crowd on his right, Perry heard a good-natured "Giddyup, Earl!" and from one of the few young people in the crowd, a rousing "Willoughby rules!" Perry also heard a few catcalls and rude hoots. He looked into the faces in the crowd and saw some that he did not recognize. He had anticipated that. Because of the town's higher profile, this year's parade had probably attracted a few tourists. He knew that they might consider the parade to be boring and "hick."

"That's okay," he said to himself as he pressed his knees inward to grip the horse. "Let 'em make fun. Let 'em point and laugh. Just as long as they spend their money here, just as long as they go back home to Houston or Oklahoma City or Fort Worth knowing that Willoughby is the Hot-Dam Mineral Water Capital of Texas and soon will be home of the Waters at Willoughby."

Among those in the crowd were Rosalee and Anita Taft, of course, roaming along both sides of the street, taking notes and photos for the *Bee*. Nearby stood David Wilson and Beverly Faulk. Beverly had offered to provide color commentary to David for his first Founders Day parade. "See the Mermaid's bikini top?" Beverly said. "I understand that some of Joyce's cotton bale found its way in there. And see Charley's lantern? Some years he fills it with scotch, not kerosene."

Nanetta saw David in the crowd and waved to him and tooted. David looked down and covered his eyes. "I have *got* to disconnect that horn," he said to Beverly.

Lilian Kreuter was also in the crowd, watching the parade with Charlene Briley and Glenda Bratcher. After all, as Lilian the martyr whined to anyone who would listen, there was little reason for her to stay home—she had no bed-and-breakfast guests to cook and clean for.

Jessie Pinkston stood across from the bank with Joe Adair's wife, Corrine, watching the parade approach from their left. Jessie turned and looked to their right. Down the block, on their bench-in-exile, Willis and Joe sat on either side of Big Un Petteway, watching but still not talking.

"Stubborn old goats," Jessie said to Corrine.

Just as Nanetta drew even with Jessie's vantage point, Vada Hoover stepped up from behind and squeezed Jessie's shoulder. "I think you're right. It's the best one ever."

Jessie was savoring those kind words when, a block away, a pickup towing a flat-bed utility trailer emerged slowly from Childress Street and drove up behind the Balaam's Cave float. On the trailer squatted Mary

Lou's hard-won claw-foot cast-iron bathtub. On the edge of the tub sat Mary Lou herself, dressed in an old-fashioned country gingham dress and wearing a bonnet to match. To the side of the tub she had taped a cardboard sign bearing the words "Stay at charming Chateau Willoughby" and her phone number.

As husband Paul kept his pickup close behind the Balaam's Cave float, Mary Lou waved a folding hand fan under her chin in what she perceived to be "mercy me" southern style. On the fan she had written "Chateau Willoughby."

Mary Lou's trailer was not on Jessie Pinkston's officially sanctioned list, of course. In fact, no commercial advertising was allowed in the parade. Mary Lou's Wyatt's tub on a trailer was a rogue float.

In the crowd, when Lilian Kreuter saw Mary Lou on the claw-foot tub and read the sign, she snapped. Mary Lou had bested her from the beginning—taking the best bed-and-breakfast name, the first customer, the real estate lady, the coveted claw-foot tub. And now Mary Lou had "crashed" the Founders Day parade with her billboard on wheels and seemed to be rubbing Lilian's nose in it all.

Lilian's half snarl-half scream drew the crowd's attention from the floats back onto itself as she pushed her way through people to the curb and then rushed into the street toward Mary Lou's float. Most people in the crowd had not yet noticed the rogue float at the end of the parade. Now everyone watched as Lilian jumped, shrieking incoherently, onto Mary Lou's trailer. She jerked the cardboard sign off the bathtub and began swatting Mary Lou about the head and shoulders with it.

Lilian Kreuter was all prayed out.

As Lilian swatted at Mary Lou, Mary Lou ducked and grabbed at the sign. She got both hands on one side and began tugging, but Lilian jerked the sign away and resumed swatting her with it. Mary Lou began to fight back by swatting at Lilian with her folding hand fan. Cardboard sign battled hand fan for several seconds until the fan fell apart. Mary Lou then began trying to dodge the cardboard sign while grabbing wildly at Lilian's hair. The trailer rocked as the women's weight shifted.

The men driving the tractors that pulled the trailers ahead of Mary Lou's rogue float saw the crowd reacting strongly to something at the rear of the parade and turned to look. When they saw the battle royal, they all stopped their tractors. But D. B. Baxter, driving the lead tractor, stopped his just a split second more quickly than the rest, causing each tractor to rear end the trailer in front of it, resulting in a five-float pileup.

At such a slow speed, no great harm was done. Lucas Elisha, the Conductor, and Queen Cotton swayed when their trailers lurched to a stop but kept their footing. The Pegasus oil drum tipped over, rolled off the trailer onto the pavement, and continued rolling until it hit the curb twenty feet later. Jason Riesel crawled slowly out of the drum and stood, dazed. He took a few drunken steps, fell down in a squatting position, and began giggling. "Neat! Can I go again?"

On the Balaam's Cave float, the Mermaid slipped off the edge of the wading pool and fell flat on her dorsal fin.

At the same time, Paul Wyatt, in his pickup at the rear of the parade, had an instant to anticipate the chain reaction ahead of him. He swerved out of line, bringing his trailer directly behind the Balaam's Cave float and causing Mary Lou and Lilian to lose their balance and fall to their knees. The sudden stop of the Balaam's Cave float had also created a tidal wave in the wading pool. Water flowed first forward and then ebbed backward, sloshing onto Mary Lou and Lilian as they grappled. Both women, now wet and on their knees, fought largely with their eyes closed. Lilian snatched off Mary Lou's bonnet; Mary Lou pulled Lilian's hair.

When Earl Perry saw what was happening, he turned his horse around and rode as fast as he dared to the rear of the parade. He was joined by Joyce Perry, waddling as fast as she could in her oversized cardboard box, and Rosalee and Anita Taft, cameras at the ready. Perry dismounted and, holding his horse's reins in one hand, edged near the two women. By now, Mary Lou and Lilian were back on their feet. Perry grabbed Lilian around her waist with his free arm and tried to pull her away. Joyce Perry tried to pull Mary Lou away, but each time Joyce approached, Mary Lou pushed her away, in the process plucking handfuls of cotton balls from Joyce's cardboard box and then throwing them at Lilian, who, ludicrously, defended herself against them by using the cardboard sign as a shield.

As Earl Perry tried to pull Lilian away from Mary Lou, Mary Lou clung to whatever part of Lilian she could cling to. Joyce Perry again grabbed Mary Lou by the arm and tried to pull her in the opposite direction. But Joyce lost her grip, and her momentum carried her backward. She stumbled and fell, landing on the back of her oversized cardboard box. She was unable to get up. As Mary Lou and Lilian fought, Joyce Perry lay on the pavement flailing her useless arms and legs, immobilized like a turtle on its back.

As the fight continued, "String" Blevins stood by and did the only thing he knew to do: He played "Red River Valley."

But before "String" reached "We will miss your bright eyes and sweet smile," Paul Wyatt and D. B. Baxter overcame their initial shock and moved in decisively to separate the two women. Mary Lou and Lilian were taken to opposite sides of the street.

It all happened too suddenly for Jessie Pinkston to step in. As she watched her parade self-destruct, she began to "go all woozy." She was a large woman, and two of her volunteers had to ease her down into a folding chair. She sat sagged in the chair, her jaw slack, her eyes unfocused. Now and then she mumbled, "The best one ever."

Meanwhile, Nanetta Wilson was not aware that the parade behind her had broken down. She blithely proceeded on the parade route back to the church parking lot—a parade of one—all the while waving regally and tooting her little horn.

Without Jessie Pinkston to bring order to the chaos, the parade simply disintegrated, stunned participants soon going their separate ways—some to their homes, some to the cafe, some back to the church parking lot. Helen Riesel tried to put Jason to bed, but he was too excited. People in the crowd, equally stunned, for a few minutes milled about talking—reliving, speculating, comparing impressions—like witnesses to a great calamity. Then they, too, dispersed in ones and twos.

Less than ten minutes after Mary Lou Wyatt's rogue float had appeared, the street was empty.

At noon, Mayor Perry went to the *Bee* office to meet with Rosalee and Anita. He was sorely distressed. He was about to attempt something that he had never had to do in his political life: spin control. "Tourists are going to see this paper," he said to Rosalee and Anita, tugging his ear and gritting his teeth. "Liggett himself might see it. For the sake of Willoughby, please report this god-awful disaster in the best possible light."

Had Rosalee and Anita taken notes of their meeting with Perry, those notes would have shown that he used the phrase "I'm begging you" six times.

Four days later, the *Bee* was on the streets of Willoughby with a front page photo of a wet Lilian Kreuter and a wet Mary Lou Wyatt snatching madly at each other's hair while Perry held his horse's reins with one hand and tried to pull Lilian away with his other arm.

The photo caption read:

"This year's Founders Day parade had a special presentation: a reenactment of the last battle fought between Indians and early settlers of Willoughby in 1878. Here, as the Indians (played by Lilian Kreuter, left) and the settlers (played by Mary Lou Wyatt, right) engage in hand-to-hand combat just after a rain shower, the U.S. Cavalry (played by Mayor Earl Perry) rides to the rescue. A good time was had by all."

❧44❧

*"I'm glad it's over. I don't know how many more times
I could have lied, 'Gee, that swimsuit makes you look so slim.'"*
——Earline Perry

During the two weeks before what Howard J. Liggett had called
Balaam's "little ceremony" on September 21, Willoughby and
Balaam Gimble were, for the most part, mutually oblivious to each
other's activities. While Willoughby was enjoying its real estate boom
and anticipating—and then getting over—its Founders Day parade,
Balaam kept a low profile. He did not come in to town. He did not
answer when David Wilson phoned. He did not answer when Lilian
Kreuter phoned.

But on a few occasions, passersby noticed Balaam traipsing around
in cow pastures in the area—Foster Jergens's nearby and even Ray Dean
Briley's on the other side of Willoughby. A few times his pickup was
seen on back roads with a blue plastic tarp over the bed.

And then, on September 18, one day after the parade and three days
before the "little ceremony," Balaam phoned Mayor Perry. When Perry
heard Balaam's voice he felt another bubble of angst rise in his throat.

"You're not backing out of the sale, are you?"

"No, Earl. I'm not backing out. But I got to thinking. We're
signing the papers in three days. I think I'd better go ahead and shut
down the cave. Liggett's not going to allow our little two-bit operation

to go on anyway. In the meantime, I don't want anyone to get hurt out here and sue me or jinx the deal."

The word "jinx" was all that Perry needed to hear. He was already worried about bad publicity over the parade fiasco. And the parade was insignificant compared to the Waters at Willoughby.

"The way things are going," Perry said with resignation, "maybe that's a good idea. We'll just explain to people that an even bigger and better mineral spring facility is coming soon. The Waters at Willoughby."

He did love to say those words.

That afternoon Balaam went down to the cave and told Earline Perry, "the friendly, knowledgeable staff" of Balaam's Cave, that he was closing the cave and that she could go home. "I'll stay here until everyone is gone," he told her.

Three people were in the cave when Balaam arrived. He sat at the metal desk until the last pilgrim left. Then Balaam removed the ladder from the mouth of the cave and sealed the mouth with a heavy iron lid, drilling holes in the limestone and fastening the hinges and the hasp to the limestone with lag bolts. Then he padlocked the lid. After he drained the two remaining bathtubs and the horse trough, he loaded Ray Dean Briley's ladder and Cliff Gholson's pump into the bed of his pickup, hung a sign reading "CAVE CLOSED" on the fence at the gate, and drove back to his compound.

The next afternoon a long-haul trucker sat at a picnic table in a roadside park on Interstate 35 ten miles north of Austin and sixty miles south of Willoughby. He paid little attention when a multicolored old Ford pickup pulled in, and the driver, a man in his mid-fifties, got out and sat at a nearby table under a live oak tree. He paid little attention thirty minutes later when a new Chevy pickup pulled in, and the driver, another man in his mid-fifties, joined the driver of the old Ford at the table.

New Chevy carried a metal ice chest, which he handed to Old Ford.

"Are you going to need any help?" the trucker heard New Chevy ask.

"Nope," Old Ford said.

In the tree above the two men, a cicada buzzed, trying to sound

276

busy.

"You know it's been over thirty years?" New Chevy said.

At that moment, a tractor-trailer truck passed by on the interstate, obscuring Old Ford's reply. Then, as the two men stood to go their separate ways, the trucker heard New Chevy say to Old Ford, "I hope you know what you're doing."

❖45❖

"I thought it was the Rapture. I always figured that Jesus
will break the sound barrier when he returns to Earth."
————Reverend Thomas Finch

O n the morning of September 21, Balaam did not dress up for the
"little ceremony." No more suits. He did not even shave. The
only concession that he made was a wristwatch—bought just a few days
earlier—which he strapped on as he left his cabin. He had not worn a
watch since Vietnam.

Balaam saw no sign of life near the cave when he passed it. He
looked at his new watch: 11:20.

The signing ceremony was scheduled for noon. Already gathered in
Town Hall when Balaam arrived were more than forty people, including
Mayor Perry, city council members, an agent from the local title company that was handling the sale, bank president D. B Baxter, the Taft
sisters, even a reporter from the county seat's weekly newspaper. Most
of the downtown merchants had stepped over to attend, as had several
other residents. Ray Dean Briley was present, proud of his early contribution to the chain of events that had led to the "big day." Willis
Pinkston and Joe Adair were present, talking to everyone except each
other.

Three of the usual faces were not present. Founders Day parade
organizer Jessie Pinkston had stayed home, "feeling a bit peaked." And

Lilian Kreuter and Mary Lou Wyatt had stayed home because each had been afraid that the other might attend.

For the assemblage, volunteers had set up a table stocked with coffee, ice tea, and, of course, plastic cups of Bounce, the Lone Star Wonder Water. Behind the table was a blackboard to which had been fastened an artist's rendering of the Waters at Willoughby resort.

As people milled about the room chatting, there was indeed much to chat about: the parade-gone-wrong, the real estate boom, and now, the first formal step toward the Waters at Willoughby becoming an economic reality. Indeed, to some in the room it seemed like ages since other major events, such as J. D. Vernon's fatal hunting accident, had been the talk of the town.

When Balaam spotted David Wilson at the beverage table, he waved and walked over to him.

"I tried to call you a few times," David said.

"I've been away from the phone a lot."

"Are you sure you want to do this?"

"I don't see as how he gave me a choice."

Balaam had just helped himself to a plastic cup of Bounce when he saw Howard J. Liggett walk his tailored clothes in the front door, followed by four of his people. Balaam looked at his new watch: 11:45.

Balaam greeted Liggett with brittle civility. Liggett soon moved on to talk with Mayor Earl Perry and others.

At 11:55, Perry made a short speech. Balaam's ears were tuned elsewhere, and he did not hear most of Perry's words: " . . . big day . . . Waters at Willoughby . . . Aquavita Company . . . happy marriage . . . partners in prosperity . . ."

When Perry finished his speech, the title company agent spread out the sales contract papers on a card table for Balaam and Liggett to sign. The Taft sisters moved in close with their cameras.

"Well, Balaam." It was the first time that Liggett had ever called Balaam by his first name, "Are we ready?"

Balaam looked at his new watch: 11:59. He sat down in a chair at the table and made himself comfortable, adjusting his chair first in toward the table edge and then back out. And then in again. Balaam cleaned his glasses with his handkerchief. Then he picked up one of the sales contract papers and pretended to read it. Then he took a sip of

Bounce from his plastic cup. He continued to look at the paper.

After a few moments, Liggett asked with a thin smile, "You did receive copies of the sales contract to look over beforehand, didn't you?"

Balaam didn't reply. He selected a paragraph at random and said, "What does this part here mean?"

The title company agent looked at the paragraph that Balaam pointed to and explained it in simple terms, but Balaam only pretended to be listening.

He looked at his watch again: noon.

"I see." Balaam pretended to read more of the contract and asked Liggett, "And how many days after we close until you take possession of the land?"

With forced patience, Liggett said, "Just as my assistant told you: thirty days."

Balaam took another sip of Bounce. "That's right. Now I remember." He moved his hand to his shirt pocket and patted it. "Okey dokey. Well, I brought my lucky pen." By "lucky" Balaam meant that the pen had no ink in it.

Boom.

Balaam left his lucky pen in his pocket and looked at his watch—just seconds after 12:01—when the boom rattled the windows of Town Hall. In the glasses of tea on the beverage table, ice cubes clinked and shivered with excitement. At the intersection, the flashing red light swayed almost imperceptibly on the cable that suspended it over the highway.

Ray Dean Briley and a few others in the room went to the front windows. Ray Dean pointed to the east toward a swirling gray cloud just over the treetops. As he pointed, the cloud began to drift and was replaced by something seldom seen in central Texas—a geyser. The geyser sparkled in the sunlight.

"What the hell?" Big Un Petteway said as he stood beside Ray Dean.

"Busted water main?" someone else speculated.

"Not way out there. That's out of town."

Others who were seated got up and walked to the windows; those already at the windows walked out onto the sidewalk. Along the main block of downtown—from the bank, the post office, the cafe—a few people came out to investigate the boom.

When Ray Dean said, "That's out toward Balaam's place," Liggett and Perry, who had remained seated, looked over at Balaam, also still seated. Balaam looked directly at Liggett. The expression that Liggett saw on Balaam's face was enigmatic—Mona Lisa with a three-day beard. Balaam shrugged his shoulders, smiled his little parenthetical smile, and said matter of factly to Liggett, "Fire in the hole."

Liggett was not certain what that expression meant. Earl Perry, who had been in the army, was more certain. Perry looked at Balaam with all-too-familiar apprehension and rushed to the window, Liggett just a step behind.

Perry pointed to the east, past the city water tower with "Will" painted on it, and Liggett saw the distant spray of water. Liggett looked around the room for his driver. "Gregory!"

To Mayor Perry, Liggett said, "Come on. Show us the way out there." It was more order than request. Liggett's driver and three aides caught up with Liggett and Perry as they walked to the Suburban parked at the curb.

"Do you know anything about this?" Liggett asked Perry as they climbed in.

Balaam had walked to the doorway of Town Hall. "Hey, come back," he called to Liggett. "Don't you want to sign the contract first?"

As the Suburban pulled away from the curb, Balaam chuckled. David joined him in the doorway. "Want to join the convoy?" Balaam asked. "Come on. We'll take my pickup."

Indeed, several others who had been at the aborted ceremony had left Town Hall and were following Liggett's Suburban east on Highway 21 toward the geyser, which was not as high above the treetops as it had been just a minute earlier. In the parking lot, as Balaam pulled his pickup into the end of the line of vehicles headed east, David looked at Balaam and said, "I guess you're not going to tell me about this, are you?"

"Let's just find out together." Again the parenthetical smile.

Outside of town, the convoy turned off Highway 21 onto a county road. The convoy raised so much dust on the unpaved road that drivers behind Liggett's lead vehicle could not see the vehicle in front of them and had to drive more slowly than their curiosity dictated. As the convoy approached the next intersection, each vehicle turned left at Walter Ridgely's German shepherd. The dog ran out from under the Ridgely house and went berserk, having to do a day's worth of chasing and barking in less than a minute. By the time Balaam's pickup approached the gauntlet, the dog was exhausted, hoarse, and coated with road dust. As Balaam turned left, Walter Ridgely's German shepherd could only stand by watching and cough an IOU.

When Balaam reached the stretch of road along the western edge of his property, he and David saw water running onto the dirt road, creating a patch of mud that had been tenderized by the tires of the earlier vehicles in the convoy. David begin to smell a foul odor through the holes rusted in the floorboard. "Oh, boy, you've done something big, haven't you?"

Balaam just took a sip from his plastic cup of Bounce and watched the dust of the car ahead of him.

When Howard J. Liggett arrived at Balaam's Cave, there was no Balaam's Cave. There was only Balaam's Lake. The lake was small, perhaps three hundred feet across, and filled with brown water. In the middle of the lake, just about where the mouth of the cave had been, was a fountain, perhaps ten feet high, gracefully splashing as the water fell back on itself.

Arriving in short intervals after Liggett were the Taft sisters and the reporter for the county seat newspaper, the agent of the title company, and others from town. They found Liggett standing with his people and Earl Perry in a small cluster at the edge of the water. Liggett had a handkerchief over his nose.

Balaam and David were the last to arrive. When Balaam saw the little lake with the fountain where the cave with the mineral spring had been, he nodded his head in satisfaction. "In case you want the recipe, one stick of dynamite and twelve pickup loads of cow patties," he said to David.

Balaam stood with his hands on his hips and admired the new landscape. Out in the lake near the fountain, the metal horse trough floated like a boat. Lumber that had once been the changing booth and the frame of the canopy over the bathtubs floated like driftwood. The two bathtubs were nowhere in sight. The steel desk under the live oak tree was overturned. Some Willoughby brochures from the desk were

caught in the branches of the tree. Chunks of limestone, some as large
as suitcases, were scattered around the edge of the lake. The blast had
pulverized most of the cow patties that Balaam had filled the cave with,
imparting the brown tinge to the water. But a few of the older cow patties, being drier and lighter, floated in the water, bobbing gently. The
air—smelling of cow patties cooking in the hot, sulfury mineral
water—was almost nauseating. In fact, some people in the convoy had
seen—and smelled—enough. They were turning to leave as David and
Balaam stood looking at the little brown lake.

Perry was the first to notice that Balaam was standing behind them.
"Why did you have to ruin it all for the rest of us?" Perry looked sad
and six years old. Earl Perry, boy mayor.

"Ask that man," Balaam said, looking at Liggett. "While you're at it,
ask him about Ernie Ruiz. But I don't reckon you'll get many honest
answers."

Liggett looked at Balaam but did not reply. Liggett turned and
looked at the fountain as it hemorrhaged money. Liggett did not know
more about geology than he needed to, but he knew that in blowing up
the cave Balaam had ruptured the hairline crack in the shale layer just
below the limestone. The hairline crack had allowed the mineral water
to seep into the cave from its source below, but the shale layer had been
solid enough to keep the seepage near the surface. With the shale layer
shattered, Liggett knew, the spring had blown itself out, and its water
was now draining irretrievably back into the earth. Even as he watched,
the level of Balaam's Lake was slowly dropping.

Balaam walked to the edge of the water and stood a few feet to the
left of Liggett. Looking out at the fountain, now only three feet high,
Balaam said, "So. There goes your water. You still gonna drill for oil?"
He felt his heart pound as he waited for the reply.

Liggett was candid in a moment of resignation. "There is no oil. I
couldn't even get the goddamned mineral rights. The son-of-a-bitch
wouldn't sell. So I bluffed. Hell, I didn't want oil anyway. I just wanted
the water. That's all. Just the water." Liggett's voice went limp as he
stared at the little brown lake. "Just the water."

Balaam narrowed his brows as he absorbed this revelation. "No
mineral rights. So I did this for nothing. I could have just hunkered
down and sat tight, and eventually you'd have had to give up and go

284

away. Well, still . . ." Balaam took a deep breath, inhaling the odor of sulfur and hot cow patties. He smiled—not just his little parenthetical smile, but a broad smile unbounded by punctuation. Balaam Gimble knew a happy ending when he smelled one.

"Still, I'd say you've lost a whole lot more today than I have."

Liggett, suddenly too apoplectic to form words, lunged at Balaam and had to be restrained by two of his people. They escorted Liggett away a few feet and talked to him soothingly while he cursed behind his handkerchief. When Liggett's people relaxed their grip on his elbows, he broke free and again lunged at Balaam. As Liggett came at him, Balaam dodged him with a passable matador's hip swivel, letting Liggett's momentum carry him headlong into the water of Balaam's Lake.

Liggett got to his knees in three feet of brown water, sputtering and dripping and cursing. His appearance triggered three reactions: The Taft sisters and the reporter for the county seat newspaper snapped his photo, Balaam began to laugh, and Mayor Earl Perry began to seriously consider not running for reelection.

Balaam laughed so hard that he doubled over and began to gasp for air. When he caught his breath, he said to Liggett, with mock disgust and an exaggerated twang in his voice, "Well, *now* you've gone and done it. You get out of there right this minute. I guess we could've tolerated cow patties floating in that good mineral water. But I reckon it ain't fit to drink now."

Liggett got to his feet and trudged out of the water. All four of his people met him at the water's edge to offer him support while touching him as little as possible.

"Get me out of here," he said to his driver.

Liggett was led to his Suburban. He never looked back.

As the Suburban turned around at the gate and drove away, Balaam bent to one knee and scooped his plastic cup full of water from Balaam's Lake. He stood and raised his cup.

"To your good health," he called out to the dust cloud behind Liggett's Suburban.

On the flight back to Colorado in his corporate jet, no one in his entourage sat near Howard J. Liggett. And only in part because he was in a bad mood.

❧46❧

*"That stick of dynamite didn't damage Balaam's compound at all.
I think two sticks might have tidied it up a bit."*
———David Wilson

"Dynamite, eh?" David Wilson was impressed. He sat on the porch of Balaam's cabin late that afternoon and looked—almost stared—at Balaam. David had a liberal arts degree, had grown up in a big city, had never been in the military. That someone he knew could know how to acquire and how to use explosives made him feel that he had led a sheltered life indeed.

"It was the only way I had left of saying 'no,'" Balaam said. Then Balaam laughed. Again. He had laughed a lot that afternoon. He was still laughing when he stood and went inside his cabin to fetch two more beers. As he walked to the door, he broke into an animated sideways shuffle and began to sing:

> I met the girl I love
> In a town way down in Dixie.

Everyone else in the convoy had long since returned to Willoughby, most disappointed, some angry, a few merely bewildered. Earl Perry had had to ride back with the Taft sisters and the reporter from the county seat newspaper. During the trip, Rosalee and Anita had expected him to ask that they not publish the photos they had taken of Liggett on his knees in Balaam's Lake. But Perry had just stared out the car window and said little.

Throughout the afternoon, the level of Balaam's Lake had continued to drop as the mineral water drained away, revealing more and more of the limestone crater created by the blast. By 2:00 P.M., one of the bathtubs had become visible in a shallow part of the lake. By 4:00 P.M., the second bathtub had become visible. By 5:00 P.M., the fountain did not even break the surface of the water.

Balaam and David had made a quick survey of Balaam's compound, finding little damage from the concussion—a cracked pane in a window of the cabin facing the blast, a framed picture jarred from its nail on a wall, a stack of plastic buckets toppled.

Balaam came back out of his cabin carrying two cans of beer, still shuffling, still singing:

> 'Neath the stars a-bove
> She was the sweet-est girl I ever did see.

He handed a beer to David and sat down and laughed some more. David did not have to ask Balaam many questions. Balaam clearly wanted—needed—to talk.

"I got the dynamite and timer from a guy I was in the army with who still keeps his hand in. Hell of a hobby to have, isn't it? Anyway, even though he'd done all the really technical work for me, I was still pretty nervous, which is not what you want to be when you're messing with that stuff. I hadn't touched explosives since Vietnam. If anything had gone wrong, you'd be sitting here now talking to a sack of meat."

"Looks to me like you cut it pretty close. When was it supposed to go off?"

"Noon. It was a minute past by my watch." Balaam had already taken off his new wristwatch. "But believe me, there was no way I'd have signed that contract. I'd still be back there at Town Hall hemming and hawing and asking stupid questions until that thing went off."

"And the cow patties?"

"Hell, I didn't know how much damage I'd do. If the dynamite didn't blow out the spring, I hoped that the cow patties would at least make it a whole lot less attractive to Liggett. I spent the last few days collecting them, walking around behind cows in pastures—getting 'em fresh from the factory."

David had two minor epiphanies.

"That's why you closed the cave this week."

"Closed it and clamped a lid on it. I didn't want anyone to get hurt after I rigged the dynamite. Yesterday I tucked my little surprise down in the cave in an ice chest with the timer set for noon today. Then I shoveled in the cow patties. Then I locked the lid on the cave and tiptoed away as fast as I could."

"And that's why you stopped working on Lilian Kreuter's bed-and-breakfast. She's been mad as hell at you, Mother said."

"She'd be a lot madder if I'd fixed up her house and taken her money and then blown up the only reason why people would be in town to stay at her house in the first place." Balaam watched a daddy longlegs spider bouncing in place on his pants leg—"bebopping," his mother had called it. "All I wanted was to be left alone. I'm sorry if other people got caught in the middle between me and Liggett. I know they made plans and had big dreams about lots of money based on what they thought I ought to do. Well, there's worse things to not have enough of than money."

For several seconds Balaam was quiet, staring at the daddy longlegs.

"Listen. Hear that?"

David had played this game before. He listened to hear whatever sound Balaam heard. But he could hear nothing. He closed his eyes. Still nothing. Just a breeze rustling the trees.

"I give up. I don't hear anything."

"Exactly. This is the first time in months there hasn't been someone else on this place. No pump running, no traffic, no tourists. And the first time in a long time I've felt like I'll wake up tomorrow and have some say over what happens out here. As of 12:01 today, I don't have anything that anybody wants anymore."

Balaam put his boots up on the cable spool and leaned back. "And that makes me feel down-right rich."

Later in the afternoon, as Balaam and David watched the sun sweep the shadows across the ground, the gaps in their conversation grew longer. Balaam saw David look at the upturned hubcap that had been Stilts's dinner plate. It had corn in it.

"Are you doing okay out here?" David asked.

"I refill it every morning. Just like I always did. No reason to stop. Corn never goes to waste out here. Squirrels and coons and possums and crows eat it."

Balaam changed the subject. "I haven't been in town much lately. How's your mother?"

"Hopelessly Nanetta," David said. "Actually, she's doing good. She doesn't even need that scooter to get around with anymore. But she's in love with it. She wants her neighbor, Mrs. Reeves, to get one so they can go 'cruising.'"

Balaam laughed and tried to imagine the two old women making loops through a Dairy Queen parking lot and not being able to get over the speed bumps.

"She says she can take care of herself just fine now and I can go back to Houston anytime. But I don't trust her to know her limitations. I'm going to stay on a while."

Now it was David's turn to laugh. "You know, when I moved in to look after Mother, I couldn't wait to move back to Houston. Living in Willoughby was like living in slow motion, like being submerged in Jell-O. But one day last week I was in Houston on business. After a few hours, I was ready to get back to Willoughby."

David leaned forward, as if putting his body in italics for emphasis. "And I'll tell you something else. The other day my boss emailed me about some ad copy I was working on. He said he needed it 'ASAP.' I emailed him back, 'WIGR.'"

"WIGR?"

"When I'm Good and Ready."

Balaam raised his beer in a toast. "To WIGR." And then he laughed some more.

"Hey, I just realized—that's my second toast today."

David raised his beer. "A toast to toasts."

David looked out across the vista of Balaam's clutter. "And lately I've noticed other things," he said with partial bemusement. "Such as I've begun to use verbs like 'fixin' to' and 'tump' and 'scootch.'"

Balaam had to remind himself that not everyone shared the rural vocabulary.

David put on his best Willoughby drawl, "Shoot, I reckon I can't go back to the big city talkin' that way."

"Nope. They'd never let you in. You're a ruint man. When you get ready to trade your little hot rod in on a pickup, let me know. We'll find you one that's good and broke in."

But David did not even hear Balaam's offer; one more dark confession was crowding in on his thoughts. "You know, I used to see Big Un Petteway and Joe Adair and Willis Pinkston and those old guys sitting on their bench and think, 'What a waste of time.' But, you know, lately I think, 'Waste of time compared to what? Compared to making up names for cosmetics?' Now I see those guys sitting there doing nothing, and I think, 'Hey, I could get the hang of that.'"

"Sure you could. Might take some practice, though. Better start slow. But you could do worse. Willoughby is a nice little town. When it's not trying to get too big for its britches."

"I guess the town has lost some of its charm lately. I'm with you—we need some peace and quiet."

"Oh, I reckon we'll have peace and quiet now." Balaam stood to go back inside to the refrigerator. "After all," in the doorway he looked back at David and winked, "that was my only stick of dynamite."

❧47❧

"Business has fallen off so much that I may be able
to keep the store open after all."
——Lawton Parker

At the flashing red light on the morning after Balaam Gimble's independence day, thirty-seven cars and trucks had passed through Willoughby's main intersection by noon. One week later, that number was down to seventeen. Two weeks later, just three blocks away, bantam roosters and their harems of hens again browsed in the grassy bar ditches alongside Highway 21.

During that first week, many residents of Willoughby were glad to see Balaam come into town now and then because that gave them a chance to refuse to speak to him. Mayor Earl Perry would have been the first in line to not speak to Balaam, but Perry had packed a fishing rod and left town for a few days. He had felt the loss of Balaam's Cave perhaps more personally than even Howard J. Liggett. After all, as Perry said, "Liggett has other resorts. I've only got one Willoughby."

Among locals who had partaken of the mineral spring water in the belief that it alleviated their various ills, there was much moaning. "What am I going to tell my feet?" Willis Pinkston asked Big Un.

"Your feet? What am *I* going to tell my *liver?*" Big Un said, patting his left side and thus giving solace only to his spleen.

The loss of the cave, the mineral water, and the proposed Waters at

Willoughby resort rippled through the town's economy. Reluctantly, the city posted a notice on its Web site: "Due to technical difficulties, Balaam's Cave and Bounce, the Lone Star Wonder Water, are unavailable." The last remaining Mason jars of Bounce on merchants' shelves were marked up and sold as "vintage."

With the sharp drop in tourism, sales slumped to former levels at Beverly Faulk's antiques store and Flora Vickers's pottery shop. The short-lived real estate boom went bust. Property values fell; houses and lots stopped selling. Real estate agent Judith Ann Giles checked out of the Chateau Willoughby and returned to Waco.

As she left, she forgot to sign Mary Lou Wyatt's guestbook.

With the drop in business at the gas station, Little Un Petteway told Big Un that he would not be able to treat him to a new liver. Big Un would have to make do with his perfectly good original equipment.

Everyone who had planned or already started expansion and other projects canceled them. At the Crossroads Cafe, Juanita Greer still would not forgive her husband for buying "that damned boat," but with the drop in business, she realized that any expansion of the cafe that she and Richard would have undertaken would have been a waste of money.

When Balaam had blown up his cave, Mary Lou Wyatt's bed-and-breakfast had already been completed—ready for the tourists who now would never come. On the other hand, Lilian Kreuter's bed-and-breakfast remained incomplete, with far less time and money invested in it than Mary Lou had invested in hers. Thus, although Lilian would never see it that way, by losing less she had actually won the Great Willoughby Bed-and-Breakfast Race.

Lawton Parker, among only a few, was pleased to see Willoughby return to "the old days and the old ways." Fewer expansion projects and fewer properties being renovated for sale meant fewer people demanding hardware. With less demand, Lawton was able to devote his time to keeping his inventory tidy and unsullied by customers.

Meanwhile, amid Willoughby's feelings of loss, some healing began. One morning Mary Lou Wyatt went to the Pinkston home to visit with—and apologize to—Jessie, who was still "peaked" after the parade debacle. While Mary Lou was there, Lilian Kreuter came to visit Jessie on the same mission. Mary Lou and Lilian were able to stay in the same room with each other without blood being shed. It was a start.

And with no real estate market, Willis Pinkston and Joe Adair no longer had their rental house as a point of contention. Day by day, syllable by syllable, they began to talk to each other again. And, as Willis said while they sat on their bench, now returned to its original location on the new sidewalk in front of the bank, "God knows there's a sure-nuff shitload to talk about."

A week later, David Wilson gave them even more to talk about. Acting on what he called a "whim ten years in the making," David quit his job at the advertising firm of Adams, Hawkins, & Jenrette. David's boss reacted as if David had suggested defying the laws of thermodynamics, telling David flatly that he *couldn't* quit, that he was too important to the Ms.-tique Cosmetics account. David repeated his intention to quit; his boss repeated his refusal to consider it.

That night David got out his long-dormant "cyanide file"—his secret list of suggested cosmetics names so outrageous that they were certain to cost him his job if submitted to Claudia Curtis, president of Ms.-tique. Instead of his usual names for lipsticks, nail polishes, eye shadows, and foundations—names such as Petal Pink, Sunrise Rose, and Rhapsody in Red—David's cyanide file contained names such as:

> Spank My Bottom 'til It's Pink
> Suck My Toes Rose
> Better Bed Than Wed Red
> I Don't Remember Getting This Tattoo Blue
> Mama Didn't Raise No Clown Brown
> Check Out This Caboose Chartreuse
> No Slack in the Sack Black
> Lick and Slurple Purple

David read over the list, making a couple of minor revisions. When he was satisfied that the list was totally unsatisfactory, he pressed the "send" button on his fax machine, sending the list directly to Claudia Curtis at Ms.-tique Cosmetics.

Then David Wilson waited for the mascara to hit the fan.

The next morning David's phone rang. "This is it," David said to himself.

"David! Phil here." It was David's boss. "You're a genius, my man. You've done it again. You should think about quitting more often!

Claudia *loves* the new names. She thinks you're a mind reader. How did you know she had been wanting to launch a new line of cosmetics aimed at the hip under-thirty market? She was toying with something edgy, irreverent, sass-mouth. She says your new names are perfect. 'You give my David a bonus,' she told me. Hey, consider it done. If Claudia's happy, I'm happy. Gotta run. We'll talk."

David's boss never gave David a chance to speak. That was just as well—David was speechless. He couldn't lose for winning.

Later that day, David phoned his boss and again politely but firmly said he felt it was time to go. Again his boss wouldn't hear of it, telling David that Claudia Curtis had threatened to take her company's account elsewhere if Adams, Hawkins, & Jenrette allowed David to get away.

An hour later, Claudia Curtis herself phoned David. "David, honey. Are you unhappy at AH&J? Has Phil been mean to you? You simply can't quit, you know. Why don't you just come to work for me at Ms.-tique? Claudia would treat her David right."

David held firm.

That afternoon David's boss phoned again, pointing out diplomatically that David already had an ideal work arrangement. "You're working from home these days, unsupervised. No staff meetings, no dress code, no traffic. My God, David, that's like being unemployed. What more do you want?"

"Out."

Finally, David felt pressured. "Phil, I appreciate your efforts to change my mind. But don't buck me on this. You can't win this one." David shifted into his best Willoughby drawl. "Phil, lemme tell ya, when it comes to sayin' 'no,' Ah've studied at the feet of the master."

✣48✣

"Nope."
——Balaam Gimble

Eight miles from the flashing red light in Willoughby, on the morning after his independence day Balaam Gimble awoke just after dawn. As he lay in bed his first thought, as it often had been lately, was "Something bad will probably happen today." But his second thought was "No, it won't. I'm untouchable now." Balaam felt that he had been away for a very long time. In late September, nights were cool enough that he could sleep with his little window air conditioner off and his windows raised. He listened to the familiar morning sounds that leaked in through the raised window: crows cawing reveille in the treetops, dew dripping off the roof of his cabin and plinking into a rain barrel, a woodpecker hammering faintly far away in the woods.

He also listened to the sounds that he did not—and would not—hear: the sound of a gasoline-powered water pump, tourists, traffic, the telephone, the guns of J. D. Vernon. And, yes, the sound of a hubcap being nudged across the ground by a black nose before breakfast.

For some reason, his third thought was that he never had finished the project that he had started six months earlier on that day in April: digging out some rocks at the limestone ridge to use as a border for his flowerbed. As he lay there, he knew that he really should attend to that. He considered it for a moment. He considered it for a second moment.

And then Balaam Gimble said "nope" aloud, fluffed up his pillow, and went back to sleep.

❧ Epilogue ❧

In the twelve months after Balaam Gimble just said "nope":
  • Howard J. Liggett, according to his chief physician, fully recovered from his cow patty apoplexy. But Liggett refused to set foot in Texas again or even to allow his corporate jets to enter Texas air space.
  • Ernie Ruiz fully recovered from his encounters with cowboy boots, Beelzebub's Bambi, Rusty's Bar F Tavern, and poison oak. And then one day the good people at Hertz Rent A Car phoned him to ask when he was going to return their pickup.
  • Big Un Petteway and his liver lived on without complication while receiving more rainfall than anyone else in the area.
  • Nanetta Wilson broke her other hip—while skateboarding.
  • Juanita Greer divorced Richard and was granted custody of the fishing boat.
  • Mary Lou Wyatt and Lilian Kreuter reconciled, united by their common desire to "snatch Balaam Gimble bald-headed."
  • David Wilson sold his townhouse in Houston and stayed on in Willoughby. The next spring, he and Beverly Faulk went bird-watching again and shared the sighting of a spectacular scarlet tanager. David was not injured.
  • The town of Willoughby continued to languish. The next summer, a bulb in the town's flashing red traffic light burned out. No one noticed.
  • J. D. Vernon's widow, because her late husband "would have

wanted it that way," leased her twelve hundred acres to a group of deer hunters from Houston.

• When Balaam Gimble, via the Willoughby grapevine, heard what J. D. Vernon's widow had done, he immediately went into his kitchen, turned on the faucet, and chug-a-lugged two quarts of plain old tap water.

About the Author

Mike Nichols is a sixth-generation Texan who has trafficked in words all of his adult life. He worked twenty-three years for the Fort Worth Star-Telegram as a copy editor, humor columnist, and travel writer. As a travel writer, he schlepped his suitcases and cameras to more than forty countries on seven continents before he realized that his favorite destination is his own back yard.

Nichols is the author of three other books: *Life and Other Ways to Kill Time, Real Men Belch Downwind,* and *Women Are from Pluto, Men Are from Uranus. Balaam Gimble's Gumption* is his first novel. He lives in Fort Worth after having spent twenty-five years living in the country, including four years just down the road from the fictional town of Willoughby.